# KING

## OF

# BATTLE

## AND

# BLOOD

## SCARLETT ST. CLAIR

Published by Bloom Books, an imprint of Sourcebooks
P.O. Box 4410, Naperville, Illinois 60567-4410
(630) 961-3900
sourcebooks.com

Cataloging-in-Publication Data is on file with the Library of Congress.

Manufactured in the UK by Clays and distributed
by Dorling Kindersley Limited, London
10 9 8 7 6 5 4 3 2 1
001-331523-Nov/21

*To Ashley*
*Who loved this book*
*before it was even written.*

ZENOVIA
VLASCA
AROTH
MOUNTAINS of AROTH
The STARLESS FOREST
REVEKKA
THE RED PALACE
CEL CEREDI
SADOVEA
ISTAS
HOUSE OF ELIN
HOUSE OF JOLA
VAIDA
THE NINE
HOUSE OF SIVA
HOUSE OF LARA
HOUSE OF LITA
The GOLDEN SEA
VIKO
TIVA
SINTA
ISLANDS of ST. AMAND
HOUSE OF THEA
The SILVER FOREST

MADOVEA

KEZIAH

FOREST
of RAVENS

HOUSE OF
VANA

HOUSES

ATOLL
of NALANI

ZUNI

OLATHE

HOUSE OF
HELA

ALO

The
VIOLET
SEA

MOUNTAINS
of LAMIA

HOUSE OF
ERIS

CORDOVA

# ONE

**There was an army of vampires encamped on the outskirts** of my father's kingdom. The black tops of their tents looked like an ocean of sharp waves and seemed to stretch for miles, melding with a red horizon that was the sky that extended over Revekka, the Empire of the Vampire. It had been that color since I was born. It was said to be cursed by Dis, the goddess of spirit, to warn of the evil that was birthed there—the evil that began with the Blood King. Unfortunately for Cordova, the red sky did not follow evil, so there was no warning when the vampires began their invasion.

They had manifested west of the border last night, as if they'd traveled with the shadows. Since then, everything had been quiet and still. It was like their presence had stolen life; not even the wind stirred. Unease crept through my chest like a cold frost, settling deep in my stomach as I stood between the trees, only a few feet from the first row of tents. I could not shake the feeling that this was the end. It loomed behind me, long fingers gripping my shoulders.

Rumors had preceded their arrival. Rumors of how their leader—I hated to even *think* his name—Adrian Aleksandr Vasiliev had leveled Jola, ravished Elin, conquered Siva, and burned Lita. One by one, the Nine Houses of Cordova were falling. Now the vampires were on my doorstep, and instead of calling arms, my father, King Henri, had asked for a meeting.

He wanted to reason with the Blood King.

My father's decision had been met with mixed emotions. Some wished to fight rather than succumb to this monster's reign. Others were uncertain—had my father traded death on the battlefield for another kind?

At least in battle, there were truths. You either survived the day or died.

Under the rule of a monster, there were no truths.

"I should not have allowed you to come so late or get this close."

Commander Alec Killian stood too near, just a hair behind me, shoulder brushing my back. If it were any other day, I would have excused his proximity, attributing it to his dedication as my escort, but I knew otherwise.

The commander was trying to make amends.

I took a step away, turning slightly, both to cast him a sullen look and to create distance. Alec—or Killian, as I preferred to call him—was commander of the Royal Guard, having inherited the position when his father, whose name he also shared, passed unexpectedly three years ago.

He returned my gaze, gray eyes both steely and somehow gentle. I think I'd have preferred only the steel, because the tenderness made me want to take two more steps back. It meant he had feelings for me, and any excitement I'd once had at catching his attention had now evaporated.

Outwardly, he was everything I thought I'd wanted in a man—ruggedly handsome with a body forged by hours of training. His uniform, a tailored navy tunic and trousers with gold embellishments and a ridiculously dramatic gold cape, served to accentuate his presence. He had a crown of thick, dark hair, and I'd spent a few too many nights with those strands wrapped around my fingers, body warmed, but not alight with the passion I'd really longed for. In the end, Commander Killian was a mediocre lover. It had not helped that I did not like his beard, which was long and covered the bottom half of his face. It made it impossible to detect the shape of his jaw, but I guessed he had a strong one that matched his presence—which was beginning to grate on my nerves.

"I outrank you, Commander. It is not within your power to tell me what to do."

"No, but it is within your father's."

Another flush of irritation blasted up my spine, and I ground my teeth. When Killian did not feel like he could *handle* me, he defaulted to using the threat of my father. And he wondered why I did not want to sleep with him anymore.

Instead of acknowledging my anger, Killian smirked, pleased that he'd hit a nerve.

He nodded toward the camp. "We should attack in the daylight while they sleep."

"Except you would be defying Father's orders for peace," I said.

Once, I would have agreed with him—why *not* slaughter the vampires while they slept? The sunlight, after all, was their weakness. Except that Theodoric, king of Jola, had ordered his soldiers to do the very same, and before they could even launch their attack, the entire army was vanquished by something the people were calling the blood plague. Those who had come down with the disease bled from every orifice of their body until death, including King Theodoric and his wife, who now left a two-year-old to inherit the throne under the rule of the Blood King.

As it turned out, sunlight did not stop magic.

"Will they have as much respect for us when night falls?" Killian countered. The commander had not been shy about expressing his opinion about the Blood King and his invasion of Cordova. I understood his hatred.

"Have faith in the soldiers you trained, Commander. Have you not prepared for this?"

I knew he did not like my reply. I could *feel* his frown at my back, because we both knew if the vampires decided to attack, we were dead. It took five of our own to bring down one of them. We simply had to trust that the Blood King's word to my father was worth our people's lives.

"No one can prepare for monsters, Princess," Killian said. I broke from his gaze and focused on the king's tent, distinct with its crimson and gold details, as he added, "I doubt even the goddess Dis knew what would become of her curse."

It was said Adrian angered Dis, goddess of spirit, and as a result, she cursed him to crave blood. Her curse spread— some humans survived the transformation to vampire while others did not. Since their incarnation, the world had not known peace. Their presence had bred other monsters—all kinds that fed on blood, on life. While I had never known anything different, our elders did. They remembered a world without high walls and gates around every village. They remembered what it was like not to fear wandering beneath the stars as darkness fell.

I did not fear the dark.

I did not fear the monsters.

I did not even fear the Blood King.

But I did fear for my father, for my people, for my culture.

Because Adrian Aleksandr Vasiliev was inevitable.

"You presume to know how a goddess thinks?" I asked.

"You keep challenging me. Did I do something wrong?"

"Did you expect complacency because we fucked?"

He flinched, and his brows slammed down over his eyes. *Finally*, I thought. *Anger.*

"So you're upset," he said.

I rolled my eyes. "Of course I'm upset. You convinced my father I needed an escort."

"You sneak out of your bedroom at night!"

I had no idea that sleeping with Killian would mean unannounced visits to my bedroom. Except, like always, he overstepped one night and found my room empty. He'd woken the whole castle, had an entire army searching the surrounding forest for me. All I'd wanted to do was watch the stars, and I'd done so for years atop the rolling hills of Lara. But all that ended a week ago. After I was found, my father had summoned me to his study. He'd lectured me on the state of the world and the importance of watchfulness and had given me guards and a curfew.

I'd protested. I was well trained, a warrior, just as competent as Killian. I could protect myself, at least within the borders of Lara.

*Don't,* my father had snapped. The word was so harsh and sudden, I jumped. After a quiet moment and a breath, he had added, *You are too important, Issi.*

And in that moment, he'd looked so broken, I hadn't been able to utter another word—not to him, not to Killian.

A week later, and I was feeling trapped.

"Since you are so keen to spill my secrets, Commander, did you admit to fucking me too?"

*"Stop using that word."*

He spoke with clenched teeth.

At least he was passionate about something, I thought. Still, his order only served to provoke me.

"And what word should I use?" I hissed. *"Make love?* Hardly." I was being unkind, but when I was angry, I wanted the recipient of my wrath to *feel* it, and I knew Killian did. It was a trait I'd adopted from my mother, given that my father rarely expressed his frustration. "You seem to think what happened between us means something more."

It was like he thought he was suddenly entitled to me, and I hated it.

"Am I so terrible?" he asked, his voice quiet.

My fists clenched, and there was a moment when guilt clutched at my chest. I shook it off quickly. "Stop trying to manipulate my words."

"I'm not trying to manipulate you, but you cannot say you did not enjoy our time together."

"I enjoy sex, Alec," I said flatly. "But it doesn't mean anything."

They were sloppy words, but I meant them. I'd only chosen to sleep with Killian because he'd been there, and I'd wanted release. That had been my first mistake. Because it made me ignore other warnings, like his tendency to keep my father aware of my every move.

"You don't mean that," he said.

"Killian." His name slipped from my mouth, a warning. He wasn't listening, and if there was one thing I hated, it was a man convinced that I didn't know my own mind. "When will you learn? I *always* say what I mean."

I started to step around him, and Killian reached for my hand. I wrenched free and punched him in the stomach. He groaned and fell to his knees as I turned on my heels.

"Isolde!" he huffed. "Where are you going?"

I kept walking into the thick wood; the leaves were soft beneath my feet, still wet from morning dew. I wished it were the middle of spring, when the trees were lush and green. I could disappear much easier then. Instead, I walked between pale, skeletal trunks, beneath a canopy of interlaced limbs. Still, I was certain I could lose Killian. I knew these woods like I knew my heart. I would make it back to the castle without him, much as I had intended to do before he followed me to the border.

"Idiot," I breathed.

My jaw ached from clenching my teeth. I did not hate Killian, but I would not accept being caged. I was well aware of the dangers in the world, and I'd been raised to fight every manner of monster, even vampires. Though I was no match for them, at least I knew it. If it were up to Killian, our armies would be battling the vampires right now, and likely, many of our people would be dead.

As humans, we had no cure to fight their diseases, no ability to outrun them, no way to counter their magic or the monsters they'd awakened. We were lesser, and we would always be unless one of the goddesses answered the many and varied prayers offered by the devout—which was unlikely.

The goddesses had abandoned us long ago, and sometimes I felt like the only person who knew it.

My pace lessened as the smell of decay permeated the air. At first, it was faint, and for a brief moment, I thought I was imagining things.

Then, the cold crept up my back, and I stopped.

A strzyga was near.

Strzyga were humans who had died from the blood plague and risen from the dead. They were horrifying creatures with little intellect, save for their desire to eat human flesh.

The smell grew in potency, and I flexed my hand, turning slowly to face the desiccated monster.

It stood on the edge of the clearing, back bent, staring with hollow eyes and cheeks. Its sparse hair clung to blood spattered on its near-skeletal face. It stared at me and then sniffed the air, a growl erupting from its throat as its lips curled back to show elongated teeth. Then it gave an eerie cry as it fell on all fours and raced toward me.

I spread my feet apart, preparing for the impact of its blow. It launched itself at me, and as it neared, I shoved my hand toward it, deploying a knife I kept sheathed in a brace around my wrist. It sank easily between the creature's ribs. Just as quickly, I pushed away, retracting my blade. Blood spattered my face as the strzyga staggered back, screaming at me, angry and anguished.

The blow would only wound.

To kill a strzyga, its head must be separated from its body then burned.

Now that the monster was weakened, I drew my sword. As the sharp metal sang against my sheath, the creature hissed its hatred before throwing itself at me again. It sank upon my blade, clawed hand slashing, tearing at my dress and skin. I gave a guttural cry as the pain registered, but it was soon overtaken by anger and adrenaline. I withdrew the sword and swung. The edge was sharp but resisted, lodging in the bone of the strzyga's neck. I shoved my foot against its chest and jerked my blade free. As the strzyga fell, I sliced through its neck again, and when the body hit the ground, its head landed a few feet away.

I stood for a moment, breathing hard, my chest burning where the creature had shredded my skin. I needed to get to the medics. Infection set in quickly with strzyga wounds. Before I began my trek, I kicked the strzyga's head, sending it rolling to the tree line of the clearing.

Returning to the castle injured would not bode well for me and my independence.

The air changed suddenly, and I twisted, lifting my blade once more, only to have it connect with another.

The impact surprised me, because I stood face-to-face with a man. He was beautiful, striking, but in a harsh way. His features were angled—high cheekbones, sharp jawline, a straight nose, all framed by blond hair that fell in soft waves past his shoulders. His lips were full and pillowy, and his eyes were hooded by defined brows. It was those strange eyes—blue, rimmed with white—that held mine as he tilted his head and spoke.

"What are you doing all the way out here?" His voice hinted at intrigue, silky in its delivery, and the sound made my stomach clench.

My brows lowered at his words, and I studied him further. He wore a black tunic secured with gold buckles and a surcoat of the same color. The edges were stitched with gold thread. It was fine work, but it was not made by my people—our designs were far more intricate.

I narrowed my eyes. "Who are you?" I asked.

The man dropped his sword, as if he no longer perceived me as a threat, which made me want to be a threat, except that I dropped my arm too, my fingers loose around the hilt. I tried to tighten my hold but couldn't.

"I am many things," he said. "Man, monster, lover."

This time when he spoke, I detected a faint accent—a slight clip I couldn't place.

"That's not an answer," I said.

"I think what you mean is that's not the answer you want."

"You are toying with me."

His smile stretched, and he looked wicked in a sinful way, in a way I wanted to taste and feel. Those thoughts made my skin prick, and I felt myself growing warmer beneath his gaze.

"What is it you want from me?" he asked. His voice was low, a purr that coaxed a shiver from the depths of my stomach.

I swallowed hard. "I want to know why you're here."

"I was tracking the strzyga when it changed course." His eyes lowered to my chest. "I see why."

Self-consciously, I lifted my hand and hissed at the sting of my shredded skin. The sudden flare of pain made me feel light-headed.

"I killed it," I managed to say, though my tongue felt thick in my mouth.

The corners of his lips curled. "I see that too."

"I should go," I whispered, holding his gaze. I wanted to move my body but felt too relaxed. Perhaps it was infection, already rooted in my blood.

"You should," he agreed. "But you won't."

An alarm sounded in my head as he spoke. And as he stepped toward me, I suddenly regained my ability to move. I drove my hand toward his stomach, releasing my knife, but his hand clamped down upon my wrist. He yanked me forward, his body pressing into mine, despite my wound, despite the blood. He bent over me, grasping my head, fingers digging into my scalp, and for a moment, I feared that he would either kiss me or break my neck. Instead, he gripped me harder, eyes never leaving mine, thumb brushing my lips.

"What is your name?" he asked. His voice shivered through me, and I found myself speaking.

"I am Isolde." The answer slipped from my mouth, at war with my mind, which raged against him.

"Who are you?"

Again, I answered not of my own accord, my voice

11

the whisper of a lover. "I am princess of the House of Lara."

"Isolde," he repeated my name, a rough growl that vibrated against my chest. "My sweet."

Then he bent, and his tongue swept across the wound on my chest. I couldn't breathe, I couldn't move, and I couldn't speak. The worst part was that this felt *good*. It felt possessive and immoral, and I found myself no longer trying to stab him but clinging to him as he worked.

When he drew away, his full lips were stained with my blood. He swallowed, and his eyes gleamed as he studied my eyes, my lips, my throat. The stare ignited something deep inside me, and the fire spread, making me ache. I was ashamed, because I knew this man was a soldier for the Blood King, a vampire.

I jerked in his grasp and was surprised when he released me. I stumbled back, my hand going to my chest, meeting smooth skin. I was healed.

"You're a monster."

"I healed you," he said, as if that made him less so.

"I didn't ask for your help," I snapped.

"No, but you enjoyed it."

I glared. "You were controlling me."

That was why I hadn't been able to grip my sword, why my body seemed to be at odds with my mind, why I suddenly felt desperate to be crushed beneath the weight of a warm body that could fill me better than anything I'd ever had before. I was out of control.

And it was *his* fault.

"I do not control emotions." He spoke so matter-of-factly, it was hard to accuse him of lying.

I lifted my blade, and the vampire laughed.

"Anger suits you, my sweet. I like it."

I scowled, but my anger just made him smile wider, his lips pulling back from gleaming white teeth, no sign that he'd just feasted on my blood. My hatred for him deepened.

"It is still daylight," I said. "How are you able to walk among us?"

Vampires could only go out during the day in Revekka, where the red sky blocked the sun's rays. *Were they evolving?* The thought brought a new kind of dread into the pit of my stomach.

"It is nearly sunset," he said. "This time is not so dangerous for someone like me."

*What did that mean?*

I did not ask, and he did not offer an explanation. Instead, he inclined his head. "We'll meet again, Princess Isolde. I'll make sure of it."

His promise shivered through me like an oath he'd sworn to the goddesses themselves. I lifted my blade and charged, but as I swung, he vanished like mist in the morning sun.

Alone, I began to shake.

I'd survived an encounter with a vampire who had tasted my blood, and the worst part about it was that he'd been right.

I did like it.

# TWO

*I had seen victims of vampires—humans who were on the* cusp of change before their hearts were cut from their bodies and burned. I'd also seen bodies drained of blood, past the point of survival. But I'd never encountered an actual vampire.

"*They look like us but are not us,*" Killian's father had warned during training. "*They are fast. They will control your mind and drink your blood, and you will not survive. If you do, you will* wish *for death.*"

Those were the truths I'd been told about vampires.

He'd never said how they were like us—that they could be beautiful, that their touch would inspire an acute desire beyond anything I'd ever experienced. Everything inside me was wound so tight, each breath was a reminder of how desperately I wanted to be touched.

"Isolde!"

*But not by him.*

Killian's voice broke through the fog of my mind. He was close, and I did not want to be caught. There was too much to explain here in this clearing—the strzyga, my torn dress, the absence of blood.

I turned on my heels and fled.

The castle felt like it had doubled in distance. The walk was agonizing, and I grew frustrated, still feeling the effects of my encounter with the vampire. My body was warm, especially between my thighs, and I was hyperaware of how heavy and sensitive my breasts felt, rubbed raw by the woolen cloak I kept close. By the time I exited the tree line, I ached.

This was torture.

Was that what this was? Some cruel form of warfare?

I skirted the high, stone walls that rose ominously and cast me in a chill shadow. The walls were a complex system of forts, bastions, and towers that ran, uninterrupted, encircling High City of Lara and Castle Fiora. They'd been built over two hundred years ago, after the birth of the monsters in Cordova—the start of the Dark Era. There were four gates that allowed entrance into High City. Two were actually useful, one for trade that led into the heart of the city. The other was for diplomats and offered a pleasing route along cobble roads to the gleaming white towers of the castle.

The other two gates were symbolic. One was for Asha, goddess of life, the other for Dis, goddess of spirit. Once, they would have opened at dawn, marking the waking of the city, symbolizing the balance of life and death. But since the birth of the vampires, Dis's gate remained sealed, a decision that had been made by the kings of the Nine Houses over one hundred and fifty years ago. There were a few priestesses of Dis who admonished the decision, claiming that the plague of the monsters would only grow worse—and they hadn't been wrong. It was why all villages across the Nine Houses had high walls and gates that closed before sunset and did not open until sunrise.

Except for tonight.

Tonight, the gates would open to allow the Blood King and his people within our walls. It would be the first time since they were built that the gates would remain open.

I approached the one for diplomats. Usually, I liked to enter through the trade gate and meander through the streets, visiting my favorite vendors for flowers and meat pies, but since my encounter in the wood, I needed to change and time to myself.

"Princess," one of the guards at the gate said. His name was Nicolae. He was young, his face doughy and pale. The other, who was silent and stoic, was named Lascar. He was olive skinned and large, his body almost too big for the sentry box behind him. Both soldiers were new to the Royal Guard. I liked the new recruits because they were easy to sway; all I had to do was smile, stroke their ego, and they'd pretend they never saw me slipping outside the gates at night.

That was before they'd all been roused in the middle of the night last week to find me, before the two guards who'd let me slip by were dishonorably discharged and relegated to the duties of a stable hand.

"Returning without escort, I see," Nicolae said. He tried to sound stern, but he had too much light in his eyes for that.

"Commander Killian stayed at the border," I said.

Nicolae's eyes shifted over my shoulder, and he raised a dark brow. "Did he?"

I turned, spying Killian as he came out of the tree line. His absurd cape fluttered menacingly behind him.

I quickly turned back to Nicolae and smiled. "He must have changed his mind."

"Do you need escort to—"

"No," I cut him off, and to soften the blow, I placed my hand upon his shoulder, holding my cloak tightly with the other. "Thank you, Nicolae."

I hurried through the gates and was immediately greeted by the towering figure of the Sanctuary of Asha on the right. The stone was white and brilliant, the colors of the hand-painted stained glass vibrant. Opposite the structure was the crumbling edifice that was the Sanctuary of Dis. The building itself looked like a shadow, crafted from volcanic rock imported from the Islands of St. Amand. The windows that weren't broken or boarded were dark, pointed, and lead-paned. Despite its ruined appearance, it was still occupied by a few priestesses, but because very few visited and the priestesses were only called when death was near, they had no money for upkeep.

I kept an equal distance from both as I passed, having never felt inclined to worship either goddess. My father would criticize me, but I had no desire to offer my loyalty—not to the one who brought monsters to our world nor to the other who let it happen.

Beyond the sanctuaries, there was a series of beautiful plaster buildings—a combination of homes, shops, and inns—all with thatched roofs and window boxes full of colorful flowers. Beyond that was a short wall that marked the start of the royal grounds. A line of trees offered privacy to those of the court who wished to use the gardens for exercise or games. Since it was nearing sunset, most were indoors, for which I was thankful. The ladies of the court fawned over me. I liked many of them, but I found it hard to tell who was genuine in their attention, given that I suspected many only wanted my favor because I would be queen one day.

I crossed the wide yard and edged along the castle wall toward the back, entering through the servant's quarters to avoid being pulled into needlework and gossip about the Blood King. I headed up a narrow staircase just to the left of the entrance, the friction of my thighs almost unbearable. I was so frustrated, both by the desire burning low in my stomach and by whatever magic still had its claws inside me. How could I possibly still be so consumed by this desperate need for release? Flight after flight, I grew more heated, my mind wandering to how the vampire had held my head, how he'd touched my lips and drew words from my mouth. I wondered what other sounds he might coax from my throat as those fingers explored other sensitive and swollen parts of my body.

*Your thoughts are disgusting*, I chided and then more kindly reminded myself that I was only thinking those things because I was under some spell.

After six flights of stairs, I made it to my room. Once inside, I leaned against the prickly wooden door. I'd held my breath for most of my ascent, because I couldn't stop thinking about sex and the vampire who looked like some kind of beautiful savior but was really a monster. I thought of him now as my hand drifted down my stomach to my center, where my swollen clit rose to meet the brush of my hand. I groaned and ground into my hand, desperate to feel pleasure thread through my body, desperate to come so that I might also release the image of this vampire and his magic. This was what he wanted—to drive me to this moment—and he had done nothing to earn it. He hadn't spoken erotic things, kissed me, or caressed my skin, and yet his face came to my mind, unbidden.

My frustration was palpable, and I thought I could hear his laugh echo in my mind—the one he'd offered in the clearing, amused, dark, arrogant.

By the goddess, I hated him.

I gathered my skirts into my hands until I could feel the curls at the apex of my thighs, then the pad of my fingers brushed against my clit. It strained against my touch, sensitive with need, still so tight, practically preening. I held my breath as my fingers drifted closer to the heat and slickness of my core, and I swore I'd never been so wet.

*It has to be magic*, I thought, and yet my stomach knotted with tension, shame, and guilt.

I drew my middle finger down my opening, gathering the slickness—before a knock erupted from behind me.

I froze, fingers poised to slip into my heat.

"My lady, are you in there?"

Nadia, my maid, was on the other side of the door. She'd been my nursemaid from the time I was born, and we'd formed a close bond. She was the only maid or servant in the castle I spent time with outside her usual duties. It was a relationship the court found strange and only the brave would comment on, but I didn't care. Nadia was the mother I'd never had, and I loved her.

Except right now. Right now, I wanted her to go away. I wasn't ready to give up the chase for release, so I slipped a finger into my flesh and released a slow breath.

"My lady, I know you are in there."

*If I ignore her, maybe she will go away*, I thought.

I was so wet, I could barely feel anything. I needed more girth, needed to feel full and stretched. I added another finger, my head pressed hard into the door behind me, my palm sliding up my body to my breast, squeezing, kneading, teasing through the ruins of my dress. All the while, I thought of that monster in the woods. The one who looked like a man, had held my head in his large hands, stroked my lips with his lithe fingers, pressed his hard body against mine. If he had kissed me, I would have succumbed. I would have let him fuck me, and it probably would have meant my death, but at least I would have known passion on my way to the Spirit.

"My lady?"

*By the fucking goddess.*

I gave a frustrated growl and withdrew, dropping my skirts. I whirled on my heels and threw open the door.

"What, Nadia?" I snapped. If Nadia insisted on interrupting, then she would have to deal with my mood, except she knew me and didn't even flinch. She stood opposite me looking very much unimpressed. Her long, dark hair was braided and threaded through with silver, those pieces whispering around her thin face, creating a frizzy halo. Her darkened skin was smooth though, and her only wrinkles were the ones around her eyes, which remained dark and lively.

20

"I have come to help you prepare for tonight."

I blinked at her, confused. "Tonight?"

"For the Blood King's arrival."

I rolled my eyes and backed away from the door, twisting so my skirt twirled around me. The movement helpfully cooled my legs and released the tension in the bottom of my stomach.

"I do not care how I look for the Blood King."

"I'd rather not doll you up either, but you are a princess and, as such, should look like one when you stand at your father's side." Nadia followed me into my room and closed the door behind her.

My room was small and the bed took up a fair amount of space, allowing for little else save for a trunk full of keepsakes and a wardrobe. I could have had a large suite, but I'd chosen this one because of the view—the window below looked down upon my mother's garden.

"What were you doing in here anyway? It took you a long time to answer the door," Nadia said as she stoked the fire in the hearth.

Even if I had noticed the chill, I would not have stirred the embers. I was afraid of fire, even contained. I did not like the sounds, the crackles or pops. I did not like the smell of smoke or even the heat, but it truly was too cold to go without, so I let Nadia keep it going and always made a wide arc around it when I passed.

"Sleeping," I said, falling onto my bed, staring up at the blue velvet canopy.

I was still insanely uncomfortable, but it was probably best Nadia had interrupted me. Otherwise, I would have continued to masturbate to the monster in the woods—his touch and smell and feel—and would have hated myself even more than I already did for it.

I sighed.

*You are a victim*, I told myself, though I hated admitting it. We'd been taught from a young age that vampires were sexual creatures, and they often cast spells that filled even the most pious with lust.

It really didn't help that I wasn't pious.

"You were not," Nadia said, straightening from her place before the fire. She pointed the poker at me. "I just watched you run up six flights of stairs."

"I was in a hurry to sleep."

She arched a brow and dropped the poker to her side. "And escape Commander Killian, I hear."

I rolled my eyes. "Commander Killian is needy. I am not."

"He would make a fine husband," Nadia countered, and I recoiled at how fanciful she sounded.

I sat up and gaped at her. "Did you not hear what I just said?"

Nadia was forty-one and unmarried—which was perfectly fine, except to her. She wanted to be married, and her thoughts on the subject were very much that of the majority of Cordovians, meaning that anyone over the age of eighteen and unmarried was considered an old maid, and the rush to marry stemmed from the fact that more people were dying young.

I was twenty-six and perfectly content to remain unwed, and I was very vocal about that—among other things—which the royal families and their peers found disturbing. It often led to unsolicited comments about how I needed to be tamed. Although the last man to

22

make that comment found himself facing the point of my dagger.

Needless to say, I had a reputation. But I would not accept a man who thought he could control me. My wish to remain unmarried also coincided with my feelings about love. Love was a risk I was only willing to take for my father, Nadia, and my people.

More love meant there was more to lose.

"I heard what you said. But what is wrong with needy? He would be devoted to you."

"He would be controlling."

*And* I'd have to sleep with him...regularly. I cringed, imagining a life of passionless sex and couldn't do it. No, Commander Killian was not the man for me.

"You should not be so picky, Isolde. You know the male population is dwindling under the vampires. Soon you'll have even fewer men to choose from."

"Who says I have to choose?"

Father had not told me I had to marry. There were no political alliances to create, because the houses were united in their determination to defeat the Blood King and had been since the rise of the vampires...until recently. Until my father decided to submit to him. Now, we'd been ostracized. If I hadn't made a suitable bride before, I certainly wouldn't now, though I had a feeling more kingdoms would soon join my father in his decision to choose the lives of their people over the alternative.

"Every respectable lady marries, Isolde."

"Nadia, we both know I am not respectable."

"You could pretend," she shot back. "You are a princess, blessed by the goddess, and yet you make a mockery of everything she has given you."

My face grew flushed with anger at Nadia's words, and I rose to my feet. If she had been anyone else in my service, I would have dismissed her. But I knew Nadia. She was devoutly religious and dedicated to Asha—she had her own reasons for her beliefs, just as I had mine. I also knew she meant well despite herself, but that did not mean I shared her views. Even if Cordova had not been cursed with monsters, I could never show loyalty to the two goddesses who had taken my mother before I even had the chance to know her.

I was surprised at how calm I sounded when I spoke.

"The day Asha rids the world of the vampires is the day I honor her blessings, Nadia. Until then, I can only be who I am."

She sighed, not in disappointment but in acceptance—her job was doomed from the beginning. She was supposed to raise me to be prim and proper, a lady who would eventually become queen of Lara. What she'd gotten instead was me. I wasn't sure what I was yet. Untamed, wild, spirited—they were all words that had been used to describe me. Whatever I was, it did not fit a mold. But I did not think that made me a bad princess or that it would make me a bad queen. What it made me was someone who was willing to rule without a king, and that was something I wasn't sure this world was prepared for.

"Well," said Nadia. "If you must be who you are, the least we can do is have you look like a princess. What did you do to your dress?"

I let my eyes drop to my chest. In my frustration, I'd forgotten it had been ruined.

"Oh. I encountered a strzyga on my return from the border."

I saw no need to lie about that. We'd all been taught to fight, having been born in the Dark Era. It was a skill as necessary as learning to walk.

"If you had stayed with Commander Killian, you would not have had to fight."

"I like fighting," I argued.

Nadia's eyes narrowed on my ruined bodice, and I knew she was connecting the dots—shredded, bloodied dress but no visible wounds.

"Besides, it barely brushed me," I said quickly. "The blood is his. You know what happens when you hit a vein."

Nadia shook her head and pointed toward my washroom. "Bath. Now."

I obeyed quickly, happy to scrub away this day. Maybe I would get lucky and the water would quench the fire raging inside before it turned my bones to dust.

# THREE

*An hour later, I was ready to present to my father. I let Nadia* choose my dress, a rarity, and I think in her excitement, she forgot the occasion, because she chose my favorite gown—a cerulean silk with pearl embellishments that ignited like fire against my brown skin. The neckline was square and low, and my breasts pillowed at the very top.

Nadia clicked her tongue, a sign of her disapproval.

"Too much bread," she said as she attempted—and failed—to force my neckline higher.

"If you think to deter me, you won't."

Nadia commented on my weight because it was another part of me that did not fit the mold. My breasts were big, my hips wide. One of my thighs was probably the size of her waist. I didn't really care though. I was fit, and I could fight. That was more than I could say for her, a nursemaid who had failed to turn me into a docile princess.

Nadia drew my hair over my shoulders, arranging

my thick, dark waves to hide the swell of my breasts. When she was finished, I promptly slipped it back.

"Can I resign?" she asked as she retrieved a pearl tiara from the wooden chest at the end of my bed. I did not own many headpieces, because what I had had belonged to my mother, and many came from her native home on the Atoll of Nalani. Her people were islanders. They were mariners, weavers, and horticulturalists, hence my mother's love for gardening.

I laughed. "And do what with your time? Stitch cushions?"

"*Read*, you insolent child," Nadia snapped, but her response was playful and not at all filled with the tension of our earlier exchange.

"I am far from a child, Nadia."

"You are a child until you marry," she said.

I rolled my eyes and smoothed my dress, studying myself in the mirror. All my life, I'd been told that I looked like my mother. As much as I longed to hear that, the compliment also left me feeling like someone had gouged out my heart. It was a reminder of her long absence from my life and the sacrifice she had made so that I could live.

"Why must I attend my father while he entertains our enemy with talk of surrender?"

I spoke more to myself than Nadia, though she offered her opinion nevertheless.

"If you are to rule this kingdom—husband or not—it will be under vampire rule from this day forward. You must learn who you are dealing with, and tonight is your first lesson."

Could that really be true? From this day forward,

Lara would answer to the Blood King, a creature who had slaughtered thousands of my kind already. It did not seem real.

"Just be glad, Issi, that the Blood King has not asked for a wife."

"Are you volunteering, Nadia?"

She glared at me. "Not even I want to be married that bad."

As much as we joked, dread had been gathering in my heart all day. Today, the world would change, and none of us knew if it was the better of two options. Still, I had to hope my father was right in his decision to be ruled by King Adrian. I had to hope that Adrian, despite being monstrous, still possessed some kind of humanity.

Nadia followed me from my room, down the narrow corridors of my wing. The walls of the castle were all intricate mason work, the brick laid in such a way that even without decor, they were aesthetically pleasing. Despite the beauty and the craftsmanship, the chill seeped through, sending shivers down my spine. Even worse, my nipples hardened, reminding me of my insatiable desire for my enemy.

At the bottom of the stairs, Nadia paused.

"Do not tremble under the gaze of the Blood King. Surrender today, live to conquer tomorrow."

Nadia's words were my hope that we would find a weapon that could defeat our enemy. She departed, leaving me to enter the antechamber where my father and I would wait for the arrival of the Blood King, at which point we would move into the great hall. My stomach knotted as I approached the door, but I paused before knocking, hearing Commander Killian's voice rising from within.

"This is a trap," Killian said.

"If the king of Revekka decides to slaughter us rather than negotiate, then it will say more about his countenance than ours," my father replied, his voice warm and resonant. It made my chest feel calm. I loved my father dearly—he was all I had from the moment I was born. I had never seen him make an impulsive decision, so I knew that he'd thought through every aspect of this surrender. Most importantly, he'd thought most about what would protect our people.

"Think of your daughter—" Killian tried.

"Know your place, Commander!"

My father's voice sent a chill through me that straightened my back, but I was glad for his anger. I was angry too. The audacity of the commander to assume my father hadn't thought about *me*. But this—it was bigger than me. Bigger than a commander whose ego suffered at the thought of being submissive to a greater power.

"It is because of Isolde that I have agreed to this truce. I do not wish for her to live in a future rife with violence."

"And yet she will face a future far more uncertain."

I took that as my cue to enter. It was either that or see Commander Killian pinned to the wall by my father's sword, and as much as he annoyed me, spilling blood when vampires were on our doorstep did not seem like the best idea.

My father's expression smoothed into a mask of calm when he saw me, a sad smile curling his thinning lips. He stood near the fire, a heavy fur-lined cloak making his slight frame look larger. My father had never been a particularly imposing man, but he had a presence, an expression that commanded attention and a voice that communicated dominance. His hair was dark but turning gray. Most of it was concentrated in his beard, which came to a point at his chin.

"Isolde," my father said. "My gem."

"Father," I greeted, approaching him, taking his outstretched hand. He pressed a kiss to my cheek.

"You look beautiful, as always."

"Thank you, Father." I smiled, despite what we were walking into. I took comfort in the fact that this surrender still meant we would be together. In the end, that was all that mattered.

"Commander Killian was just telling me you went to the border today and left without him."

If Killian was going to betray me, the least he could do was tell the whole truth, which included how I'd gotten away from him.

*How is your gut feeling?* I wanted to ask but kept silent. I didn't want this lecture to get any longer.

"Commander Killian caught up," I said, glaring at him.

"Issi," my father said, a note of warning in his voice. "You know the danger that lies upon our doorstep."

"I fail to see what Commander Killian could do if we were set upon by a vampire. It takes an army to defeat *one*."

My father sighed. He knew I had a point.

"There are other monsters, Princess," Killian argued, his voice tight.

I shifted my gaze and met his stare, which dipped to my breasts. I wanted to roll my eyes but refrained.

"Monsters I was taught to kill. Again, I fail to see why I need your escort."

"Because I have ordered it." My father's voice was

like a whip, cutting through the air and drawing my attention. "It is not up for discussion, Isolde. Clear?"

"Crystal," I replied tightly, my skin flushed with frustration.

My father sighed again, but it sounded more like relief. He was probably glad I hadn't argued. It was only for his benefit. I knew how taxing this surrender had been for him. I knew his concern for me stemmed from the invasion of the Blood King. I wasn't going to add to that. I would, on the other hand, ensure that Killian heard—and felt—my rage.

There was a knock at the door, and Miron, the herald, entered. His uniform was a dark-blue tabard with gold fringe. Usually, it complemented his burnished skin, but today, he looked sallow, and as he spoke, I thought I knew why—he'd just seen the Blood King in the flesh.

He bowed.

"Your Majesty." His voice trembled, and he cleared his throat. "The Blood King has arrived."

A strange tension filled the small room. Somehow, this felt different. The Blood King wasn't just beyond our borders; he was within them. He would rule us from this day forward.

My father looked long at me and then turned, grasping his cloak as he went so it whirled around with him. Commander Killian held out his arm. I'd have rather shoved a knife through it, but I accepted it instead.

"Why are you wearing that?" he asked, dipping his head so that his breath coated my cheek as he spoke.

*I should have gone with the knife*, I thought.

I did not look at him as I replied. "It is not your place to comment on my wardrobe, Commander."

His hand tightened on mine.

"You are showing too much skin. Are you trying to tempt the vampire king?"

"Know your place," I said, my voice just as icy as my father's.

"That is not how I meant—I only mean to protect you."

"From what? Hungry gazes?" I asked. We had just come through the doors of the antechamber and into the great hall when I turned to him, challenging. "Yours is just as threatening, Commander."

I crossed the precipice upon which my father's throne sat and moved to his left, my gaze sweeping the great hall. It was a grand room, richly decorated with gilded mirrors and elaborate candelabras. A canopy of blue silk curtained us, and throughout the room, gold larks—our house emblem—adorned banners of the same blue that hung from the ceiling.

The room was silent and still, though it was crowded with people—guards and lords and ladies who had come from their estates to watch the surrender. My father had spent weeks in this very room, hearing their concerns, mediating their arguments for and against surrender. By the end of it, I began to loathe many of them whose fears amounted to losing their lands, wealth, and status under the Blood King, as if that mattered when the decision wasn't between losing status and retaining it. It was between life and death.

"His majesty King Henri de Lara welcomes King Adrian Aleksandr Vasiliev of Revekka."

This time, Miron's voice was steady and strong. Holding my breath, I fixed my eyes on the doors at the other end of the hallway. The crowd, who had stood on either side of a carpeted runner, drew farther back as the guards pulled them open to reveal the Blood King.

I swallowed a gasp as a heady flush unraveled within my body, and I wanted to crawl out of my skin as my eyes connected with a familiar, gorgeous face. The vampire who had found me in the clearing, the one who had licked blood from my skin and sent me into a spiral of desire, was Adrian, the Blood King.

He had changed since our encounter, wearing bloodred instead of black. Gold rings gleamed upon his middle finger and pinkie, and upon his head sat a spiked black crown. His status was evident in the way he carried himself—regal and confident—and yet he walked like a predator, his black boots clicking as he took lethal step after lethal step toward my father.

*I should have known it was him*, I thought, staring at him now, but it had not occurred to me to expect the king of vampires to have gone in search of a strzyga. Were they not monsters born of their kind?

As he approached, his gaze slid from my father to Killian and then to me. Our eyes met, and I let out a slow, quivering breath as he assessed the length of my body. Something about him opened a chasm in my stomach, and I was again overwhelmed by the same keen hunger as before. I wanted to be devoured by this creature.

My legs began to shake, and I shifted my gaze to my father as he spoke.

"King Adrian. It is a grim welcome I extend to you," he said, his voice resonating within the great hall.

"A welcome all the same," Adrian said. His voice drew and held my attention, and I watched his lips as he spoke, not with the voice of a monster but the voice of a lover. "I accept."

"You and your army have quite the reputation," my father said.

"A reputation that has you contemplating surrender before bloodshed," Adrian said and inclined his head slightly. "Smart."

"Some have called me a coward," Father said. "For considering your proposal."

The tension in the great hall grew.

"Do you care what others think, King Henri?"

"I care about my people," he said. "I want them safe. Is that your offer, King Adrian? That you will keep my people safe?"

The vampire stared at my father for a long moment, studying him with a different intensity, as if he were trying to decide if he was being truthful.

"How much freedom do you wish for your people to have?"

My father did not answer immediately. Finally, I shifted my gaze and saw him lean forward.

"Are we bargaining, King Adrian?"

The vampire offered a small shrug. "I have an offer."

Father waited, and when Adrian did not continue, he prompted, "What is this offer?"

"I want your daughter. To wed, of course," he added, as if it were an afterthought.

"No," Commander Killian said instantly.

Adrian glared and so did I, even though I was still trying to process the enemy king's words. Had he just asked for my hand in marriage? My legs began to shake for a very different reason now, and for a moment, I feared my knees would buckle. Instead, I curled my fingers into my palm, letting my nails pierce the skin. I would not show weakness before this creature, though I'd already managed to do that in the clearing.

"You wish to wed my—no," my father said definitively.

I did not want to be married, least of all to this man.

Adrian stared at him. "You would choose war so quickly? I thought you cared for your people."

"He does care," I said and took a step forward, angered by his accusation.

"Issi." My father made to reach for me, but it was Commander Killian who intervened and stepped between me and the Blood King.

"King Adrian has asked for my hand," I said. "Am I not allowed to speak?"

"These are matters for kings," Commander Killian said. His voice was low and grated against my ear.

I wanted to push him away, but I reined myself in, offering a command instead. "Back to your post, Commander."

He was reluctant to obey, and if we had been alone, he wouldn't have. Still, he fell back and returned to my father's side. When my gaze turned back to Adrian, he looked amused.

"If you wanted a wife, why did you wait until now to ask for my hand?"

"I did not know I wanted one until today," he replied.

My frustration spiked. Had he decided when we'd met earlier in the wood? Had I had the same effect on him as he did on me?

"Attraction hardly makes a marriage, King Adrian," I said.

"It makes a bearable one," he said. "Wouldn't you say, Princess?"

*So you want to fuck me*, I thought, narrowing my eyes. We did not even need vows for that, but somehow, offering myself to the Blood King without a marriage contract felt worse than losing my freedom.

"Unless it is marriage to a monster," I said. "Then it is merely captivity."

There were a few murmurs from the crowd, quickly silenced by Adrian's reply. "If you will not agree, then we will have war," he said simply.

"A battle I will gladly fight!" my father shouted, getting to his feet, and a few members of the crowd cheered along with his declaration. His words were visceral, and I knew he meant them, even if I also knew he would die, and it was that reality I could not face.

How had I suddenly become the prize to be won in battle?

"Father—" I started to speak but was silenced.

"Isolde, leave. Immediately."

The arms of the guards at the exits rattled as they hoisted their weapons, and the lords and ladies who had crowded into the hall began to scream and murmur, pressing into the walls.

This could not happen. It would mean slaughter. Commander Killian had come around my father's throne, his hand taking my arm before I jerked away.

Why was he *always* touching me?

"I will not be dismissed!" I said.

"Princess—"

"Your princess wishes to speak," Adrian said. "*Let her.*"

The last two words were spoken with warning. My heart was still racing, adrenaline surging through my blood. I looked to my father, whose watery blue-green eyes were desperate.

*Don't*, he begged.

*I have to*, I mouthed. As much as he did not want to lose me, I could not lose him. I could not lose our people. I'd wanted to be their queen to protect them, and I still would, but not in the way I expected.

I turned to Adrian, taking a step toward him. I could feel everyone in the room stiffening, tightening their holds on their weapons. The tension was already a battle, and the phantom smell of blood permeated the air although none had been shed yet.

Still, I held the Blood King's gaze, focused on him so completely, it was as if he were the only person in the room. The longer I looked, the easier it was. It helped that he was beautiful, but I also became interested in things I shouldn't, like the bow of his lips and the faint scar over his cheek I had not noticed earlier.

I refused to take a breath before speaking, fearing it would sound more like a shudder. "King Adrian, if you maintain you will protect my country, my people, my father, then I will agree to marry you."

Adrian's lips curled, but it was a smile that did not last long when Commander Killian protested. "My princess, you can't marry this monster! I won't let you!"

Adrian scowled. "You won't *let* her?"

"Quiet, creature. You are a curse upon our lands!"

The commander drew his sword, and the guards followed.

I turned, facing Killian, blocking Adrian. It was not

a smart decision. I did not know Adrian, he was the enemy, and I was giving him my back, but I could not let things progress.

"Lower your sword," I seethed. He glared at me, his fingers tightening around the hilt. "*Now!*"

My command echoed in the hall.

"I will not see this land covered in the blood of my people. I agreed to King Adrian's terms."

"You forget, Princess. It is your father who rules here and rules your fate."

I glared at Killian before shifting to look at my father, gaze softening. "I love you, Father. I would never willingly leave you, but you know this is the right decision. You know because you made it before Revekka was on our doorstep."

I knew what he was thinking—*that was before he wanted you.*

"I am one person," I said. "I am not worth a slaugh-tered kingdom."

"You are worth every star in the sky, Issi," my father said, and for a moment, my heart sank. Would his decla-ration of war follow? But instead, his gaze lifted to Adrian. "My daughter has a habit of ensuring everyone else's safety before her own. I trust among those you protect, she will be one."

I turned to face the Blood King. I wanted to look upon him as he answered my father. For the first time since he arrived, he bowed, placing a hand over his heart as he answered, "I vow it upon my life."

His words surprised me, and I had to admit, I didn't believe him. I narrowed my eyes. What was his motive? Why me?

"Father, I would like to speak with King Adrian alone."

"Absolutely not."

"Do you doubt my vow?" Adrian said.

"You are an enemy, you have slaughtered thousands of our people, and you have just asked for my daughter's hand in marriage. You will forgive my wish to protect her for as long as possible."

"Father," I said quietly. "I will ultimately be alone with King Adrian many times in the coming weeks. What is a few minutes here in the walls of our home?"

He watched me, frowning, and then glared at Adrian.

"I will give you five minutes. No more."

I looked at Adrian and then turned, leading the way into the anteroom. I clenched my teeth and fists, feeling so violent, I shook. It did not help that when I faced him, he looked completely calm.

Of course he was calm. He would end this day with a new kingdom and a wife.

*Wife.*

My stomach sank at the word.

"Is this some kind of joke?" I demanded.

"Which part?" he asked, as if he could not guess.

"The part where you asked for my hand in marriage," I spat.

"That part," he said, his voice deep, his words deliberate, "is very serious."

"What need have you for a wife?" I asked. "You cannot sire children."

Vampires were not technically living creatures and could not reproduce; they created more of their kind by turning existing humans into monsters.

Adrian narrowed his eyes, and I wondered if I had struck a chord. Still, kings married for many reasons: if not heirs, then alliances, and occasionally love. Adrian could not have children, he did not need alliances, and love was a ridiculous notion for someone like him.

"Do you wish to be a breeding mare?" he challenged.

I scowled. What did it matter? I did not want to be a wife, but here I was, suddenly engaged. "Will you take a wife for every house you conquer?" I countered. Perhaps he wished for a harem or bodies he could drain.

Adrian seemed amused, his brows lifted, his lips pursed. "I think you will be challenging enough. Why would I wish for more?"

"I don't understand."

"What is there to understand?"

"Why me?"

He stared at me, and I got the impression he did not know how to answer my question.

"You assume I want a wife," he said. "But I came for a queen."

It was my turn to stare.

"So our marriage will be one of pageantry?"

"Oh, I think we are both too passionate for that."

His words had an unnerving effect on me, and I could not figure out if it was because of the way he said them—his voice low and erotic, the voice I imagined he used in the dead of night as he spoke to his lovers—or the words themselves.

I stiffened, and yet heat blossomed in my chest. "You did not have to ask for my hand if all you wanted was my body. I am sure we could have come to an agreement."

Adrian's eyes flickered, and he took a step forward. I could not tell if the action was from frustration or if he'd taken my comment as an invitation. Either way, it took everything in me not to step back. He must have seen my apprehension, because he paused.

"You have nothing to fear in my approach."

"I have everything to fear. The blood of the Nine Houses is on your hands."

"Not your house," he said, as if that made everything better.

Perhaps I should have said it differently. "Do you intend to continue your war upon Cordova, even with my father's surrender?"

"I did not set out to conquer the House of Lara only, Princess Isolde. I set out to become king of Cordova." His eyes dipped. "And I need a queen."

"Are you trying to tempt me with power?"

"Eventually, as it tempts all."

"Is that why you are doing this? For power?"

"It is not my main motivation," he said. "But a result of it."

"And what is your main motivation?" I asked, my eyes slipping to his lips, which lifted at my question.

"I'm afraid I cannot be tempted to reveal all my secrets, Princess."

"Really?" I breathed. "Not even a little?"

He lifted his hand, and I took a step away. He chuckled, as if I'd proven his point.

"No, not when you flinch at my approach."

I glared at him.

"I swore an oath to your father. I will not hurt you."

"Do you uphold all your oaths?" I asked.

"I have never sworn an oath until now," he answered. "And I will swear no more after this."

Once again, he held out his hand. My eyes fell to it—scarred, strong, graceful—and I gave him my fingers.

"See?" he whispered. "Nothing to fear."

Though he spoke the words, I still held my breath as he turned my hand over to reveal my palm. It was bloodied from earlier when I'd clenched my fingers tight in an effort to keep standing after he'd asked to wed me. Now the blood had dried into the cracks of my skin.

He clicked his tongue.

"You should be more careful, Princess."

Then he bent and his tongue swirled over my palm. That was twice in one day this vampire had tasted my blood and, once again, healed my wounds. This time, I let him, even as guilt crept over me.

When his gaze lifted to mine, there was something deadly within his eyes—a darkness that seemed endless. He licked his lips.

"Your blood is truly a homecoming," he said.

I pulled my hand away, disgusted and suddenly afraid he would want more.

Adrian chuckled, as if he knew my thoughts. "Not to worry, my sweet. I will not feed from you. Not until you ask."

"I will *never* ask."

The Blood King's lips twitched, and when he spoke, his voice was reverent. "You will. You will beg for it."

I could not imagine begging for anything from this…creature. I took a deep breath and let it out slowly. The rise of my chest drew his gaze.

"Are you threatening me?"

"No. I am offering the promise of pleasure."

I thought my throat would close up, because as much as I hated what he was, as much as I hated him, he spoke a language I wanted to learn.

Still, he could never know that.

"Believe me, King Adrian," I said and was proud of how steady my voice sounded. "Nothing that comes from you will ever be a pleasure."

His lips lifted higher. "I accept your challenge, Princess."

The doors opened then, and my father's voice beckoned. "Isolde. Come."

Why, when given a reprieve, did I not move? I stayed, standing before Adrian, rooted to the spot, feeling as if I'd been dragged to the edge of a cliff, body on edge, completely wound.

I wanted to fall, and I could tell by the hungry look in Adrian's eyes he was ready to catch me.

"Run along, Princess," he said. "I'll see you soon enough."

# FOUR

*"You gave her to that monster!"* **Commander Killian's** voice rose. He stood before my father, who was slumped in his chair. Usually, Killian's words would incense me, and I'd form some kind of snide reply that illustrated how much I disagreed with him, but right now, I had no words. Tomorrow night, I would marry our conqueror.

I'd never imagined myself married, even with all Nadia's talk about how it was expected of me. *Queens do not rule alone. Queens do not rule at all*, she'd say. They held no power beyond what they could do for their king.

I was supposed to change that. I'd felt as though that was my purpose, a feeling so strong, it had filled my whole heart with excitement and determination.

Suddenly, that was gone, and the absence of it was a greater weight than I'd ever imagined.

Now, I'd rule just like other queens.

*Do you wish to be a breeding mare?* Adrian had asked

me. Was it too early to hope that perhaps he wanted something different from his queen too?

I lingered near the window, staring out over my home, my kingdom, the one that now belonged to the Blood King. It was still dark, but the moon was heavy and full and cast the land in silver. Absently, I wondered if Adrian would think it was as beautiful as I did. Would he appreciate what Lara had to offer, our colorful textiles, sweet wines, and lively culture? Or was it just another country to mark off his list of conquered kingdoms?

"You cannot mean to *let* her leave with him!"

"Commander Killian." My father's voice was low, roughened, tired, and I turned from the window to watch the exchange. "Leave us."

Killian froze for a moment and then looked to me, as if I would beg my father for his presence.

"You were given an order," I said instead, which caused him to frown. "You should obey."

Another moment of hesitation, then he bowed and left.

At first, neither one of us spoke. The air was too heavy, the shock of what we'd both agreed to not quite registering.

"This is never what I intended for you," my father said at last.

Something thick gathered in the back of my throat.

"I know," I whispered, my mouth quivering. "I would have never left your side."

My father swallowed and wiped at his eyes before he stood and approached, placing his hand upon my face, his thumb brushing my cheekbone. I hated the way he looked at me, like he was alone in the world without me.

"You are the hope of our kingdom, Isolde."

Then he dropped his hand, turned, and left the room, shutting the door quietly, and I felt like he had taken my whole heart with him.

––––––

Returning to my room was a nightmare.

I hardly made it down the corridor without encountering a stricken gaze. I held my head higher, refusing to lower my eyes. I was not ashamed of my decision, and I knew that my people only looked at me this way because they were afraid—for me and their future.

"Princess Isolde!"

Lady Larisa shimmied forward; the folds of her gown seemed to restrict her movement. She had her younger sister, Gabriela, in tow. Their father, Lord Cristian, oversaw one of three vineyards in Lara. He had been the first to sweeten the bitter drink, which had heightened the demand across all Cordova. He had also loudly declared his concern for the loss of his title and land upon surrender to Adrian, which had lowered my opinion of him considerably. Though Larisa and Gabriela were well meaning and sweet.

"I just heard the news. How are you?"

"I am fine, Lady Larisa," I said. "Thank you for your concern."

I meant that genuinely. She had been the first to ask if I was all right.

"I cannot imagine how shocked you must be," she continued. "I always thought you would rule as our queen."

"Becoming queen of Revekka does not mean I will not also one day rule Lara," I said.

"So you will support your new husband, then, in his conquest of Cordova?"

I whirled to find Lord Cristian hovering. He was a tall man with dark features, and he stared down at me, his hands behind his back. I hated the way he looked at me. It was clear he thought I was nothing more than a child, even at my twenty-six years of age.

"Certainly not, Lord Cristian," I replied, trying to keep my frustration at bay. "Though I am still heir of Lara."

"Of course," he said and came to stand beside his daughters. "We are all watching with bated breath, Princess, to see your next move."

"Excuse me?"

"You will be close to the Blood King," he said. "Closer than anyone ever has been."

He did not need to be explicit for me to understand his implication—they were waiting for me to kill Adrian. To speak such words, however, would be considered treason to the Blood King. Though that did not matter to me so much as this man's perceived power over me.

"The only thing you should be watching, Lord Cristian, is your crop," I said.

The man stiffened. If he wanted to play a game of subtlety, I could too, especially given his concern for himself and not those over whom he ruled.

"Have a good night, my lord," I said, and then my gaze shifted to his daughters. "Lady Larisa, Lady Gabriela."

By the time I made it to my room, my adrenaline had crashed, and I was left feeling exhausted. As I opened my door, I found Nadia waiting. She looked up at me from her spot before the fireplace, shoulders hunched, hands grasping her apron. I did not need to ask if she had heard the news; I could tell by her expression she knew. Her eyes were wide, glassy, and she was pale.

"Nadia." Her name fell from my mouth, quiet and distant. I had not expected her to be waiting for me. I'd really hoped to be alone, especially because she looked at me—in the same way everyone was looking at me—as if I were already a ghost.

"Oh, Issi," she said as she advanced. Her arms encircled me, hands digging into my back. "I cannot believe what I have just heard. Tell me that vile king did not ask for your hand."

"He did," I said, and she pushed me to arm's length to study my face. I looked back at her but did not really see her. I couldn't focus.

"You did not have to say yes. Your father would have gladly fought for you."

My father rarely made rash decisions, but something else had overtaken him when Adrian had asked for me. I had never seen that kind of fire in his eyes, but I could relate, because it was how my insides felt—a kind of angry fear, a desperation to hold on to the person you love most.

"But I did say yes," I said.

Nadia knew that, and my father did too.

I took a breath and released her, crossing the room to my bed. I slipped out of my shoes. It was my way of telling her I was ready for bed.

"If only you had wed Commander Killian," she said as she loosened the ties at my back.

I cringed. "Even if I had known what today would bring, I could not face marrying Alec Killian."

"It would be better than marriage to a monster," Nadia said as she finished unlacing my gown. It puddled to the floor, and I was left wearing only a cream-colored shift.

I turned to face her.

Killian had all the potential of becoming a monster, though I did not say that, because at the end of the day, that wasn't what I cared about.

"What would be better is if I could remain alone," I said. I had gotten too comfortable, assuming I did not have to fill the traditional roles of a princess. I had thought I would blaze my own trail, that I would become the first queen to serve in the Nine Houses, but I was wrong, and that hurt me more than anything. "At least this marriage will save a kingdom."

If I could not blaze the trail alone, then perhaps I could save our kingdom. My spirits rose a little at that thought.

"I cannot imagine what that creature could possibly want with a wife."

"*You assume I want a wife,*" he'd said. "*But I came for a queen.*"

Except that Adrian had conquered and ruled over Revekka for more than one hundred and fifty years— and he'd been alive far longer—without a queen. At one point, it seemed, he too had desired to be alone, so what had changed?

*Your blood is truly a homecoming.*

I shivered as I recalled his words and the way his fingers felt as they clasped mine. It must have been noticeable, because Nadia reached for a blanket, wrapping it around my shoulders. I hated how I reacted when he touched me—my head felt light, my face grew flushed, my whole body felt alive and yet on edge, unprepared for the next sensation he might urge to the surface.

I hated it because my body acted as if he were not the enemy.

*Nadia was right. You're a child*, I scolded myself and reasoned. *Any man can make you feel this way.*

"I shudder to think what he has planned for you."

Nadia was still talking, but my mind had gone into a full spiral. While I wondered what he wanted with me, I thought of the immediate future. What duties did the Blood King expect me to perform? He'd been open about his wish to drink my blood, and he'd offered the promise of pleasure—did vampires consummate marriages differently? If it was done by drinking blood rather than sex, could I abstain for as long as possible to prevent a true marriage?

"Issi?"

My eyes lifted and connected with Nadia's concerned stare.

"Yes?" I asked.

"Are you okay?"

I hardly knew. I had begun the day hating vampires with every fiber of my being and ended the day engaged to one. I had been through a whole range of emotions—a passionate high and a devastating low. I felt exhausted and yet lustful. The need to be full and stretched and utterly shattered had never really gone away. It had ebbed and flowed.

"Can I be alone, Nadia?" I asked.

She hesitated. "Are you sure?"

"Please, Nadia."

I rarely said please.

"All right."

Nadia moved toward the door and cast me a forlorn glace. "Call if you need me."

When she was gone, I fell onto my bed, sinking into the velvet covers, my eyes fixed on the ceiling.

"What have I done?" I said aloud before closing my eyes. As I exhaled, I relaxed, then drew my legs up and apart, the hem of my shift gathering around my thighs as I trailed my fingers along my skin. I thought about how much I would have preferred another's touch, because I did not think my own would ease this ache.

Perhaps that was the hold of Adrian's magic. Was he the only one who could release me?

Suddenly, Adrian hovered over me, his mouth close to mine, his hair, like the sun, curtaining my view, curling softly against my skin.

"Why are you here?" I asked.

"Because," he said, "you were made for me."

"You could say that to any woman, just as I could say that to any man."

"But would it be true?"

"There is no truth where magic survives."

"There is only truth if magic survives," he said, and he bent toward me, lips touching my throat as my head pressed into my pillow, and my fingers teased my aching flesh. "Come for me, my sweet, so that I may taste you."

My body was primed and heated, my entrance slick with need, and just as I was about to dip my fingers into my swollen flesh, the door to my bedroom flew open. I jerked into a sitting position, meeting Killian's gaze.

"What?" I snapped, angry that I had been interrupted

51

again, that I could not untie this knot deep in my stomach.

"Am I interrupting?" he asked, eyes darkening as he took in my position on the bed.

"Yes," I hissed, angrier because he knew what he interrupted, furious because of what he dared to say next.

"It isn't anything I can help with?"

"If I'd wanted help, I would have called for you," I snapped as I slid off the bed. I crossed the room, putting distance between myself and the commander. "I wish to be alone."

Instead of listening, he closed the door, and I sighed loudly.

"What did the creature say to you?" Killian demanded.

"Nothing that means much," I said. "I can barely recall his words."

Which was a lie. I remembered every word. They still slid across my skin, much as his tongue had done this evening, promising pleasure. I hated myself for wanting what he offered, but I was standing opposite a man who could never give it. How could I possibly be blamed?

"You can't really mean to marry him," Killian said.

"What do you mean?" I gazed at him, even though I didn't want to look at him. I'd rather he left.

"I mean exactly what I'm asking. You aren't really going to go through with this wedding, are you?"

"I don't have a choice, Killian. I—"

"You *have* a choice!" he cut me off. "Kill him, Isolde. Drive a knife through his heart, and then you and I can wed."

I stood opposite Killian, stunned. "I would never marry you."

"You would marry the Blood King with no argument but not me?"

"It's not as if I have a choice. This will save so many lives, Killian. What can you offer?"

He clenched his fists and lifted them, as if he wished to strike something—maybe me—but he did not move from his place. After a moment, he spoke. "Before your father decided on a truce with the vampires, he promised you to me," Killian said. "I only had to kill the Blood King."

"Promised?" I repeated the word, because his admission shocked me. My father had never spoken to me of marriage, least of all to Killian.

"Think about it, Isolde. Would you not rather live a long life with me than one with him?"

"If it were my choice, I'd have neither of you."

"You don't mean that."

"I mean every damn word."

I started to pass Killian, intent on opening the door and demanding that he leave, but he grabbed my arm and jerked me toward him. I lifted my hand and slapped his face, but he didn't release me.

"Let. Go," I said between my teeth.

"You do not think I could kill him. I could. I would for you."

"And I am telling you no. Do nothing for me, Killian. I don't want it."

I jerked on my arm, and he loosened his grip.

"Are you telling me you want him?" he asked, a note of disgust in his tone.

"I will not dignify your questions with a response. Not that you would hear me if I gave one."

I turned from him and swung the door open.

"Leave. *Now.*"

Killian's stare was lethal, but he still managed a courteous bow before storming from the room. I stood for a moment, rubbing my sore arm. There were a lot of reasons I'd never consider marrying the commander. Aside from bland sex, he was quick to anger, a trait I never wanted in a husband. I saw it too often among nobility, especially among the kings of the Nine Houses.

Once he was gone, I walked to the window and stared out into the night. It was well past sundown, and every gate that led into High City and the castle grounds would be locked and under guard, though that meant nothing for Killian, and I wondered if his anger was acute enough to send him beyond those gates to attempt his assassination of the Blood King.

I had no faith that Killian would succeed in his effort to kill Adrian, but I wondered what his betrayal would mean for our truce? For the protection Adrian had offered my people? I wanted to ensure they would be safe despite one man's rogue choice.

I lingered at the window a moment longer before slipping on my cloak, arming myself, and leaving my room.

The cold seeped through my slippers as I made my way out of the servants' quarters and into the night. I hadn't exactly decided how I was going to make it past the guards at the gate, and I was no closer to figuring that out when I arrived. Nicolae and Lascar had retired; in their place were two older guards who were not as easily swayed by my charm—one named Avram, the other Ivan.

"Princess," Avram said. "You best get back to the castle."

I ignored him. "Has Commander Killian come through these gates?"

"Minutes ago," said Ivan. "Can we pass along a message?"

I hesitated and tried to look coy, clearing my throat. "I'd rather surprise him."

The two exchanged a look. Avram looked amused, but Ivan frowned.

"You cannot blame her," Avram said. "She's got to marry the Blood King tomorrow."

By the fucking goddess, I hated asking permission from anyone. Perhaps becoming Adrian's wife would afford me some level of freedom again.

"At least let one of us escort you to the commander," said Ivan.

"You said he was minutes ahead of me," I responded. "I can catch up."

"There are monsters in the woods, Princess," Avram warned, as if I did not know.

"I'm armed."

"If you want the commander, you must have an escort," said Avram.

"Fine," I said, haughty, and stepped between the guards. "Come along, Ivan."

I did not wait to see if he began to follow, but I had chosen him over Avram, who I knew was far more athletic. Ivan would have a harder time catching me when I made a run for the border.

We entered the tree line. There were three paths where the vegetation had been worn down. Each led to a different stronghold on the border of Lara. I did not usually stick to paths when I entered the woods—mostly because I never wanted to be caught by the soldiers who used them.

"He went this way, Princess," he said, pointing straight ahead.

My stomach dropped a little further. It was the direction of the vampire's camp.

*He isn't this stupid*, I told myself. Though I could not be sure, given how determined Killian seemed to handle me. That being said, Killian was loyal to my father's orders. I wondered if my father retracted his offer to make me Killian's bride once he'd decided to make peace with the vampires. Or was it still on the table?

That thought had me walking faster.

Ivan chuckled, already falling behind. "Slow down, Princess. You'll get there with enough time to say your goodbyes."

While it was my fault Ivan believed I was headed into the woods to have a tryst with Commander Killian, I still hated the implication in his tone and voice.

I paused abruptly.

"Did you hear that?" I asked.

Ivan went rigid and peered into the night. Slices of moonlight pooled throughout the forest, cutting between the canopy of branches overhead. A part of me felt guilty. Ivan was kind, he meant well, and I could tell he had transitioned, going from playful to soldier, his hand on the hilt of his blade.

"What exactly did you hear, Princess?" he asked, a serious edge to his voice.

"It was a rattling sound," I said, which was usually a sign

that a virika was near. Virika were creatures that moved with the shadows. They were impossible to see until they bared their bloodred teeth. They could be stealthy, unless they were hungry. Hunger made them stupid.

"Follow closely, Princess," said Ivan.

I let him walk ahead, trailing behind him as I bent to pick up a rock. We continued for a little while longer before I tossed the stone into the wood nearby.

"What was that?" I whispered frantically.

Ivan turned in the direction I'd thrown the stone, eyes searching cautiously as I slipped away into the darkness. I did not take off at a run until I heard Ivan yell.

"Princess!"

I wasn't made for running, and I certainly wasn't dressed for it, but I pushed forward, running until I could see the vampire's camp through the trees, then I paused within the shadows. Unlike this afternoon, the camp was alive with activity, and I was taken aback by how *human* everyone appeared. They were dressed in Adrian's colors, the colors I imagined decorated the halls of Revekka— red and black. Flashes of gold armor that looked almost featherlike ignited like flame as they milled about, some gathered around the fire, while another group looked to be playing cards. They seemed carefree—as if they were not an army encamped in enemy territory.

Then again, they had little to fear. They were unbeatable.

I did not notice Commander Killian. I expected that if he'd attempted to enter the camp, he would have been captured by now.

Just as I was about to dart from the tree line and head straight for Adrian's tent, a voice sounded from behind me.

"That was very unkind, what you did to your guard."

I whirled to find a vampire I did not recognize behind me, and I hated that I had not been able to sense his approach. I stumbled back and, consequently, out of the tree line, and the vampire advanced. The moonlight cast beams of light over his body, illuminating slivers of dark skin and a pretty face—wide cheekbones, full lips, and a set of dimples on either side of his mouth.

"How long have you been following me?" I asked.

"I wasn't," he said.

My back met something hard, and hands clamped down on my shoulders. I reached back, grabbed them, and released my daggers into the person's forearms. A scream that sounded more like a wounded growl erupted into the night, and I twisted to find another vampire. This one was slimmer, his hair hanging straight and lanky around a thin face. His fists were clenched, and blood dripped from his forearms.

"Fuck, she stabbed me!" he cried.

Behind me, the other vampire laughed. "Serves you right for assuming she was unarmed."

"Sorin, what is going on?" another voice joined the mix. This one was female.

"I caught a mortal sneaking into camp," said the dark vampire. "She stabbed Isac."

The woman who approached was blond, her hair pulled into an intricate braid that ran from the top of her head to the middle of her back. She was beautiful and fierce, and she sounded as if she were laughing.

"Stabbed *you*, Isac?"

"Shut up, Miha," he snapped.

There were now three vampires standing in an arc

before me, and I was shocked I was still alive. Even the one I'd stabbed seemed relatively calm, and I'd expected him to retaliate quickly. Instead, his arms quit shaking, and blood stopped dripping from his wounds. Soon, he let them fall to his sides, healed.

An explosion of cheers sounded behind us suddenly, and I turned to see the group of vampires who had previously been playing cards on their feet. Two men were on the ground, fighting.

Miha rolled her eyes while Sorin and Isac chuckled. "I knew that game would end in a quarrel."

"Four kings always does," said Sorin.

I did not ask what four kings was. Instead, I started to shift away from the trio of vampires, until their attention returned to me and I froze.

"So what are you doing here, little one?" Miha continued. "Have you come to seduce and kill our king?"

I was too surprised by her question to complain that she'd called me little one. My brows rose. "Excuse me?"

"It wouldn't be the first attempt," Sorin said.

"I—no," I said and paused. "Did you just say it wouldn't be the first attempt?"

"That's right," Sorin quipped.

"What happened to the woman who tried that?"

I couldn't help myself. I was curious. Was Adrian capable of being seduced, or had he murdered every woman who tried?

The three of them exchanged a look, and before Sorin could speak, another voice joined the fray.

"Princess Isolde. What a surprise."

I whirled to face Adrian while the three vampires behind me acknowledged him.

"My king," they said.

"I caught her sneaking into camp, Your Majesty," said Sorin.

"She stabbed me," said Isac.

"We stopped her before she could reach your tent," Miha added.

Adrian looked at me for a long moment and then spoke. "Princess Isolde is my betrothed. She may come to my tent whenever she wishes."

It wasn't a wish. This was business, but I said nothing.

"You could have said that," said Isac, "instead of stabbing me."

I turned to look at him. "You were the one who touched me."

"On the *shoulders*," he added, as if to clarify for Adrian's sake.

"Your point?"

The other two vampires were smiling, and behind me, Adrian chuckled, which drew my gaze. When he wasn't laughing at my expense, the sound was actually...warm.

"You laugh," I said and tilted my head back to better meet his eyes, "but he is not the only one who will feel the sting of my blade."

Adrian touched my chin, and this time, I managed not to flinch. "My sweet, I look forward to that."

Someone cleared their throat, and I looked at the three vampires, who had all averted their eyes, lingering awkwardly.

"We're just going to...go," Sorin said, and I watched the three fall back into the shadows of the wood.

I returned my attention to Adrian, who was still watching me.

"You were heading to my tent?" he asked.

"I need to speak with you," I said.

He stared and, after a moment, indicated for me to follow. "Come."

We walked side by side, and as we came around to the front of his tent, I got a better look at their camp. The first thing that took me by surprise was the sight of several fires, over which a mortal man cooked. The smell of sizzling meats and seasonings wafted toward me, and my stomach turned.

"What is he cooking?" I asked, my stomach turning. I didn't think it was human meat, but I wanted to be sure nevertheless. Vampires did not eat as far as I knew.

Adrian raised a brow. "Lamb. For the mortals who travel with us."

"You let mortals travel with you?"

"How do you think we eat?" he asked.

His question was so casual, and yet it made my blood run cold. I was not aware that mortals traveled with his army, though there were stories of people who fled to Revekka to gain immortality by offering their blood in the hope that they would eventually be turned into a vampire. The practice was called bloodletting and seen as treasonous to all kingdoms of the Nine Houses. It was also an automatic death sentence.

Adrian directed me into his tent, letting me enter ahead of him. Inside, it was warm, the heat wafting from a brazier at its center. The sight of it caused me to hesitate at the entrance, and Adrian bumped into me. Instead of staggering away, his hand touched my waist.

"You are safe here," he said, mistaking my fear of the fire for a fear of him.

I moved forward quickly. At my feet plush rugs covered most of the ground, and a round table and several wooden folding chairs were arranged to one side. There was also a desk, upon which a map of Cordova was spread, and I fought every urge to approach and read his plans for my world. A bed took up the other side of the tent and it was that I focused on, because it was occupied by a very naked woman. She was stretched out, completely exposed, creamy skin burnished by firelight. She jerked into a sitting position when she saw us enter, not bothering to drag the blankets up to cover herself. She only stared, wide-eyed, as if she had not expected Adrian to bring a visitor.

"Out," Adrian snapped, and she fled. I watched her go, feeling irritated that he hadn't been alone.

"Will your mistress join us on our wedding night?" I asked, glaring at him.

"Already dreaming of our time together?" he countered and then offered a smile. "She is not my mistress."

"So you wouldn't have slept with her?"

He stared. "I suppose it depends on how I'm feeling."

I narrowed my eyes upon him. "You're supposed to say no, at least to my face. Unless you wish to conduct our marriage openly. In which case, shall I start scouting for potential lovers?"

Adrian's mouth hardened. "Are you demanding fidelity?"

"I will follow as you lead," I said. It was a taunt.

"It is early to make demands. We have not even wed yet."

"If my request is such a burden, then call off the

engagement," I challenged. I walked farther into the tent, keeping my distance from the fire at the center. The flames seemed too high and too angry.

"Oh, my sweet, things have become far too interesting for that," he said and then tilted his head to the side. "Why are you here?"

I hesitated for a moment. Maybe this was a mistake. As the words came out of my mouth, they seemed ridiculous. "I need a promise from you."

Adrian's pale brows rose over his strange eyes. "Go on."

"It won't surprise you to know that Commander Killian hates you, even more after today. I think he believes he could kill you and free me from our engagement. I need you to promise that if he tries to attack, you will not seek retribution against my people."

Adrian stared at me for a long moment.

"What will you give me in exchange for this promise?"

"I warned you of Killian. Is that not enough?"

"You have told me nothing I did not already know. Your commander has been planning ways to kill me since I landed on your doorstep."

I stared at him. "What do you want from me?"

"Everything," he said. "But for now, I will settle for the answer to why you do not walk near the fire."

I stared at him, surprised he had noticed, and then looked toward the flames. Acknowledging my fear of fire seemed so minimal compared to anything else he could have asked, so I answered truthfully.

"I am afraid of fire," I said. "I have been since I was a child."

"Were you burned as a child?" Adrian moved closer.

"No," I said and then inhaled an involuntary, shaky breath. There was more to this than I wanted to admit, an unexplainable panic that came at night when I closed my eyes. It was a horror Adrian had no right to access, so I said nothing more.

Still, he was staring, and his gaze burned worse than any fire.

"Why do you ask?"

"You are to be my wife," he said.

Now he was behind me, and though he did not touch me, I felt him through the tension between us. His body called to mine, a magnetic pull that grasped my hips and shoulders. It took everything in my power not to bow into him.

I was so focused on keeping my body in check that when he spoke against my ear, I gasped. "Tell me, does Commander Killian visit your bed often?"

Jealousy was a strange trait between strangers, and yet it had reared its head twice between us now. At least I was not alone in my irrationality.

I turned my head, eyes falling to his lips, which were only an inch from mine.

"What makes you think he visits my bed?"

"I know jealous lovers," he said. "Does your commander think that if I am dead, he can have you?"

"No one *owns* me, King Adrian."

"I do not seek to own you," he said but did not elaborate.

Again, I found myself wondering why he had chosen me. I turned to face him, my shoulder brushing his chest as I moved, glaring up at him.

"Do I have your word you will not retaliate?" I asked.

"I will not seek revenge against your people, but I will not promise to spare your commander."

I felt the color drain from my face. "And if I ask you to spare him?"

I could not explain the look on Adrian's face, but I thought that maybe he felt triumph at my question, as if he'd snared me into another bargain. He took a step away and sat in one of the folding chairs. He was relaxed, one large hand resting on the arm, his long legs spread wide, as if in invitation.

"Would you spare a man who tried to kill you?" he asked.

I hesitated but answered truthfully. "No."

"Then why should I spare your commander?"

*Because he's an idiot*, I wanted to say. "Because I asked you to."

He stared, and my eyes wandered down his strong frame.

"You ask for much."

"Think of it as a wedding gift," I said slowly.

"A wedding gift," he repeated.

"Do you not wish to please me?" I asked.

Adrian's head tilted again, and his lips quirked. "Of course I wish to please you."

I approached, driven by a need to extract my promise but also a curiosity—how close would he let me get? And if I could get close...could I kill him myself? I recalled Lord Cristian's words, wondering if everyone in the kingdom had the same expectation of me.

Adrian watched me, eyes aflame as I settled my knee between his thighs.

"Then please me," I whispered and gingerly placed my hands on his chest. He was surprisingly warm, and the muscles beneath my palms were hard. He still had not moved, had not placed his hands upon me, and the only indication that he was aroused was the hard length pressed against my knee.

I slipped my hands up his chest. If he would let me, I could shove my blade into his neck and jerk it through. My knives were sharp enough to cut bone if I got the angle right.

"Is that what you really want?" he murmured, his eyes never leaving mine.

"Yes."

He smirked and lifted his head just an inch so that I could feel his breath on my lips as he spoke. "Because I think you want to kill me." In the next second, he moved. One of his hands gripped beneath my knee, and the other moved around my waist as he stood, sealing our bodies together, trapping my hands between us. I gripped his shirt in my fists, and my leg hitched around his hip, his erection pressed against the softness of my body, a hard edge I wanted to ride, but I kept still, glaring at him as he spoke. "And if that is the case, I should warn you now that any attempt will be met with my wrath."

"As if your wrath could be any worse," I spat.

"Oh, my sweet," he said and moved to grip my face. He was so quick, so fluid, I could not react, and as he spoke, his words whispered across my lips. "I could turn you in an instant."

Then he tilted my head back, lips trailing along my neck. My fingers squeezed his shirt tighter. "And then what would you be?"

He waited until he drew back to look me in the eyes before he answered. "Nothing more than the undead you hate."

I shoved against him, and he released me. We stared at each other for a moment, and I wondered what Adrian was thinking. Was he torn between fighting and fucking?

I was.

Instead, I came to my senses and returned to why I had come here to begin with.

"Do I have your word that you will not retaliate against my people?"

Adrian glared, as if now the question annoyed him. "We made an agreement," he said. "I swore to protect your people so long as you agreed to be my wife. I will uphold my promise, even when others do not."

I knew his final words were directed at me, but I had promised to marry him, nothing more, nothing less, and as much as I wanted to fight him—to kill him—I managed to contain my hatred and instead expressed my gratitude.

"Thank you."

Adrian's expression softened a little. He did not speak but bowed his head in acknowledgment.

"I…I should go," I said and took a step away.

"I will escort you," he said.

"That won't be necessary."

"It is," he said, "if I am correct in assuming your commander gave you that bruise."

I looked at my arm. In our earlier…struggle…my cloak had fallen over my shoulder. My gaze cut back to Adrian.

"I will take care of it," I said.

"Of that I have no doubt, but what if I wish for a turn?"

"Are you offering to defend my honor? How chivalrous."

"It has nothing to do with chivalry," he answered. "I insist."

I did not argue, if only because, in Adrian's presence, I might escape a lecture from the guards. We exited his tent and headed toward the woods once more, but at the border, we came to a halt, face-to-face with Killian and Ivan—Killian whose face was twisted with anger, and Ivan who looked pale and embarrassed. I hoped Killian wasn't too hard on him.

"Isolde," Killian said, and his eyes shifted to the vampire beside me. "King Adrian, I will take her from here."

He started to reach for me, and Adrian's hand shot out, clamping down upon Killian's with a hard smack.

"You have already touched her once without invitation," he said. "You will not do so again."

I saw Ivan glance warily at Killian as the commander jerked away.

"You will forgive me if I do not trust you to see to my fiancée's safe return."

"As if she is safe with you," Killian sneered.

"We will let the bruises speak for themselves," Adrian said.

The commander paled, and it was the first time I think he realized just how hard he had handled me. Still, his hand flexed over his blade, but before he could pull it, I stepped between them. It was the second time I'd given Adrian my back, the second time I'd put myself between him and Killian.

"I have accepted King Adrian's escort, Commander. You may return to your position."

His lips pressed thin, and his eyes shone with anger. It was the same anger that had led him to reach for me earlier.

"Fine," he said at last, and my ears bled with the words he didn't say: *Your father will hear of this.* But what could either of them really do? I was Adrian's betrothed, and this time tomorrow, I would be his wife. I watched him go, disappearing with Ivan in the dark.

After, I walked a step ahead of Adrian all the way to the castle. As I had predicted, Avram said nothing as we passed, alone since Ivan had yet to return form the border, probably still in the middle of a severe tongue-lashing from Killian. I would have to apologize tomorrow. I passed through the gates without stopping, and I intended to continue to the castle without looking back at Adrian, except as I swept past the sentry box, he called to me.

"All the stars in the sky," Adrian said.

The words made my heart race, and I halted as an answer that was not my own formed in my mind—*are not as bright as my love for you.*

But when I turned to look at him, he was gone.

# FIVE

*I spent my morning in my mother's garden surrounded by*
midnight roses—one of few flowers that bloomed in our
winter. I had been told they were my mother's favorite, with thick, velvet petals that were so rich in the
color purple, they almost looked black. The cold could
not manage to burn away their smell either, which was
strongest in the early morning—a sweet, warm scent
that reminded me of the woods and warm kitchens.

The garden was one of my favorite places in the
whole kingdom, and I tried not to think about the fact
that this would be one of my last visits. Each flower here
had been carefully selected, planted, and cultivated by
my mother. After she died, my father had seen that the
care fell to the palace groundskeepers. It was much the
same as when she died, except that there were far more
blooms, the shrubs were lusher, and the trees were taller.

She would have loved it, but since she couldn't, I
loved it for her.

It wasn't until Nadia came to collect me that I had to face what this day truly meant—change. She informed me that Adrian was meeting with my father again to go over the details of my departure tomorrow and that my trunks were already being packed.

"So soon," I said, my voice quiet, and I looked around the garden through hazy vision, my chest tightening. I had not expected to stay long after the marriage. I did not imagine Adrian felt comfortable here—even being unstoppable, he was not welcome. Still, I had thought I'd have more time to say goodbye.

"Your father extended his welcome," Nadia said. "But the Blood King refused. I cannot imagine why he is in a hurry to return you to his kingdom, unless he hopes to isolate you from us."

I did not know Adrian well, but I did not think his reason for leaving Lara quickly was to isolate me. That seemed more like something Killian would do.

"I just cannot believe that in two days' time, you will no longer be here." She paused and took a shuddering breath, and it was then I realized she was crying. "What will I do without you?"

"Oh, Nadia," I said and reached for her hand. I did not react well when others cried, especially Nadia, and my instinct was always to make her laugh. "I suppose you will read."

We laughed together before leaving the garden to prepare for the wedding, which would take place at sunset.

We decided to use my mother's suite, since my room was being packed. When I was younger, I spent much of my time here, pretending she was alive and that she might catch me at any moment playing with her things. Of course, Nadia was the one who found me, not my mother. Though she never made me leave. Instead, she told me stories about how my mother's marriage had been arranged—a bridge between the inlands and the islands. How nervous my mother had been to marry my father, but how confident she had been that she would love him, because he had been kind—and because her people believed in fate and destiny.

I believed in neither.

I sat at her vanity now with dread and darkness in my heart and no hope for love, while Nadia worked my curls into a tight bun of braids and twists.

"Ouch!" I seethed as Nadia gouged my head with another hairpin.

"Do not touch!" she commanded, slapping my hands away as I reached up to soothe the place she'd jabbed.

"Then don't stab me!"

Nadia placed her hands on her hips and huffed. She'd done my hair my whole life, and this was how every attempt ended—with her frustrated and my scalp bleeding.

I sighed and rubbed the space between my brows where a faint ache was forming.

"I didn't mean to snap, Nadia."

"It's all right, my love. I cannot imagine what must be going through that head of yours."

She couldn't.

Because I was thinking about Adrian, once again wondering why he wanted a queen. What role did he envision for me? Was I to sit at his side as an equal? I could not imagine a vampire treating his mortal wife as more than food, and yet he had demanded my voice be heard when others would silence me. He had also promised not to feed from me…unless I asked.

I cringed. We were taught in sanctuary that the act of drinking blood was vile because it was the act of stealing goddess-given life, but I felt it was vile for a different reason: because of what it made us—prey. Why would I ever ask to be made a victim? And how could something that had caused so much death, resurrection, and pain be pleasurable?

Perhaps Adrian was a sadist.

I supposed I would find out tonight. Thinking of our wedding night should make my stomach sour, but instead, I found I felt warm at the thought.

Once my hair was done, Nadia helped me into my dress—a black, sleeveless gown that flared at the waist. Gold lace created a halter that clasped around my neck and danced down the skirt of my dress. Trini, the seamstress, had woven larks into the design. It was beautiful work, regal work that spoke of power and elegance.

I had only worn it once—at the Reaping Feast, which was a celebration of the fall harvest. It was the same night I'd pointed a dagger in Lord Sigeric's face for suggesting I needed to be tamed. I wondered now, as Nadia laced me into the dress, would Adrian try the same?

Nadia crossed the room to open a gilded cabinet where my mother had stored her tiaras. They'd always been unlike anything another royal wore throughout Cordova because they'd come from the Atoll. Some were circlets made from exotic-looking flowers I'd never seen before, others were made of pearl, and some of precious shell. Among them was her gold coronation crown, each fringe inlaid with white and black diamonds from her homeland. Nadia turned with it between her hands and said, "Today you will become a queen."

I allowed her to settle the crown upon my head. It was heavy with the weight of my past, present, and future.

I turned to stare at myself, and I looked sad, grieving and uncertain, but proud. I knew duty, especially to my people, and I would marry Adrian to save them.

"You should kill him," Nadia said, and I shifted to meet her gaze in the mirror. Adrian's words from last night returned—the threat he'd made with my body pressed against his.

*Oh, my sweet. I could turn you in an instant.*

"Nadia—"

I wasn't sure what I was going to say, but I knew I was going to protest, and that thought really did make my stomach clench. Despite his threat, I should still be planning the Blood King's death.

I turned toward her. As I did, she drew a dagger from her pocket. It was beautiful, the hilt and scabbard made with gold-plated steel and red rubies.

"*Nadia.*"

This time when I said her name, I sounded breathless.

"Take it," she said. "It is a gift."

She urged the dagger into my hands, and I unsheathed it with a snick. The blade was narrow, sharp, and unmarred.

"Kill him, Issi," she said. "Don't give him the satisfaction of claiming victory over the House of Lara."

I met Nadia's gaze.

"It is the honorable thing to do," she added, holding on to my chin. She leaned forward and pressed a kiss to my forehead before leaving the room.

I stared down at the dagger and then at myself.

*You are the hope of our kingdom, Issi,* my father had said. Did that mean I should fulfill my agreement to marry Adrian and step into the role as queen of Revekka, or did that mean I was one who could get close enough to kill him?

There was a knock at my door, and I jumped, not prepared to be disturbed so soon after Nadia's departure.

"A moment!"

I slipped the blade into its sheath and shoved it between my breasts—a snug and uncomfortable fit, but it was the only place to hide it on my person, and I wanted to be armed at my wedding.

I turned toward the mirror and pretended to adjust wisps of my hair.

"Come in."

My hands fell to my sides as I glimpsed my visitor in the mirror. King Adrian had entered my suite, dressed in a black tunic and an overcoat lined with intricate gold stitching. It did not escape me that we matched.

I turned to face him, taking in his overwhelming presence. The king was tall and filled my chamber like evening shadows. His hair fell in golden waves past his shoulders, and upon his head, he wore a crown of black spires. His strange white-blue eyes held my attention and then lowered, tracing a path down my body that left me holding my breath, warm in places that should be as dead as his lifeless heart. The fact that they weren't made me feel like a traitor to my people—and angry with him.

"You aren't supposed to see me before the ceremony. It's bad luck."

It was a ridiculous thing to say. Bad luck had proceeded this whole thing, but I was growing nervous under his stare, which only seemed to darken the longer he looked.

Adrian's lips curled. I couldn't really call it a smile. Then he spoke, his voice trickling down my spine like drops of cool water. Suddenly, my mouth was dry.

"Considering the reasons for our marriage, I think I will chance it."

He closed the door behind him, and I heard the distinct sound of my lock clicking into place. My back straightened painfully, and I was hyperaware of the metal hilt digging into the softness of my breasts.

"Can I help you, Your Majesty?" I asked curtly.

His approach was graceful, his eyes locked on mine.

"I merely wished to look upon my bride before we are to exchange our vows."

I refrained from rolling my eyes.

"Having second thoughts?" I asked, elevating my voice to what I thought sounded hopeful.

He chuckled.

"No, if anything, I am more determined to make you my wife."

He paused before me, and now I could smell him, and it reminded me of cedar forests. A fresh, crisp scent that hit like cold, misty mornings. It was calming, but only for a moment, because when I realized what was happening, I stiffened, glaring up at him.

"Why is that?"

He lifted his hand slowly, studying my eyes as his

palm fell flush against my cheek. I swallowed and let a shuddering breath escape between my lips as his thumb brushed my skin.

"Do you tremble because you fear me?" he asked.

"Yes," I breathed, because I would never admit otherwise—that his touch had a heat forming low in my stomach.

He dropped his hand.

"Then why do I sense arousal?"

"That is…" I couldn't find words.

"Deny it," he said. "If it will make you feel less of a traitor."

"I wasn't going to deny it," I said. "But it is vulgar nonetheless."

"Hmm." The corners of his mouth tilted again. "I am vulgar."

I looked away, no longer able to maintain eye contact, and asked, "Did you come here to taunt me?"

"I would never taunt you," he said.

"It sure doesn't seem that way."

"That is because you are ashamed," he said.

His words drew my gaze back to him. This time, he moved quickly, securing his hand behind my head. "Soon, however, I hope you will find pride in being my wife."

Then he brought his lips to mine, sealing our mouths together, and something dark and frenzied flourished within my body. It was like a spell overtook me, and every inch of my skin burned with the need to be touched by *him*. My hands skimmed over his chest and into his hair, and when he groaned, I rewarded him by opening my mouth so he could taste me. As our tongues twined and slid together, he took me by surprise, driving me into my vanity, my back bowed beneath him as he devoured, my hands pressing into his hard muscles, his erection grinding into the softness of my heat. I found myself gasping at the feel of him between my legs, and as my hips moved against his, I knew I'd give anything to know what it would be like to have him inside me.

"Say that aloud to me," he growled against my lips, and as he spoke, I froze. His face was inches from mine, his white-rimmed eyes holding my gaze.

"What?" I asked, breathing hard.

The corners of his lips lifted. "You want me inside you," he said. "Say it aloud."

I shoved against him, and to my surprise, he stepped away.

"You can read minds?" I asked. I still couldn't catch my breath, and I hated that because it was a reminder of how I'd let him take advantage of me.

"You welcomed me with open"—his eyes drifted down my body and then back up—"arms."

"Get out of my head!"

I pushed him again, but he grasped my wrists and pulled me flush against him.

"Do not be ashamed by your thoughts, Sparrow. If it's any comfort, I wish to know the same thing."

I narrowed my eyes at the sudden use of a nickname I had not approved and jerked in his grasp, but he held me tighter.

"Your hair is beautiful."

My brows knitted together. "What?"

It wasn't until that moment that I realized the tight coil Nadia had worked so long to style had sprung free. I tore myself from him, staggering back. His stare pinned me, dark and lustful.

"At least we can be sure of one thing, Sparrow."

"And what is that?" I asked, seething. I hated him for how he'd made me feel and that he knew it.

"We both know what we have to look forward to tonight." Then, as if he thought I could not guess what he was implying, he added, "When we consummate our marriage."

He had no idea we would not even get that far. It was my turn to smirk.

"I think you should leave, King Adrian," I said and brought a hand to my hair. "I must restore my appearance."

His eyes glittered darkly.

"Of course, my queen," he said and bowed.

When he left the room, it took everything in my power to remain standing.

I had just finished pulling half my hair back, leaving the rest to curl down my back, when my father arrived, dressed in royal blue. The contrast between us was stark, our colors clashing. He looked grim today, and the lines around his mouth seemed deeper.

"Father," I said, rising to my feet. I threw my arms around his neck and hugged him.

"My Issi," he said, and as we parted, he brushed a curl off my shoulder. "You look beautiful."

I smiled. "Thank you."

His compliment was genuine, but I could feel the strangeness between us. We were both thinking the same thing—I should not look so beautiful for *him*.

"I brought you something," he said and held up a

small, rectangle package. I took it and sat on the bench in front of the mirror before tearing away the beige paper to reveal a carved wooden box inlaid with mother-of-pearl. It reminded me of the things my mother kept from her homeland.

"Open it," my father encouraged, and when I did, a pure lullaby chimed.

"A music box," I whispered.

"Yes. I had it made for your birthday…but since you will not be here, I thought it a fitting gift for today. The song is one your mother would hum before you were born."

My eyes watered. "What is the song?"

"I do not know the name," he said. "Only a few words."

He was quiet for a moment, and then he spoke the lines:

*"Moon above and earth below,*
*Bring my love stars that glow.*
*Far past midnight, shadows sneak;*
*Bring my love dreams that speak."*

His voice trailed off, but the music continued, and when it died, I hugged the box to my chest, my vision blurred by tears.

"I intended this day to be happier," my father said.

I looked at him and reached for his hand—the skin was thin and spotted.

"I'll be all right, Papa."

Right now, I could speak those words with some level of belief, because tomorrow still seemed so far away. Tomorrow, when we would leave Lara for Revekka.

"Will you?" He stared at my hand on his for a moment and then placed his other atop mine.

"So long as you are safe, I will be well."

There was a knock at the door, and Nadia entered. Her expression was grave as she spoke. "Your Majesty." She bowed. "It is near sunset."

Which meant it was time.

My father stood and held out his hand for me to take. I left the music box behind and walked beside him down the cold corridors of our castle, out the main entrance. We made our way to the Sanctuary of Asha, flanked by the royal gardens.

I had been to other weddings, both royal and nonroyal, and none had been this morose. Lara weddings were vibrant and exciting, grand affairs that lasted all day and all night. Well-wishers would line the walkways to cheer for the couple and toss amaryllis, clematis, and baby's breath at their feet, all of which would be gathered by flower girls who would make a bouquet for the bride.

But as I walked with my father, there were no well-wishers and no flowers—only guards who led us and followed us. Killian waited at the temple doors, radiating anger. It hit me in waves, crushing my chest, but his fury only ignited the same within me, and I glared at him. I knew what he was thinking—that I chose Adrian over him—and I supposed, in a way, I did. But that didn't matter when it wasn't a choice. I held to what I said before—I would choose neither if it had been an option.

A set of Killian's guards were stationed outside the temple door, and as we approached, they opened. The Sanctuary of Asha smelled like damp earth, and as we crossed the threshold, we were shrouded in a dim, red–orange light. It came from behind the altar—a large, twisted tree that reached to the darkness above—and there, before it, was Adrian.

Once again, I was struck by his beauty—by the glow that seemed to rise from his skin and hair. I hated how my eyes held on to his, how forceful his gaze felt, how immediately my body responded. I had no ability to catch myself or repress the thoughts, and I was sure Adrian had read my mind by now. Beside him was a vampire I did not recognize, but he was handsome—just as tall, lean, but athletic. He had short, dark hair and a defined jaw, his lips were thin, and pronounced brows made his eyes shadowy.

I held Adrian's gaze as I approached. A heavy silence followed us, and it was Adrian who broke it as I released my father's arm to face him.

"You are stunning," he said, smiling down at me, his eyes glittering darkly.

"You forgot to say so earlier," I said.

He smirked. "Are we talking about that?"

"I don't see why not," I replied. "We learned valuable information about one another."

"It sounds as though you would like to learn more."

"I want to know everything about my enemy," I said. "But I am in no hurry. As you so delicately reminded me early, we have all night."

Adrian smiled, showing his teeth. "Oh, Sparrow. There will be no time for talking."

It was my father who cleared his throat as another person joined us in the sanctuary—Imelda, a priestess of Asha. She was dressed in deep-blue robes, her hair covered with a hood, and a piece of silver rested against her forehead, disappearing under her hood. She held a gold cord between her hands—it would be the cord that bound us as husband and wife, king and queen.

"Princess, Your Majesty," she said and held out her hands for each of us. There was nothing to indicate the start of our vows, no welcome for those who gathered, no talk of the importance of union to bear children, as was common. Instead, Imelda moved straight to vows. Her voice was clear and warm—a beautiful tone that put me at ease despite what she was about to do. "This handfasting symbolizes your pledges to one another. Do you swear from this day forward to honor, respect, and commit to each other?"

She did not mention love, and I had to admit that my heart squeezed, mourning the loss of something I would never have, even as I had determined I'd never wanted it.

"I do," Adrian and I said in unison, our eyes holding.

Then Imelda joined our hands. Adrian's swallowed mine, and his palms were rough. I liked the feel, though, because mine were no smoother. It was a sign of the lives we'd lived. Always on the defense, always ready to fight.

"As your hands are bound together by this cord, so too shall your lives be bound as one." As the priestess spoke, she began to tie the cord around our hands. I couldn't look away, couldn't stop thinking about how Adrian's hands had captured my face, how they would descend down my body tonight. These were blasphemous thoughts—thoughts I was certain he could hear.

The priestess continued, instructing us to repeat her next words, and as she did, the slither of the cord caressed my skin, and my fingers tightened around Adrian's, an unconscious move that came with the vows I spoke.

"These hands will feed you, protect you, and guide you. These hands will ease your pain and carry your burdens. They will hold you and comfort you…"

My gaze lifted to Adrian, who watched me with fire in his eyes, and I wondered if his hands would ever offer anything our vows promised. At my thought, his lips curled, and I already knew his mind well enough to guess his vulgar retort.

"And so the binding is made," the priestess finished. "As your hands are bound together, so your lives and souls are joined."

With our hands bound and our vows sworn, Adrian's mouth covered mine. I braced myself for his kiss, expecting something akin to the passion he'd displayed in my chamber, but all he offered was a quick press of his lips to mine, then another on the edge of my lips before he straightened.

We turned together, facing our small gathering, and I noticed my father waving a servant forward. The man carried a tray upon which was a loaf of hard bread. I looked to my father.

"We thought it best you break bread here."

Part of the handfasting tradition was the practice of breaking bread as husband and wife, usually at a banquet that would follow the ceremony. I had not considered that there would be no feast in celebration of my new husband. This was meant to be a quiet affair, except that while everyone in my kingdom could pretend it never happened, I would still be living this nightmare.

Adrian did not argue or challenge the arrangement.

It was likely he knew this was for the best. If we had held a feast, it would have included human and vampire, and despite the agreement, it would have been wrought with tension that inevitably led to bloodshed.

Adrian took the bread and pulled a piece from the loaf.

"Hungry, Sparrow?"

"Starving," I said, meaning to sound sarcastic. Instead, I sounded breathless.

Adrian placed a hand upon my face while he brought the bread to my lips. I opened for him, and as he pushed the food into my mouth, I bit down on his thumb.

He inhaled between his teeth, his hand tightening in my hair, and he brought my head close to his as if he meant to kiss me. There was movement around us as Adrian tugged his finger free of my mouth, his lips pulling away from his teeth as he smiled.

"I am sure you meant to harm. Lucky for you, I like teeth."

He released me and I glared at him, breaking a piece of bread to feed him, but before I could, his finger caught my wrist, holding my hand in place as he took the bread into his mouth, sucking my fingers before he released. I inhaled as my cheeks flushed, embarrassed by Adrian's display. Even if he had not been the enemy of my people, I was not keen on public displays of affection.

He released me suddenly, and I swallowed hard, my eyes leaving his to look anywhere else.

"Isolde, go with Nadia," my father said.

Every sense that had been heightened within me bottomed out. My face drained of all warmth, and my stomach twisted and soured. Even the air changed, thickening. Everyone, even my father, knew what I was being sent off for—to prepare for tonight.

My hand was still tied to Adrian's. I lifted it between us, but before I could move, his lithe fingers were already in motion. It was strange to watch his lethal hands carefully work the cord free. I expected viciousness from this man, knowing that he was capable of it, and yet here, in the Sanctuary of Asha, one would never guess he was a warlord.

The soft cord slipped from my hands, and Adrian's eyes lifted to mine.

"I'll keep this on hand," he said. "For tonight."

I knew he wasn't joking, and it wasn't his words that frustrated me so much as his tone. He had made light of our consummation during this whole event, and in front of my father. My anger boiled over, and I gathered as much saliva in my mouth as possible before spitting in his face.

"Isolde!" Commander Killian spoke my name, and I felt his hand on my arm as if he wished to whisk me away before Adrian retaliated, except that Adrian's cold gaze turned to him instead of me.

"Release my wife, Commander," Adrian said. "You insult me by assuming I would harm her."

"Let her go, Killian." It was my father who spoke.

I could tell by Killian's grip that he did not want to release me, so I jerked in his grasp until he did and glared at Adrian.

"I anger you," he said. "I am sorry. We will speak of this later. Go with your maid."

I could not hide the shock I felt at his sincerity, and for a long moment, I was rooted where I stood, staring.

Then he reached out a hand, and I let him brush his fingers along my lips and across my cheek.

"I will be along shortly," he said.

I swallowed hard and turned on my heels. Before I knew it, I was running out the sanctuary doors—the doors I'd entered as a princess and left as a queen—while Nadia followed after me.

# SIX

**"Issi, wait!" Nadia called.**

I didn't stop running until I was halfway across the garden. The evening had faded, and there was no hint of the setting sun, only darkness and starlight. My chest rose and fell, and I turned my head toward the sky.

I had married the Blood King.

I was his wife.

I had never been so conflicted, so frustrated with the push and pull of my body. I felt in extremes—deep hatred and burning desire. There was no middle ground, no safe way to go about this. We would come together, and we would erupt.

Nadia finally caught up with me, breathless.

"By the goddess, you run fast!" she complained. Once she was recovered, she asked, "Are you all right?"

I could not answer, and Nadia must have taken that as a sign of shock.

"Of course you aren't," she said. "You just married a monster."

I flinched, though her words were true.

She continued. "I cannot believe the vulgar—"

"Can we not talk about it, Nadia?" I knew well enough what Adrian had said. His words had burrowed deep under my skin. "Let's just get this over with."

I started toward the castle, and Nadia followed. "You will kill him, won't you?"

I didn't respond. It was not that I wouldn't try; it was that I didn't know if it would work.

I did not return to my room or my mother's. Instead, Nadia led me to another suite in the east tower where guests usually stayed. Except that no one had come to the borders of Lara since the Blood King had begun his invasion, save for Adrian himself. Inside, the room smelled like dust. A large bed took up the far wall, the four posters decorated in swathes of dark velvet. A set of windows looked out over the woods and would offer a remarkable view of the sunrise tomorrow. A metal bath waited, full of steaming water.

Nadia helped me out of my gown, and before it could puddle at my feet, I turned to face her. I kept my hand over my chest, in part to hold the dress up but also to keep the blade I'd shoved between my breasts from falling to the ground.

"Can I be alone, Nadia?"

It was the second time I'd dismissed her, but this time, she didn't hesitate.

"Of course. I'll…check on you tomorrow."

"Wait until I summon you," I said. "Please."

I did not know what tomorrow would bring, but I knew I'd want time to collect myself.

She stared, and after a moment, she took my face into her hands, pressing a kiss to my forehead. "If he hurts you…"

"He won't hurt me," I said and then thought, *unless I hurt him*. "I can take care of myself, Nadia."

"But should you have to?" she asked.

"Perhaps you should ask your goddess," I said.

It wasn't a fair thing to say, but it was how I felt.

Nadia sighed, and I noticed the shadows beneath her eyes as she spoke, "I love you, sweet girl."

"I love you," I whispered, the words barely audible as she closed the door behind her.

Once she was gone, I released my dress, and as it fell to the floor, I pulled the blade from beneath my chemise and crossed the room to shove it behind the bed where the mattress met the frame. I only hoped I could reach it when I needed it.

When my weapon was in place, I discarded the shift and lowered myself into the bath, reveling in this time to myself, because I knew, at least for the next week, I would not be alone again. I pushed those thoughts away and instead focused on my bath—on the heat of the water, the steam that made me sweat, the vanilla-scented oil that pooled on the surface.

I stayed in the water until it was cold and then scrubbed my skin, probably too hard, trying to remove the still-lingering feel of Adrian's touch. It was futile since I would see him soon, but I hoped that maybe I could erase the feeling of want, of need, of desire he had inspired inside me.

It didn't work.

I left the bath still humming with an electric energy I needed to expend. I toweled off and slipped into nothing but a sheer red robe, not bothering to tie it. The point of this wasn't to hide. I was putting myself on display—meat on a hook for the predator to taste—but it would also show Adrian I was unarmed, and hopefully he would let his guard down.

I walked the perimeter of the room. I could tell no one had used this space for quite some time. A thick layer of dust covered everything, and the only clean item in the room was the bedding. I stared at it for a while, unable to move from the spot where I was supposed to consummate my marriage, willing myself to feel disgusted rather than this strange stirring excitement, and when I could not manage, I moved to the window, just as the door behind me opened.

I'd half expected to see Killian and felt guilty for the dread that thought had given me. Instead, it was Adrian. As I turned to face him, he halted, unable to hide his surprise. I was sure he had not expected me to wait for him like this—in skin and red lace.

"You are not modest, my queen."

"Have I need to be?"

Adrian closed the door, his boots thudding against the floor as he approached. He slipped out of his coat and tossed it on the bed. His tunic followed. I swallowed hard as I took in his bare chest—his shoulders were wide, his waist narrow, and his muscles sculpted with a precision only achieved through constant training. As much as I marveled at his body, I also marveled at his forwardness.

"You have done this before," he said. It wasn't a question.

I wasn't sure why I hesitated, but he smiled, rueful, dark, almost like he was promising I'd think of no one else beyond this night.

"Don't worry. I shall not annul the marriage, but I will look forward to a good fucking."

I narrowed my eyes, and he held out his hand.

"Come."

I did not move, his command anchoring me.

"Before we fuck, I have questions."

He let his hand fall to his side. "I do not wish to talk," he said, eyes darkening.

I scowled. "Am I to lie back and be silent?"

His lips quirked. "I'd rather hoped you'd be just as vicious as you are in battle."

"I draw blood in battle. Is that what you want?"

"If you make that a promise, I'll let you ask your questions."

"You read minds?"

He answered by telling me what I was thinking. "Only when you are very...passionate. Like right now, you hate my smirk. Earlier, you wondered what my skin would feel like against yours, what I would feel like inside you."

I clenched my teeth and quickly turned my thoughts toward my next question.

"Yesterday in the woods, you drew words from my mouth against my will."

"Is that a question?"

"I wasn't finished," I said, taking a step closer. "If you *ever* do that again, I will cut off your balls and shove them down your throat. *That* is a promise."

His infuriating smirk never left his face. "Anything else before we begin, my queen?"

I had more questions, especially about his magic, but asking those would mean admitting to the insatiable desire I'd felt for him the past day, and while I knew he was probably well aware, I could pretend it wasn't real so long as the words never left my mouth.

"That was not magic," he said, answering my thoughts.

"What do you mean it wasn't magic? I would *never*—"

"Desire a monster?" he asked, then tilted his head. "Tell me how many times you touched yourself and imagined it was me."

I reached to shove against his chest, but he caught my hands.

"You mock me," I snapped.

"I am only asking you to confront your desire for me. Will it help if I admit to mine?"

My eyes lowered to where his flesh bulged. I didn't need him to admit to it; I could see it.

He reached out and his fingers brushed my lips. My hand clamped down on his wrist.

"I will keep my promise to you," he said, holding my gaze, and after a moment, I guided his hand down my throat to my chest where, against my better judgment, I wanted his touch. Then his mouth collided with mine and both hands kneaded my breasts through the lace robe. The fabric created a rough friction that teased as his fingers rubbed my nipples. I drew my arm around his neck as his tongue plied my mouth, tasting of wine.

I wondered absently if he had fed before coming here and had only drank wine to hide the taste, but I could not continue with that thought as Adrian lifted me off my feet and guided my legs around his waist. One hand splayed across my back, the other gripped my ass, and he ground into me, sending waves of pleasure coursing through my body. I felt volatile in his hands, and I wanted to explode.

He guided us to the bed, and as I sank into the covers, Adrian's mouth moved from mine to my neck. His teeth grazed my skin, and I went rigid.

"I won't feed," he whispered, breathless. "Though you are sweet."

He kissed down my body, between my breasts, along my stomach. His body parted my legs, brushing my clit as he sat back on his heels and looked down at me. He did not wait, did not tease. His fingers just parted my hot flesh, and it was more than I could have ever imagined. I arched my back, and as I did, my hands disappeared under the pillows. Briefly, I remembered that I should not be enjoying this.

Above me, Adrian hissed and then descended, mouth closing over my clit. A sound I'd never heard, a feeling I'd never felt erupted from the bottom of my stomach. I hated him for this as much as I wanted it. Instead of reaching for my blade, I pushed against the headboard, pressing into his mouth. One hand reached for his wrist, and I pulled him deeper inside me, his fingers curling. The pressure crested, and when I came, I was overcome by the need for his cock.

The frustration divided me—part of me wanted this, but I hated that part of myself. Adrian was my enemy, and his mouth had just driven me to climax, a mouth that took blood from others. A monster who only had me beneath him now because he'd threatened to go to war with my kingdom unless I married him.

Adrian kissed up my body once more—tongue gliding, teeth scraping, and as his face leveled with mine, I reached for my blade and shoved it into his side.

He snarled. It was a sound I didn't expect him to make. He was quick to rear back and plucked the dagger from his flesh. Blood gushed from the wound, and he looked at me, eyes full of anger and lust. He turned his attention to the blade and snarled again, tossing it across the room. It clattered as it hit the stone floor.

"Oh, my sweet, you will regret that."

He gripped my face, leaning close. I glared, waiting for his retaliation—for the bite that would end my mortal life. My attack had done nothing. But instead of turning me, he left the bed.

"What are you doing?" I asked, sitting up.

"I find it a little hard to continue where we left off, considering you just tried to kill me," he said. "I'll wait until you're ravenous once more, and if you're lucky, I'll fuck you then."

I scoffed. "As if I would ask you to return to my bed."

Adrian drew his fingers into his mouth, tasting my come as he smirked. "I think you will, Sparrow."

The moonlight scattered across his back as he retreated, and for the first time, I saw raised welts crisscrossed over his shoulders and down his back. They were scars, long healed, at least outwardly, and I wondered what horrible thing he'd done to receive such a horrific punishment.

I woke in a cold sweat, the space between my thighs

aching. I squeezed them together and then gave in with a frustrated cry, parting them and drawing my knees up. If Adrian were near, I'd stab him again for this, for this unending ache that had driven me to pleasure myself—and fail—three times in the last two days. I let myself circle my clit and parted my flesh, but the attempt to find release was in vain. Frustrated, I sat up and found Adrian watching me from across the room. He sat, reclined, eyes full of things I'd never seen. The moonlight hit him—a sliver over his face and his chest. He'd changed and was now wearing what looked like a robe. He looked predatory and sexual, and I knew I had to have him.

I stood from the bed and shed the robe. He said nothing as I approached. I expected him to let me do what I wished, with the way he was looking at me. But as I moved to straddle him, he caught me around the waist and stood.

"Oh no, my sweet," he said and turned me so my back was flush against his chest, his arousal settled against my ass. "You will not have the control here."

His tongue touched my jaw and then my neck, where he sucked the skin into his mouth until it stung before he pushed me toward the bed.

He kept one of my hands secured behind my back, and the other I used for purchase against the footboard where he bent me over. His knee dipped between my thighs, widening my stance, as he guided the crown of his cock against my opening. My breath escaped in a shuddering gasp.

"Can you handle this?" His words were laced with barely restrained lust, and though all his movements up to this point had been rough, his question offered a strange sort of comfort. I knew if I said no, he would release me.

And I should have said no, except that as I spoke, I knew it was the surest I'd ever been.

"Yes."

The word turned into a guttural moan as Adrian filled me in one brutal thrust. He paused to release my arm, only to bury his fingers in my hair. With both my hands free, I gripped the footboard as his hips moved, driving into me. The bed knocked against the wall. It was a sound that worked in tandem with the ragged cries coming from my throat.

"Yes," Adrian hissed. His hand tightened in my hair, the other moved to my neck, and he guided me so that my back was bowed, my shoulder blades meeting his chest. In this position, he could not thrust, but he ground his hips into me, eliciting a new sensation that had every nerve ending in my body on fire.

"Scream my name, Sparrow, so that your commander may hear how loud I make you come," he said against my ear, and then his teeth scraped my skin, once again trailing a path down the column of my neck to my shoulder, where he licked and sucked until I was certain I would bruise.

This was his claim to me, and right now, I could not even hate it because this pleasure…it was exquisite.

He released me, and I just had time to reinstate my hold on the bed before he drove into me harder. My breath escaped me in a strange sound—a guttural moan that could only communicate the pressure building in my core, the tension tightening every muscle—until my body burst, leaving me weak and shaken. I did not realize what was happening until Adrian lifted me into his arms and carried me on to the bed.

Compared to the ferocity with which we'd just come together, his movements were gentle as he settled me atop the covers. My body relaxed, despite my enemy's hold. Too exhausted to fight or to speak, I just held his gaze, still clouded with desire and a strange warmth that seemed misplaced given what it had taken to get to this point.

Adrian hovered over me, his face inches from mine.

"How are you?" he asked.

I did not know how to answer. I felt like a traitor to my people.

So I stayed quiet, and Adrian asked a different question.

"Are you hurt?"

I shook my head.

He stared at me a moment longer. I expected him to leave then, but instead, he brought his hand to my face, his fingers brushing lightly over my cheek before he pressed a kiss between my breasts, down my stomach, until he hovered between my thighs. From that place, he stared at my whole body, as if I were the only thing he had ever wanted—a prize he had desperately sought and finally claimed.

Then I remembered who I had between my thighs— the Blood King, a conqueror whose true desire was to bring Cordova to its knees.

As my thoughts turned unfavorable, he parted my flesh and his mouth closed over my clit. He drew it against the tip of his tongue, sucking lightly before releasing to lick. He followed that pattern, slow and controlled, and I lost my grip on the anger and hatred while I writhed.

I could not decide where my hands should go—over my head or in his hair. My heels could not find a safe place to anchor, slipping on the bedding the tighter my muscles grew, and when his fingers speared my flesh, I wanted to arch off the bed, but he held me in place, devouring.

Once again, I found myself unable to control the sound or volume of my voice as I focused on the illicit sensation of his long fingers curling inside me, the vibrating pulse of his tongue against my clit. My breath caught, and suddenly my lungs froze. My chest wouldn't heave as every part of my body tightened.

I came harder than before, in a fit of desperate gasps and quivering muscles, and it was only then that Adrian released me to climb up my body. His lips hovered over mine as he spoke.

"Sweet," he said and dipped his tongue into my mouth so I could taste myself. I understood that as much as this had been about pleasure, it was more about power. Adrian had proven my unrelenting need for his body, and I wondered who in the castle was bearing witness to my shame, to how loud he had made me come. I did not doubt that curious staff and even court members lingered down the hall listening, though I was certain they'd expected a different outcome—a beheaded king rather than a pleased one.

My fury at myself and him was sudden, and it gave me renewed strength. As he shifted to lie on his back, I followed, straddling him; his engorged cock sat between my thighs, still wet from my release.

"You have not come," I said.

He smiled. "This was about you."

"Do you not believe in my ability to pleasure you?"

"Oh, Sparrow. You do please me."

"And yet your cock is full," I pointed out and rolled against him.

Adrian drew in a breath, and his fingers gripped my thighs.

"Would you like to come?" I asked. I could take him again, and he would cry my name just as loud, an even exchange.

"I would," he said, his eyes boring into mine.

"Where?" I whispered and bent to press a kiss to his chest. It was intimate, but he had done the same to me. "Inside me? Or in my mouth?"

My question was met with silence, and when I looked at Adrian, he was staring at me like he couldn't believe what I just asked him. But the corner of his mouth lifted, and he answered, "Take me into your mouth."

I shifted off him and took his hands, guiding him into a seated position at the edge of the bed before kneeling between his thighs. I watched him as my fingers closed around his hard length, applying pressure from the base of his shaft to the crown, where my thumb lingered, teasing and massaging as his come beaded at the tip.

"What do you like?" I asked, my voice breathy.

"Show me what you are capable of, Sparrow."

So I tasted him, licking him as he had done me, before my mouth closed over his cock. He groaned, and his hands threaded through my hair. I let him, while I alternated between swirling my tongue over his length and balls and pressing kisses to his thighs. Then I pulled away to wet my palms with as much saliva as I could manage before wrapping both my hands around the base of his cock. As I stroked him, I paid attention to the head, lavishing it with my tongue and hollowing my cheeks. It was a give and take that left Adrian groaning and his hands tightening in my hair, fingers scraping my scalp. The muscles of his legs bulged against my body.

"Fuck!" Adrian's curse was a hiss, and I looked up to find his head thrown back, his throat working, his breaths ragged and quick. Then his eyes returned to mine as he gritted out, "Yes."

I held his gaze, willing him to think of this moment, to never forget it. From this day forward, he would never be rid of me. He would never escape the need that had plagued me since our encounter in the woods. I would haunt him, filling his cock until he was ready to burst with no outlet save my body.

The thought made me smile around his length, and I moaned, closing my eyes. I didn't think it was possible for his hands to grip me tighter, but they did, and my eyes watered at his hold, but I continued until he released into my mouth. As I swallowed, I rose to my feet and gripped his face, bringing my lips to his, parting his mouth with my tongue. He tasted me hungrily, hands guiding me to straddle him once again.

When I drew back, I stared into the Blood King's eyes—my husband and enemy.

"I knew I liked your mouth," he said, his thumb brushing over my bottom lip. I bit down hard, and he chuckled before twisting and pinning me to the bed once more. As I stared up at his hungry eyes, my legs parted, welcoming whatever he would bring, because as much as we were fighting for dominance, he'd given me the one thing I'd been searching for.

Pleasure.

# SEVEN

*I woke to movement, lying on my stomach in the bed I'd* shared with Adrian. Peeling my eyes open, I found the door open as maids hauled steaming pails of water to the metal tub. I shifted onto my back and sat up, holding the blankets to my chest. My body was sore and sticky, and I was pretty sure I'd only fallen asleep an hour ago.

I found Adrian standing by the window, staring out at the night. He was fully dressed and in different clothes than those he'd worn at the wedding. These were not as fine as what he'd worn last night, but they were travel clothes. Still, he looked every bit the ruler, clad in black and crimson. He wore no ornamentation, but he did not need it. His presence spoke of his power.

How was he functioning after the night we'd had together?

At that thought, he looked at me over his shoulder.

"I do not need as much sleep as you to feel recovered," he said.

"That hardly seems fair."

He turned fully toward me, and there was a moment when all I could think about was how his skin had felt against mine, how his body had moved inside mine, how desperate I'd been to come and make him come. Tendrils of desire curled inside my body, flushing my skin.

I may have borne his marks, but his body also bore mine—and that was where I was torn. As much as I'd met my match in pleasure, it was through my enemy's body.

"I know what you think of my kind," he said, and there was a glimmer of amusement before his expression turned more serious. "But there is more to us than the monstrous parts."

"Are you trying to suggest you have redeeming qualities as a murderer?"

"Why not ask your father that question?" Adrian said.

"My father is not a murderer. He has fought bravely to defend his kingdom."

"So it is only murder when *your* people are killed?" Adrian asked.

I glared at him. "You were created to curse us."

Adrian stared, and I could not tell how he felt about my comment. But after a brief pause, he licked his lips and answered, "Well, I cannot argue with that."

The vampire king crossed the room to the chair beside the fire where I'd found him sitting last night before our coupling began. He retrieved a fur-lined cloak and clasped it around his shoulders.

"Bathe," he said. "You will not have the chance for the next week."

I glared at him but rose, wanting to wash all evidence of his claim to me from my body. At my thought, he chuckled.

"That is not possible."

I reached for the closest object, which happened to be a heavy brass candlestick, and launched it at him. It soared past him and hit the wall, damaging a painting that hung just behind his head.

"Stop reading my mind!" I snapped.

"That is like asking you to stop feeling," he said.

I sighed, frustrated. "I hate you."

"You hate parts of me," he said.

"I hate all of you," I said. I let my eyes shift down, but he was fully dressed, and it was impossible to tell if he was aroused.

"Then why are you wondering if I am aroused?" he asked.

"Because I wonder if you get off on arguing," I said.

"Yes," he said. "To answer both."

I scowled. "Stop reading my mind."

He chuckled, and I turned on my heels, hips swaying as I headed for the copper bath. I hoped his cock grew tight and his balls heavy with need.

The water steamed, making my face sweat as I neared. I sank into it, groaning as Adrian approached, swiping a few items off a nearby table.

"Soap?" he asked.

I met his strange eyes first, then let my gaze fall to his hand, hesitant, wondering if it was some kind of trick.

"You can call for Nadia," I said.

"I did not think you would want her to see you like this," he replied.

I knew what he meant. I looked down at my breasts, my skin covered in dark bruises from Adrian's hungry mouth. It was bad enough that the Blood King lived, worse that I had let him touch me, enter me, destroy me—and he knew that. Except that instead of forcing me to face my people in a state that would expose me to shame, he was protecting me from it.

I took the soap and the washcloth he offered next.

"Thank you."

He inclined his head before turning his back and walking toward the window again.

"We will depart for Revekka tonight?"

"Yes."

"If you intend to conquer the rest of Cordova, why not leave me here until your conquest is complete?"

"No."

"So you will leave me in Revekka while you conquer my country?"

"I will return to Revekka with you and remain until you are established as my queen."

"You would risk the Nine Houses plotting against you in your absence?"

"The Houses can plot all they want. I am inevitable."

He wasn't afraid. He believed he was truly untouchable.

And he was—as far as anyone knew. I'd stabbed him in the side, and he'd healed immediately. My father must have believed so too, which was why I was now married to the king of Revekka.

I stared at him. "And what does it mean to be established as your queen?"

It was the only question that mattered to me now.

"My people must respect you," he said. "But they are predators and you…you are a sparrow."

"Are you calling me weak?"

The thought had me squeezing the washcloth, and when he looked at me, his gaze was both gentle and oddly proud.

"We both know you are not weak," he said. "But not even you can survive the Red Palace without someone to teach you our ways."

I'd never thought much about the ways of vampires, but now I wondered—what was their culture? Were they as barbaric with one another as they were to my kind?

Adrian certainly made it seem so.

There was a knock, and both our heads snapped toward the door. Before either of us could speak, Nadia entered, cradling towels. She paused, staring down at something before bending to pick up the knife I'd used to stab Adrian last night. She held it by the pommel, between her thumb and forefinger, the blade crusted with Adrian's blood.

"Good morning, Nadia," I said, folding my knees to my chest, as if I could hide the bruising on my skin.

Her gaze shifted from the knife to me, then to Adrian, and I knew she was trying to figure out how it had gotten there and how both Adrian—and I—were still unharmed. After a moment, she seemed to come out of her shock and spoke.

"Issi," she said. "Good morning." She crossed to the bed, where she set the dagger on the nightstand. "I brought fresh towels and your travel clothes," she said, draping them on the bench at the end of the bed. "Shall I help you dress?"

I opened my mouth but hesitated. My gaze shifted to Adrian. I hated that I looked to him for guidance. After a moment, he offered a small nod.

"We leave in an hour," he said. "You will want to say your goodbyes before then."

Adrian's boots thudded against the floor as he headed for the door. Nadia and I stared at each other until it clicked shut and we were alone.

"Issi." Nadia's hands fell to her sides. "Are you well?"

"I'm fine, Nadia," I said quickly and returned to scrubbing my skin and my hair.

"Let me help," she offered, and I sank beneath the water, holding my breath until my lungs hurt. When I surfaced again, I rose to my feet and stepped out of the tub, facing my maid.

She stared, her mouth hanging open.

"Issi," she breathed.

"Bear witness to my shame, Nadia," I said. "I could not kill him."

*And I let him fuck me.*

Nadia seemed to overcome her shock enough to reach for a towel and fold me into it as she brought me in for a tight hug. I let her hold me, because this would probably be the last time I saw her. She pulled back, and I held on to the towel as she cradled my face.

"Did he hurt you?"

"No."

It was the truth. He had been rough, brutal even, but it was nothing I had not willingly accepted.

"Do…you…favor him?"

"What? No," I said, but as I rejected her inquiry, her eyes drifted to my neck and shoulders. I sighed and pushed past her, reaching for the clothes she'd brought me.

"You cannot blame me for asking, Issi. You let him—"

"Fuck me," I interrupted. "It doesn't mean anything, Nadia."

She glared. "It does where I'm from."

"It has nothing to do with where you are from. You are well aware I've had other lovers. It is only because it is Adrian that you are appalled."

"Adrian? You're calling him by his given name?"

I shoved my feet in the leather leggings and pulled on the blue tunic she brought.

"Did you even try to kill him?" Nadia asked.

I leaned toward her, shoving my hand toward the table. "Did you not see the bloody knife?"

"How many times did you stab him?"

"It doesn't matter," I snapped. "Because you know what happened within seconds of stabbing him? He *healed*."

Not even a scar remained, which meant that the scars on his back and the one on his face were there before he became immortal.

Nadia looked a little shaken by the news. Still, she said, "I never knew you to give up so easily."

"*Give up?*"

"Will your first attempt at assassinating the Blood King be your last?"

I stared at her. "Have you heard nothing I said? He cannot be killed, Nadia."

"Everything dies, Isolde." She crossed the room and retrieved the knife from the bedside table before approaching me again. "You could be the savior of your people, of the whole country, and when you have conquered him, you can come back to Lara where you belong."

My chest ached already, and my eyes stung. *Back to Lara.* I hadn't even left yet, and I was already desperate for home.

"This is an opportunity, Issi," Nadia said and placed the knife in my hand. "The Blood King has a weakness, and you must find it."

Nadia left after her lecture, and I finished getting ready. I arranged my weapons, securing my retractable blades at my wrists. The blades themselves weren't long, and they had sat against my skin so long, not having them felt wrong. I also cleaned the knife Nadia gave me, washing away Adrian's blood, though afterward, I thought perhaps I should have kept it as proof that I'd at least tried to murder him. When I was finished, I sheathed the knife at my waist. The last item I layered was a cowl-neck cloak; it was practical for the icy nights but hid my shame as I left the room that bore witness to my treason.

I was still angry because even now, I wanted him, because last night I couldn't stop myself from touching him, because I had taken every chance to ride his cock and let him come inside me. He swore it wasn't magic that had me in his hold, and I believed him. Last night, I had been claimed in ways I'd never been before, and I had acted in ways I'd only ever dreamed, but there was something about Adrian that made me feel I could be passionate, rough, erotic—without restraint.

And so I had.

Wherever my desire came from, it was primal, and he matched it.

The goddesses were cruel.

I found my father in the great hall where my nightmare had begun. Today, it looked much different, with wooden tables arranged in a large rectangle, the benches crowded with courtiers, both eager to please my father and witness my fate. King Henri sat elevated behind a similar table, beside him Commander Killian, whose gaze I avoided. Except he proved to be the least of my worries, because as I entered, silence descended, and so did my embarrassment.

There was no hiding how I'd spent my night. My father had known he'd sent me off to consummate a marriage, and so did the kingdom, despite my union being a quiet, lackluster affair. They'd expected to wake this morning and discover I had killed the Blood King. Had my father thought the same?

I made my way toward him when I was halted by Marigold, the daughter of Lady Crina Eder. Marigold liked to stay at court rather than her home province of Belice, and she'd tried to become my friend, but she did not like what I liked. One day in my shadow, traversing the wood to explore, and she had given up. I'd understood then that she'd expected something very different from a friendship with me—days at court in pretty dresses and silk shoes, only walking along the worn paths of the royal gardens and trading palace secrets.

But I was not that kind of princess, and today, I was not that kind of queen.

"Princess Isolde," she said and curtsied, wearing a dress made of scarlet wool. This particular fabric had been dyed a deep purple, which contrasted with her vibrant green eyes and yellow curls.

I considered correcting her address but declined. I was fine with being Isolde, princess of Lara, another day.

"I did not have a chance to see you yesterday after the...*arrangement* was made. I wanted to express my condolences."

Her voice echoed in the hall, not because she was speaking loudly but because everyone was still quiet, watching our exchange.

"Your condolences?" I repeated.

I knew marriage to the Blood King was not ideal, but I wished everyone would stop treating this as if it were my funeral.

"You must be devastated," she continued.

I imagined that everyone in Lara thought they could guess how I was feeling. They only had to consider their hatred for Adrian to relate, but there was something about being in this room on the first day of my marriage to the vampire king, beneath the judging eyes of my people, that made me want to speak on my courage.

"I am not dead, Lady Marigold," I said.

She hesitated.

"I may not have had a choice in my partner, but I have a choice as to how I move forward, and you can be certain I will use that power to my people's advantage, so perhaps you should be congratulating your queen."

Marigold's cheeks turned pink, and she stammered, "Of course. I apologize, Queen Isolde."

She brushed past me and headed for the exit. I continued toward the dais and curtsied.

"Good evening, Father," I said quietly and took my

seat beside him. The food laid out at the center of our table was traditional fare—cheeses, dried meats, and vegetables. There were also tankards of wine and mead. I took in the sight and the smells, knowing that this was my last night of familiar food and drink.

My last hour at home.

After my send-off, my father and his kingdom would retire to bed and perhaps be less fearful of the night.

"Isolde," my father said. "Are you well?"

"I am."

I kept my eyes on my empty plate, my cheeks flaming. I could not bring myself to reach for food. There was silence again, and then Killian spoke. "Eat. You must be hungry," he said. I lifted my gaze. He could have stopped then, but he added, "You barely slept."

It was his way of telling me he knew how I'd spent the night, and his jealousy was apparent.

I narrowed my eyes. "I will eat when I am hungry, Killian. As it stands, I am rather sated."

His eyes flashed, a mark of his surprise and shock at my open challenge. The commander set his fork down, and I expected him to pounce, to expose some part of my life to the entire room, but my father intervened, setting his own utensils down and pushing away from the table. As he stood, so did the whole room.

"Come, Isolde," he said quietly. It was his tone that told me I wasn't in trouble, and yet my heart raced at facing him alone. Still, I rose and followed him into the adjoining anteroom where we'd waited yesterday for Adrian to arrive. Once inside, I turned to him.

"Father—"

Before I could finish speaking, he hugged me tightly.

I said nothing. As soon as I felt the weight of his arms around me, I burst into tears.

"I have disappointed you," I sobbed.

"You could never disappoint me."

I was certain if he knew the extent of my truth, he would disagree. Instead, he clasped my shoulders and drew me away. Our eyes met, and he touched my chin.

"Feel no shame, Isolde," he said. "You are but a victim here."

A victim.

I hated the word. I was also princess of Lara and now a queen, though I did not completely understand what I ruled—a nation of monsters, a country of my conquered people? Still, there was power in the ruins of the life I was about to leave behind. I refused to fall under the weight of these circumstances, not when I had so much at my fingertips.

We did not return to the great hall. Instead, we made our way outside, into the cold evening, and followed the stone path that cut through my mother's garden. The gardeners had lit lanterns, and the flames cast dancing light along our path. I kept my arm looped through my father's, passing barren plots and leafless trees, our breaths frosting as we spoke.

"I tried to kill him," I said, and my father's steps slowed. "I knew vampires were hard to kill, but I did not think it was impossible. Adrian, though, is impossible to kill."

"Perhaps it is not Adrian who must die," my father said at length.

My brows furrowed. I did not understand. "What do you mean?"

"There is a greater evil than the Blood King, Issi," my father said. "And it is the power that created him."

"You mean magic?"

He nodded.

Over two hundred years ago, before the Nine Houses united, Cordova's countries were advised by witches, women who were initially thought to be blessed with the ability to harness magic, until they turned upon their kings. For their treason, they were burned at the stake in an event known as the Burning. It was said that in the aftermath, Dis, the goddess responsible for witches and their magic, cursed Cordova with a plague of mortal fears. Shortly after, vampires manifested from the darkness and, with them, other monsters.

"If Adrian is a curse...can curses not be broken?"

My father's gaze leveled with my own. "Only the king himself knows," he replied.

It was my father's way of telling me to find out. He turned and picked one of my mother's midnight roses, reminding me once again, "You are the hope of our kingdom."

He was giving me a mission—one I accepted as I took the rose.

We continued through the garden, and when we returned to the castle, Adrian waited with the same dark-haired vampire who had been present at our wedding.

"My queen," Adrian said as he lifted his hand to his heart and bowed his head. "Allow me to introduce my general, Daroc Zbirak."

As my gaze shifted to him, the general bowed, though I got the sense he did so begrudgingly—which was fine with me, because I did the same.

"General," I said, inclining my head, biting my tongue so I did not say the things I truly wished. *So you are the man responsible for the fire, the destruction, the death in Cordova.* Still, I let those thoughts cycle through my mind, hoping my emotions were high enough for Adrian to hear them. Then I wondered if Daroc possessed the same abilities as Adrian.

"Daroc has arranged your escort," Adrian said.

"I have appointed my best soldiers as your guards, my queen," Daroc said. "They have been instructed to ride outside your carriage during our journey to Revekka."

"Carriages are targets," I said. "I will not ride in one."

There was a beat of silence, and I looked from Daroc to Adrian. Neither of them blinked. I could not tell if they were surprised by my response or irritated.

"Our journey will be long, my queen," Adrian said.

"I am a princess born of Lara," I said. "I can ride for hours."

He lifted a single brow, and the corners of his lips followed. "Very well. We shall find you a horse."

Adrian looked to Daroc, who bowed and left, presumably to find my horse.

There was a strained silence that followed his departure. I could not help feeling completely awkward in the presence of my new husband and my father, and I was relieved when Adrian spoke. "You are welcome at the Red Palace in two weeks' time," he said to my father, "when Isolde's ascent to queen is made official. I will send an escort to ensure your safe passage into my lands."

"That is generous of you, King Adrian," my father replied, his tone wavering toward sarcasm. "I welcome any chance to look upon my daughter again."

Something thick gathered in my throat, and I wondered who I would become in that time? Would my father even recognize me? Would I recognize myself?

"Issi is my greatest treasure," my father added, and while I looked at him, he kept his eyes upon Adrian. "I trust you will place her safety above your own."

It was the second time he'd asked Adrian to ensure my well-being. It was a little ironic given that my father could do nothing against the vampire king if he decided to harm me, save go to war.

"Without a second thought," Adrian replied. "She is my wife."

Those words were like a strike to my chest. They should have sounded false, but they didn't. I stared at him, half in disbelief. I did not expect him to respect our marriage vows so fully, especially when I was still plotting ways to murder him.

The thought brought a smile to Adrian's lips, and I scowled. I would have to figure out what triggered his mind reading or a way to veil my thoughts. Was that possible without magic?

"It is time, Isolde," Adrian said.

Up until this point, I thought I could handle leaving my father, but suddenly I was faced with the reality, and it hit me so hard, it stole my breath. My throat closed up, and my eyes burned as I faced him.

"I will see you soon, Issi," Father said and kissed my forehead. I closed my eyes against his affection, wanting to memorize this moment. It felt as if it would be the last time I inhaled his scent, felt the warmth of his touch, heard the sound of his low, rugged voice.

I swallowed thickly.

"I love you," I whispered through lips that quivered.

"I love you," he replied, and I tucked those words into my heart, spoken so softly and so rarely, as I held his calloused hands for what felt like forever. Slowly, I let my fingers leave his, immediately wishing I could return to his side even as I backed away. I turned and faced Adrian, whose stare was curious and remorseful, and took his outstretched hand. He said nothing as we walked side by side, exiting the castle at the very front where a crowd had gathered beneath the night sky to watch my departure—a mix of guests from High City and courtiers.

Once again, I could not help feeling that this event should be filled with more celebration, and if I had become a queen to any other king, that would be the case. Instead, my people looked on in fear, disappointment, and horror.

My father followed and stood atop the steps as I descended them, only to meet Nadia at the bottom. Her eyes were swollen and red from crying, and she dabbed at her face with a white kerchief.

"Dear girl," she said and drew me into her arms. I had managed to keep a cap on my emotions until that moment, when a cry burst out of me. It was only for a moment—a strangled sob that I grabbed on to and shoved deep down as Nadia whispered against my ear, "Remember what I told you."

Then she kissed my hair and released me.

I moved on from her, turning toward Adrian, who waited patiently beside two horses. Both were gorgeous steeds with shiny, black coats. I approached the one Adrian stood near and stroked his nose.

"Their names are Midnight and Shadow," he said. "Shadow is mine."

"And who did Midnight belong to?" I asked. Adrian had not planned on returning to Revekka, least of all with a bride. An extra horse usually meant a death. The question was, had it been a vampire or a mortal?

Adrian did not answer but instead said, "Come. We must depart."

I took the reins from Adrian and grabbed a tuft of mane with the same hand. With my other, I grasped the cantle of the saddle and placed my foot in the stirrup, pushing off the ground as I swung my leg over. Once I was settled, I stared down at Adrian.

"What place do I take in line?" I asked.

"You ride beside me," he said. "It is where you will be safest."

My brows drew together. "I am safe with my people."

"Perhaps you were as princess of Lara," he said. "But today, you are queen of Revekka." He left my side and then mounted his own steed. "We will ride until sunup," he said.

Daroc, who appeared to be the only vampire who had accompanied Adrian into the city, rode ahead of us, and as we fell into step behind him, I looked over my shoulder one last time at my father, who stood wreathed in the lantern light at the front of Castle Fiora, poised and regal and alone.

# EIGHT

**When brides departed with their new husbands, people** gathered to offer gifts—small things like flowers, polished stones, and gold and silver coins.

For me, there was nothing, not even a crowd gathered within High City, though when I turned my head from left to right, I saw people peering through windows and from behind their doors. They were curious but afraid—both of the dark and of Adrian.

We came to the gate where Nicolae was on duty with another guard I did not recognize. I started to smile at him as I passed, because that was what Nicolae usually did when he spotted me. This time, he frowned and cast a dark look at both Daroc and Adrian, then me. His expression hit me in the chest, and I quickly looked away, knowing that he did not understand. He, like my people, did not know why Adrian still lived when I had gotten so close.

As I passed, I heard Nicolae say something under his breath, and I pulled on my reins, halting Midnight.

"Do you have something to share, Nicolae?"

The guard stared at me, and then his gaze flickered to his left, where Daroc and Adrian lingered.

"No, Your Majesty," he said and bowed his head.

"I would hate to think that you would disrespect me," I said. "Because that would mean I would have to dismiss you."

His eyes connected with mine, his jaw clenched.

"With all due respect, Princess, I am beholden to the king of Lara."

I went rigid, and after a brief pause, I slid off my horse to stand face-to-face with Nicolae.

"It's Queen to you," I said, and then I smiled. "Enjoy your last night on guard, solider. I will be sure to send Commander Killian notice of your immediate dismissal."

I turned from him then, mounted my horse, and guided him past Daroc and Adrian. The two looked at me but said nothing as they followed me into the tree line. Once we were in the woods, I slowed my pace, unsure of where we were going. Adrian had brought a whole army to our border. Where were they?

"Part of the army has continued on to occupy other territories," Adrian responded, and I wondered what he meant by other territories. Would he continue to Thea next? "A small party waits for us just outside the capitol to accompany us home."

"Revekka will never be my home," I said.

Adrian remained quiet.

We continued to where the vampires waited, in a small clearing not far from High City. Only a few remained of Adrian's army, all mounted upon horses, covered in armor. I recognized only Sorin, Isac, and Miha.

I watched Sorin elbow Isac.

"Look, it's our queen—the one who stabbed you!"

Miha grinned and Isac glared. "You say that as if I've forgotten."

"I think you do not appreciate the gesture. Who else can say they were stabbed by their queen?"

"Your king," I said, and the trio exchanged both surprised and amused looks.

Beside me, I felt Adrian's eyes on me. "I have met my match," he said.

His comment made me shiver, and I met his gaze, which seemed far too serious. I wasn't sure Adrian and I were a match for anything but hatred, though I also wasn't sure he hated me at all.

"We travel until dawn," Adrian instructed, and as Daroc rode forward, Adrian and I followed while Sorin, Isac, and Miha fell in line behind us. After, the rest of the group joined, which included several vampires dressed in the same feathered, gold armor and mortals, both men and women, who were dressed in regal silk and fur, as if they were not part of an army.

We would travel north through Lara to the border of Revekka. I had not ventured north since I was a little girl. Those territories were beyond the mountain pass, too close to Revekka, and as Adrian's power had grown and new monsters were born, the visits stopped. Now, only Killian and his soldiers made rounds close to the border near the Blood King's kingdom.

Despite being with monsters, I was excited to see the villages in the north. They were so far from the castle, they had their own traditions and cultures, but I wondered…would they welcome me?

The wood was dark, but the naked limbs of the trees allowed for a view of the stars, and I found myself watching them, seeking light, mourning that I would not see the sun for a few days.

"Do you miss the sun?" I asked Adrian.

"That is a curious question." He glanced at me.

"And why is that?"

He was quiet for a moment, and when he spoke, he answered my first question, "I do not miss the sun, not anymore."

"And what if *I* miss the sun?"

How bright was the sky in Revekka—what would the sun look like beaming from behind red clouds? Would I even be able to see it?

"Then I will find it for you," he replied.

Our eyes locked, and I saw a human sincerity in his expression that made my chest and cheeks feel warm. I quickly looked away.

Silence stretched until I noticed a few of Adrian's soldiers breaking ranks, disappearing into the darkness. My heart picked up pace, wondering what they were doing.

"They are scouting," Adrian said.

"But we are still in Lara."

I didn't see the need to be on guard. Adrian and I had made an agreement, and no matter how angry my people were about the arrangement, they would honor my father.

"Do monsters not lurk in your shadows?" he asked. He was referring to things that lurk in the dark—the strzyga, the virika, revenants, the ker—all creatures that were like Adrian but different in how they appeared and the way they fed upon life.

"Are you not their king?" I retorted, frustrated by his sarcasm.

"I am the king of vampires," he said. "I am not the king of monsters."

"There is no difference," I said.

I did not know Adrian very well, but I could tell my comment frustrated him. That shapely jaw tightened, and I felt triumphant. I'd learned that the true measure of men was how they handled their anger. Would he be like Killian and lash out if I pushed too hard?

"You seem to believe I spawned all dark things," he said, his voice maintaining that silky quality, and he delivered his words with no hint of frustration.

It was what we were told—that all dark things came from the Blood King. That when he partook of sacred life, the blood that dropped to the earth created monsters.

Beside me, he laughed. "That is a lie."

"Enlighten me, Your Majesty," I said.

"I turn humans into vampires," he said. "But even I have rules. The monsters you know of—the strzyga, the virika, revenants, the ker—they were created by Asha."

"No," I said immediately. "The goddess of life would never corrupt it."

I was not a worshipper of the goddesses, but even I did not think Asha would create such heinous creatures.

"Never forget, my queen, that goddesses are just humans with great power."

With his comment, he moved ahead to Daroc's side as if he no longer wished to ride beside me. I watched him, wishing that I could pitch an arrow into his back, but I considered what he said about the goddesses and found that I did not think so differently. There were many others who suffered worse attacks, worse experiences, and yet were far more devout. They wore their hardships like badges of honor and their faith like weapons, and I did not understand it.

I glanced to my left as Sorin meandered up beside me and extended his hand, a piece of dried...*something* clutched between his fingers.

"What is that?" I asked, eyeing it suspiciously.

"Beef," he said with a grin. "You want some?"

"Why are you eating beef? *Can* you eat beef?"

I only knew vampires to sustain themselves with blood. I wondered how long it would be before I witnessed a vampire feed from a mortal, and was not looking forward to the display.

"The mortals seem to love it," he said, and then he sniffed. "And I can eat anything I want."

"He'll throw it up later," said Isac from behind us.

"It's disgusting," Miha added. "But he keeps doing it."

"Let me live my life," Sorin snapped, glaring at them. I tried hard not to smile but failed. When Sorin looked back at me, he wiggled the beef stick in my face. "Take it. I know you're hungry. I can hear it."

I raised a brow. "Is that another power I should know about? Superior hearing?"

"I'd say yes but even the mortals at the back of the line can hear your stomach growling."

I frowned. I *was* hungry, and I hadn't been able to bring myself to eat dinner this evening, so I took the dried beef and tore a piece off, chewing vigorously. The meat was hard and papery but not unpleasant. I was just glad to have something in my stomach.

"Thank you, Sorin," I said.

"Of course, my queen."

We continued for a few hours more, stopping once to water the horses.

Instead of leading the horses to water, the vampires filled buckets for the horses to draw from. I left Midnight's side, hoping to sink my hands into the cool river, but as I knelt on the bank, a hand clamped down on my shoulder.

"Do not touch the water."

I looked up into Daroc's severe face and rose to my feet. With his warning issued and no explanation, he left me.

"Ignore him. He isn't very polite, though he means well," Sorin said, coming to stand beside me.

"I think he hates me."

"He doesn't, but he is very focused on duty. You are his responsibility. He will take personal offense if you are hurt on his watch."

"Sounds like you know him very well."

Sorin raised his brows. "I do. Very well." Then he pointed to the water. "Animals attract creatures just as humans do, some that live in the water. Alps, in particular, feast upon horses, but they are not picky when they are hungry."

Alps were creatures that could morph into varying sizes depending on the prey they were hunting. They had frightening, demon-like faces, and their features were large, taking up most of their face—a wide, tooth-filled smile, a large, bulbous nose, dark, endless eyes, and tall, pointed ears.

"I have never heard of alps in Lara," I said. Commander Killian took these paths with his soldiers; I was certain he had stopped to water his horses as well and never reported attacks.

"You do not have to hear of them for them to exist," Sorin said.

"I suppose that is true enough," I said.

It was also frightening, but that was the world we lived in. I stared at the dark water as it shimmered over the rocks beneath rays of moonlight and couldn't help feeling a little betrayed.

"Allow me," Sorin said. Retrieving a bucket, he then dipped it into the water.

"How are you able to approach the water?"

He smiled ruefully. "The only blood that pumps through these veins is that which I drain." I did my best not to cringe, but Sorin caught my discomfort and laughed. "In time, you will come to understand."

"I beg to differ," I said.

His smile widened, but he said nothing as he held the bucket for me. I dipped my hands in the cold water, hating how much I mistrusted it after what Sorin had told me. As I pressed cool hands to my heated face, I looked at him.

"How did you come to be part of Adrian's army?" I asked.

"I have known Adrian since the beginning," he said.

I wondered what he meant by that. Was he referring to the time of Adrian's curse? Or before that when he'd been nothing more than a man?

"You did not answer my question," I said, and this time, when he smiled, it was not as wholesome.

"Nothing gets past you, does it, my queen?"

He looked off to where Daroc and Adrian stood

together. My gaze followed, and I noted how Daroc stiffened and glanced toward us.

"Are you…lovers?"

"Daroc and I are two souls," he said. "One cannot go where the other does not follow."

"Why do I get the sense you did not choose this life," I said.

"Mount up!" Daroc shouted suddenly, and I jumped at the abruptness of his voice. I wondered again if all vampires could read minds.

Sorin looked back at me and said, "I chose Daroc. I am happy with that."

We continued. I'd felt a brief reprieve from my lethargy when I'd dismounted, but the steady sway of my horse made my eyes feel heavy. The next thing I felt was a hand grasping my arm. I jerked and straightened, looking into Adrian's white-blue eyes.

"I will hold you if you wish to sleep," he said.

His words sent a shiver up my spine that felt too thrilling.

"I'm fine," I said curtly and scrubbed my face with one hand. I could not imagine what sort of line I'd be crossing if I agreed to share his horse and sleep in his arms. Sex was one thing—that required no trust and no affection—but this was a level of trust I wasn't prepared to offer.

He did not argue, and once again, I found myself alone in the procession as I continued—and failed—to fight sleep. It wasn't until Daroc halted his steed and held up his hand, signaling for the others to follow, that my body awakened, now pumped full of adrenaline. I tugged on my reins, staring into the darkness, feeling unease creep along the back of my neck.

"Attack!" Daroc barked.

"The queen!" Adrian commanded, and he yanked his horse around as if to charge for me. But I was confused. Nothing seemed to be amiss.

Then a fiery arrow cut through the air, lodging in the carriage behind me. Others followed, breaching the curtained window, igniting the interior, and within seconds, it was consumed in fire.

*Carriages are targets*, I thought just as an arrow whizzed past my face. Another hit my horse near my leg.

"No!"

Midnight neighed and snorted, a mark of her pain. She bucked and then tried to walk, wobbling until she stumbled forward as her legs folded under her. As she hit the ground, people emerged from between the trees—my people, dressed in gray shrouds, bellowing fierce battle cries. Some were armed with weapons, while others carried equipment from their farms—pitchforks and axes, sickles and slashers.

"Stop!" I commanded, but my voice was buried beneath the clash of weapons as my people met the skilled end of a vampire's sword. The blood sprayed immediately, and I watched in horror as my people were slaughtered by creatures who moved faster and hit harder. I felt helpless, sitting near my horse, unsure of how to proceed. I could not raise my weapons against them. I could not raise them against my husband's army—not when I was expected to continue this journey to Revekka.

A trio of vampires made an arc around me—Sorin and Isac and Miha. Their movements were controlled, their blades catching each blow aimed at their bodies, and I got the distinct impression they were moving slower than they were actually capable of. I had expected different behavior from them. I'd been told vampires fought with nails and teeth, that they lunged in battle, flying through the air to attack their victims with a viciousness I did not see here.

Were they trying to spare my people?

My gaze shifted to Adrian, who was in the middle of cutting down a man who had an arrow pulled back on his string, but he had no chance to even loose it as Adrian's blade found a home in the hollow of his neck. A spray of blood followed as he pulled his weapon free. Another arrow raced toward his back, and he twisted, knocking it out of the air, eyes narrowing on the culprit—a smaller man who stumbled back at his approach.

I rose to my feet.

"Stay down, my queen!" Miha ordered.

But I couldn't. I wanted the bloodshed to stop, and I bolted through their barrier. I was not sure what I really intended to do. Perhaps I thought if Adrian ceased fighting, others would. What I had not expected was the determination of my people to kill me.

No longer guarded by the trio, I became a target.

"The queen!" someone shouted just as a man, one of my own, came toward me, blade overhead. I turned, moving at the last second and letting my knife release into his back. There was a moment when he paused, his body arched unnaturally as he stared, wide-eyed, at me. Once, I'd been his princess, and now I was his murderer. His blade clattered to the ground, and he followed.

I took up his sword in time to face another opponent. The word felt so wrong, to look at the man opposite me as an enemy, and yet as he charged, an ax in hand, that was exactly the side he took. He swung his weapon violently, and as I ducked to miss his attack, I swung my blade out, cutting into his legs. His cry was silenced as I released the knife at my wrist into the bottom of his chin. His blood coated my hand and sprayed across my face, and I shoved him away in horror, blinking through hot tears even as another gripped my hair and yanked me backward. I stumbled and fell, saved only by the knife I was able to release at my wrist to counter a blow aimed for my head.

A large man stood over me, wielding a blade like an ax, swinging down as I rolled away. I reared up, kicking my attacker in the face, and as he released his hold on his blade, I took it and rose to my feet, shoving it through his stomach.

The fight continued like that with my people charging, calling me traitor. Each time I cut down one of my own, a piece of me went with them. My face was wet with tears as I faced a young girl. She could not be any older than me, with the same dark hair, the same dark eyes, the same dark skin.

"Why are you making me do this?" The question tore from my mouth, a devastated demand.

"No one is making you," she replied. "You *chose* the Blood King. You are the traitor."

Those words were an even harder blow, and I took a step back.

"You know nothing of my sacrifice." My voice was visceral, my hurt and anger so acute, I felt like my skin was on fire. I'd done this to protect them. I'd done this so that they could have some kind of life beyond yesterday's surrender, and here they were, squandering it all.

"It doesn't look like sacrifice," she said. "Queen of Revekka."

She lifted her blade and charged. My hands were slick with blood and sweat, and my grip on my sword was faulty. I could barely hold the hilt as her blade clashed with mine. Two more blows and my weapon flew from my hands. As triumph flashed in her eyes, I shoved my other hand toward her, losing my knife in her soft stomach. Her eyes widened, her body went slack, and I caught her as she began to fall.

"I'm so sorry," I said, but even as she stared blindly at the night sky, she spoke, her words harsh.

"If you were truly one of us, you would have killed him."

Blood dripped from her mouth, and as I settled her upon the ground, she went slack. My body shook, angry. Sitting there on my knees, I gave a frustrated cry and shoved my dagger into the earth beneath me.

The sounds of battle died around me, but I did not rise until Adrian approached.

"Up," he said, dragging me to my feet.

"We have to bury her," I said, staring into his blood-spattered face. "We must bury them all."

I might not abide by the goddesses' doctrines, but they did, and they deserved the burial rites they'd prayed for. If they were left exposed, they were left to be fed upon, and their souls would never make it to the afterlife.

Then my eyes shifted to the dead littering the road, and a small group of survivors who were now on their knees before the vampires, swords pointed at their throats.

"What are you doing?" I demanded. "Let them go!"

"They have committed treason," Adrian responded. "They must be punished."

I understood his inclination to punish, because what they'd done was wrong, but this was different…these were my people. They had a right to their anger.

"You think these are your people, but they are not."

My brows lowered. "I was born of this land."

"You will come to find that blood has no bearing on who you become."

"Adrian, please," I breathed, but he just stared back, unmoved by my plea.

"I have already spared one life for you."

My gaze shifted to the few who were left, all glaring back at us. It was clear they considered me the enemy. How had I gone from the savior of my people—*you are the hope of our kingdom*—to this?

"Daroc," he said. It was a wordless command.

"No!"

I bolted for them, but Adrian's arms snaked out, winding across my shoulders and waist. He turned me at the last second before the kill was ordered, and a wet thud followed as the bodies hit the ground in unison.

It was done.

Adrian's chin had settled in the hollow of my neck, and as he spoke, I felt his breath on my cheek.

"They do not deserve your tears."

I did not know if I cried for them anymore or if I cried for myself. I thought I'd lost my future the moment I agreed to marry this monster. Tonight, I'd lost my home.

I pushed away from him and whirled. "You didn't have to do that!"

"If they can attack their princess," he said, "what is stopping them from attacking their king?"

His words hurt, and it was worse because I knew they were true.

"Come," he said, placing a hand upon my shoulder. He guided me to his horse, but before I mounted, I turned to look at him.

"You will bury them," I said. It wasn't a question.

"It will be done," Adrian said, taking my face between his hands. "But not by you."

I stared. "You promise."

"I promise," he said.

"Why should I believe you?"

His eyes fell to my lips, and he brushed his thumb against my cheek. "Because I only make promises for you."

*Why me?* I found myself thinking as I had so many times over the last two days but said nothing. I'd take his promises now because one day, they might run out.

"Up," he commanded, and this time, I obeyed. Adrian followed me onto the horse, and I settled against him, cradled by his arms as we took off into the dark. I felt as though my chest were unraveling as I left the souls of my slaughtered people in the hands of my enemies.

Except that the vampires hadn't been my enemies in that fight.

It had been my own people.

The shock of their anger, of their conviction reverberated through me, striking in new places—my heart and chest, my stomach and throat. It was a blow I had not anticipated. I had thought they would understand my sacrifice. I had chosen to marry Adrian to ensure their lives never changed under his rule, but that had not been enough. They'd wanted him dead.

And now they wanted me dead too.

I was beginning to think Nadia was wrong.

There was no coming back to Lara.

Adrian set a brutal pace through the wood that took us away from the main path. The ground was uneven, which caused my body to rock against his, my thighs unable to grip Shadow's sides. Adrian's arm slipped around my waist, tightening so that I was sealed against him. He leaned forward, his cheek against mine. It was an intimate hold, but it was a stance that kept me in place and urged our horse forward.

We did not stop until the sky was tinged light blue, a sign of the coming sun. Scouts were sent ahead, and by the time we reached them, an encampment had been erected. The same tall, black tents that had loomed outside Lara made a haphazard circle upon a balding patch of earth surrounded by thin trees.

Adrian dismounted near his tent.

"Isolde," he said, drawing my attention. When I looked down at him, he was waiting for me to follow. I considered taking off, riding hard into what remained of the wild night. I didn't know where I would go. Back to my home? To the castle where I was now known as a traitor?

Adrian's hand closed over mine, once again drawing my attention.

"Dismount, Isolde."

It was the closest thing he'd ever given to a command. He did not say it, but I read the message in his eyes—*If you run, I will catch you*, and I knew he would. For a moment, I let myself think about what that would be like, watching Adrian's power and aggression descend upon my body. We would fight like we fucked—brutally.

"Isolde," he said my name again, tinged with a harshness that told me he knew my thoughts. I looked at him again and swung my leg over Shadow's body. Adrian reached for me, his large hands splaying across my waist as he lowered me to the ground. He did not let go for a few moments, and I knew it was because he did not trust me not to bolt, but my thoughts were giving way to something else—a tangle in my chest that built as the tension between us grew.

"If you flee, you flee into the hands of your enemies now," he said. "Do not forget what transpired here."

I scowled. "You do not have to remind me of my treason. I think of it when I look at you."

He did not respond, and I found myself wishing I could antagonize him instead of amuse him, because I was angry. He kept his hand on the small of my back as he walked me to his tent. Inside, it was spacious and similarly arranged as it was on the border of Revekka, but the fire he'd had blazing the night I'd come to ask for Killian's life appeared to have been reduced to only hot embers. I tried not to wonder if he'd made that concession for me.

I stood at the center of the room, unmoving.

"I am sorry," he said, and the words hit me wrong.

I spun to face him and pushed him. He didn't budge, but the act felt like a release, so I did it again and again. It did nothing to him, and that only made me angrier.

"Are you done?" he asked.

I scowled and reared back, ready to release my blade

and shove it into his heart—not that it would do any good—but Adrian's hand latched onto my wrist, halting my strike.

I met his gaze.

"No."

I shoved my other hand toward him, releasing my blade again, but he caught me, and this time he pinned my hands against my sides, stepping in to me.

"Enough, Isolde! I know you grieve—"

"What do you know of grief?" I spat. "You made me their enemy."

"They made you the enemy. Your people could have just as easily tried to protect you."

I flinched, knowing he was right, and the words took all my fight. He walked me backward until my knees hit the back of the bed, and I sat. My eyes were in line with his stomach, and after a moment, he tilted my head up, his fingers poised beneath my chin, so that my gaze met his.

"You had every right to defend yourself," he said. "Take comfort. If you had not killed them, I would have, and I would not have been merciful."

I swallowed hard, wondering what sort of justice he would have executed on my behalf.

"You must know my father had nothing to do with the attack."

Adrian stared, unblinking, as if he did not believe me. "You are so certain?"

"Yes," I whispered fiercely.

For a brief moment, Adrian let his fingers trail from my chin over my jaw and across my cheekbone. The movement was gentle and surprised me. As soon as the shock shuddered through me, he dropped his hand.

"Sleep," he said and took a step away.

Again, I found myself surprised. I expected him to demand sex or at least tease it.

He raised a brow. "Unless you would prefer another activity."

I looked down at my clothes, spattered with blood.

"A bath," I said. "Or...whatever can be managed."

Adrian nodded and left the tent.

A short while later, he returned with a bucket and a cloth. While he'd been gone, he had washed his face, though his clothes were still stained with the carnage of our battle.

"It is all we can manage," he said, setting it down at the center of the tent. After, he took a seat opposite me, spreading his legs wide.

"I...don't have anything to wear," I said.

"It is no problem," Adrian replied.

I glared at him, but honestly, I did not care as much as I pretended. I liked my body, I liked being unrestricted, so I removed my cloak, then my boots and the rest of my clothes. My legs and lower back ached, and it wasn't until now that I realized how much damage I'd done to my hands during the fight. They hurt, my knuckles were bruised, and my fingers were cut. I submerged them in the water and watched the blood dance away in ribbons of red, ignoring Adrian's burning gaze. After a few moments, I used the cloth to begin scrubbing away the remaining blood. Some of it was mine, but most of it was my attackers.

*My people*, I kept reminding myself, still in disbelief.

"What happened to your mother?"

I froze at his question, not expecting it but also

unsure if I wanted to share what little I had of her with him. I focused on my task.

"She died," I said.

"A while ago?" he pried.

"When I was born."

Adrian was silent, and I moved on from cleaning my hands to my arms, my chest and stomach. I felt his gaze on all parts of me, even as he asked these serious questions. "What do you miss most about her?"

His question shocked me, and I hated being shocked by him. It was both curious and sincere, and I had an answer.

"I miss her potential," I answered, staring at him. "I miss what could have been with her as my mother."

He seemed strangely thoughtful. I assumed the questions were over and had returned to my task when he continued. "Who taught you to ride?"

I paused a beat, my frustration growing. "My father."

"Who taught you to fight?"

"My commanders."

"Alec Killian?"

Once again, I halted my task, and this time, I turned to face him fully. My eyes roamed from his face to his powerful shoulders to his cock, which strained against the fabric of his clothes.

"Jealous, King Adrian?" I taunted.

He tilted his head up, mouth and body tightening.

"I am just trying to ascertain what is left for me to teach."

His words inspired heat to blossom in my stomach, and I wanted to tremble, but I tightened my muscles to keep from showing weakness.

"I don't know there is much you can teach me, Adrian, except hate."

A smile curved his lips, and then he rose to his feet. As he did, the edges of his clothing brushed my skin, and the shiver I'd fought so hard to keep at bay shook me. I bent my head back to hold his gaze as he towered over me.

"Sparrow," he murmured, lifting his hand to hold my jaw, thumb brushing my cheek as he'd done earlier. "I think you are right."

I felt his lips brush mine as he spoke, and I thought he would kiss me, but instead, he dropped his hand and slipped from his place between me and his chair, leaving the tent.

As soon as he was gone, I realized how much I'd wanted him to kiss me, because I'd wanted the pleasure he promised. I'd wanted to get lost in him so I could forget my reality.

It was good he'd left me alone.

I turned back to the basin and finished washing up. After, I curled into the furs covering Adrian's bed. It took me a while to fall asleep, my mind racing with my recent past. It followed as the dark descended, and all I heard was the clash of metal and the screams of my people.

# NINE

**Those screams continued, but when I woke up, it was to** silence. The only thing that clung to me was a feeling of dread that had settled deep in my chest. Beside me, Adrian was asleep. He was naked and lay atop the covers. The low light from the brazier reflected off his lean and hard muscles. The curve of his erection drew my eyes, and I wondered if he was ever not aroused. I considered that he was too trusting to fall asleep beside me like this, and yet I did nothing but slip from bed and dress, stepping into the fading day. All around, the woods looked as if they were burning, set aflame by the sun.

The camp was quiet, eerie, and I did not feel as safe as I expected, given that I was still within the borders of my home. Even outside the tent, the icy feeling in the pit of my stomach remained, and I couldn't shake the feeling that something horrible was about to happen.

A high-pitched mewling drew my attention, and I turned in the direction of the sound. Between the dead boughs of the trees, I saw buzzards circling. Again, that strange dread overcame me, sharper this time. *They're looking for food*, I thought and hoped Adrian kept his promise to bury my people.

A chill wind swept from behind me, dragging my hair into my face and carrying the distinct smell of death, but we were too far from those who had perished last night, and this smell was strong, indicating days of decay. Another cry erupted from the vultures, and I watched as one peeled away from the volt. As it did, the others followed.

And so did I.

I cut through the trees, following the birds in the fading daylight. I started moving at a walk, but my pace increased. As I went, tree limbs caught my hair and thorns gripped my clothes and scratched my skin, but I was urged on by a sense of alarm that turned my stomach, despite a growing fear of what I would find.

The trees began to thin, and I came upon a village that was surrounded by a tightly woven wooden fence. In Lara, most of the villages were given the name of the family who founded them. In this case, a carved sign indicated the name to be Vaida.

The gate, which faced me, was closed. That was not unusual, as it was almost sunset. What was unusual was the quiet...and the smell.

There was death here.

The vultures cawed, and I saw them swoop down to land inside the gate as I approached.

"Hello!" I called, and my voice echoed in the trees around me. It was unsettling, and as the wind picked up, swirling the smell of rot, my skin prickled.

I pushed on the gate, rattling it to get someone's—anyone's—attention, but there was no response.

*A soldier should be stationed here*, I thought. One of Killian's guards.

I squeezed my hands between the fence and the gate and tried to pry open the door. There was enough of a crack that I could peer through, and what I saw elicited a cry from my throat.

I released the gate, turned on my heels, and vomited.

"Isolde!"

The voice that called my name was familiar, and I didn't expect its presence. I looked up, sobbing, and screamed at Killian, who rode toward me upon his horse.

"They're dead! They're—"

I couldn't say it. I'd only seen part of two bodies, but they seemed to have been skinned alive. As I recalled what I'd witnessed, my stomach roiled again.

Killian dismounted and came to me.

"We need to leave," he said and took my shoulders, pulling me from the fence. I wrenched away.

"Did you not hear me?"

"I heard you," he said through his teeth. "And if we don't leave now, we're next!"

"Release my wife, Commander."

Adrian's voice was cold, but his presence surprised Killian enough that he loosened his hold, and I whirled toward Adrian, who stood apart from us. He looked just as callous as his voice had sounded, his face and hair pale, his clothing immaculate.

"They're all dead," I said again.

"He knows," Killian said. "He's responsible."

If Killian's words angered Adrian, he did not show it. He remained calm as he asked, "You are so certain, Commander?"

I shook my head and swallowed, feeling the bile rise in the back of my throat again. "No. This wasn't vampires. This was…"

I did not know, but I knew vampire attacks, and vampires did not leave humans looking like what I'd seen…did they?

Adrian's eyes met mine, and in an instant, Daroc, Sorin, Isac, and Miha appeared. I blinked, shocked by how quickly they moved.

"Open the gate," Adrian commanded.

I watched as Daroc effortlessly scaled the wall.

"Do not look," Adrian said as the gate groaned open.

All the while, Adrian held my gaze, even as Daroc returned to summon him.

"Your Majesty, you will want to see this."

Adrian's eyes did not waver, and it was if he were asking me if I'd be okay.

I swallowed and nodded before I was left alone with Killian. I had words for him anyway. I didn't watch Adrian disappear into the village, because I had seen enough to know that the bodies lay right before the gate. It wasn't until Killian himself stopped watching and shifted to look at me that I spoke.

"Your men should have been patrolling. How long has it been since they ventured this far north?"

"You berate me for not protecting them yet turn to the man who slaughtered our people. We found the graves, Isolde." Killian stepped in front of me. "Leave with me. You aren't safe with them."

"I am not safe *here*," I argued. "Our people, the ones you found. They tried to kill me."

"You were just caught in the crossfire—"

"No, Alec, I wasn't."

There was a pause, and then he said, "You cannot be angry with them. You did not even resist when he took you away."

My lips flattened as I glared. My anger was acute, a flush that made my whole body hot. Killian had been present during the discussion.

"You know why I didn't resist."

"Why? Because you feared for your people? Or because he fucked you the way you wanted?"

I narrowed my eyes. I'd guessed that he'd lingered outside my door on the night of our wedding, and this confirmed it.

"Do not shame me, Killian."

"I am only pointing out that despite professing to hate him, you appear to enjoy his company."

"So you are justifying the attack," I said.

"Isolde—"

"I am your queen," I cut him off. "You will address me as such."

Killian's jaw tightened, and his eyes flared. "So this is how it will be."

"If what you have said is truly how you feel, then yes."

He blinked, and for a moment, I could see his doubt and confusion warring.

"If you are finished trying to convince my bride to leave me, then I think it would be wise for you to inform your king of what has occurred here."

I flinched at Adrian's words and turned to face him. As I did, I caught a glimpse of the corpses beyond the fence and felt the blood drain from my face once more. Adrian shifted to block my view.

"And what exactly will I tell him?" Killian asked.

"That a whole village was slaughtered," he said.

"By whom?" I asked.

Adrian's eyes settled on mine, and despite the fierceness of his expression, his gaze seemed to soften.

"My guess would be magic."

"There is no magic, save yours," Killian accused.

"That is a myth of our existence," Adrian said. "I have abilities, not magic."

"I thought magic had been eradicated with the Burning," I said.

"So long as spells exist, magic will prevail," he said. "This is the kind of chaos humans make when they summon magic they cannot control."

Magic was considered a gift, not a skill. Even before King Dragos ordered the Burning, those who were not born with magic were forbidden to speak spells.

"You are saying one of our own spoke this"—Killian gestured toward the village—"into existence?"

"Not necessarily," Adrian said. "The spell could have been cast from anywhere."

I felt even more dread at that thought.

"And do you really think my king will believe that? Knowing you were here?"

"My father will believe you, Commander," I argued. "Adrian has told you what he thinks occurred. You should communicate that."

Killian stared and kept his jaw tight, but after a

moment, he bowed. Part of me wanted to go with him so I could tell my father what I'd seen myself. I knew Killian would not want to admit that his guards had neglected to travel this far. I also wondered if this village was destroyed, were the others?

The commander departed, and after a moment, I felt Adrian draw a piece of my hair behind my ear.

"How are you?" he asked.

I stared at him, my mouth slightly ajar. I didn't know why it always surprised me that he asked if I was all right, and yet this was the third time.

"Will this happen again?" I asked.

I did not know much about magic. Once a spell was cast, was it like a plague? Did it continue until it had nothing to consume?

"It is hard to say without knowing what kind of spell was cast or by whom," Adrian replied.

So he was telling me there was no way to fight it. I swallowed the thickness gathering in my throat.

"We have to bury them," I said.

"We'll have to burn them," Adrian corrected, and despite the gentleness of his tone, I still flinched.

Until corpses began to rise from the dead, burning was for witches and those who were caught using magic—not victims of it.

"Do you think they will rise again?" I asked.

"No, but since we do not know what killed them, fire is best. It will cleanse the ground."

———

Adrian returned to camp with me, and I managed to keep my tears at bay until we were inside the tent. He left me to cry, for which I was thankful, and returned later after I'd composed myself. We rode to the clearing together, the cold air stinging my wet face, and as we approached Vaida, I could see several bodies piled in the center of town through the open gate, all covered in white cloth. Adrian's soldiers had been hard at work in my absence, and I admired the care they'd taken to wrap and stack them, even if it was only so they could be consumed with fire.

We kept our distance from the open gate as the vampires dropped torches upon the bodies and made their way out, closing the gate behind them. It wasn't long before the smoke rose, spreading the smell of burning flesh.

As I watched the smoke rise, I spoke, not looking at Adrian. "How did you know this was a spell?"

"I am over two hundred years old," he said as a way of answering.

It meant that he had lived during the Burning.

I had questions for him—questions about magic and witches and the world that he had existed in long before I was born—but I did not ask them, because there was a part of me that wondered if I could trust his answers.

After a moment, Adrian turned to me. "I will leave one of my men behind to aid your father, but we must continue on to Revekka."

I hesitated as he spoke, the hate I felt for him overpowered by a sense of gratitude.

He called to one of his soldiers. "Gavriel!"

A large blond vampire strode forward, his gold armor glinting in the firelight.

"Return to Castle Fiora," Adrian said. "Take Arith and Ciprian with you."

"Yes, my king," he said and then looked at me. "My queen."

The three wasted no time mounting their horses and setting off in the direction of my home. I worried at their return but hoped my father, at least, would accept their aid.

"Thank you," I said to Adrian, though the words sounded strange in the space between us.

He did not smile, did not act as if the words affected him.

He crossed the field to his horse. It took me longer to move as I stared at the flames that were now consuming the wooden wall, effectively erasing Vaida from existence. I could not explain the grief I felt for my people or the guilt that burdened me as I prepared to leave them to face this unknown enemy.

But there was a part of me, a small one, that felt like it was some kind of retribution.

I relented and went toward Adrian, mounting his horse. He followed behind me, his body cradling mine as we continued through the darkness.

---

I had expected to relax more as the hours passed on our journey. Instead, I found that I was even more on edge, waiting for the next attack or to find the next massacre. It had only been a day since leaving High City, and yet those hours had been filled with a horror I'd never expected—something far greater than the arrival of vampires at our border.

"You are safe," Adrian said, and I was conscious of how his hand pressed against my stomach.

"I am safe," I said. "But what about my people? You said you would protect them."

"I have given you all I can against magic," he said.

I wanted to be angry at him for not being that powerful, but I couldn't muster the energy. Instead, I asked, "I did not think there was anyone left who could speak spells."

"Do you really believe a king let that kind of power slip through his fingers?" Adrian asked. I turned my head toward him, but with my back to his chest, I could only feel the brush of his jaw against my cheek. He was referring to Dragos, the former king of Revekka, whom he had killed.

"Is that why you murdered him?" I asked. "Because you wanted what he had?"

He did not answer the question. Instead, he said, "So you know my history."

"Everyone knows your history," I said. "You stormed the Red Palace and murdered King Dragos and his pregnant wife in their sleep."

"I did not murder them in their sleep," he said. "They were dragged from their beds, and when Dragos faced me, he begged for his life to be spared and offered his wife as a gift. I slaughtered him. His wife I spared, but she jumped from her tower window." He paused and then added, "I did not know she was with child until after her death."

"Do you think that somehow excuses your actions?"

"I am not seeking a pardon," he replied.

I expected him to explain himself, to tell me that the murder was justified, but he didn't, and after that, we did not speak.

We did not travel as long as the previous night, stopping a few hours before sunrise. Once again, when we reached our chosen campground, the tents were already up, and the vampires who had ridden ahead to prepare camp had already lit fires for warmth and food.

"Tomorrow, we will be in Revekka," he said, following me into our tent. "Do you need anything?"

He seemed in a hurry, which I found strange. I thought he would linger, and I hated to admit that I'd hoped he would. I had questions about spells and witches and the Burning, but if he could read my mind, he did not jump to offer answers. I wasn't sure if that was due to my emotions not being extreme enough for him to sense what I was thinking or because he wanted to leave, so I shook my head. "No."

I noted how he swallowed and inhaled a sharp breath. "Then get some rest."

I would ask him where he was going, but I did not want him to think I was asking him to stay, so I let him go.

Once he was gone, I shed my clothes and curled into Adrian's warm furs, but I could not sleep. I kept thinking of how quickly those in the castle, at the gates, and in the villages beyond High City had turned on me. Even Killian seemed to think my choice to marry Adrian meant I had chosen a side. Except now, I felt like I was being forced to the only side that had defended me, that had sworn to keep me safe and had actually done so.

Why did it have to be Adrian who kept his promises?

I sighed and sat up, too restless to sleep, and left the bed. I dressed in my tunic and cloak, deciding to step into what remained of the night. If I was in High City, I would have wandered beyond the gates of the castle in search of stars, but there were few left as the early morning grew brighter. Even if I had wanted to be alone, I did not trust these woods or the monsters I might have attracted, so the camp would have to do.

I peered through the tent opening, finding a few of Adrian's soldiers lingering near the fire that had been built between us and the rest of the camp. I had a feeling they'd been stationed there to guard me until Adrian returned, and I wondered where Sorin, Isac, and Miha had gone. I was growing fond of the trio, but I thought it would be harder to convince those three to let me walk around the grounds alone than it would these four strangers.

I stepped out of the tent. The air was cold against my skin and my tunic too short for this weather, but being outside in the open made me feel as though I could breathe again. The vampires who were gathered around the fire looked over and scrambled to their feet.

"My queen," one said. "May I be of assistance?"

"I cannot sleep. I am going to walk the perimeter of the camp."

The three exchanged a look. "Can she do that?"

"I think what you mean is will Adrian like that?" I said. "And for the record, I do not care."

"At least allow one of us to escort you," another suggested.

"I can defend myself."

"We are aware, Your Majesty, but—"

"I appreciate the offer, but I would like to be alone," I said, and drew my cloak tighter around my body, and though they allowed me the space to stroll between the tents, I felt their eyes on me—no one was letting me out of their sight.

This was the first time I'd wandered farther than Adrian's tent, which was some distance from the others, and as I cut through to the edge of the wood, I was not prepared for what I heard as I passed—passionate moans, chanted names, desperate pleas to *let me come*.

I suppose I should have expected more grotesque displays of sexual behavior based on what I'd learned about vampires, but I had not even thought of it beyond my own experience with Adrian. Hearing these pleasurable sounds, however, made me stiffen, and suddenly I worried over why Adrian had been in such a hurry to leave our tent.

What would I do if I found him with another woman? The thought filled me with an acute rage. In part, it was due to the fact that I had to give up my life to exist with him in a foreign land and also because I had asked him not to sleep with other women after we were married. If he broke that promise, I would make him suffer.

But I never heard his voice, only the cries of his army—in particular those of Sorin, who gasped Daroc's name so loud, my heart jumped into my throat. I wondered at Adrian's second-in-command. The stoic guard seemed far too serious to have any passion, but hearing what I was, I had clearly been wrong.

I turned the corner and glanced to my left, my eyes catching on a sliver of light that cut across the ground from a tent. I halted. There, through the opening, I saw Adrian holding a woman. Her head was bent back, her pale hair spilling into his lap, his lips pressed to her neck, and while their embrace looked sensual, I knew it had nothing to do with sex. He was feeding. Behind him were other vampires, mouths molded to necks and wrists, crimson spilling onto their skin and clothes.

Now I understood why I'd never seen any of them feed on the road and why we stopped traveling before sunrise. I should feel grateful that I hadn't had to witness it before, but seeing this now, I found that I was both horrified and angry. The act was despicable but also intimate, and a horrible jealousy tore through me as the woman Adrian was holding arched into him, her fingers digging into his skin.

At my flare of anger, he looked up, his bright eyes meeting mine even at this distance. My horror overpowered my jealousy, and I turned on my heels and returned to the tent. I half expected Adrian to follow, but he didn't. I crawled beneath his furs, taking a breath that rattled my whole chest before closing my eyes against threatening tears.

I was living in a whole new world.

I woke later and rolled over to find Adrian reclining in a chair across the tent. Candle flame flickered on a table beside him, highlighting his grim features. He was so pristine, so beautiful, I was glad I'd seen him with the woman earlier. I'd let a few kindnesses blind me to who he really was—a monster.

"Did you fuck her?" I asked. "The woman whose blood you took?"

His eyes connected with mine. "No."

I studied his expression for a long moment, trying to decide if he was lying, but the Blood King had never been anything but honest—frustratingly so.

"Who…was she?"

I assumed she was now dead, but Adrian corrected

me. "She *is* a vassal," he said. "She—like many mortals—have agreed to serve me and my court."

My gut reaction was to be disgusted. "Serve you?"

I did not know what that meant. Did that only mean bloodletting? Or was he suggesting more?

"They offer their blood and are richly rewarded," he explained.

"So you bribe them?"

"You may call it whatever you like," he said. "In the end, I am fed, and they are rich."

"So you pay them from the treasury you stole?"

He stared at me, his hand propped against his face, lithe fingers fanned against his cheek. While I got the sense he did not like my reply, he also did not let my comment antagonize him as he answered, "At least I pay them."

I wanted to roll my eyes at him, but I refrained and asked, "How often do you drink?"

"Every day," he said.

"What happens if you don't?"

"It is my sustenance," he answered.

"You told me before I would beg you to take from me. Why would I ever want that?"

I could not imagine how he would think I would want him to *feed* from me.

He smiled. "Because as much as I draw life from it, all you will feel is sweet release," he said, and then he tilted his head. "You like release, don't you, Sparrow?"

I ignored his question. "I fail to see how something so vulgar could mean pleasure."

"There are a lot of vulgar things that bring pleasure," he said. "I am one of them."

"So you are telling me this…bloodletting…brings your vassal pleasure?"

There was something about that knowledge that felt like betrayal.

Again, there was a pause as Adrian replied, "You are more than welcome to take her place."

"I'd rather not," I said.

I'd already offered my body to this man. Offering my blood would be an even greater betrayal. Besides, I did not like the idea of being connected to him in that way—of being sustenance.

"Have you been…fed from?" I asked.

"No," he said, and there was a strange sadness to his eyes. "No one feeds from me."

"Why?"

"Because I do not allow it."

"Why?" My voice seemed to grow smaller and smaller. Adrian paused, staring at me before rising and approaching the bed. His robe hung open, exposing his chest and his erect cock, which was where my eyes caught until he placed his hand on my face, hooking his fingers into my hair.

"Because only my queen may take from me, and she is mortal."

Then his mouth closed over mine. I tried hard to keep my hands to myself, refusing to show him how much I wanted this, but I arched to him, like a puppet attached to a string. I released the furs from my grip and twined my fingers in his hair. He lifted me, my legs wound around his waist, and he turned to sit with me in his arms. My tunic rode up, and my naked flesh sat against his swollen length. The feel of him had my stomach tightening into a hard knot. His lips left mine to trail along my jaw, down my neck, over my shoulder. As he moved, I felt the scrape of his teeth. All the while, his hands pressed into my ass as he guided me along his cock. I gasped at the feel of him, thick and heavy between my thighs.

Then he dipped his head, his mouth closing over my nipple, peaked with arousal, and he spoke against my skin. "I could drink from you, you are so wet," he said.

I found myself pushing him onto his back while I straddled him.

"Then drink," I challenged, and he grinned as he guided me to his face. I kept most of my weight on my knees, staying still as he began, his tongue licking and thrusting, his lips sucking and kissing, but soon I started to rock against his mouth, tilting my hips, grinding harder. The more I moaned, the harder Adrian's hands pressed into my thighs, my ass, my breasts. He was everywhere all at once, and I was lost in this, addicted to the feeling building inside me. I chased it, raced for it, setting a faster pace that Adrian seemed all too pleased to maintain. I came with a guttural cry, and he held me a few moments longer, drinking between my thighs just as he promised.

Then he helped me slide down his body before he rolled, pinning me beneath him on the bed. His legs parted mine, the crown of his cock poised at my entrance.

"How is tasting your come different from drinking your blood?" he asked.

I stared at him. "Drinking blood is sacrilege."

"According to your goddess," he said. "It's not the first time Asha has villainized something she wished to destroy."

My brows knitted together. I was confused by his statement—what else had she villainized? I was also desperate to feel him move. "That is blasphemy."

"Are you pretending to be pious?" he asked, a small smile on his lips. Perspiration had formed on his face, and I felt heat building between us.

"I don't know what you mean by pretending," I said. "I am a saint."

"Oh, Sparrow, no one who fucks like you is a saint," he said and filled me in one brutal thrust. I cried out at the feel of him, instinctively lifting my hips and widening my legs to accommodate him deeper. When I focused on his eyes again, he bent to press his lips to my neck and jaw.

"Sing for me, Sparrow," he commanded and set his pace, moving inside me steadily. It was neither slow nor rapid. All the while, he watched me, his long hair teasing my skin, and I did exactly as he bid—I sang for him, I cried for him, I screamed for him.

# TEN

*As the sun set, I stepped out of the tent, finding that most* of the camp had already been packed. I was exhausted and my body ached; both things would make tonight's ride difficult. I was also unreasonably frustrated with myself and my feelings for Adrian. I even hated to call them *feelings*, but I was finding it harder to hate the actual person behind the monster, and that was something I had not expected in our short time together. I reasoned that the answer was simple: Adrian had been kind. He had buried my people according to our customs. He had left his soldiers to aid my father against an unknown threat. He had kept his promises to me.

But those promises were for Lara, not Cordova—and those were my people too. In the end, he would kill anyone who did not submit to his will.

I *had* to remember that.

"Princess Isolde."

I turned toward the feminine voice that had used

my old title and met the dark stare of Adrian's vassal. As I studied her, I remembered what Adrian had said—that they were richly rewarded, which was evident in the furs and blue silk she was draped in. Half of her blond hair was pinned up, and the rest fell in curls around her shoulders. Her features were pretty, small and pointed, but there was something vicious in her gaze: a dark thing that lived beneath her slight facade.

I had no trouble showing her my own vicious side, seeing no need to hide it. "I am married to your king, which makes me your queen," I said.

Her mouth opened, her face paled, but she recovered well, offering a laugh that grated against my ears. "Of course, I apologize. I am Safira, Adrian's favored vassal."

My eyes dropped to her gloved hand, which she extended to me.

I did not take it and lifted my gaze to hers once more. "As *King* Adrian's favored vassal, I would think you would be familiar with the etiquette of approaching a royal," I said.

Safira's fake smile fell. "Of course I am familiar with etiquette," she answered, though she still did not move to bow. "I merely felt that we were more equal, given we are responsible for Adrian's pleasure."

"You thought wrong," I said. "If you approach me again, I expect you will curtsy and address me by the appropriate title."

I was a little relieved when Safira dropped her false warmth. Her expression became icy, her cheeks rosy, as she answered, "My, you certainly have adjusted well to your new position."

"I was bred to be a queen," I said and took a step toward her. "Just as I was bred to dispose of things that bother me. Will you continue to bother me, Safira?"

Her mouth pressed into a tight line, and she lifted her chin, glaring at me. "If you touch me, you will face Adrian's wrath."

I had not been married to Adrian long, but last night, he'd essentially offered me her place. I did not think she was as irreplaceable as she thought. I took another step toward her.

"Do not threaten me with my husband. If I come for you, *no one* will protect you." I straightened. "Best to begin planning how you will fight your own battles, Safira. I have a feeling you'll need it."

The woman stood there a moment, chest heaving, and I had the fleeting thought that if she had a blade, she would go for my heart, but I did not think she was brave enough to go head-to-head with me—not after she'd seen me fight my own people.

She curtsied, and I offered a cold, triumphant smile.

"Your Majesty," she said in parting before she turned on her heels, curls bouncing, and cut a path through camp.

"Making friends?"

I turned to find Sorin standing behind me, an amused smirk on his face.

"More like managing expectations," I said.

"Safira is jealous," Sorin said, as if I could not guess. "Though after what I heard last night, even I am jealous."

I raised a brow, glaring. "You were across camp."

"Trust me, *I know*."

"Sorin," I warned.

"All I am saying is your cries of pleasure were heard for *miles*."

"Does Daroc punish you often for your mouth?"

"All the time," he said with a wink, and then someone cleared their throat behind us. We turned and found Daroc looming. He obviously did not appreciate my humor as much as Sorin. Adrian's second-in-command gave me a pointed look before his gaze slid to his lover.

"Sorin, King Adrian has a job for you."

"Good afternoon to you," Sorin said, and though he was being playful, Daroc's eyes widened, and he hesitated.

"I'm sorry," Daroc mumbled. "Good afternoon."

I looked between them, thinking how odd it was that they were still so awkward…hundreds of years later.

Sorin rolled his eyes. "It is, thank you." Then he looked to me as he bowed. "Another time, my queen."

Sorin left, and when my gaze returned to Daroc, he was staring at me, his lips pressed thin, a hard line between his brows. I got the feeling he did not trust me, and that was just as well, because I did not trust him.

"Any news from Lara?" I asked, wondering what had transpired since Commander Killian had returned to High City with Gavriel. I was anxious about how my father would handle the massacre at Vaida and could not deny that I dreaded the rumors that would spread. It was inevitable, no matter the truth, that vampires would be blamed, and normally, that would not bother me, except now it did. And it had nothing to do with Adrian's kindnesses and everything to do with how my people thought of me since my marriage.

I hated to imagine an even greater divide between me and my people.

"None," he said. "Perhaps today."

Daroc excused himself, and I turned my attention to the sky. Above me, the clouds were white and wispy, but tendrils of red bled through like blood in water. I followed those threads to the horizon, where the shades of red stained the sky. I would be beneath that sky within hours, within the borders of Revekka, surrounded by an enemy who sustained their lives by stealing mine. I did not know the politics of Adrian's court, did not know if vampires could ever respect a mortal queen, but I would do my best to survive.

*No, not just survive*, I thought. *Conquer.*

"Mourning the sun?"

I turned to find Adrian standing beside me. I found his question strange, considering the direction of my thoughts.

"A little less," I admitted and then said something that even shocked me. "Since you seem to keep your promises."

I was offering him as much as I could give—a kernel of trust that was as valuable as a blade in our world—but also reminding him of his vow.

His eyes seemed to glint at my compliment, but I frowned, wondering how long until I was left feeling like a fool for my belief in a monster.

Adrian held out his hand.

"Come," he said. "I am eager to depart. We will be in Revekka soon."

Taking his hand was easier now. His fingers closed around mine, and when he settled behind me in the saddle, a warmth bloomed in my chest that flushed my face. I was glad that my back was to him so he could not see how his touch was affecting me. I could hardly be blamed with thoughts of last night fresh on my mind. Even now as I recalled our passion, phantom threads of pleasure twisted through my body, and I shivered.

Adrian's hand came around my stomach, and he pressed me tight against him, his mouth near my ear.

"As eager as I am to be within my kingdom, I will delay our progress if you continue to think these thoughts."

I turned my head slightly, his lips close to mine.

"Am I hearing that you are not as eager for me?"

His answering chuckle sent a thrill through me, and then his hand lowered, dipping between my thighs as his mouth closed over my shoulder, teeth scraping through my clothing.

"Adrian." His name escaped between my teeth, and I inhaled.

"Yes, my queen?"

"What are you doing?"

"Proving myself," he answered and jerked my head toward his, fingers digging into my skin as he parted my lips with his tongue. He tasted cold but sweet as he kissed me hungrily while cupping my heat with his other hand. It was indecent. It was carnal. It was lust. I didn't want it to end, but as that thought blossomed in my mind, he released me all at once, and I was left dizzy and aroused as he urged Shadow forward into the thick of the woods, putting distance between us and his army, still making our way toward Revekka. Now all I could focus on was the hollow feeling in the pit of my stomach. My fingers curled into my palms as I thought of how I wanted to be full of him.

"Hold on to that passion, Sparrow. I will make you sing again."

I did as he guided me against him, my head resting on his shoulder. He drew his cloak about us and lifted my tunic, hand dipping beneath my leggings, where his thumb brushed my clit. I heaved a sigh that shook my bones.

"Are you always this insatiable?" he whispered against my ear.

I swallowed hard and answered truthfully—there was no reason to merely think it. He would hear, though I kept the answer short, clipped. It slipped between my teeth angrily. "Since you," I said.

Even so, he rewarded me, sliding into me while his thumb teased and circled. The closer I came to release, the harder he breathed, the more kisses he peppered down my face and neck. He stayed deep, curling inside me, and as my muscles clenched around him, he siphoned pleasure from me until I came.

When he was finished, he pressed a kiss to my temple, and it sent a strange rush through me. It was the first time he had kissed me like that, but I felt as if I'd been here before—held by him, touched by him, just like this. It wasn't just the action, it was the way he had done it—gentle and sure, as if to ask *are you all right?*

I lingered on those thoughts as we slowed our pace so the soldiers and their vassals could rejoin us, and then I fell asleep in his arms.

Later, when I woke, we were beneath the red sky. From a distance, it always looked one shade of red—a crimson color that reminded me of fresh blood—but now that I was here, I saw it for what it was: shades of red that deepened even to black. It felt so ominous—a representation of the threat vampires had presented over the last two hundred years. How else had this landscape changed over time, I wondered. Did the rain fall in crimson sheets? Did the rivers run red?

Behind me, Adrian chuckled. "That is ridiculous," he said.

I glared at him over my shoulder. "You live beneath a red sky and spread plague at will. How are my thoughts so ridiculous?"

He did not respond, and I sat up a little straighter in the saddle.

The sky wasn't the only part of Revekka that had an unnerving effect on me. All around us were tall, naked trees, and while it was winter, it was evident that even in the spring, nothing grew here. The bark was scorched and black, the earth at our feet barren, and it was like that for as far as I could see.

I had never felt so uneasy, especially in nature, but this place felt wrong, and the only way I could think to describe it was that something horrible had happened here. I could feel it—a heavy dread that was just as present as the clothes upon my body.

"This is the Starless Forest," Adrian said. "The trees—they sprang from blood."

"What happened here?" I asked.

"Witches were hung from these trees during King Dragos's reign," he said.

I shivered. Revekka belonged to Dragos over two hundred years ago—before the Dark Era—and had declared that all who possessed magic should burn. Mobs formed, hunts began, and people who thought they would never kill were suddenly happy to murder anyone they suspected possessed the ability to use magic, even without proof.

It was the will of Asha, Dragos had said, to destroy evil.

"Do you think you would feel such horror if those who died here were truly evil?" Adrian asked, and I flinched, both at the fact that he had been listening to my thoughts and by his tone.

"Even the worst of us fear death," I said.

I wished I could see Adrian's face as I spoke. I wondered if he feared death, or did he feel like his existence was already some kind of end? Still, this wasn't just the horror of those who had deserved it; it was the horror of the innocents who had died during the Burning.

"If they were not evil," I said quietly, "what were they?"

"Powerful," he said.

"Is that not the way of kings? To destroy those who would make them weak?"

"It is the way of cowards," Adrian said.

"And yet you attack those who have no defense against your onslaught. What does that make you?"

"A monster," he said without hesitation.

"Do you really believe that?" I asked, curious.

There was a difference between a monster and someone who could be monstrous. As much as it felt wrong to consider it, I wondered if I had mistaken one for the other. Once again, I was treading into dangerous territory. The moment I began to see the humanity in Adrian was the moment I truly betrayed my people.

"I can be anything. Your jailor, your savior, your lover." His mouth was closer to my ear as he added, "Your monster."

We continued in silence for a few moments as I turned over Adrian's words. The more I considered what I'd learned of the past, the more questions I had.

"If your witches were so powerful, why did they not defend themselves?"

"What do you know about witches?"

I hesitated. I knew what I had been told. We had been taught to fear witches since we were young. *Quiet*, Nadia would tell me, *or the witches will steal you away and gobble you whole!* As I had gotten older, they had morphed into something far more evil, their atrocities shared via the histories transcribed by royal librarians and scholars of Cordova. They described a group of women who conspired to starve and kill kingdoms, spelling kings to tax and go to battle, hoping the people of Cordova would turn to them for support.

It was a twisted road to power.

But Dragos had discovered their plan and called for the hunt. The years following were full of fire and a fear of magic.

"None of that is true," Adrian said.

"And I am supposed to believe you over a lifetime of history?" I challenged.

I felt him shrug. "History is just perspective. It changes depending on your side."

"Then tell me yours."

He took a moment to continue, and I wondered what gave him pause. At last, he spoke. "Two hundred years ago, a coven governed magic in Cordova. They were called High Coven, and they were dedicated to ensuring the practice of magic remained peaceful. These witches you think of as evil, they only wanted to nurture humanity and earth.

"But their leader saw opportunities to grow, to cultivate peace, so she assigned a witch to each kingdom. They would be a bridge between the king, his people, and the land. They were never meant to be weapons, but that was what Dragos wanted, and when they refused, he had them—and thousands of innocents—killed. So you see, your hero is really the villain."

"No one is that good," I said, unwilling to believe that the witches had motives so pure.

"No one should be."

I was not completely willing to change my mind about witches and witchcraft, and it was difficult to believe that Dragos wasn't merely doing what Adrian would do as a king. Had he not chosen to execute my people for their treason too?

"And you? Who were you all those years ago?" I asked.

Adrian wished to lecture me on the past but never brought up his own, and I wanted to know—who had he been before the curse?

I felt his body go rigid against mine as he answered, "A different person."

We did not speak after that, traveling only a few hours more before stopping to camp. Adrian brought a pail of hot water from a nearby spring that I used to freshen up. Once we arrived at the Red Palace, the first thing I would do was order a hot bath. My body and bones demanded it.

Since we had been on the road, I'd developed a bit of a routine, going straight to the tent to sleep, but as dawn drew nearer, I felt restless. I stepped outside, scanning the grounds for Adrian, who was nowhere in sight. A few feet in front of me was a fire the vampires had built Where Sorin sat there with Isac and Miha. When they saw me, they waved me over.

"Join us, my queen!" Sorin said, holding up a wooden cup.

Curious, I approached but kept my distance, not liking how close they sat to the sparking fire or the way the wind blew the flames this way and that. Perhaps it was an irrational fear, to catch aflame, but it was my fear all the same.

"What are you drinking?" I asked.

"Mead," he said.

"Is that something you will throw up later?"

He shrugged. "We'll find out."

Isac laughed and Miha rolled her eyes.

"Where is Adrian?" I asked.

"The king is feeding," said Isac. His long hair was pulled into a knot at the back of his head, and he lounged on the ground, his back propped up against a rock.

My mood instantly darkened at the news. Feeding meant that he was with Safira.

Miha paused what she was working on, which looked like a carving of some kind, and asked, "Have you need of him? I can relay a message."

"No," I said, gritting my teeth. I realized I could not expect Adrian not to feed, especially when I was unwilling to give him my blood. Still, I could not escape what I'd seen in the tent—the way he had held her, how she had clung to him. His mouth, his skin, his body, it was mine. I did not like that Safira felt she was somehow entitled to my husband because he fed from her.

I sat beside Sorin with my back to the fire.

"If it bothers you that much, just offer him your vein," Sorin said.

I glared at him. "That will never happen."

He gave a wry smile, exchanging a glance with both Isac and Miha. Still, as I watched them, I found I had questions about that too.

"Tell me more about it," I said.

"What do you want to know?" Sorin asked.

"I don't know. Blood is your sustenance, correct? Does everyone feed from vassals?"

"Not everyone. Lovers feed from each other."

My face flushed. "Every day?"

Sorin and Isac chuckled, but Miha remained quiet.

"Most days," Isac answered. "But we feel most of our hunger after sex."

"Why?"

Isac shrugged. "I don't know. It is a need, an impulse, and when we satisfy it, it is like the rush you feel at the peak of release."

Now my skin felt impossibly hot. I thought of all the times Adrian and I had come together—had he left my side to feed on Safira? Or perhaps he fed before to ensure he didn't bite me. Either way, I did not like that he would do either.

"If you are to live among us, you must understand our bloodlust," Sorin said. "As much as it is life-sustaining, it is also a bond. Granting Adrian access to your blood is the highest show of trust."

"But it is *your* choice," Miha added, looking up momentarily from her work.

My throat felt tight. All this talk of lovers and sex and blood, it made me feel heated and light-headed. Still, hearing the way Sorin spoke of it was different. It sounded sacred to them, which made the fact that Adrian took from Safira nightly even worse.

"And…how can I trust it will only be bloodletting?" I asked.

Sorin's brows lowered. "What do you mean?"

"Well, you became a vampire somehow," I pointed out. "How were you turned?"

"That," he said, "is a deeper bite."

"It is a great insult to hear another man teach his wife of bloodlust," Adrian said, suddenly appearing from the darkness around us.

My eyes collided with his, and I rose to my feet.

"I asked Sorin to explain," I said quickly. "Would you have him deny his queen?"

Adrian glared, baring his teeth before turning on his heels and entering the tent. I offered a quick, apologetic glance to Sorin and the others before following Adrian inside, stumbling when he twisted toward me suddenly, his eyes alight.

"You should have asked me," he said, jamming his finger at his own chest. "I would have told you. I *wanted* to tell you."

I stared, shocked by how strongly he was reacting to this.

"Was I supposed to assume blood sucking was a sacred process when you feed from anyone with a heartbeat?"

"I do not feed from just anyone," he said.

"Forgive me," I mocked. "You feed from your vassal, who feels responsible for your pleasure. You expect me to believe in a sanctity of something you also offer to her?"

"It is not the same," he said.

"You fuck her and drain her blood. How is it not the same?"

"I have never fucked her," he snarled.

I felt like my chest was going to explode. After a moment of quiet, he tilted his head back, which made the shadows darken the hollows of his cheeks.

"If I were to partake of your blood, I would have no use for her," he said. He was attacking my jealousy, as if to say *the way to end this is to give me everything*.

"And if you fucked her, you would have no use for me," I said.

"You say that as if you would not mind," he said, closing the space between us.

I shouldn't, but he already knew I cared. By the fucking goddess. Why did I care?

"Think of how I touched you last night." He trailed his fingers down my face. "Imagine another woman in your place."

I gripped his wrist to keep him from continuing his exploration, but I did not pull away from his touch.

"I don't want to care," I said. I was desperate not to care, even as resentment built inside me—toward Adrian, toward Safira.

"You do not have to be embarrassed by your desire, even if it is for me. Sex is a primal need. You have every right to satisfy it."

At his statement, I wondered when I'd departed

from my original idea of what sex was supposed to be like between us. It was meant to be a passionate release, not an emotional investment, and here I was, fighting jealousy over all of it, even the bloodletting.

We stood chest to chest, my head bent back so that I could meet his gaze, and I wasn't sure I liked who stared back—a man with gentle eyes and a soft expression, a man who longed for a connection I could not give.

His palm pressed to my cheek; his lips hovered near mine. "One day, I will make love to you, and I look forward to that day."

"Are you a dreamer, Your Majesty?" I whispered.

A small smile curled his lips. "No," he said, his breath caressing my mouth. "I am a conqueror."

Then Adrian kissed me, lifting me off my feet as he guided my legs around his waist. I twined my fingers in his hair and pried myself free to look into his strange, hungry eyes.

"I want you to stop feeding from Safira," I said. "Find another vassal."

I expected him to argue, but he didn't. His grip tightened on me, his erection pressing hard against me.

"I will do as you wish," he said and then consumed me.

# ELEVEN

***We would arrive at the Red Palace today.***

My thoughts were chaotic, and I was confused. I'd spent the last three nights on a journey to my new husband's home, and I knew little more about him than when I'd left Lara. No one seemed to be willing to give up information—not about themselves or him. Even asking about their powers seemed to be a topic that was off-limits. These people did not want to have weaknesses.

Despite dreading my arrival at my new home, I was eager to put distance between myself and Adrian. I should be encouraging his betrayal so that I would feel justified in running. Instead, I'd demanded he find another vassal for my sake. I was too invested, which I attributed to the fact that we had been together nonstop since our encounter in the woods. At the palace, Adrian would need to attend to his own agenda while I could consider my future, process the betrayal of my people, and decide how I was supposed to rule a kingdom of monsters—or destroy it.

"You are quiet today," Sorin said, coming up alongside me.

I stood just outside my tent, close enough to what remained of the fire to stay warm. The evening was colder than all the rest, and I was not looking forward to riding in this chill.

"Well, I am about to enter a den of wolves," I said.

"We're not that bad."

I glared.

"Okay, maybe we are, but it isn't anything you cannot handle."

"What do you know about what I can handle?" I asked.

Sorin gave a breathy laugh, his dimples deepened. "I have only needed to spend a few days with you to know you will survive our court."

I hoped he was right.

I went in search of Adrian and found him beside Shadow. He held the reins of a new horse; this one was white. I hesitated as I approached, wondering why there was suddenly another horse available for me to ride.

"This is Snow," Adrian said. "I thought you might like to ride into Cel Ceredi upon her."

Cel Ceredi was like High City in Lara—it was the town that had formed around the palace.

I took Snow's reins. "Who did she belong to?" I asked.

Adrian stared, and I could tell he did not want to answer my question.

"Her rider was a mortal," he finally said. "Who died last night."

I paled, and a number of possibilities ran through my

head—like they had been drained of too much blood—but Adrian was quick to shut those thoughts down.

"She wandered away from camp and was attacked by a wight," Adrian said.

"A wight?"

It was a creature I had not heard of before, but I was certain there were several monsters I had yet to encounter, especially in Revekka.

"It is a creature born of death. They are attracted to life—to the beat of your heart."

I stared at him for a moment, my eyes shifting to his chest as I fought the inclination to press my hand to where his heart had once beat. As much as I wanted distance from my new husband, I did not like what was forming between us now. It was not hostility so much as uncertainty. I had always been sure about my hatred for Adrian, but these new feelings…his concern for me…scared me.

"Mount up!" he called then, and the camp jumped into action.

We made our way through what remained of the Starless Forest, and as we neared the edge, I felt its grip leaving me, one finger at a time. I thought of what Adrian had said about the witches who had died there and did not realize how heavy of a burden it was to exist beneath that canopy until I was outside it and could breathe again.

My gaze shifted to Adrian. He rode a few paces ahead beside Daroc. He looked just as ominous as the red sky overhead—a powerful man with a long history, and I wanted to know what had made him. How had the history he felt so passionately about—Dragos, the witches, the Burning—shaped him into the Blood King?

Once I was at the Red Palace, I would find out.

The landscape of Revekka was much like Lara—rolling plains, mostly treeless with the exception of a few clustered pines. Beneath the sky, everything was tinged in a red hue varying from pink to crimson. It was beautiful but strange, and I wondered how long until I grew tired of it.

"We are coming upon the first village now," said Sorin, drawing his horse beside mine. "It is called Sadovea."

"Who lives there?" I asked. I wasn't sure about the population of Revekka. What was the ratio of humans to vampires?

"Revekkians," he said.

"Are they human or vampire?"

"You really don't know much about us, do you?"

I did not honor his question with a response since it seemed to be obvious to him.

"Adrian only allows a select few the privilege of becoming a vampire," said Sorin. I tried not to cringe at his use of the word *privilege*. "Those who go rogue and attack or change others without his permission are destroyed."

Destroyed was not an exaggeration when it came to vampires. They were hard to kill, but hearing it from Sorin sounded far more ominous.

"What are his criteria?" I asked.

"You must be useful to Adrian if he is to grant your change," Sorin said. "People petition him often when he holds court. You'd be surprised by their offers."

I was intrigued, but more curious about Sorin.

"Why were you chosen?"

He smiled softly, and though he did not look at me, I knew it was sad, which made me want his answer even more.

But when he looked at me, he surprised me by saying, "Because I am useful."

"You never give straight answers," I said. "Why? Are you afraid to be honest with me?"

"I am not afraid, but you are not ready to hear what I have to say."

"I would not have asked if I weren't ready."

He shook his head. "That is a lie," he said. "You still believe we are monsters."

"And?"

Nothing Sorin had to tell me about his past would convince me otherwise.

"Your humans are far more cruel, Isolde. You have no one to blame for our existence but yourselves. I fear the day you come to know it."

I blinked at him, confused by his words, but before I could say anything, a horrified scream erupted. My whole body felt the shock of it. A familiar routine played out in front of me as Adrian turned to look for me before disappearing around a bend in the road with Daroc.

I expected to be told to halt, but instead, my trio created a perimeter around me—Sorin and Isac to my left and right, and Miha behind me.

"Come," Sorin said, and we matched Adrian and Daroc's pace as we headed toward the sound of the screaming. The path ahead widened and turned from a dirt lane into a stone bridge. Beyond the creek was a village. Pointed roofs and chimney smoke billowed from over a wall that encircled the town, but that was where the quaintness ended as a man raced from a heavy mist, through the open doors of the gate, terrified. When his feet could no longer carry him, he went to his knees, and when those would not work, he fell, facedown, and did not move again. I did not need to approach to know that he was dead or that he had died from whatever magic had killed my people, because his skin looked as if it had been eaten away as if he were freshly skinned.

Silence fell, and then Sorin said, "Welcome to Sadovea."

A few of Adrian's soldiers entered the village first, returning to report that whatever had attacked seemed to be gone. After, Adrian gave the order to search for the dead. He waited at the gate, and as I approached, he placed his hand upon my forearm, halting me.

"Can you handle this?" he asked, his eyes searching mine.

"I'll be fine."

I knew he meant well, but his question made me feel weak. No, I hadn't been able to look upon my own people, but I had also been in shock. I knew what to expect now, so this would be easier...I hoped.

Besides, I wanted to help in whatever way I could.

Inside the walls of the village, I dismounted as the vampires began to kick in doors and drag out bodies that looked just like the ones found in Vaida. I wandered down a side street, past a storefront, a tavern and inn, and what I suspected were houses, though they looked different from the ones in Lara. These were made from slats of pine, not wattle, which was a weave made of twigs, and the roofs were covered in clay tiles, not thatch.

The bodies in the street were dressed warmly and contorted in a way that made me think they'd been fleeing from whatever had attacked. I paused, staring down at the form of a young woman. Her hair was dark like mine, and her hand was curled beneath her head as if she had merely fallen asleep. I wondered what her name was, if her mother and father lived, or were they here among the dead?

My gaze shifted to my left, and I saw someone staring back from inside a home. A woman with long, ginger-colored hair and sharp eyes.

*A survivor*, I thought, but I blinked, and she was gone. Confused, I approached and looked through a dirty window into a kitchen, but I did not see the woman, only the bodies of a mother and two children. I backed away from the house, an eerie feeling crept along my spine.

As I did, I noticed movement in the corner of my eye and caught sight of a bare, dirty foot as someone fled down an adjoining alleyway.

"Wait!" I called and began to follow.

I turned the corner and saw a small girl ahead. She turned to stare with wide, blue eyes. Her face was dirty, her hair a pale yellow. She was dressed in a pair of leggings, a tunic, and a thick woolen scarf.

"I can help you," I said, but she took off once more.

This time, when I came around the next curve, I saw no sign of where she'd gone, but I continued, thinking that perhaps I could draw her out of hiding.

"Hello?" I called. "I know you are here. Please, let me help you."

I passed several quiet homes and shops, all of which had been built side by side. There were a few people in the road, all skinless, all dead. I drew my cloak tighter around me as I passed them. If I had not seen this in Lara, I would have assumed some kind of plague had taken them, but for so many to die at once? It was like their entire town had been blanketed by death.

A creak drew my attention, and I twisted to find the door of an apothecary shop ajar. Pushing it open, I discovered the girl cowering in the corner, shaking.

"Hi," I said quietly as I stepped into the shop. "My name is Isolde."

The girl continued to shiver.

"I'm not going to hurt you," I said, standing in the doorway. "Are you hurt?"

The girl shook her head.

"Can you talk?"

The girl said nothing, just remained silent.

"Did you see what attacked your village?"

The girl nodded, and I inched toward her.

"Can you tell me what it was?"

She shook her head. I did not know if that was because she did not want to talk or because she truly did not know. It would make sense, considering she seemed to be the only one who was alive.

"And...are you parents...do you know where they are?"

I did not want to ask if they were dead. She shook her head.

"It's not safe here," I told the girl. Now I stood in front of her. "Will you not come with me?"

I bent and held out my hand, hoping she would take it. She stared at me for a long moment before reaching out, her small hand touching mine—and then gripping. I was shocked by her strength, and when my gaze returned to hers, her eyes had become red, her lips had peeled back to show jagged teeth, and she gave a horrible cry.

I wrenched my hand away and stumbled back into shelves of glass jars. The smell of pine and mint filled the air as they cracked and shattered beneath my weight. The girl bellowed and charged at me on all fours. I barely had time to draw my knife, but before she could reach me, something caught her in midjump and flung her across the room. She landed as I had—against a wall of jars. The crash of shattering glass couldn't overpower her angry screams as she rose from the rubble and glared, body heaving with anger as she faced Daroc, who now stood in front of me.

She hissed, baring teeth that did not resemble a human's, and charged once again. Daroc moved quickly, and it was as if he were teleporting—one moment, he was in front of the creature, the next behind, his hands on either side of her head. A quick snap and she was dead, her wide eyes meeting mine as she fell to her knees, no longer the monster she was moments ago but a girl again.

Daroc lowered her to the ground and then looked at me.

"Are you all right, my queen?" he asked.

I could not answer because I could not say. My body hurt, my arm burned where the girl had reached for me, and I had just watched Daroc kill a creature that looked like a girl. He rose to his feet and yanked a curtain panel from the window, using it to cover her.

"What happened to her?" I asked. I couldn't take my eyes off her limp body.

"Hard to say," he said. "We will have to take her to the Red Palace for an autopsy."

Daroc approached, helping me to my feet, though my legs were shaking.

"You're injured," he said, eyes falling to my hand. I

looked too, finding that there was a burn on my skin in the shape of a hand.

"Oh," I said and swallowed. "It doesn't hurt...not really."

He frowned. "Come."

I followed Daroc out of the apothecary and through the maze of buildings. As we emerged, Adrian turned toward me and frowned, his strange eyes brilliant against the gloom of the day. He started toward us, and when he came upon me, his hands cupped my face.

"You're pale. What happened?"

"She found...something," Daroc said. "A human... possessed by some kind of magic."

Adrian's severe gaze shifted from Daroc to me. "She looked like a girl," I said, and my mouth began to quiver. "A little girl."

I had watched her die.

"She is injured," Daroc said. "Her hand."

Adrian's eyes fell to my arm, which I was now cradling with my other hand. He frowned as he studied the wound.

"The creature did this to you?"

"With only a touch," I confirmed, staring at the wound almost blindly. My skin looked much like that of the dead—red and raw.

Adrian reached for me, and I let him take my hand as he examined it. I expected him to try and heal it. Instead, he said, "I cannot heal this. It is magic."

He looked at Daroc, worry etched across his severe face.

"We will be at the Red Palace soon," Daroc said. "Ana Maria can look at it."

I did not know who Ana Maria was, but I wondered what she could do that Adrian couldn't. Still, his jaw tightened, but I was not so much worried about my injury as I was about what had happened here.

"I don't understand. Was that girl responsible for... all this?"

"Not her, but whatever possessed her," Adrian said. He looked at Daroc again, offering a wordless command before the vampire bowed and departed, returning in the direction we'd come to retrieve the corpse of the girl, if I had to guess.

Alone with Adrian, he tilted my face toward his, and I got the impression he was trying to ensure that whatever had consumed the girl had not consumed me, but as I stared into his eyes, I could not help seeing hers, wide with the shock of death. I closed my own against the image and asked, "Who would do this?"

When Adrian did not answer, I opened my eyes again to find him staring off into the distance, his jaw set tight.

"Adrian?"

At the sound of his name, he looked at me.

"It's hard to say," he replied.

"But you have an idea, don't you?"

Suddenly, all Adrian's talk of good witches and gentle magic seemed like a trick. If a witch's magic could create something like this, how could it ever have been good?

"Anything can be evil in the wrong hands, Sparrow."

As the vampires gathered bodies to burn, another vampire tended to my arm. I had seen him around camp but never asked his name. I stared at him now, a handsome man with sharp cheekbones and dark skin and eyes. His hair was thick and braided, his hands gentle as he bound my burned arm.

"What's your name?" I asked.

"Euric," he said.

"Are you a healer?"

"No," he said. "At least not in the same capacity as they once were."

"What do you mean?"

"A true healer can mend by touch," he said. "Your people called them witches and had them burned."

"They healed by touch. That is magic."

"It is a miracle, not magic," he said. "Think of all the ways you cannot fight us. Now think if you had healers, at least you could fight our plagues."

I stared at him, considering his words, and thought of what Adrian had said yesterday—that history was all a matter of perspective.

Euric rose to his feet and bowed.

"My queen," he said before departing.

I watched him go and did not move until I saw Sorin, Daroc, and Isac light torches to burn the corpses. I rose to my feet and headed for Snow. As I reached for her reins, Adrian stopped me.

"I won't allow you to ride alone," he said. "Your pain will worsen, and it will make for a difficult ride. I will not have you injuring yourself further."

"Okay."

I did not argue, because I was already in pain, and I did not really wish to make it worse. The tension in his brows eased at my agreement, and we mounted Shadow while the others followed suit.

I did not think I was imagining the way Adrian enveloped me. His thighs pressed into mine, and one of his arms wrapped around my waist. During the ride, his lips trailed my neck, dusting kisses across my skin. I found myself holding my breath as each one lingered longer than the last.

"What are you doing?" I asked, my voice breathless, betraying what his actions were doing to my body.

"Distracting you," he said.

It was working. I was warm, my stomach was knotted, but the longer we rode, the less Adrian's distraction worked, and the pain in my arm was beginning to give me a headache. Coupled with the ride, I felt sick.

"We'll be home soon," he said against my ear.

Those words helped me relax, and I leaned against his shoulder, my head too heavy to hold up.

It wasn't until I saw a town that I sat up straighter. We passed through an open wooden gate, and before us, a winding road made a slow incline up the side of a hill, through a large market town, to a castle that loomed, both terrifying and beautiful. The wall of the castle seemed to span for miles, a series of grand arches. Behind it rose the stronghold itself, a cluster of tall and pointed towers, each carved with fine, floral details. At times, the castle itself appeared to be black, but when the light shone just right upon its glassy surface, I could see a deep red gleamed from within.

"Welcome to the Red Palace," Adrian said.

He continued through the town, and as he made his way along the path, villagers emerged to watch our procession. Some waved from windows while others threw flowers, wheat, or coins into the road at our horse's feet. It was a far better welcome than the send-off I'd had at home, and the thought hurt my heart.

"Were they ordered to do this?" I asked, having not expected this.

"Do you really think so poorly of me?"

It wasn't that. It was that I had expected to find that Revekkians were no happier to be under the rule of the Blood King than Lara.

"I take care of my people," he said. "Just as I will take care of your people."

"Were you Revekkian?" I asked. "Before you were cursed?"

"I am Revekkian," he said and added, "And I am not cursed."

His comment made my heart beat harder in my chest, and I had the thought that if he was not a curse to be broken, what was he? How had he become this?

Adrian did not speak and continued on through the valley, up a steep incline to the Red Palace. As we came to the gate—a large one with black iron bars—I realized I could not see the wall that surrounded the palace for all the trees. Once inside the gate, Adrian rode right up to a set of wide stairs. These were black, unlike the walls of the castle, and a crowd had already gathered upon them.

He dismounted and held his hand out for me. I accepted, tired of the pain that had at first only been in my arm but was now reverberating throughout my body. Despite this, I pulled myself together and watched as a man approached. He was older, his hairline receding almost to the middle of his head, and yet he kept this hair long. He wore dark-blue robes, embroidered with silver, and unlike many of the vampires I'd encountered, his skin was paper-thin and creased.

"Your Majesty," he said.

"Tanaka," Adrian acknowledged.

The man looked as if he were about to speak when Adrian stepped past him, pulling me alongside him. The crowd parted. Unlike Tanaka, they seemed to know he was not in the mood to chat.

"Who was that man?" I asked.

"He is my viceroy," Adrian said and left it at that.

We entered the palace through a set of large, wooden doors and were immediately greeted by a grand staircase, heavily embellished with ornate carvings of the old goddesses I knew from our myths—Rae, the goddess of sun and stars, and Yara, the goddess of forest and truth, and Kismet, the goddess of fate and fortune—who were no longer worshipped by the world at large. I wondered if Adrian had worshipped them two hundred years ago, back when the whole of Cordova had multiple goddesses instead of just two.

The walls and ceilings of the castle were the same deep red, intricately cut with sweeping designs—vaulted ceilings, interlaced arches, high and pointed windows. If the windows were in Lara, they would have allowed for the halls to be filled with light, but because they were in Revekka, a strange hazy red loomed outside.

"Come. I will take you to your rooms and send for Ana," Adrian said.

I did not argue. My head was pounding, and my arm still burned from the girl's touch. We took the steps slowly, and just as I was about to comment on Adrian's patience, he paused on the step and shifted toward me.

"Let me carry you," he said.

"That is hardly the introduction I need to your people."

It would be hard enough to be human in a castle full of vampires without Adrian encouraging them to see me as weak.

"They will not think you are weak," he said.

But he did not ask again, and we continued, cresting the stairs, heading to our left where another set of stairs led into a darker hallway. My suite was at the very end. It was large, with a four-poster bed, velvet coverlets and curtains, and plush rugs covering every inch of cold stone. I was glad that the fireplace felt so far away from the bed, as it contained a healthy fire.

I expected Adrian to leave me at the door, but instead, he followed me inside.

"Ana will need the fire when she looks at your wound. After, it will not get above an ember, I promise."

"Thank you."

"You will rest after she leaves."

I arched a brow at his command, though my body softened at the thought of sleep in a real bed.

"You must be well enough to attend tonight's festivities," he added in response to my questioning stare.

"What is happening tonight?"

"We are celebrating my return and our marriage," he said. "It will be your first introduction to my people, and while I know you are not eager to meet them, I'm sure we can both agree that first impressions are everything."

"You do not count our rushed entrance to the castle as a first impression?" I asked.

He smiled then. "I think my people will assume I was more eager to be alone with you."

"Except that you are depositing me in a room and leaving others to care for me."

I wasn't sure why I said that, and Adrian's brows drew together over simmering eyes.

"Missing me already?" he said, amusement in his tone as he tilted my head upward, his hand splayed across my neck as if he wished to feel my pulse as I spoke.

"Hardly," I said, clenching my jaw and averting my eyes.

He laughed, unfazed by my curt reply. "This would be easier if you would admit that, against your better judgment, you like me."

"This would be easier if you would admit that the only reason we remotely get along is because of what our bodies do together, nothing more."

He stared at me for a long moment, unmoving. His face was near to mine, lips hovering close, his hand around my neck, his fingers tightening, a gentle squeeze that had my pulse racing against his skin.

"All this hate for what I am," he said. "Would you feel the same if I were human like your commander?"

I glared. "You would still be the enemy."

"You do not even know why I am your enemy," he said.

"You are a threat to humankind," I countered. "You have killed kings and conquered countries! No one, not the strongest among us, stands a chance against you."

"Such a speech and yet all I hear is your fear of something not like you."

"Do not reduce my hatred of you to difference! You are more than different. You burned whole villages, spread plague, and killed hundreds. You are a spineless, murderous—"

Adrian stepped closer and gripped my head, his hand tightening in my hair, his body flush with mine. I was not certain of his intentions, even as he bent his head to mine, even as his breath caressed my lips, because his eyes glinted with a sharp, frustrated anger.

"I know what I am," he said, voice quiet. "Can you say the same?"

*Once.*

I could have said that once, a week ago, when I had been Isolde, princess of Lara. That was until I met Adrian, and from that first encounter in the woods, it had become clear I had never really known myself at all.

"You call this treason," Adrian whispered, his fingers trailing down my face, a soft, careful caress. "But this— *us*—is beyond choice."

"You're right," I replied, and though I knew he was talking about something that went far deeper between us, I ignored it and spoke through my teeth. "I didn't have a choice."

He released me, and I had to admit, the distance he placed between us pulled heavily at my heart. Maybe it was because of his expression, which seemed both pained and defeated.

"I have much to attend to," he said and turned to leave. At the doors, he paused. "I expect you will be eager to explore the castle, but do not do so on your own. You will find those who reside here are not as easily restrained, and I'd hate to have to murder my council for turning you before I have the chance."

With that, Adrian was gone.

# TWELVE

**Once Adrian left, my legs gave out and I sank to the bed.**
*Turning me?*

We had talked a lot about bloodletting, but the only time he had mentioned turning was in the form of a threat.

*I think you want to kill me, and if that is the case, I should warn you now that any attempt will be met with my wrath.*

So far, he had not upheld his warning. Now, I wondered if he would truly turn me without my consent, or if he assumed I would beg for it, much like he'd assumed I'd beg him to partake of my blood.

Exhaustion settled heavily on my shoulders. Adrian had stolen my energy. Every encounter with him had me on edge, my whole body twisted and knotted, waiting for his next move—would we fight or fuck? Would I always feel so torn between him and my people? As I sat here upon this regal bed, so much more extravagant than the one in my small bedroom in Lara, I realized I had not thought much beyond my arrival at the Red Palace, aside from how I would defeat Adrian. And while I was still dedicated to that mission, I was beginning to think that I needed to consider how I would reign.

Perhaps the more I embraced my role, the more willing Adrian would be to open up about his past—a past I hoped unlocked the key to some kind of weakness.

A knock drew my attention and was followed by a voice.

"My queen, it is Ana Maria. Adrian sent me to attend to you."

I rose to my feet and opened the door, my gaze colliding with a pair of striking eyes, fringed by thick lashes. They were the color of a summer sky, her hair was thick and almost silvery, her lips plump and pink. Ana Maria was beautiful, and I was momentarily taken aback by it. She wore an emerald gown that reminded me of Lara, of the spring when the trees were blooming and the sun was bright, and suddenly, I was homesick.

I could only guess at what the woman was thinking, but as she stared at me, she seemed just as stunned by me, though I doubted it was because of my beauty. There was a flash in her eyes, something akin to disappointment, and the smile she'd prepared for me faltered. I wondered if she had expected someone different, and what sort of investment she had in what Adrian's wife looked like? Perhaps she had not expected someone of island descent.

To her credit, she quickly recovered. "My queen," she said again and bowed. "I heard you were injured."

"Yes, come in," I said, stepping aside to let her enter. I worried once the door was closed that things between us would become awkward. I was not familiar with this space or how to entertain, and the only chairs were near the fire—which I was not going to approach—but once Ana Maria was inside, she asked, "May I see your arm?"

I extended it toward her, and she peeled back the dressings Euric had wrapped. As the bandage came free, it felt like another layer of my skin was being removed, and I inhaled sharply.

Ana Maria frowned. The wound looked far more irritated than it had earlier.

"Adrian could not heal it," I said. "He said it was because of magic. Do you know why?"

She glanced at me and then said, "We do not even know why he is able to heal at all."

That surprised me. I'd thought all vampires could heal others, but it appeared only the Blood King had that gift. "If he cannot fix this, how will you?" I asked.

"I studied medicine."

"Oh," I said, feeling silly, and my face flushed.

She offered a small smile and crossed the room toward the hearth. "I hope you don't mind. I took the liberty of setting up before you arrived."

"No, of course not," I said. Then I hesitated. "How did you know I was injured?"

"Adrian sent Sorin ahead," she answered.

I hadn't even noticed. I realized I had no idea how quickly vampires could actually travel without the burden of mortals. The closest I'd come to witnessing their speed was when Daroc had killed the...*girl*. I flinched at the thought, recalling how swift his actions had been. How human she'd looked in death.

Ana Maria hung a cast iron teapot over the fire and

arranged her supplies. I admired how comfortable she was near it as I kept my distance, choosing to sit on the bed.

"How well do you know Adrian?"

She laughed—a sound that made my chest feel warm. "Well enough. He is my cousin."

"Your...*cousin*?" I asked, surprised, though now that I thought about it, they did look alike. I had not thought about Adrian having family. "Did he...turn you?"

"He did," Ana Maria answered but offered nothing else.

"Is it...rude to ask?"

"For some, it is," she explained. "It depends on the circumstances by which they were turned. The oldest among us did not have a choice. We were not...in control then."

I swallowed thickly, understanding.

"And...Adrian. Did he have a choice?"

Ana Maria did not answer as she took the teapot from the fire, setting it upon a cast iron trivet. Finally, she met my gaze. "I suppose it depends on who you ask," she said.

She placed a few herbs into a mesh bag, soaking it in the hot water before placing it upon my skin. It smelled like peppermint and wintergreen, and once the heat of the water wore off, it began to cool and soothe. While the medicine took effect, Ana Maria made a cup of tea with a few of the supplies in her bags. As she poured water over the mixture, a strong, minty smell wafted toward me.

I wrinkled my nose.

"It is willow bark," she said. "It will help with your pain."

I was skeptical but encouraged by how good my arm was feeling. After a few sips, I set it aside.

"I do not know why I am here," I said almost absently.

"You are here because Adrian wanted you," Ana Maria said.

"But why?" I asked, meeting her eyes. "He could have had anyone, *taken* anyone else."

He could have wed his vassal, and no one would have thought twice, because he did not need a union to conquer.

Ana Maria looked at me, and as she did, she slid her palms together. "You're wrong," she said, and her voice shook, but not from nerves. She seemed almost frustrated with me. "It could have only been you. There is no one else."

I stared, confused, both by her reaction and her words. Then she took a deep breath and swallowed, and I thought she was trying to hold back tears.

"I apologize, Your Majesty. I spoke out of turn," she said. "You should rest. Your lady-in-waiting will be along shortly to help you get ready for tonight's feast."

She curtsied and practically fled.

*How strange*, I thought as I fell heavily upon the covers of my bed. I did not realize I had closed my eyes until I was roused by a knock at the door.

"Your Majesty? It is Violeta. I have come to help you get ready for tonight."

I rose from the surprising warmth of the bed, still groggy, and made my way to the door where I found a young woman waiting. She was short and thin, her limbs pale white and her hair a dull brown. She had delicate features—round eyes, a small nose, and thin lips. The only color in her face was her cheeks, which were rosy. I did not know if it was a natural tint, the cold, or perhaps she was nervous to meet me.

"You're human," I said, surprised.

Her blush deepened, and she bowed her head, turning the movement into a curtsy.

"Yes," she said. "King Adrian has appointed me as your lady-in-waiting. He also advised you would want a bath."

My eyes shifted to see a set of servants behind her holding a large copper tub.

"Yes, thank you," I said, stepping aside.

Violeta hesitated, probably at my expression of gratitude, but she entered the room, instructing the servants to place the tub before the fire.

"Not there," I said.

Violeta and the servants halted, staring at me in surprise.

"Can you place it near the window," I said, and because I felt like I needed to offer an explanation for why, I added, "I'd like to look at the view while I bathe."

I did not even know what was outside these leaded windows, but anything was better than being near fire.

Violeta did not hesitate. "Of course, my queen," she said.

After a few trips back and forth by the servants, the tub was full of steaming water.

I shed my clothes and entered the bath, groaning with relief as I relaxed against the edge and closed my eyes. After a moment, a sensual and rich scent filled the air. I looked at Violeta, who froze, arm suspended over the water as she dropped something into my water.

"What is that?" I asked.

"J-jasmine," she answered. "Lady Ana Maria said it would relax you. I'm sorry. I should have asked—"

"No, it's…fine."

I had only asked because the smell was familiar, and yet I could not pinpoint why. I watched as Violeta finished adding the drops and then reached for a cloth.

"If you'd like, I can scrub your back and your hair."

I let her, and when I was finished, I stood from the bath, happy to feel clean. I toweled off, and Violeta helped me into a silk robe. I expected her to ask me to sit by the fire while she brushed my hair to help it dry, but instead, she waited by the vanity—an ornate piece of gold furniture with an oval mirror.

Violeta did not seem overly concerned that my hair would be wet for the feast. She brushed it, leaving it slick to my head, and when she was finished, she asked, "What would you like to wear tonight?"

She walked across the room to a wardrobe and threw open the doors to reveal a set of gorgeous dresses. I rose slowly and approached, reaching to touch one of the plush skirts.

"Who did these belong to?" I asked.

"King Adrian had them commissioned ahead of your arrival," she explained.

That felt strange. Still, I could not deny that I was pleased.

"They're all so beautiful," I said.

"Shall I choose for you?" Violeta offered. I looked at her, and she hesitated. "If, that is, you are having a hard time choosing."

I smiled at her. "Of course."

She grinned and then reached for a red gown, clearly having already decided what I should wear. There were so many layers to the skirt, it took some time to get it over my head, and the laces at the back of the bodice had me regretting letting her pick, until I turned to face the mirror.

The gown was beautiful, and it accentuated every lush curve of my body—from the neckline that cut low between my breasts to the skirt that flared at my hips and dusted the floor. The long sleeves, though lace, still allowed me to holster my knives, which was a comfort to me. Despite not having any trouble with Adrian's army on the way to Revekka, I did not trust the castle at large—and neither did Adrian, or he wouldn't have warned me not to leave my room alone.

"Your jewelry, Your Majesty," Violeta said. She approached with a wooden box lined with red velvet. Inside was a pair of dangling gold and ruby earrings and a matching necklace. They were far more extravagant than anything I'd ever owned, even being princess of Lara. I tried to ignore the fact that once they were on, they reminded me of blood. Still, staring at myself in the mirror, I hardly recognize the woman I'd been a week ago.

A knock at the door announced Ana Maria's return. She had changed and was now wearing a black gown with a halter neckline that made her hair look like a glowing halo. Her skirt was full, crafted from layers of tulle, and it swept the floor as she moved.

"Oh, my queen, you look beautiful."

"Thank you, Ana Maria," I said.

"Just Ana," she said and held out a small box. "I brought you something. A gift from Adrian."

My brows lowered as I took it. "Can he not give it to me himself?"

"I think, perhaps, he wants to be surprised when he looks upon you tonight."

It was ironic considering how he had visited me on our wedding day. Still, that was better than my reasoning. I had thought he was avoiding me after our earlier conversation. Except that since I'd met the Blood King, he'd rarely avoided confronting me about anything.

Inside the box was a tiara. It was stunning and, while simple in appearance, heavily embellished with diamonds on each fringe.

"Do you like it?" Ana asked.

"Of course," I said, and as I placed it upon my head, I felt that it belonged there.

"Adrian will not look away," said Ana.

"I suppose that depends on whether or not his favorite vassal is there," I said. I imagined Safira would be present despite the fact that I'd asked Adrian not to drink from her.

Ana gave me an odd look.

"You do not know Adrian very well," she said.

"You are right. I don't."

Ana frowned, and for the first time since I met her, I considered that perhaps she had expected me to be happy about this marriage.

"Are you ready?" she asked. "I shall escort you to the great hall."

I supposed I was as ready as I would ever be, though I hated how my stomach roiled. I did not want to fear my enemy, and yet, I could not help feeling apprehensive. This was different from my wedding, different even from the small army I'd traveled to Revekka with. I was about to be surrounded by Adrian's entire kingdom.

I was a sparrow in a den of wolves.

We left my new suite. Violeta stayed behind with instructions not to tend to the fire. I hoped by the time I returned to my room tonight, it would be nothing more than burning embers like Adrian had promised.

Unlike Castle Fiora, the hallways of the Red Palace were warmer and wider, which meant that Ana and I could walk side by side comfortably. Now that I felt better, I could appreciate the decor of the castle—black sconces dripping with crystals, tipped with tapered candles, large landscapes framed in thick, gold frames, and lavish, woven carpets. I wondered how much of it Adrian had changed since he had killed Dragos.

And how much of it he had scavenged from conquered villages.

As we ascended the stairs, I could see the entrance to the ballroom—gilded doors opened wide, inviting.

"What is expected of me tonight?" I asked Ana.

"You and Adrian will dance," she said. "And after, you will stay close to him."

"Perfect," I said and took a breath which I held the closer we drew to the hall. *I shall do the opposite.*

The room was crowded, full of laughter and revelry. Humans feasted on food from a table while vampires pulled those same humans aside to drink from their veins. There was dancing and drinking and music, and above it all, elevated upon a precipice, was Adrian, who lounged upon his throne, looking exceptionally bored until his eyes found me and held, touching every part of me. He straightened, and the movement drew attention—first to him and then to me. Suddenly, the chaotic celebration ended, and as gazes turned to me, the crowd parted and then bowed, creating a path for me straight to Adrian.

But my eyes had shifted to Safira, who lingered near his throne, dressed in powder blue and silver. I had never seen them like this side by side, and it occurred to me how right they looked together. Her expression was tense, her eyes and mouth pinched, and I wondered if Adrian had spoken with her about no longer feeding from her. Still, why did she linger? Why was she in a place that elevated her above the rest? Not even Tanaka, the viceroy, lingered upon the dais with the king.

I did not follow the path made for me. Instead, I turned away, sweeping the crowd, my eyes narrowing upon a waiflike human.

"You," I said, turning toward him.

His eyes widened. "M-me?"

"Come," I said.

He hesitated.

"Do not make me ask again," I said.

His throat bopped, but he obeyed and approached.

The silence in the room pressed against my ears, and I felt Adrian's gaze growing fiercer as the human approached me.

"Your Majesty," he said, bowing.

"Dance with me," I said.

"Your Majesty, I really must de—"

"It was not a question," I said.

I did not think it was possible for him to grow any paler, but he did. I lifted my hand for him to take.

"You may touch me," I said and happened to glance

at Adrian, who looked murderous. I refrained from smiling, but it was more than a pleasure to stroke his fury.

The man's hand was cold and clammy as he took my own.

"What's your name?" I asked.

"Lothian," he said.

"Lothian," I repeated his name. "Do not tremble. It is embarrassing."

"Apologies, my queen. It's just that I had not planned on losing my balls tonight."

I laughed. "Your balls have my protection, Lothian. Now, at least act like you enjoy my presence."

The music began—a painfully boring song that made my dance with Lothian tedious. It was punishment, I was certain, for disobeying rules, so instead, I tried to focus on the mortal at arm's length.

"What do you do, Lothian?" I asked, determined to enjoy my time enraging Adrian.

"Your Majesty?" he asked, confused.

"Your trade. What is your job here?"

"I am a librarian," he said.

"A librarian." I smiled. I thought he would say he was a vassal. "Will you take me on a tour?"

"Of course," he said, suddenly sounding much more confident. "Any particular area of interest?"

"Oh, all of it. I am a *voracious* reader."

"I will do my very best to please you," he said, grinning, and I decided that I very much liked excitable Lothian.

"Very good. Let's start this week," I said, unsure of what Adrian might have planned for me. "I am eager to learn the history of my new home."

As our song came to an end, Lothian bowed.

"Of course, Your Majesty," he said. "You will not be disappointed!"

He spun and practically floated off the dance floor. Now that my dance was complete, I hoped to go in search of wine, or something to further aid in my enjoyment of the evening, but when I turned, my way was blocked by a large man. He had long, dark hair and a pointed beard. There was something about him that made me feel uneasy, and that only worsened when he smiled.

"Your Majesty," he said as he bowed, extending his hand. "A dance?"

"I would rather have a drink," I said and walked past him. If Nadia were here, she would lecture me.

*A lady never declines a gentleman!*

*What is the point in being a princess if I cannot shun men?*

*The point is to set an example!*

I had set an example, just not the one she wanted.

A hand landed on my shoulder. It startled me, and I jumped, turning to find that the dark-haired vampire had followed me.

"Do not touch me," I said. Each word I uttered sounded like a threat.

The vampire chuckled. "Adrian has found himself a lively mortal," he said, his eyes trailing my body. Again he said, "Dance with me."

My eyes narrowed upon the man. His were glazed and distant, and I wondered what he had been consuming before arriving at this event.

"So you are one of those," I said.

"One of what?" he asked.

"A man who does not listen," I said.

His slick smile spread, and he took a step closer to me. "Perhaps I should introduce myself. I am Noblesse Zakharov."

"Well, Noblesse Zakharov, I don't care who you are. I will not dance with you."

I did not linger to hear his reaction, turning to leave, but Zakharov once again reached for me, his fingers digging into my arm as he jerked me around. This time, I drew my knife holstered at my wrist. I twisted the hilt in my hand and brought it down into the hollow of the man's collarbone.

The only sound he made was a choked gurgle as he fell to his knees, blood oozing from his wound. Vampires might be able to heal themselves, but they still felt pain, and it was possible this was worse, given that I did not think Zakharov thought I would fight back. The room went quiet, and none moved as I stood opposite the vampire who had accosted me.

The tap of boots upon the marble floor interrupted the silence, and slowly, a path was made for Adrian. He seemed to tower over everyone, a force that commanded attention. He certainly had mine as he approached, his features a cool mask of indifference.

"He touched me," I explained.

Adrian's eyes left mine, falling to Zakharov, whose hand was around the hilt of my dagger, blood seeping from between his fingers. But just as he was able to pull it out, his eyes lifted toward Adrian.

"M–my lord," he managed.

Adrian said nothing as he plucked the knife from his flesh, wiped it free of blood with a handkerchief he pulled from the inside of his jacket, and returned it to me.

"Thank you," I whispered, and he offered the softest smile before drawing a blade sheathed at his guard's side and swung. No one spoke as Zakharov's head rolled across the ballroom floor, his body left to fall against the marble with a wet thud.

Adrian returned the bloodied blade to his guard and then looked at me, offering his hand. Once I took it, he spoke, addressing the gathering.

"Your queen is a warrior first, a noble second. I suggest you keep that in mind if you decide to place your fate in her hands." Then he looked at me. "And if, by chance, she spares you, I will not."

I held his gaze and felt the promise of his words shudder through me.

"Clean this up," he said and led me away from the body. Pausing at the center of the room, he brushed a strand of hair from my face. "Are you all right?"

"I am," I said. "What is a noblesse?"

"It is a title that means royal birth," he said. "Zakharov has always been a problem. Now he is not."

I looked to where he had lain, his body already cleared. Another vampire carried the head by its long, black hair toward the exit.

"Dance with me," Adrian said.

I bowed my head, accepting his invitation. He smiled and lifted my hand to his mouth. His lips touched my knuckles, a soft caress that reminded me of the kisses he'd offered on our ride through Cel Ceredi to the Red Palace. Then he drew me close and began to move, his body a solid guide I followed effortlessly around the room.

"You are beautiful," he said, his eyes lowered, lingering on my breasts.

"I thought you would disapprove," I said, but I'd only thought that because Killian would have chided me for the amount of skin I was showing.

Adrian, though, seemed to like it.

"My feelings are far from disapproving," he said, and as if to drive the point home, he drew me closer, the hard swell of his cock pressing into my stomach.

I held his gaze, a fire igniting in the pit of my stomach.

"You are not angry with me?"

"Why would I be angry?"

"Because I danced with Lothian," I said. "When I was supposed to dance with you."

"Hmm," he said, understanding. "You are lucky I like him."

"I promised to protect his balls," I said.

"Suddenly, I like him less," Adrian said.

"*I* am angry with you," I said.

Adrian raised a brow. "As if I could not guess by your actions. Safira?"

"You said you would cease feeding from her."

"I have," he said.

There was a pause as we continued to dance, slow and controlled, the skirt of my dress swaying and tangling around my legs and Adrian's.

"I had only told her a few moments before I entered the great hall. Poor timing, perhaps, but it is done. As you wished."

I bristled. "Do not guilt me."

"It is not my intention," he said. "I would do anything

you asked if it meant you might see me as more than a monster."

I could not quite isolate how his words made me feel, but it was something akin to shock.

"So you danced with Lothian because of Safira?" he asked.

I shrugged. "I don't like being told what to do."

A cruel smile spread across his face. "I think you wanted to drive me mad."

"Did it work?"

"It made me want to fuck you," he said. "Right here in front of my kingdom."

"How primal of you," I said, though his words opened a chasm in the bottom of my stomach that burned hotter than any flame.

He did not deny it. "Primal, possessive," he said. "It is in my nature."

It was in my nature too. I could feel it every time I thought of Adrian's vassal.

At least we could be honest with each other.

"You would do well to remember it," he said.

"Or what?" I challenged.

Adrian kissed me.

There was nothing gentle about it. He grasped my head in both hands as he bent over me, parting my lips. I clung to him, meeting the thrusts of his tongue with my own, feeling both desperate and reckless. Our bodies were so close, our fingers digging into each other's skin. I wanted him, to be stretched by him, filled with him, possessed by him, and I hoped he could hear *every single thought*.

Adrian growled and released my mouth, gleaming

eyes meeting mine. But before he could fulfill my wish, my eyes slipped from him over his shoulder, to the doors where a man—a vampire—entered, flanked by two others. In his hand, he gripped the head of Zakharov.

Adrian turned to face the newcomers.

"I will have vengeance, King Adrian, for the death of my son."

I tried not to react to the presence of the newcomer, but my heart was racing, and I gripped Adrian's arm a little tighter. He held me close, a hand on my waist, lips still gleaming from our kiss. As I looked up at him, he seemed unconcerned.

"Your son accosted my wife, your queen, Noblesse Gesalac," he said. "And for that, he was punished. It is your choice to kill him now. Burn him or not, it is for you to decide."

"That is no choice at all," Gesalac snapped.

It wasn't. If vampire bodies were not burned after decapitation, they would reanimate, not as they were before but as revenants—essentially vampires with no humanity. They attacked humans and animals alike, thirsting endlessly for blood. We had learned this at a young age during training, but it had never occurred to me that vampires also practiced this, mostly because I had never imagined they had any sort of justice system.

"Then you have your answer," Adrian said.

Gesalac threw his son's head at our feet. It rolled, landing with his half-opened eyes facing me.

"You risk my allegiance for a woman—a mortal one at that?"

"Careful of your words, Noblesse," Adrian said. "No one is irreplaceable."

"That also goes for you, my king," Gesalac replied.

There was a moment of tense silence when I wasn't sure Gesalac would leave, but he bowed his head and left with his men.

The celebration resumed, and I got the feeling that this wasn't an unusual occurrence. I lifted my dress to keep the hem out of the blood draining from Zakharov's head and used my foot to roll it away, unnerved by how his eyes watched me.

Adrian stared at me, and I knew that look well enough. He was asking if I was okay, and I shrugged.

"It wouldn't be a ball if I didn't make enemies."

Shortly after Gesalac's departure, a vampire retrieved his son's head and announced that his body was being burned in the courtyard if anyone wanted to watch. As the ballroom emptied, Daroc appeared, his expression a harsh mask. He approached us and bowed.

"Your Majesties," he said. "I have heard from Gavriel."

My heart raced.

"Has there been another attack?" I quickly asked, fear draining the blood from my face.

"Of sorts," he said. "A group of your people attempted a coup. They stormed the castle but got no farther than the courtyard. Your father is safe, and no lives were lost."

"A coup? Why, because my father surrendered to Adrian?"

"That," he said, "and they believe the attack at Vaida was us."

I was not so much surprised as disappointed, but I could not say that I blamed my people for their assumption. They had not seen the bodies; all they knew was that now a whole village had been wiped out and their remains burned—a practice against our customs. It looked like a cover-up.

I looked to Adrian as he asked, "What would you have me do? I could send guards for your father."

"I think that will only make the situation worse," I said.

"Perhaps, but if it means your father is safe, does it matter?"

It didn't.

"Gavriel and his men are as good as ten of my father's men," I said, and it was becoming harder to trust those closest to him at all. At least I knew Adrian's soldiers were beholden to me through our marriage. I cringed at the direction of my thoughts but had more than enough reason to think them.

Adrian grasped my chin, brushing his thumb across my lips. It wasn't until then that I realized I'd been worrying it with my teeth.

"Just ask it of me," he said.

Finally, I relented. "Send your best men," I said. "And send more before he travels here for the coronation."

"It will be done."

And I believed him.

I had to.

Because I wasn't certain I would survive if something happened to my father.

———

Violeta was waiting to help me undress.

She had taken the liberty of preparing another bath. I thanked her and dismissed her, wanting to be alone. She left a table nearby with soap, washcloths, and the jasmine oil. I added a few drops, hoping the smell would ease the ache that had formed at the forefront of my head where words and thoughts and emotions were building. I felt like I was on the precipice of breaking but not quite there. Something heavy had nestled within my chest, and a pressure had built behind my eyes that threatened tears, and yet I did not weep.

I lowered myself into the tub, rested my head against the edge, and closed my eyes.

A cool breeze roused me, and I found myself in a dark lake, but all around me were willows and trees with white flowers that smelled like the jasmine oil that was in my bathwater. The moonlight bathed my naked skin in silver, and the water was cool. Though I was no longer in my room, this place was familiar.

It wasn't long until I felt the presence of another behind me, and I turned to find Adrian standing on the shore. He watched me, staring with a familiar hunger in his eyes. I sensed that something was different about him, though I did not know exactly what. It tugged at the edge of my mind, a memory too far to grasp.

"You looked beautiful tonight," he said.

"Looked?" I asked, raising a brow.

He smiled, and it was so beautiful, it stole my breath. I had never seen him smile like this, and I wanted to see it more. Still, the longer I looked, the more troubled I became. There was something different about his expression—something far more lighthearted. He did not have the sharpness to his face I had come to know well or the depth to his strange eyes.

He entered the water, fully clothed, and placed his hand upon my cheek.

"Yes," he said, and his hand slid to my neck. "Right now, you are radiant."

His lips crashed against mine, and I sighed into his mouth. My arms slid around his waist, and I sank against him, comforted by his presence.

"I've missed you," I found myself saying as his mouth left mine to kiss along my neck. "You were gone so long."

I did not understand the words pouring from my mouth or their context, but I spoke them and I felt them so harshly, it hurt.

"I'm sorry," he said. "Never again."

But I knew that was a lie. Still, I hoped.

I drew away, my naked flesh pressed against his clothed body. I could not wait to feel him against me, skin to skin. To have him inside me, and yet I could not shake this strange fear that someone might catch us here together. It gripped my heart and threaded along my spine.

"Promise," I said—begged.

Adrian's brows knitted together, his hands sliding to my face once more. "Did something happen in my absence?"

Tears pricked my eyes at his question, and to hide them, I kissed him. "No," I whispered against his mouth and my hands drifted down to pull his sex free from his trousers. As he lifted me into his arms, I spoke. "Just promise me…"

But before I could even finish my sentence, he answered.

"I promise," he said as his flesh parted mine and he slid inside me.

I gasped and opened my eyes as I was lifted from the

water. Adrian's face hovered over mine. For a moment, I thought I was still in the lake, but the firelight reflected off his face, harsher in this light than it had been beneath the moon.

I had been dreaming.

"You will catch your death," he said, the notes of his voice rumbling in my chest.

"I was just tired," I whispered.

I couldn't stop looking at him and thinking about how different he was in my dream. That Adrian had looked so young, so carefree, so in love. The Adrian who held me now carried his age within his eyes, which were burdened by heartbreak, and I wondered if that was what had made this man a monster.

"You are soaked," I said.

"Is that your way of asking me to disrobe?"

"It would be warmer," I replied, and he settled me upon the bed before straightening. My body grew heated under his gaze, my nipples taut. I felt very aware of my own emptiness, of the wetness gathering between my thighs.

Adrian discarded his clothing. His movements were graceful, and as each part of his body became exposed to the light, my hunger grew.

I swallowed thickly. "Thank you for protecting my father," I said.

"I made a promise," he said simply.

"Have you always kept your promises?" I asked. I was curious about his response, given my dream.

The last piece of his clothing fell to the ground, and he stood naked beside the bed, meeting my gaze as he answered.

"No."

His hands sank into the mattress on either side of my face as he straddled my body, leaning to press a soft kiss to my lips. There was an ease and comfortability to his movements, as if we had been lovers for a lifetime.

He drew back and spoke, low and rough. "But for you, I will do anything."

It was the second time he had spoken like this tonight.

My brows drew together as I studied him. The crown of his cock touched my stomach, and the feel of him cradled between our bodies made me feel hollow inside. I was restless, and as much as I wanted to draw him inside me then, I resisted. "But I am your enemy."

His white-blue eyes were shadowed as he searched my face, fingers brushing a few strands of hair from my cheek.

"You were never my enemy," he replied and pressed his lips to mine. My breath caught in my throat, and I sighed into his mouth as I opened for him, my legs rising to frame his body. My fingers dug into his back so that his hard chest was pressed into mine, and when his tongue slipped past my lips, tangling with my own, I arched into him. There was a spice to the sweetness of his mouth that told me he had drunk wine tonight. I usually did not enjoy the taste, but this I wanted to siphon. His strokes were slow, savoring, even as he left to kiss my jaw, my neck, and between my breasts. He settled back on his heels and pressed a kiss to the inside of my knee, another higher up, another against my hip, and I let my breath out in a rush, my fingers twining into the sheets. It was sheer anticipation, and he let it build as he riddled my skin with kisses.

I twisted beneath him, desperate to feel the release that would come with his mouth on my swollen clit and his fingers deep inside me. Instead, his hands came down upon my legs, pressing my knees into the bed. The open air teased my heat, and I felt manic and frustrated as he lingered there, so close to my center.

Then his eyes fell to the nest of curls at the apex of my thighs.

"So fucking beautiful," he said, and he dipped his head to lick my clit. My head rolled back as he caressed it again before dipping into my slick heat.

"Yes," I breathed, and Adrian chuckled, increasing the pressure of his tongue. When he added his fingers, I vaulted off the bed, my shoulders pressed into the mattress, my hips surging forward into his thrusting fingers. Adrian moaned at my reaction, and his mouth closed over my sensitive nerves, sucking and teasing until the sounds coming out of my mouth were no longer within my control. I had given myself over to him, a weapon to be wielded. He kept pressure on me, kept driving inside, building me up and up and up, and I climbed with him, my insides humming and twining, my muscles clenching and knotting, and when the release hit, I screamed with the rush of it. It was like he had fed off my essence, but somehow, I was better for it. Brighter.

I was still catching my breath as he climbed back up my body and kissed me hard on the mouth. And though I felt completely weightless, I bent toward him, bound to his direction. He shifted behind me, his chest to my back. His hand drifted behind my knee, and as he opened me, he slid inside. One of his arms cradled my head, the other gripped my leg, and as he began to move in slow, sensuous strokes, I held his gaze. I couldn't look away. I studied every part of his face—the way his hair clung to the perspiration on his cheek, the way the blue of his irises seemed to consume more of the white while he was inside me, the way his teeth clenched with each deepening thrust.

Then Adrian kissed me again.

A bruising kiss that kept going as he moved, and I was left feeling the effects of something I did not understand. A heavy wave of emotion built inside me, burning my eyes, and I realized that we had crossed a line into something that felt too close to lovemaking. I had been too caught up in this moment, in the feelings Adrian drew to the surface of my skin, to stop it.

We couldn't have this. We were enemies. We were supposed to be angry, our intimacy a fight, a battle won, or a body conquered. This...this was tenderness. This was sweet and lush and...intense.

I froze at the thought, and Adrian did too. One of his hands cupped my jaw, the other splayed across my stomach.

"Isolde?"

I never thought I would beg to be called Sparrow, but to have him speak my name, thick with lust and an undercurrent of affection...it frightened me.

I couldn't do this. I was already a traitor to my people. I would be nothing...*nothing* if I let this progress.

"Stop," I said and pushed away from him.

All at once, he let me go, and I climbed out of bed, needing to put distance between us. I crossed the room and slipped into a robe Violeta had left.

"Did I do something wrong?" Adrian asked.

"You should leave," I said. I kept my back to him. I couldn't look at him, or he would see the tears gathering in my eyes—tears that were attached to emotions I couldn't explain.

There was a long pause, and then the bed creaked as he stood and dressed.

"At least tell me," he said before he departed. "Tell me I didn't hurt you."

I shouldn't have looked at him then, but it was the desperation in his voice that caught me off guard, and no matter how chaotic I was feeling right now, I couldn't let him think he had harmed me.

Even as I met his gaze, a thickness gathered in my throat, and I could not clear it before I spoke.

"No."

After I answered, he looked away. I thought that perhaps it was shame that turned his head.

He bowed.

"Good night, Queen Isolde."

With those words, I had gotten what I wanted—a wedge driven between us—and as he closed the door to my room, I crashed to the floor.

# THIRTEEN

*I rose early the next morning and dressed. My options* were limited to the gowns provided by Adrian, all of which were tight and heavily embellished. I would have to speak to him about providing me with something I could train in regularly, though at the moment, the thought of facing him at all sent me into a spiral of confusing emotions. Perhaps I could convince Ana to communicate my need for something that included a place for my blade, even as I worked it into the bodice of my gown. I left my cuffs on the table by my bed. This dress, a high-necked, sleeveless gown with a minimal flare, would not serve to hide the weapons.

Violeta and Ana had arrived. Violeta carried a tray with bread, butter, jam, and tea. Ana followed behind, dressed in a structured silver dress that moved like liquid as she walked.

"We thought you would prefer breakfast in your room," Ana said.

"Is there no formal breakfast?"

In Lara, my father dined with the court every morning and evening; the only meal he took on his own or with me alone was lunch. It was almost ritualistic—he rose, dressed, and dined. After, we would take a walk in the garden.

"Among vassals, yes," Ana explained. "But they are rarely joined by Adrian or the noblesse."

She did not need to tell me why. I could guess the reasons for their sporadic visits.

"I would like to walk this morning," I said. "Is there a garden here?"

"Yes, a beautiful one," she said. "Adrian tells me you love midnight roses."

I opened my mouth to respond but hesitated, wondering when they had spoken about me.

"I do. They remind me of my mother."

Ana only nodded, and I got the sense that Adrian had told her about that too.

"Then we shall begin with the gardens."

The gardens of the Red Palace were very different from what I had formulated in my mind. I'd imagined something slightly more grand than what my mother had created and my father had maintained at Castle Fiora. What I walked into was far more magnificent. In addition to lush flowers, trees, and plants, there were statues, fountains, and decorative stones that created a maze of distinct gardens, each with their own theme and flair. I was enchanted, to say the least.

"This is beautiful," I said as I walked ahead of Ana, down a bank of white marble steps that led into a formal garden, encased by a frame of box hedges. The center design, crafted from aromatic florals, reminded me of the stained glass windows in the palace. "Did this survive from King Dragos's reign?"

"It was very small," Ana said, keeping a few paces behind me. "It was Adrian who insisted on something far more extensive."

That both surprised and intrigued me. "Why?"

"He felt it was important," she answered. Just like when Sorin answered questions about Adrian, I felt she was being evasive, which was even stranger given we were discussing the design of a garden.

I looked up at the red sky and wondered how things survived here since the sun could not shine directly on anything, but clearly the flowers had no trouble thriving. There were several varieties—datura and foxgloves, oleander and lily of the valley, irises and larkspur. I wandered farther, losing sight of Ana as I slipped between openings in the stone walls. Each garden had a different centerpiece: some a pool, others a fountain, this one a gazebo with a delicate, filigree roof. I took the steps one at a time and stood for a few minutes at its center, enjoying the quiet of the garden.

"Queen Isolde."

I turned and found a woman standing outside the gazebo; her arm was looped through that of a younger companion. One was dressed in lilac, the other in gray. I did not recognize them or know their names, but they were vampires, not human, and I wondered how they had come into existence, what use had Adrian found in them.

"Yes?" I inquired, and they both bowed.

"We wanted to welcome you to Revekka," the woman in gray responded.

"Thank you," I said and looked away. If I were in Lara, it would have communicated my dismissal of their presence. Here, it only seemed to encourage them.

"The whole kingdom is intrigued by you," she continued. "The mortal who managed to snare our king."

*What a coincidence. I never suspected I would be snared by anyone either*, I thought, still not looking at them.

"We, of course, thought that if he married at all, it would be one of the women at court," she added. "But it seems he merely enjoyed sampling."

"Have you *merely* come to boast about how you fucked my husband before me?" I asked, finally looking at the woman. Her eyes widened slightly and then narrowed, mouth hardening into a tight line. She did not need to tell me she had—her jealousy had to have sprung from somewhere.

"He is not a man you can satisfy on your own," she said. "He needs more. You would do well to remember that."

"Are you suggesting you can somehow make up for what I lack?" I asked.

The woman in gray straightened, lifting her head. "Everyone knows you have not let him feed from you," she said. "He has to receive blood from somewhere, and now that you have forced him to dismiss Safira, well, one of us must take her place."

I should have anticipated that Safira would not make a secret of her dismissal, least of all that I had commanded it. Still, that did not surprise me so much as this woman suggesting she could satisfy my husband in other ways.

"Adrian doesn't fuck those he feeds from," I said.

Both women laughed.

"Is that what he told you?" the woman in gray asked between laughs. "Oh, and you believed him!"

"He must care for her at least a little," said the woman in lilac. "Or he wouldn't spare her the details."

They continued to laugh, but as I turned toward them fully, they quieted.

"Are you suggesting my husband, the king of Revekka, is a liar?" I asked, and their amusement died. I took a step toward them. "Because if you are, I think he should know what you think of him."

The two exchanged a look. "We only meant to inform—"

"You meant to mock me," I said. "But I will not play this game. You will either respect me or be eliminated from this court. Do you understand?"

"There you are!" Ana said, joining me beneath the filigree awning. Her eyes shifted to the women, who were now retreating across the lawn. "Are you all right?"

"Who were those two?" I asked.

"One is Lady Bella, the other is Lady Mila. They are cousins. Lady Bella is the daughter of Noblesse Anatoly." She paused. "Did they say something to you?"

"More than something," I replied and then met her gaze. "What more do you have to show me?"

I did not wander far from Ana as we continued through the gardens. I did not think it was possible for them to get any more beautiful, but they did. Each layout was different, each path offering a different route through gardens of roses, hemlock, and amaryllis, past great pieces of art—glass prisms that shown like rubies beneath the sky and statues carved of volcanic glass depicting the lesser goddesses.

"Does Adrian...worship the old gods?" I asked.

"He worships no gods," said Ana. "That does not mean he doesn't believe in them."

"Why would he offer them a place in his royal gardens then?"

"You can respect someone and not worship them," Ana said. "Rae and Yara and Kismet, they are peaceful goddesses."

Her statement suggested that Asha and Dis were the opposite, and I was curious about her thoughts, but just then, we stepped through a set of high hedges that backed up against an encroaching line of trees, distracting me from my question.

"This is the grotto," Ana said.

I was momentarily taken aback by this place because I had been here before—just last night—and while it looked different in what light the red sky offered, there was no mistaking that smell or the presence of jasmine trees all around.

The pool, which had appeared dark in my dreams, was full of clear, crisp water from which steam rose as the heat met the cold morning air. Part of the pool was tucked beneath the castle, creating the grotto. Under the canopy, the walls appeared to be painted into a soothing swirl of calming colors.

I wandered closer to the edge of the pool and then turned in a slow circle, recalling my strange dream. How I'd felt when Adrian had approached, how desperate I was for him to never leave my side again, and yet how afraid I was we would be caught, and despite all that, I still took him into my body. My thoughts were a chaotic storm—a mixture of the Isolde who had loved Adrian in the dream and the one who wondered how I'd imagined a place I'd never been. Was this some kind of magic? Perhaps something residual that had followed me from Sadovea?

"Isolde?" Ana asked, a note of concern coloring her voice.

My gaze snapped to hers.

"Are you all right?" she asked. It wasn't lost on me, the number of times I'd been asked that since leaving Lara.

"I—"

Before I could speak, a bell began to toll, and I looked to Ana for an explanation.

"It is noon," she said. "The castle gates are opening for court. I must get you to Adrian."

"Court?"

"Adrian has been gone for so long. While he is here, his subjects will petition him to end feuds, send aid, or even turn them."

"Turn them? Into vampires?" I'd been told this but still couldn't seem to believe someone would ask for it.

"Immortality is desired by many, Isolde," Ana said. "The question is who will present as useful to Adrian and, now, to you."

To me? Was I expected to grant immortality too?

Our return to the castle was through an alternate entrance. The corridors were narrower and colder, but Ana promised it was the best way to travel the castle without interruption.

"There are maps," she explained. "You can get just about anywhere except the library."

I frowned. "Why?"

"Because it was added during Adrian's reign, and the passages were from Dragos."

We exited the corridor into a closet, which led into a hallway, and from there, Ana escorted me to a room just off the great hall.

"You only need to knock," she said. "He knows to expect you."

I waited until she was gone and did so, finding Daroc on the other side.

"My queen," he said and bowed as I entered. I wondered if he hated bowing to me, if he hated me. At least, unlike others in the castle, he did not show it.

"Commander." I nodded as I swept past him, halting as soon as I was inside the room.

"I take my leave," Daroc said and left me alone with Adrian.

He stood opposite, dressed in black, holding a small book. His surcoat was far more embellished, with a design embroidered all over in gold thread. Over the top, he wore a black fur vest and over that a collar of gold. He had pulled half his hair back, so that some fell in soft waves around his face. A black crown of spikes made him appear far more imposing.

I had dreaded this moment, facing him after asking him to leave last night. My chest felt heavy, full of a static that increased the longer I held his gaze, which took effort, because I did not want him to see how I felt. Even I did not know.

"Isolde," he said.

"Adrian."

We stared at each other, and before he could broach the subject of last night, I spoke.

"What do you expect of me?" I asked.

Adrian's brows drew together. "What do you mean?"

"During court. Am I merely an ornament to adorn the seat beside your throne? Because if that is the case, then I decline your invitation."

Adrian set aside the book he had been reading and faced me fully.

"You make many presumptions, wife. Your presence by my side is not up for discussion, nor is it for show. You are my queen. I expect we will rule together, which means your participation during court."

I blinked at him. "Does ruling together mean you will listen to me when I beg you not to continue invading the Nine Houses?"

Adrian said nothing.

"I thought not."

"Isolde," he said my name again, quiet and almost desperate. I didn't like it. *My sweet* or *Sparrow* were far less personal than my actual name.

"Do not pretend to give me an equal say in the ruling of your land if it only extends to court politics."

I whirled on my heels, intending to leave, but as soon as I touched the handle, Adrian's hand covered mine. I turned my head slightly, only to find his lips hovered near. He stood close, but his body did not touch mine, and in that space, something like a current began to run between us. It took everything in my power not to lean into it.

"You are infuriating," he said.

"You are the one who married me on a whim."

"It wasn't a whim. It was very much intentional."

"You forgot to inform me," I said.

Part of me knew how he would answer. There was something undeniable between us, something completely electric that even hate could not dissolve. It kept me rooted to the spot now, when I would usually fight to be free.

I turned toward him, though he still caged me against the door.

"Give me time," he said. "Soon you will beg me to conquer the land you wish to save."

"Now who is making presumptions?"

"I am offering truth," he said.

I glared at him, and there was a knock. It came from the opposite side of the room, where a door led into the great hall.

Adrian did not immediately answer, just stared at me a moment longer, somehow looking both fierce and mournful. He wanted to talk about last night, but I was more eager to talk about vampires like Lady Bella and Lady Mila. More importantly, who would he choose as his next vassal?

Another knock, and I pushed against his chest.

"We are being summoned," I said.

He grabbed my wrist and pressed my fingers to his lips.

"I meant it, Isolde. I would have you make your own judgments today."

I believed him.

He held on to my hand and fitted it into the crook of his elbow as we entered the great hall. There were people gathered, many with variations of Adrian's gold collar. Noblesse, I guessed when I spotted Gesalac in the crowd fitted with silver and emerald. His gaze was dark and made me feel dread. Still, I thought it said something about his loyalty to Adrian—and this court— that he presented despite his son's death.

Though perhaps it said more about how feared Adrian truly was.

"Who is Noblesse Anatoly?" I asked.

Adrian looked down at me and then nodded toward the far wall.

"He is the dour-looking one," he said.

He did not need to give me any more of a description than that. Noblesse Anatoly stood aside, dressed in black and silver, an almost sleepy expression on his face due to large, round, half-lidded eyes.

"You will have to tell me later of your relationship with his daughter, Lady Bella," I said.

Adrian raised a brow. "I will tell you now. There is no relationship."

"Really? She seems to know a lot about your sexual exploits," I said. "And your bloodlust."

Adrian held my hand aloft as I made the short walk up the precipice where two identical thrones now sat. He paused before them and touched my chin, a gentle movement that made my face flush.

"You will find within these walls many profess to know me," he said. "You must trust what you have come to know."

"You are asking me to trust you," I said.

Adrian guided me back, a subtle invitation to sit, our private conversation finished. He released my hand and turned.

"Open the doors," he said and settled himself on his throne.

Adrian's court was already crowded against the walls of the great hall, leaving the center of the floor free for petitioners. I was not certain what to expect, but the line seemed to go on forever, from the opening of the hall out the front doors of the castle.

The first villager shuffled forward.

"Your Majesties," she said, bowing. "My name is Andrada. I am from the village of Sosara. Our crops were destroyed by a creature we have yet to catch. Our animals have followed. We are in the middle of winter and do not have enough food to sustain our village until summer. We humbly ask for more protection and food. We are dying."

I looked to Adrian, whose posture reminded me of someone who was bored, and yet his expression was serious. There were any number of creatures that could kill cattle and destroy crops, the rusalka, koldum, and leyah just to name a few.

"You have traveled far, Andrada," Adrian said. "Tell me, have you brought this matter to your noblesse?"

So the noblesse of Revekka were like the lords of Lara—they represented various territories and were supposed to provide a buffer between the people and their king.

She swallowed. "I have, Your Majesty. Our pleas have gone...unanswered. Though I am sure Noblesse Ciro is very busy."

"Is that what you would claim, Noblesse Ciro? That you are too busy to attend to your people?" Adrian asked, his attention shifting to a man with short blond hair and brows who stood just at the edge of the crowd. He wore rich robes, far more extravagant even than Adrian's. His collar was silver with purple gems.

"Of course not, Your Majesty," Noblesse Ciro said, casting a hardened glance at Andrada. "This is the first time I have heard of Sosara's plight."

"Then perhaps you should spend more time among your people," Adrian said.

"I will take care of it," Ciro replied, and my pulse thrummed heavily.

"Of course," Adrian said. "Ciro will escort you back to your village. I will send members of the royal guard with food as well, and they will stay until the monster destroying your crops and slaughtering your cattle has been killed. Does that satisfy your request?"

"M-more than," Andrada stuttered, her eyes darting to Ciro.

She feared him. I started to protest the noblesse's return to Sosara when Adrian spoke.

"Do not fear Noblesse Ciro," Adrian told her. "He has already failed in his duty to protect you and your people. Once more, and he will be executed."

It was a clear promise and threat that made Ciro paler, but I was glad to see consequences for absent nobles. There was nothing more infuriating than a man or woman who did not care for their people, as I had been reminded during my father's negotiations with Adrian.

"May good health and abundance bless your marriage, Your Majesties," Andrada said, bowing low. As she moved to leave the great hall, she was joined by three of Adrian's soldiers, who flanked her as if to create a barrier between her and Noblesse Ciro, who lingered farther back, following slowly.

There were a few other requests just like that, though they came from attentive noblesse. In one horrible instance, a lamia had managed its way into a home and stolen away a child. It was never found, but a trail of blood had led back to the water. Another story came from the west where men were being lured by an iara who would hypnotize them and drain them of both blood and semen.

I was surprised by the number of monsters that dared to ravish Revekka, given that vampires ruled, but hearing these complaints and concerns made me realize they were no different than the Nine Houses. Perhaps the only superior thing they had was an army of vampires to fight.

I watched the next villager approach. He was an older man who had a graying beard and short hair he kept hidden under a cap. His clothes were mostly rags, though the woman who lingered behind him, blond and beautiful, wore a far nicer gown, and I guessed they'd spent their last bit of coin on it to be here.

"Your Majesty," the man said, addressing only Adrian as he made a sweeping exaggerated bow. "I am Cain, a farmer from Jovea. My wife and I have three daughters, but Vesna, she is the most beautiful. Do you not agree?"

I instantly felt disgust, both for this man's ability to single out the beauty of one of three daughters and because of his probing question to my husband. I looked to Adrian, whose mouth hardened.

"My village relies upon me to sow crops and harvest every year, but I am growing older and in poorer health. As the years pass, it will become more difficult to provide. So I ask you—please, make me an immortal. In exchange, I offer my daughter as a concubine to serve you."

The shock of his statement reverberated through me,

stiffening my spine. I saw Adrian glance at me from my peripheral, and I wondered what my astonishment had looked like to the people crowded in the great hall. Cain did not seem to notice me at all, his gaze lingering upon Adrian. I suspected that was because he was the target of his request—I could not turn this man into a vampire.

My gaze shifted to the young girl, whose head was bowed. Her hair fell straight, and she let it curtain her youthful face. She had yet to raise her eyes to anyone, and I noted how her shoulders hunched as if she wanted to crawl into herself. She did not wish to be here.

"You say you are a farmer and a cornerstone of your village," Adrian began. "Yet I have heard differently. I have heard that you hold crops hostage in exchange for coin or favors. It does not sound like you are all that necessary to me."

The man's eyes widened, and I had to admit, I was impressed by Adrian's own knowledge of his kingdom.

"Your Majesty," Cain said and laughed awkwardly. "Why would you listen to these lies?"

"Are you calling your noblesse a liar?" Adrian asked.

"I am merely saying that Noblesse Dracul has been misled."

Even as they spoke, I could not keep my eyes off the woman lingering in this man's shadow. Her fingers were turning white and all I could think was that I had to free her from this.

I rose to my feet, and whatever the man had been saying ended abruptly as his eyes found mine. I repressed the urge to scowl, maintaining my placid expression. There was a hunger in his gaze, and I did not know if it was for power or my flesh.

"Cain, is it?" I asked.

"Y-yes," the man said, and then he bowed, as if seeing me for the first time. "Your Majesty."

I shifted my gaze to Vesna. "Your daughter, how old is she?"

"She is sixteen, my queen."

"Sixteen," I repeated and descended the steps, stopping a few feet in front of them. "Come."

The girl glanced at her father, and he waved her forward hurriedly. She made a wide arc around him, as if she feared he would reach for her. As she approached, she curtsied but would not meet my gaze. I guided her eyes to mine.

"Vesna, what are your skills?"

"I can cook, clean, sew," she said, and her voice was soft, almost musical.

"Can you sing?" I asked, my heart hopeful for her answer, and for a brief moment, I imagined teaching her songs from my mother's home and felt a surge of happiness.

"I can," she said.

"Then you will stay here in the castle with me. I could use a mortal companion," I said.

Before she could reply, her father clapped his hands loudly. "That is most generous of you, my queen!"

I stared at him, and despite the look of disgust I cast his way, he maintained his enthusiastic expression. After a moment, I returned my attention to Vesna.

"My queen, that is very generous of you. I fear...I fear to leave my sisters behind."

"We will do something about those fears," I replied and then summoned Ana, who had positioned herself near the dais. "Take Vesna to my quarters. I will join her after this is over."

I watched until they disappeared into the adjoining room, and as I turned, I drew my knife from between my breasts, hiding it in my skirts before turning back to her father. I took two deliberate steps to face him.

"You will not regret your decision, my queen!"

"You are right," I said. "I won't."

The knife slid home between his ribs, and as his eyes widened, I withdrew it with a jerk so that he fell heavy and dead at my feet, blood dripping from his mouth. I stared out at those gathered before me and those who were waiting for an audience.

"Anyone else wish to offer their daughters as a concubine to my husband?" I asked.

There was only silence.

I turned and made my way back up the precipice.

Adrian held out his hand. "Your knife."

I hesitated but offered it to him, as he didn't seem to be so much disappointed as pleased. Then he took it and cleaned it as he had done last night, returning it to me immediately. Another set of guards dragged Cain's body from the center of the room, leaving a streak of blood as they went.

No one else left me out in their address after Cain, and he was not the last to ask for immortality, though no one bothered offering their daughter as a sex slave. What surprised me most was that Adrian declined every request from a mortal to be turned, and I began to wonder what would convince him.

The final person to ask was familiar to me, and seeing him in the great hall of the Red Palace shocked me.

"King Gheroghe."

His kingdom was Vela and had yet to be conquered by King Adrian.

"Prin—Queen Isolde," he said, bowing. "A pleasure. It has been a long while since last I looked upon your beauty."

I felt Adrian's eyes upon me as I spoke.

"It has been a while," I said. "Since I put a knife against your son's throat. How is Prince Horatiu?"

He had been one of several to suggest they could both please me and lead my people, insinuating that I could not do it on my own, and when he'd cornered me in the dark to kiss me, I'd reacted by drawing blood.

"Much recovered," Gheroghe replied.

"What is the reason for your visit, King Gheroghe?" Adrian asked, a note of irritation in his voice.

"I have come to surrender," he said. There was a surprise quiet that flooded the entire room, and then he added, "In exchange, I ask only to become immortal."

"Surrender does not usually include negotiating where I am concerned, King Gheroghe," Adrian said. "You surrender and keep your title and ensure the safety of your people. There are no other options."

"Vela has much to offer, my king. Not only would you inherit a wealth of iron ore, but you would have access to launch an attack on the Atoll of Nalani, a kingdom rich in pearls and gems."

I straightened and my hands fisted, hearing my mother's homeland thrown into talks of conquering.

"You would inherit so much more than a wife with a penchant for knives."

"I like my wife and her knives, and while I'd prefer

your surrender over battle, I will gladly go to war nevertheless."

King Gheroghe's eyes widened, and as Adrian rose, I followed.

"I-Isolde," he said, as if begging me to come to his defense.

"You lost my support when you suggested that Adrian invade my mother's lands," I said. "Return to your kingdom and await the war."

The memory of Adrian's words were not lost on me; I had just approved of the invasion of one of the Nine Houses.

Adrian took my hand, and we returned to the adjacent room. He pushed me against the door, dragging my hips against his, and kissed me.

I held his head between my hands and freed myself.

"How many women have you accepted as concubines?" I asked.

"None," he said. "But I have never executed a man for the offer either."

"He was a snake," I spat.

"I am not disagreeing or disapproving," he said, and he ground into me further. The hard length of his cock settled against my stomach. Then his voice lowered to a low rumble, and it was as if he were confessing a sin. "You are everything I have ever wanted."

I stared at him and saw the same gentleness, the same raw emotion I'd seen last night. And I couldn't indulge.

I pushed him back and slid out from between him and the door. He reached for my wrist, and I met his gaze.

"Isolde, tell me what I did wrong."

"Can you not read minds?" I countered, frustrated, though I really hoped he couldn't in this moment. I didn't want him to know the truth—that I could not handle the care with which he had looked at me, that I felt more emotion than I could manage when I looked at him.

"I'm *trying* to give you privacy," he said, and it was the first time I sensed his exasperation with me.

"I just...did not know you would make a habit of visiting my bed every night. It is not as if we need to produce an heir, so it is hardly necessary."

He released me but turned fully toward me, towering, eyes narrowed. "Are you saying you tire of me, my queen?"

I hated the way those words hurt my chest, and I hated how uncertain I sounded as I answered, breathless. "Yes."

Adrian stared a moment longer, as if he thought I would change my mind beneath his scrutiny, but I didn't—I couldn't—and I hoped that if he had chosen to read my mind in this moment, my thoughts reflected the same. Adrian and I were supposed to be enemies, and I could only stand our closeness so long as I still felt anger toward him.

Finally, he took his leave, offering only a single bow. I wondered how long I'd be able to keep my distance before that unexplained need for him took over and betrayed my self-control.

I returned to my quarters after court to find Ana sitting with Vesna. The two looked up as I entered and then stood to curtsy.

"My queen," Vesna said, keeping her eyes on her feet.

"You will have to learn to meet my gaze if you are to work for me, Vesna," I said, and when she did, she blushed a deep crimson.

"I apologize, my queen."

"Do not apologize," I said. "Ana, will you summon Violeta?"

She nodded and left the room. Alone with Vesna, I invited her to sit beside me on the bed, once again keeping my distance from the hearth.

"I must inform you of your father's death, Vesna," I said. "I..."

I did not know what to add.

*I murdered him*, I thought, but I did not have the chance to add anything to my statement. Vesna burst into tears. It was a torrent of emotion that lasted only a few seconds before she was able to compose herself.

"I'm sorry," I said. I wasn't apologizing for killing her father, but I was apologizing for her hurt.

"No, please. Do not be sorry. I just...do not know how to feel. He was terrible, to be sure, a true monster not only to me and my sisters but our mother and the townspeople. To be truthful, I do not know how he survived this long."

She told me of instances when her father's food or drink had been poisoned, but he'd escaped any attempts by feeding the contaminated fare to their animals. I felt sick at the thought.

"Still, he was my father," she said.

"You do not have to decide how to feel today or tomorrow or ever if that is your choice," I said. "But I cannot have men selling their daughters without consequences."

"I understand," she whispered. "I am only glad that I can protect my sisters from him."

"Tell me about them," I said.

Vesna smiled when I asked. They were nine and eleven, and their names were Jasenka and Kseniya. She told a story of how much they loved flowers and how they would shriek with delight when they spotted white butterflies resting on petals, and as they flew away, the girls would follow, dancing as they went.

"We called it the butterfly dance," she said, smiling even as tears stained her face. "I think I remember those times so well because there was sun just beyond the border, and sometimes, we would run beneath it."

The sun.

It was strange how the thought of it filled me with mourning as I remembered how I'd sought the tallest hills in Lara just so I could lie closer to its rays. Homesickness swamped me.

"What about your mother?" I asked, swallowing hard, blinking back the tears burning my eyes.

At the question, Vesna's mouth began to quiver. "I do not know what will become of her. I…" She fell forward and sobbed into her hands, and the only thing I could think to do was hold her. After she had cried a while, she was able to tell me more about her mother. "She used to sing," Vesna said. "But my father would yell, so she only sang when he was gone. Then he began to hit, and her singing stopped altogether."

I sent her with Violeta after that, promising before she left, "You may leave to visit your family as often as you wish."

She smiled at me. "Thank you, my queen."

Alone, I lay upon my bed, and as I stared up at the canopy, the tangled pattern blurred with my tears. I missed my father and the presence of my mother so much, my chest ached. I closed my eyes against the pain and rolled onto my side, humming my mother's lullaby, the one that had played from the music box my father had given me—the one he would bring me in less than two weeks' time.

*You still have him*, I reminded myself.

And yet his absence burrowed deeper, and for the first time since I'd left Lara, I felt very much alone.

# FOURTEEN

*I had no self-control.*

Adrian did not visit my bed that night, and while I knew he was honoring exactly what I'd asked for, I'd never wanted him to defy my wishes so much in my life. It was not dramatic to say I writhed. I was so uncomfortable in my skin. Each caress against my nipples and engorged clit was a reminder of Adrian's absence. I pushed the covers away until I was exposed to the night. The chill air blanketed my body, and as I closed my eyes, fingers parting my flesh, I heard Adrian's voice.

"Dreaming of me, Sparrow?"

When I opened my eyes, he stood near, watching me. He was the same Adrian I'd witnessed in the grotto, untroubled and unmarred, surrounded by jasmine trees and darkness, and while he was just as beautiful, I realized I liked the severity of his face now—the way life had etched anger into his eyes and the set of his jaw.

"I dream of you always," I said, embarrassed by the

words, and though they were true, they were nothing I would ever say aloud. I started to pull out of myself, but Adrian held my hand against my heat, guiding my fingers to return.

"No, let me watch," he implored, and my whole body flushed with his request. He knelt between my legs as I pleasured myself. Within moments, he joined me, drawing his cock into his hand and stroking himself. We didn't touch, but we held each other's gazes, and our breaths quickened, moans rising together. I watched him until I could no longer keep my eyes from rolling back as I found release. I lay there a few moments, expecting to feel his body pressed against mine in the aftermath, but there was nothing, and when I opened my eyes, he wasn't there.

---

The next morning, I rose early, unable to rest, and headed for the garden, despite the fact that Adrian had told me not to leave my room without an escort. That had been upon arrival, and since, I had been responsible for the death of one vampire and one mortal.

I felt I was pretty safe.

I wasn't sure how long it would take for me to get used to Revekka mornings, but they were not crisp and golden like those of Lara. The horizon blazed crimson red, and blades of the same light cut across the garden, casting other parts in deep shadow. There was nothing cheery about it—it was a bloodbath.

As I wandered along the paths, I wrapped my cloak tightly around me to fight the chill. It was no colder in Revekka than it was in Lara, for which I was glad, because I had heard winter here was long and harsh, with the land accumulating several feet of snow. I preferred summer—the height of it when the sun was hottest. Blinking up at the bloody sky, I doubted I would feel those rays anytime soon.

My meandering brought me to the grotto, and I lingered at the edge of the pool, enjoying the heat wafting from the water before shedding my cloak and the remainder of my clothes.

The pool was shallow where I entered and grew deeper as I waded into the center. Suddenly, I wanted Adrian here, body slick and warm. I would coax come from his cock and slide him between my thighs. I would climb his body until he could fit himself in mine, and I would ride him until he came inside me. Those thoughts gave way to a reel of images, and I could not help squeezing my legs together, fighting the urge to once again pleasure myself.

This connection to Adrian was abnormal.

I dipped beneath the surface of the water to stop my thoughts from spiraling and stayed until I could no longer hold my breath. When I surfaced, I came face-to-face with Gesalac.

In my haste to break through the water, I had come up too far, exposing half my body to the noblesse. Gesalac did not lower his eyes, even as I retreated so that the water rose to my shoulders.

"You did not come up for air," he explained. "I was concerned."

"How long were you watching me, Noblesse?"

"I was not watching," he said, but he offered no other explanation. "I would be mindful of where you choose to swim, my queen. The king's rage is rarely rational."

I did not like his warning or his comment about

Adrian. Even if Adrian was irrational, in this instance, his anger would be justified.

"No one asked you to linger, Noblesse," I said, ready for him to leave. I was too exposed and weaponless, and I did not trust his intentions.

The vampire stared a moment longer, then bowed his head and left. I did not exit the pool immediately, fearing that Gesalac still lingered nearby. When I felt enough time had passed, I dressed, pulling the hood of my cloak over my head to keep the chill at bay.

I made my way to the castle, deciding to take the passage Ana had showed me rather than return through the garden. Once in my room, I changed into dry clothes and braided my still-wet hair. As I worked, Violeta and Vesna arrived with breakfast.

Vesna held the tray, and though she looked far more composed than she had yesterday, there was a soft sadness to her features. I could not imagine how she felt—to grieve her abuser—but the expectation of the world was that we loved our parents no matter their crimes against us.

As she set the tray at my bedside, I noticed she wore the same clothes as yesterday.

"Do you have a change of clothes, Vesna?" I asked.

"No, my queen, but I have sent for them," she said. "I'm not sure when they will arrive."

"Perhaps we should have some made," I suggested.

"Tomorrow is market day in Cel Ceredi," Violeta said. "I had hoped to take Vesna anyway."

"Good," I said. "Pick out some fabric while you are there."

"Is there anything you require, my queen?"

The question caught me off guard because I did not know enough about my future circumstances in the castle to answer.

"Perhaps I will go with you," I said. "To get an idea of what I may need."

Violeta hesitated.

"Is that a problem?"

"No, my queen. I am only surprised. I have never known a royal to visit the market," she said.

"Then I shall be the first," I said and then glanced down at my tray, finally paying attention to my food. "What is this?"

"Oh, it's yetta," Violeta said. "It's a traditional Revekkian breakfast, though you'll find *everyone* has their own way of making it."

"And what is in yetta?"

It looked like a stew, and while it did not smell horrible, it certainly looked questionable.

"Oh, many things," she said. "Sausages, bacon, spinach, tomatoes, tons of spices…that's a goose egg on top, if you were wondering."

I had been.

I dipped my spoon into the thick broth and took a tentative sip, surprised by how flavorful it really was. It came with a hard piece of bread that Violeta explained was supposed to be used at the end to soak up what remained of the dish.

"Nothing goes to waste," she said.

I finished the bowl, partly because I found I wanted to please Violeta who had been so excited about the dish. After, she collected the tray and left with Vesna in tow. I was not alone long when there was another knock at my door. I was expecting Ana, who still needed to dress my wound.

Instead, it was Adrian.

I couldn't describe the feeling his presence triggered inside me, but it was like shattering. My heartbeat swept into a frenzied pulse that made my body flush. Beneath his gaze, I felt uncertain of how to present myself—conscious of his eyes on every part of me, conscious of the words I'd said that had driven him from my bed and how we had parted yesterday.

"Adrian," I said, his name sounding more like a question.

His expression remained passive and a little cold.

"I've come to invite you to High Council. I will be meeting with the noblesse," he said. "We will be discussing the attacks at Vaida and Sadovea. I…thought you would want to join."

"Of course," I said and attempted to imbue my voice with as much authority and control as his.

There was a strained silence that followed, as if he wished to say more, though he did not speak. After a moment, he took a breath. "Ana will bring you. She will be in attendance as well."

He started toward the door, and I fought the urge to call him back to me, feeling uncomfortable with his coldness, knowing it was because of what I said. Why did I feel this way about our distance? Hadn't I hoped for exactly this upon arriving at the Red Palace? I should be relieved it had worked so well.

"Adrian." His name slipped from my mouth, and I wished I could take it back. He halted and stared at me, and my lips parted as I searched for words to speak.

"I..." What was I going to say? *I'm sorry? Come back?* Those words made me cringe. "Violeta is going to market tomorrow. I would like to go with her."

"I am not opposed," he said. "But I will have to send Isac and Miha to accompany you."

"Not Sorin?" I asked.

I was used to all three acting as my protectors.

"Sorin is on assignment," Adrian said.

Oh. Despite my curiosity, I did not ask for more information. Instead, I thanked him.

The way he looked at me made me think he wasn't used to expressions of gratitude, and I supposed that was fitting, given that he was the Blood King.

He was about to turn once more when I called him back again. "Adrian."

This time, I saw the frustration in the set of his jaw.

"Yes?" the question was clipped, almost a hiss, and I fought my own irritation.

"I'd like to send for Vesna's family, her mother and two sisters."

"You wish to relocate them?" he asked.

I hesitated. "Is that possible?"

"I will have to speak with Tanaka."

"Please."

He nodded, and with that, he left.

Ana arrived a short time later and dressed my wound. She wore white today, which made her hair look pale, her skin near translucent, and her lips far more crimson. The color made me think of fresh blood, and suddenly I wondered who Ana had taken as a vassal. I hesitated to ask, considering I had insulted her at our first meeting when I'd asked if Adrian had turned her, but drinking blood seemed far more common than siring another vampire, so I did.

She surprised me by blushing.

"Her name is Isla," she said.

Now I was even more curious. "Have I seen her? Was she in the great hall the other night?"

"No, she is visiting family in Cel Cera."

"If she is gone, who do you take from?"

I was mostly curious because of Adrian. Did he have a line of mortal women to cycle through if Safira was unavailable? She'd called herself his favored vassal—did that imply he had others? And now that I'd asked him to stop drinking from her, who would he choose?

Ana hesitated and then answered, "I don't."

My brows knitted together. "Won't you starve?"

"I won't starve," Ana said with a small, amused smile. She focused intently upon my arm, smoothing a cooling salve evenly upon my skin. "She will only be gone four days."

"Why wouldn't you drink from someone else?"

"Because I do not wish to," Ana answered.

It took her looking at me for it to sink in. Isla was not only her vassal but her lover.

"*Oh*," I said. "Does she know?"

Ana's laugh was lyrical, and she returned to her task of wrapping my arm. "She knows I will not drink from anyone but her. It is why she will only leave for as long as I can abstain."

Again, I found myself think of Adrian and Safira. Had he been loyal to her in this way? A knot of jealousy twisted in my stomach as I realized how close the relationship between a vampire and his vassal must be.

"Do you love her?" I asked as she knotted off the gauze.

She took a moment to answer, rising to her feet first and smoothing her palms on her dress. "I do," she answered quietly.

"Will you turn her?"

"She does not wish to be like me," Ana said, and I sensed a note of pain in her voice.

"But she is your vassal. I thought…"

I thought all vassals agreed to offer their blood in hopes that they too would one day know immortality.

"She offered her blood to show me she loved me," Ana said. "And that is enough."

Except that I got the sense it wasn't.

"Are you sure?"

"It is a decision she must make, and I will not make it for her."

I considered how their society seemed to be built around consent—vampires had to have permission to drink from vassals or turn them.

"Is that what happened to Sorin? Was he not given the choice?"

"I cannot speak for Sorin," she said. "But what I can say is that many of us were not given the choice in the beginning, which is why there is choice now."

I frowned, thinking back to what I'd learned of the Dark Era. We had been told that it was a time of great fear, that new vampires were being born at an alarming rate. In the early days, they were not in control, their fierce hunger overtaking any humanity. I wasn't sure how they'd come to handle their desire for blood, but eventually, the number of new vampires decreased. As they did, Adrian Vasiliev rose to power.

I had never considered, though, the horror these vampires had gone through.

I suppose Adrian was right. History was just perspective.

We spoke no more on the subject, and I left to attend High Council. The meeting would take place in the west wing of the castle, which happened to also be where Adrian resided. I wondered why he'd placed me in the south—was it to provide the distance I'd wanted? Or was it so that he could continue his trysts as he had before he'd left?

As we went, Ana pointed to Adrian's chambers.

"In the event you…desire his presence," Ana said as we passed. It made me think she knew he hadn't come to my bed last night. I had to admit, I wondered what was behind those carved, black doors. Did he live in simplicity, or would his room reflect the extravagance present in every detail of the castle?

We continued up a set of stairs, now to the third floor, which opened into the most beautiful room in the entire palace. It was a long hall that created a bridge between one tower and the next. The walls alternated between large, rounded windows and gold mirrors. The floor at my feet was carpeted and crimson, made to look even darker by the red light streaming into the space. A row of chandeliers, lit with hundreds of taper candles, hung down the center, and I walked beneath them, taking in every detail—from dark paintings depicting the Burning to relief carvings of the goddesses Asha and Dis.

"Was this here before Adrian's reign?" I asked.

I did not think he would have commissioned such

art to decorate his palace, but then again, I could not be sure.

"It was," Ana said. "He keeps it as a reminder."

My brows lowered at her comment.

"A reminder for what?" I asked.

"Why he conquers."

We continued walking, and I glanced at a mirror to my right. Just as I was about to walk out of frame, I caught site of something—a reflection that was not my own. It was a woman with ginger hair—the same one I'd seen in the reflection of the window at Sadovea.

I halted and stepped back, finding her staring back.

I could see more of her features this time—light olive skin, freckles across her cheeks and nose, full lips, and green eyes. She was beautiful, and as she stared back at me, the corners of her lips lifted.

"Are you a ghost?" I whispered.

"Who are you talking to?" Ana asked.

I whipped my head to the left and found her at the end of the hall, waiting.

"There is a woman." I turned back to the mirror, but only I looked back. "In the mirror..." My voice trailed off as Ana came to stand beside me. I blinked and shook my head, confused. "I...must have been imagining it."

Perhaps this was just another strange vision like the one I'd had of Adrian in the grotto.

Ana frowned. "Come. We'll be late."

The hall of mirrors emptied into a large corridor. A flight of steps inclined upward to higher floors. To the left, the hall curved out of view while the right led to a set of doors that reached the ceiling. We turned right through the doors, only to be greeted by a room full of men.

My disgust was immediate as they all turned to look at us. At least they bowed at my presence. The room where Adrian held council was far narrower than it was wide. A large marble fireplace framed the Blood King as he stood before a round table with Daroc only a step behind. I noted how the hearth was not full of raging fire, only glowing embers, and I wondered if he had done that for me. The rest of the room was just as extravagant as the hall we'd exited, with towering, gilded mirrors and chande- liers dripping in crystals. The ceiling was covered in a fresco that appeared to detail the creation of the world. I noted Asha and Dis, one depicted in white, the other in black, one haloed by the sun, the other by the stars, surrounded by the lesser goddesses, the ones we no longer worshipped in Cordova.

I did not have long to inspect every inch of this room, as my attention fell to the noblesse present. I only recog- nized a few—Tanaka, Gesalac, Dracul, and Anatoly. I noted that Ciro was absent from the mix, which was just as well. He had done his people a disservice and needed to rectify it. There were five other men I did not know, but none of them looked at me with as much mistrust as Gesalac, whose gaze made my stomach sour. I wondered if he was thinking about earlier when he'd found me in the grotto.

My gaze shifted to Adrian, who seemed on edge, his eyes burning with an infernal light. I wondered if he could hear my thoughts at this moment. If he was trying to guess what happened at the grotto.

"How unfortunate," I said, "that no women advise you."

"You advise me, my queen," Adrian said.

"One woman and nine men—how revolutionary of you."

I held Adrian's gaze as I moved to his side. He stared down at me, and a little of his coldness had melted away.

"Your concerns are noted, my queen," he said.

Tanaka cleared his throat, and Adrian shifted his attention to the older vampire. "Do you have something you wish to share, Viceroy?"

Tanaka hesitated, mouth working. Clearly, his interruption did not have the intended effect.

"Uh, no, Your Majesty."

There was a strange silence, and my eyes shifted to a map that was spread upon the table, and I noted three small, red pins—one in Vaida, one in Sadovea, and one in a place called Cel Cioran.

"Was there another attack?" I asked, my chest tightening at the thought.

"Yes, but it was not recent," he said. "Like Vaida, it was discovered late."

I wondered if it was another one of Ciro's territories but did not ask as Adrian jumped into an explanation of what we'd discovered on our way to the Red Palace. I felt more and more dread as he spoke of the state of the bodies, of the horror of hearing the man's screams as he ran from the gates of Sadovea, and the child who had attacked me.

"A child?" one of the noblesse asked, looking just as devastated as I had felt. His name was Iosif. He was a tall man with blond hair that came to his shoulders and a smattering of facial hair.

"She was possessed by whatever magic was unleashed," Adrian said. "And it turned her into a monster. We brought her here for an autopsy, which Ana performed."

My eyes wide, I looked to Ana, who'd been hovering along the edge of the room. I had no idea the task would fall to her.

"During my analysis, the only thing I found of note was that her blood seemed to be crystalized," she said. "Which, after a lot of research, leads me to believe that a spell was cast, specifically one for something called the crimson mist."

A mist.

It made sense, considering how everyone had seemed to perish, like something had covered the entire town, crawled beneath doors, and seeped through windows. Still, I wondered how she was so certain it was a spell. Could a vampire also not possess this power? They could spread plague, so how was this different?

"Whoever is casting, however, is either not a witch or not gifted in blood magic," she continued. "If the spell was successful, every villager would have been possessed by the crimson mist just like the girl."

"I thought all witches were dead," I said.

There was a strained silence, and Adrian answered, "It is likely a few survived. And even more were born after the Burning. Witches are not created, they are born. It is in their blood."

I did not know what to make of this information. I'd grown up believing witches were a part of our past, that no more would walk this earth. Suddenly, Adrian was telling me that wasn't so, which meant...where were they? Was the mist their attempt at retribution?

"Could this be Ravena?" Tanaka asked, and beside me, Adrian stiffened.

"Who is Ravena?" I asked, looking up at him. He

stared for a long moment, and I wasn't certain he wanted to tell me, but finally he relented.

"She was Dragos's witch," he said. "After his death, she escaped and has never been found."

This was new information to me. I never knew that Dragos had employed a witch. Was that not contrary to his mission? That was a question for another time. Right now, I wondered why someone from Adrian's past, someone who had been in hiding, was suddenly making herself so obviously known.

"If she is your enemy, why attack Vaida then?" I asked.

"We do not know that it was Ravena who conjured the spell," said Adrian.

"Whoever it was likely did not intend for the mist to strike Vaida," Ana said. "I believe they lost control of the magic, which is also why the spell has only managed to work on one person and killed the rest."

"So the spell is intended to create monsters?" I asked, shivering as I recalled how dangerous something like this could be if it worked. The girl in Sadovea had looked so innocent, and she'd lured me in with no issue.

"I think it is intended to create an army."

There was a stretch of silence.

"Can the mist affect us?" The question came from a noblesse named Julian.

"As long as the mist can attack the blood in our veins, I imagine so," Ana replied.

More dread.

If the mist could successfully possess vampires, there would be no stopping the terror they might inflict. The worst part about this was that no one really seemed to know who was responsible.

"We should double down on our efforts to locate Ravena," said Julian.

At his suggestion, Adrian's jaw tightened, and I was curious about his reaction. Then he said, "Do you not think I have tried, Noblesse?"

"I did not mean to suggest otherwise, my king," Julian said. "It's just that you have been distracted."

It was the wrong thing to say. I knew it in the way the air changed around me. It became thick and heavy, and beside me, Adrian tilted his head.

"Please enlighten me as to what has distracted me, Noblesse."

Julian swallowed noticeably, and his eyes slid briefly to me. I was not sure if he was looking to me for help or suggesting I was the problem.

"The conquest of Cordova has taken up much of your time, Your Majesty, not to mention…your new wife."

A long pause followed his words, and then Adrian spoke. "Do you think I lack the ability to conquer the world, fuck my wife, and search for a fugitive witch, Noblesse?"

I flinched at his words, and Julian did not answer.

"Does anyone else agree with Noblesse Julian?" Adrian asked, and as his gaze swept the crowd, he left my side, coming around the table as he twisted a gold ring upon his finger. No one spoke, and a sense of unease crept along my neck. I noted the way Daroc took a step closer to me, as if he were preparing to whisk me away the moment something horrible happened. Tanaka tensed, his fingers splayed across the map as if to give him added support.

Adrian came to stand in front of Julian, towering over the vampire.

"It seems you are the only one who thinks I am not worthy of this crown I wear," he said, and he leaned forward, both hands on Julian's shoulders, squeezing. "Would you like it?"

"N–no, Your Majesty," Julian answered quietly, his gaze falling to the floor.

"Look at me when you lie, Julian," Adrian said. "It will make this next part far easier."

What next part?

But I soon found out, because just as Julian lifted his head, Adrian clasped his face between his hands. The ring he'd been twisting turned out to also be a small, curved blade, which he slid right into Julian's eye. My nails bit into my palms as the vampire screamed, and Adrian continued to push the blade farther until he wrenched his thumb free and the eye came with it, hitting the ground with a slick splat.

Julian fell to his knees, rocking forward, holding his hands to his eye socket. I trembled but managed to remain steady as Adrian spoke, his hand dripping with Julian's blood.

"*Never* assume you understand my purpose." Then he turned, gaze sweeping the crowd. "You will all instruct your territories to light fires around their gates to keep the mist at bay until we are able to locate Ravena or the person responsible for the spell. You are all dismissed."

The noblesse filed out silently, passing Julian as they went. Adrian placed his boot against Julian's side and kicked him. The vampire fell with a groan to the floor.

"Get out!" Adrian yelled.

I flinched and watched as Julian scrambled to his feet.

"I'd like to be alone with my wife," Adrian said to Daroc and Ana, as they still lingered.

I looked at both of them, a note of hysteria climbing up my throat, but they were already retreating. When the doors were closed, Adrian and I stared at each other.

"Do you feel justified in your belief that I'm a monster now?" he asked after a long bout of silence.

"That was indeed monstrous," I said. "And all because he said you could not multitask."

"It wasn't what he said. It was what he was thinking," Adrian said.

I stiffened. Sometimes I forgot Adrian could read minds. And apparently not just mine.

"And what was he thinking?"

"He called you a whore," Adrian said.

"I see," I said, suddenly feeling far less sorry for the noblesse. My eyes fell to Adrian's clenched hands. I took a step away from the table, closer to him.

"He is lucky he left with his head."

"Why were you so generous?" I asked.

Adrian's lips twitched. "Eager for a beheading, my sweet?"

"I only wish to know why he is so valuable to your council."

"He is an excellent huntsman," Adrian said. "And he teaches his people to live off the land. It is a valuable skill."

"And no one else can teach such skills?"

"Not as well as he does. Not yet," he said.

Which told me he would eventually be expendable.

We were quiet for a moment, and then I asked, "Do you think Ravena is responsible for the mist?"

"I think she is likely responsible," he said. "If the attack only occurred at Vaida, I would have continued to think it was a mortal who happened upon a rogue spell. It wasn't until Sadovea I began to suspect otherwise."

"Why did you not tell me as soon as you suspected?"

I thought I knew why, and it had everything to do with his past—a past no one seemed inclined to tell me about. I wanted to know why and how Adrian had become the first vampire. I wanted to know why he was so invested in the High Coven. I wanted to know why this witch wanted an army.

He watched me for a moment and then answered, "I wanted to be certain."

Suddenly, he reminded me of my father, but not in a good way.

*I want to protect you*, my father would say as he barred me from attending his council meetings, but really it was just an excuse, a way to keep me from knowing exactly what was going on while men discussed things like barring shipments of blue cohosh and silphium— two methods of birth control for the women of Lara. I'd been so angry, I hadn't spoken to my father for two weeks and only relented when he agreed to a compromise. He would remove the ban and allow healers to administer the herbs. It was not the best circumstance. Healers could be bribed, and some, themselves, did not believe in preventing pregnancy, but it was better than no access.

"That is an excuse," I said. Even now, I could recall the moment I suspected Adrian knew something—it had been the way he'd set his jaw and stared off into the distance. He'd been connecting the pieces, searching for confirmation. "You could have told me, but doing so would mean telling me about your past, and it seems you value its secrecy over winning the trust of your wife."

"Isolde," Adrian began, and there was a spark of hurt and frustration in his eyes.

"*Don't* say my name," I said, closing my eyes against the sound of it, the way it burrowed under my skin. "Just...tell me the truth."

He stepped closer. "You want truth?" he said. "Ravena may be building an army to come after me, but her target is *you*."

"What?"

"Your father told you to find my weakness," he said, a lithe finger twining around a piece of my hair. My eyes widened at his words—words that had been spoken only between me and my father. He smiled at my reaction, and it was wicked. "Little did he know...it is you."

# FIFTEEN

*I was not surprised when Adrian did not visit my bed for* the second night in a row. I spent most of the evening turning his words over and over.

*Ravena might be building an army to come after me, but her target is you.*

I did not like admitting to fear, but those words had an effect on me, and I wanted to know more about Dragos's witch. Why, after all this time, was this woman coming out of hiding to create an army, and did it really have anything to do with me?

*Your father told you to find my weakness. Little did he know...it is you.*

How was I Adrian's weakness? He had known me for *days*, and yet even I could not explain our connection. Sometimes, it was like our bodies knew each other and our minds hadn't caught up, and I was left reeling in the aftermath.

The night continued like that until I rose the next

morning, exhausted with a headache. It was made worse as I headed into Cel Ceredi with Violeta and Vesna, while Isac and Miha followed behind. Vesna had broken out into song. I did not recognize the lyrics, but they were fun, and the beat was a steady thrum.

> *And when the snow falls on the ground,*
> *I'll come, my love, I'll come on down.*
> *Down from the mountains and into the town,*
> *The town where our love was found.*

At first, it was a contained affair, with Miha singing along and Isac clapping, but as we reached the village, others joined in, and Vesna became the center of attention as she skipped and clapped and sang. When she finished, it was to a round of applause.

I liked seeing her smile, and I hoped she would grow happier the longer she stayed. I imagined relocating her mother and sisters here to Cel Ceredi would help, though I had yet to hear confirmation of the move from Adrian.

"You have a lovely voice, Vesna," Miha said as the girl fell into step beside me and Violeta.

"Thank you," she said, blushing, and then sighed. "Cel Ceredi is so much nicer than Jovea."

I wonder if she meant the people or our surroundings. I liked the uniqueness of the village, to be sure. Parts of the town were far older than others. I could tell because the homes and shops were all constructed differently—some had pine walls and clay roofs, others were made of woven twigs with thatched roofs, others were covered in plaster. We walked along a cobble road, past carts of vegetables, fresh meat, linen, and wool while the smell of roasted pork and mutton, evergreen and tobacco permeated the air. They were scents that also reminded me of winter in Lara, which carried a nostalgia that suddenly made me homesick.

Despite this, the markets here were far less exciting than those in Lara. Perhaps it was because Lara's market came once a month while Cel Ceredi's was weekly, but the villagers always used it as an excuse to celebrate. Jugglers and dancers would entertain while other shop owners would host games and contests. It was festive, colorful, and fun, but here, there was a strange melancholy in the air that I did not understand until I spotted several people stacking wood into perfect squares.

"Are those...pyres?" I asked, the thought making me uneasy.

"Yes," Violeta replied. "We are a week out from the Burning Rites."

"The...Burning Rites?"

"It is the anniversary of the night High Coven was executed. King Adrian orders every village to burn bright for a week to memorialize their deaths. The fires begin tonight, and there are events every night. The most anticipated is the Great Hunt."

"What is the Great Hunt?"

"Exactly what it sounds like," she said. "It is the night we hunt monsters."

"What is the purpose?"

Many of us did not hunt monsters by choice, it was necessity, survival, though I supposed vampires were different.

She shrugged. "It is a sport," she said. "And there is a prize."

"What is the prize?" I asked.

"A place beside the king at the feast on the last night of the Rites."

I wasn't sure what I was most uncomfortable about—the celebration of witches or the fires—but I could acknowledge the horror of the Burning and the need to memorialize the innocent people who had died during Dragos's hunts.

"What do your people think of High Coven?" I asked, uncertain of how those who resided in Revekka felt about vampires or witches or anything that had to do with King Dragos's reign. Did Revekkians view him like the Nine Houses did? As a hero who had been murdered by a monster? Did they believe witches to be cruel and corrupt? Or did they believe as Adrian believed? That the witches were innocent?

"You will find that most of us think very differently about High Coven than you, my queen." Violeta spoke carefully, but I sensed an edge to her voice that she could not hide.

"How so?" I asked.

Violeta hesitated, so I spoke.

"Never fear to speak your truth, Violeta."

She pressed her lips together and then took a breath, explaining, "Some of us are the sons and daughters of those who died during the Burning, and the stories that survive within our families tell a very different tale than what is shared outside Revekka."

"Tell me of your ancestor then," I said. "Who was she?"

She offered a small smile but did not look at me as she spoke, choosing instead to watch the cobbles at her feet as we walked.

"Her name was Evanora. She was a member of High Coven, and she was sent from her home to Keziah to serve King Jirecek. She wrote home often. Her letters were beautiful. Even when I read them now, I can feel her hope. I do not know if she truly believed in the future she thought she was cultivating or if she was only trying to protect her mother from the truth. Either way, the night of the Burning, she was pulled from her bed along with twelve other members of High Coven across Cordova and burned."

I shivered. I could not imagine a worse death.

Violeta met my gaze when she said, "Do you know the way my family was informed of her death? They woke to discover their house burning. King Dragos had declared that the relatives of every witch should be hunted and murdered. It was a relief when King Adrian came to power. It meant we no longer had to hide."

I had never heard this side before, and I had to admit I was stunned. "I'm so sorry."

They were the only words I could find to speak. Inside, I felt a mix of emotions—I was confused and ashamed and angry, and there was a part of me that could not completely disregard what I'd been taught. I could feel myself hanging on to the stories and the fear of magic. It was not as if I hadn't seen it firsthand—the villages of Vaida and Sadovea remained as horrors in my mind.

Still, there were monsters among us all. Now, I wondered how many had stories like Violeta's.

"Do not be sorry," she said. "You are here now and our queen. You can learn."

We visited several vendors at the market, many greeting Violeta and even Isac and Miha by name. It was then I learned that Violeta had worked in the kitchens at the Red Palace before becoming my lady-in-waiting. It explained why she'd known exactly what was in the breakfast stew and why she insisted I try every Revekkian delicacy offered in the market.

"You never know what you might like," she said, and despite her enthusiasm, I could tell that the vendors, shopkeepers, and farmers were not so keen to serve me. They were polite, they curtsied and bowed and called me "Your Majesty," but they were guarded, and some gave me sharp looks. I wondered if it was because I wasn't Revekkian, because they knew my beliefs conflicted with their own. In the end, I tipped everyone who gave me samples of their treats and drinks, and we managed to find fabric for Vesna's clothes.

We returned to the castle, and Violeta took Vesna with her for more training while I headed to the library. I was excited at the idea of having so much history at my fingertips. Lara's library was minimal—some large tomes that had been scripted by our local historians and a book that offered a few details about my mother's home. Even so, it felt like such a small sampling of a world with hundreds of years of history. If I was going to be queen of Cordova, I wanted to know more. I had to know more.

Miha escorted me to the library, for which I was thankful, as it kept me from being waylaid by any noblesse.

"How are you liking the palace?" she asked. "Cel Ceredi?"

"The palace is beautiful," I said. "Cel Ceredi is quaint. I only fear these people will never truly see me as queen."

"They will," Miha said. "Though you can begin by calling them your people."

I had the urge to fight her comment, but I knew she was right. I was trying to keep everyone at a distance, too afraid I might find something I liked.

Miha's remark made me pay closer attention to my surroundings, and I found myself appreciating the palace activity rather than avoiding it. Servants carried heavy, silver trays stacked high with plates and metal chalices while others lit multitiered candelabras and hung garlands that smelled of rosemary and sage. It was preparation for the Burning Rites, I realized.

"My queen," servant after servant said, offering a bow or a curtsy.

I acknowledged each, nodding or smiling as I passed, though I found myself more than eager to escape the scrutiny, and felt a rush of relief as we turned down an empty carpeted hallway. At the end was the library, which lay beyond two large ebony doors, each inlaid with colorful stained glass. Miha did not follow me beyond them as I stepped into a room full of black shelves lined with embossed books. I tilted my head back to observe a glass ceiling through which the red skylight filtered, illuminating floor after floor of overflowing shelves.

A large circular desk at the center of the library was vacant, and the first floor appeared to be void of people. I walked along the first few stacks, trying to decipher the language written on the spines of each book. Some were in Old Revekkian, which I did not know how to read but could identify by the older characters and accents over certain letters. I spent a while looking for familiar words among the titles and gathered that many of these books were myths and history.

A noise suddenly drew my attention upward. It

sounded like a book had fallen to the floor, or several. I followed it up a crescent of stairs that wound to the second floor.

"Lothian?" I called.

Different noises followed my ascent to the second floor—groaning and moaning and a steady thud. As I came around a corner, I found the source. A man had Lothian pinned against the shelves and was moving inside him, their moans echoing throughout the library. For a moment, I was too stunned to move, watching as the man, who was only slightly taller and just as thin as Lothian, pounded into him. Then he took a tuft of Lothian's dark hair into his hand, pulled back his head, and bit down on his neck.

I fled to the first floor, unsure of what to do. I didn't want to leave, so I continued my exploration, endeavoring to ignore the sounds from above. I discovered a line of glass cases amid the stacks, each displaying a different artifact. One held two different knives, one white and one black, each engraved with the phases of the moon. Another held a gold chalice inlaid with fine filigree and small rubies. A third box contained a stave, which looked more like a weapon with a piece of pointed bone bound to its tip. The final case held a book so worn, the letters were barely readable, but as I shifted, a faint silver sheen spelled the title—*The Book of Dis*.

It was a spell book.

I wasn't sure what it was about being so close to one that made my heart beat out of my chest, but I was suddenly frightened. I thought of the crimson mist and Ravena. Why would we so publicly display a book from which evil might spread?

"What do you think of my library?" Lothian asked.

I looked up, watching him approach. He was surprisingly composed after what I had witnessed in the stacks upstairs. His dark hair was smoothed back, and the high collar of his black and silver tunic hid the bite I knew he had sustained.

"It is very beautiful," I said.

"I see you have found a few of our relics," he said.

"These all belonged to witches?" I asked.

"They belonged to members of High Coven," he said and nodded to the spell book. "We believe *The Book of Dis* belonged to Karmina, their leader. It's blank."

"Blank?"

He nodded. "We believe it is either a replica or a book of spells she intended to write."

"Even blank, do you not think it is dangerous to display such items?"

Lothian hesitated, but he was saved from answering as another man approached—the vampire who had fed from him. He was dressed similarly, in black. His hair was curly and stuck to his forehead, and his thin, pale face made his cheekbones look hollow and his eyes dark.

"These relics give us access to our history," the man said. "We display them so that we—and others—might learn from them."

Still, I wondered if magic was the type of thing we wanted people to learn about.

As if he could read my mind, he added, "Secrets only make the world curious. Better to display than to hide."

"Your Majesty," Lothian said. "Allow me to introduce you to Zann."

270

The vampire swept into a graceful bow. As he straightened, his cheeks flushed.

"A pleasure," I said.

"Zann is an archivist," Lothian explained. "Recently, he has been busy overseeing the collection and maintenance of items sourced from the ruins of Jola and Siva."

I flinched. "What will you do with those materials?" I asked.

"King Adrian is in talks with ambassadors from each House. He would prefer preserving the history, of course, unlike previous kings."

I knew he spoke of Dragos, but I also knew he was referring to what he saw as the inaccurate history of the Nine Houses.

"And what of the old history remains?" I asked.

"Nothing," Lothian said. "All we have is what has been written within the last two hundred years. Anything that came before that was burned with the witches, including spell books...minus, of course, this book, which can hardly be called a spell book but more of a...journal."

"A travesty," Zann said, and I looked at him questioningly.

"Why a travesty? Are those not dangerous in the wrong hands?"

I thought of the attacks on the villages, the way average mortals were turned into killers with a string of words that had some kind of power behind them. It was frightening.

"Of course," he said. "But anything can become a weapon in the wrong hands, even people. The truth remains that our world suffered far less when magic was present. There were fewer droughts, less hunger, and more peace."

I narrowed my eyes.

"Were you alive then? When the High Coven oversaw magic?"

"No," Zann replied. "I was born much later, but I am an archivist, which means I have read many accounts of that era."

"Could I read those accounts?"

"Of course," Zann said.

"While you find those volumes, I will take the queen on a tour," Lothian said.

"Perfect. I will meet you in the great room," Zann said, and we watched his lithe form retreat into the back of the stacks.

Once he was gone, I looked at Lothian. "Are you... his vassal?"

He cleared his throat. "Yes. We are...a new pairing. I think it's going well."

I resisted the urge to smile as he began his tour on the first floor.

"This is the original library. The first king of Revekka only had a few dusty volumes that amounted to a work journal and ledger. It was his brother who began the first collection."

"Who expanded the library beyond the first floor?"

"King Adrian," Lothian replied.

"To make room for his spoils?" I asked.

"If that is how you choose to see it," Lothian said. "But we have been tasked with preserving them, and when the countries rebuild, we will go in and craft their libraries."

Well, that was something.

The second floor was dedicated to biographies, poems, plays, and fictional stories gathered from countries across Cordova and the islands.

"Do you have anything from the Atoll of Nalani?" I asked, hopeful.

I knew very little of my mother's home country, only that when people saw the color of my skin, they knew I was part islander. One of the things I mourned along with her was the loss of her culture. I resented knowing nothing of their traditions and always wondered if my love for the sun came from her. My father refused to discuss it with me, saying it was too painful for him.

"I will look for you," Lothian promised. "And if not, I will secure as many items as possible."

It was the third floor that held most of my interest as it was dedicated to the history of Revekka.

There were rows of black-bound books and rows of red ones.

"The black are histories from the Dark Era, the red are from other countries."

Lothian led me to the great room. The far wall was made up of floor-to-ceiling windows; the ceilings were high and crowned with carved crossbeams, and lit sconces ran the length of the room on either side. A large rectangular table took up most of the space, and it was there that Zann stood with a series of stacked books and loose papers.

"Much of what you will find here are personal journals of common folk who lived during the Burning," Zann explained. "It is a unique perspective. One, I imagine, many who live south of us are not aware of."

"How did you come by these?" I asked, pulling a loose piece of parchment toward me. The writing was spidery—long loops and pointed lines.

"When the Burning began, items that professed criticism of Dragos were considered propaganda. Anyone caught with such items was accused of sorcery and killed, so the people of Revekka began to hide their journals however they could—within the brick of their fireplaces, buried in their gardens."

"Dragos's campaign against witches was mostly just an excuse to murder his enemies," said Lothian.

It took me a moment to make out the letters on the page I'd pulled toward me, but soon my eyes adjusted and I read:

*Dragos's witch held another Reaping today. She claims to possess no magic and yet professes to sense it in others. Today, she pointed to anyone who accused her of witchcraft, and they were all burned in the square. These are dark times.*

I looked at Lothian and Zann.

"Dragos's witch?" I asked. "Ravena?"

"Yes," said Zann. "She was excommunicated from High Coven for her support of Dragos's agenda. Of course, when it came to the Burning, he protected her."

I was not so surprised now that Adrian had made it his mission to find her.

Zann took me through a stack of items he'd pulled from his archives, organizing information by type. Most of them were journal entries and letters, and some were sketches depicting momentous events like the first night of the Burning. I found it horrific, maybe because I feared fire so much, but the series of images before me were ones from which I could feel the terror, woman after woman bound and burned at the stake. I knew from what I had already learned that there were thirteen members of High Coven, but here there were only twelve drawings.

"Someone is missing," I said.

Lothian looked over my shoulder. "Ah, yes. Yesenia of Aroth. Dragos blamed her for the High Coven's insubordination, so he forced her to watch each member of her coven die. She was last."

"Was she their leader?" I asked.

"No, but she was appointed by High Coven as his court advisor," said Lothian.

"I thought Ravena was," I said, confused.

"She came after Yesenia was imprisoned. To the public, she claimed to have the ability to identify witches by sight, which meant she condemned anyone she did not like. She was truly evil."

"Why was Yesenia imprisoned?" I asked.

"She was also said to be a powerful seer, though Dragos did not like what she foretold."

"What did she foretell?"

"His downfall," he answered. "Here she is."

Lothian handed me another sketch, and I was startled both by this woman's beauty and the lifelike way she was portrayed. She appeared to have dark features and darker skin. Her hair was long and black and her eyes matched, though they gleamed with a liveliness that felt a little unsettling given that this was a drawing made in charcoal.

She did not look evil, and as my eyes shifted back to the depiction of the first night of the Burning, I could only think about the terror she must have felt, watching twelve of her own perish and knowing that was her fate.

I learned more about High Coven. In particular, the names of the other twelve members. Each of them had a strength ranging from Yesenia's gift of prophecy to manifestation, mediumship, healing, or shapeshifting. There were others too, powers I'd never heard of, like binding, which was the ability to take away someone's magic, and bilocation, the ability to be in two places at once, and portal magic, the ability to create gateways to other places out of objects or from thin air. In addition to their specialization, each member of High Coven was responsible for their own minor covens.

Among the items Zann had brought were detailed notes from High Coven's meetings, which itemized the issues they were presented with. In one instance, a terrible plague hit the northern part of Revekka. Ginerva, the healer, put forth a proposal to send her covens into the territory to perform spells to prevent the spread and heal those affected, but before it could even be considered, Yesenia was made to read the timelines and determine if High Coven could even interfere. Some things, it said, were by divine order. After Yesenia approved the measure, the coven set about establishing rules, namely that Odessa, the necromancer, was not allowed to reawaken any of those who had already passed, and Ginerva would be prevented from healing anyone who was fated to die, which required the skills of Yesenia's coven.

I was beginning to see how they worked to care for

their people, and I stayed, continuing to read until my eyes grew weary.

"How often may I return to read?" I asked before departing.

"As often as you wish, my queen," said Lothian. "This is your library, and I am your librarian."

"I knew I would not regret dancing with you," I said, grinning.

"That makes one of us," Lothian said.

We laughed, and I realized it was one of the few times I'd done so since I'd arrived at the Red Palace.

———

I could not sleep.

As tired as my eyes had been when leaving the library, I was now wide awake—or rather, my body was. I wasn't sure what it was about this room or this bed or the person I'd become since I'd met Adrian, but I could hardly think about anything other than him. And this time, it wasn't just thoughts of his body against mine that kept my mind going—it was every subtle nuance of our time together. It was the way he'd said my name, that he'd said my name at all, desperate for me to hear whatever he wasn't saying. It was the way he trusted me to take on my role as queen without really knowing who I was as a princess or a person.

It was how he kissed me.

Like he possessed a true, unnatural passion for me that I could somehow match, and I did not know why. I reasoned that I felt this way because of all that had transpired since leaving Lara. My people had betrayed me and attempted to overthrow my father, and despite once understanding their fear and anger, the more I learned about the Burning, the less I could excuse their behavior. Not that I'd been able to really forgive them before; they had reduced my sacrifice down to nothing, just as Killian had. *Did he fuck you the way you wanted?* he'd asked.

Once, I'd felt such shame, but no longer.

I'd made my sacrifice, and now my people would live in a world ruled both by me and Adrian, and I was not sorry for it.

I kicked off the blankets and pulled on my robe. If I couldn't sleep, I'd return to the library. I cracked the door and peeked into the hallway. The corridor was empty, except for shadows that danced in tandem with the candle flame. After a few seconds passed with no sign of activity, I slipped out the door, tying off my robe.

I paused at the top of the stairs as the sound of revelry reached me. There was singing, strange growls, and moans. The Burning Rites had begun, and it seemed the celebration continued even into the early morning. I took a few steps down and halted, ducking so that I could assess the risk. Below, the tall windows were full of flickering fire that looked more red than orange as it was filtered through the glass. The doors to the front of the castle were wide open, giving me a view of the courtyard where a fire raged and people danced. The air was heavy with the scent of flesh and blood and smoke, tinged with spice and resin.

Even from this distance, I could see bodies before the fire—a woman taking a man into her mouth, a man taking another into his. There were others too, engaging in various sexual acts, and some who embraced in the same manner I'd watched Adrian hold Safira, and I knew they were drinking each other's blood.

If the act was so sacred, why was it being performed in public, I wondered. Then again, I'd always thought of sex as a private act, and yet among these people, it seemed to be a form of entertainment.

Then I caught sight of Adrian, who stood with Safira on his arm.

A rush of jealousy thickened the blood in my veins. Had he sought his vassal since I'd sent him away? Had he partaken of her blood against my wishes? There was an undercurrent to my jealousy, a strange feeling that held on to my heart. I did not want to put a name to it, because acknowledging that this...*hurt*...was ridiculous. How could I, a human princess of the Nine Houses, feel hurt that a vampire would betray me?

I ground my teeth and tamped down the pain. I would not let him have that kind of control over me. I rose to my feet, renewed in my mission to explore the library and discover more from Adrian's past. I descended the stairs, racing into the adjoining corridor before anyone spotted me from the open doors, except that just as I was about to round the corner, I caught sight of Daroc and Sorin. I wasn't sure what was happening, but neither one of them looked pleased. Daroc leaned close, a finger pointed in Sorin's face, whose jaw was set so tight, I could see it popping. Whatever words were being exchanged, I could not hear them, but I sensed I had stumbled into a fight.

I took my chance and darted across the hall as I tried to retrace the path I'd taken with Miha earlier, but the hallways branched off in so many directions, I was not exactly sure I'd taken the right way. I got halfway down one hall and turned around, feeling as though I'd gone the wrong direction.

The next route I took seemed even more wrong. The walls were intermittently recessed, and while I'd originally thought I was alone, I soon found out I was not and that some of the alcoves were occupied. A man had a woman pressed against the wall. His hand was around her neck, his mouth there too. Blood dripped down her skin. I watched her for a moment—eyes closed, lips parted, body arched into his—she was lost. Farther down, a woman openly fucked another with her fingers. I was not appalled so much as uncomfortable. What was the purpose of this exhibitionism? Were others meant to watch or mind their business?

I chose the latter, quickly turning another corner only to pause and stare at a series of portraits. They were paintings of beautiful women dressed in black. There was an insignia on their breasts, a twelve-spoked wheel, crowned with a different image. As I studied each portrait, I noticed the wheel turned, which meant a different symbol crowned each wheel.

This was High Coven, I realized, and the symbols communicated their power.

I lingered before each picture longer than I should have, given that Adrian had advised me not to leave my rooms, but they made me curious. Some were young, others were old, and most were in-between. Some looked like me, and I wondered if their ancestors were islanders. Others were pale, like mountain folk, but the woman who drew my gaze was the one whose portrait hung at the very end of the hallway where the corridor split in two. I recognized her because of her eyes—Yesenia.

She had strange-colored eyes, a shade that appeared both violet and blue. They were fringed with thick lashes that cast a shadow upon her cheekbones. Her hair was thick and dark, pinned back, which only served to sharpen the structure of her face. Her lips hinted at a smile, and her skin was a warm brown that made me think she'd lived beneath the sun. She was beautiful, her expression peaceful. It was a feeling I could relate to, a feeling I wanted to recapture—one that I had known before I'd discovered this world was so harsh.

Again, my eyes fell to the symbol on her robes. The symbol that topped her wheel was an eye, the symbol for prophecy. Had she known her life would end in smoke and flame? What a horrible gift, to know one's death.

I turned, eyes sweeping the walls again, recalling the names I'd learned earlier. I had never truly seen the members of High Coven as people, but here they were—beautiful and serene and real, not at all violent or wild as I had imagined. They were...like me.

"I see you have found the portraits of High Coven," a voice said.

I pivoted to find Gesalac watching from a distance, and I shuddered, wondering how long he had been there before he'd spoken. I turned fully, staring, hoping he would not linger. Had he hoped to corner me?

After a moment, he bowed his head.

"Queen Isolde," he said, dark eyes meeting mine once again. "It is late to be outside your chamber."

"And yet the halls are full of people," I said.

"Vampires," he corrected. *Predators*, I thought he might be saying.

"Who have learned the consequences of not leaving me alone."

I expected Gesalac to show his anger, but his expression remained the same, though that wasn't much better.

"Perhaps I can help you find what you are looking for," he offered, and I hesitated, unsure of his motives.

"I can find my own way."

"I understand your fear—"

"I am not afraid of you," I said. "But I do not trust you."

"Likewise, and yet my king killed one of his own for you, a mortal woman he met a week ago. It is any wonder I am angry that my son is dead?"

"Perhaps you should have taught him no means no, but I see where he inherited his inability to listen."

Gesalac's mouth hardened into a thin line.

"I do not wish to be enemies, Queen Isolde," he said. "I rather hoped we could be allies."

"If you are allied with my husband, you are allied with me."

Though I was not so certain he was.

He raised his brow and spoke slowly, deliberately. "Are you allied with your husband, Queen Isolde?"

"What are you suggesting?"

He shrugged. "It is no secret you two are enemies. Unless, of course, you have developed a fondness toward him."

"Do you have a purpose, Noblesse?" I asked, growing impatient and far too uncomfortable.

"I merely wish to caution you about the crimson mist," he said.

"Excuse me?"

He stared, pointedly, and said, "Curious that the mist came so shortly after your marriage. If I were you, I would be wary. Perhaps it is Adrian's way of endearing himself to you."

"What are you suggesting?"

"Well, what better to gain the trust of your enemy than saving her people?"

I started to protest that the crimson mist would only result in my greater hatred for him, but I considered that Gesalac was right. The mist had endeared Adrian to me because of his actions following the discovery at Vaida. He had sent Gavriel, Yeva, and Ciprian to Castle Fiora, and after my people had attempted their revolt, he sent even more soldiers. Still, I did not wish for Gesalac to know that I was considering his words.

"You make a bold claim, Noblesse," I said.

He shrugged. "We are not aware of the breadth of Adrian's powers. Who is to say he is not responsible?"

I stared at the man, and though I did not trust him, I wondered if what he was saying had some truth.

"There you are," Sorin said. "I thought I saw you sneaking around."

Gesalac turned, stepping out of my path as Sorin approached. His handsome face was alight with amusement, but I sensed tension in the air between us.

"Noblesse Gesalac, I'll take it from here."

Gesalac looked from Sorin to me as if he wished to protest, but at last, he bowed, adding before he left, "Careful of where you wander, my queen."

I watched until he had disappeared around the corner.

"By the goddess, I hate that man," Sorin said.

I looked at the vampire. "Where have you been?"

He held up as hands as if to ward off my demand.

"Easy," he said. "I've been busy. Adrian has me on the hunt."

*On the hunt?*

"Have you been searching for Ravena?"

"I have, but I lose every trail," he said. "It's like she's disappearing into thin air."

I raised a brow. "Is that your special power? Tracking?"

"Something like that," he said with a chuckle. "What are you doing out of your rooms?"

"I was heading to the library," I said. "I guess I got lost."

"Did you ever," he said, grinning, his dimples deepening. I liked Sorin's smile. "Come. I'll take you."

I felt far more comfortable with Sorin and accepted his escort.

"How did you know where to find me?" I asked.

"Does the word tracker mean nothing to you?"

I glared at him, and he grinned.

"I saw you sprint down the hall," he said. "You're lucky I distracted Daroc, or you'd be back in your rooms right now."

"Were you...in trouble?" I asked.

"Yes, and not in the good way." As he spoke, his tone shifted, and I heard a note of frustration in his voice.

"What did you do?" I asked as we turned a corner, finding the familiar ebony doors of the library at the end of the hallway.

"It's what I didn't do," Sorin said, coming to a stop. "Or rather that I wasn't where I was supposed to be."

Sorin did not offer any more of an explanation than that, and I thought perhaps it was because he was embarrassed.

I looked at the doors.

"Do you...want to come inside?"

He grinned. "No thanks, my queen. I don't read."

I raised a brow.

"Kidding," he said. "I have a witch to hunt."

Before he left, I called to him. "Sorin."

He halted and faced me.

"If you find anything on Ravena, I want to know."

"I'm sure Adrian will tell you."

"I asked you," I said.

He bowed his head. "Of course, my queen."

I slipped inside the library, lit with low, amber flame.

I was not completely ready to return to the great room where most of my research still waited. Instead, I made my way to the third floor where the histories of the world were shelved. I touched the spines of embossed books, reading the carefully painted titles. There were several volumes of *The History of Cordova*, one for each year since its incarnation by the goddess Asha.

I was about to choose a book on the Burning when I noticed a symbol on the spine of a different book. It was the same twelve-spoked wheel I'd spotted in the paintings of the witches, and it was titled *High Coven*. I took the book from the shelf, and when I opened it, I found that the middle had been carved out, and inside was a knife.

*Strange*, I thought, taking the blade in hand. There was nothing extraordinary about it. In fact, it seemed crudely made; the blade itself was crooked, the handle too small, and yet it was heavy. It would make for an awkward weapon, and I wondered why it was hidden here.

Then my body went rigid, and I spun as two hands landed on either side of my face. A man blocked me with his large body. He seemed familiar somehow, with short, dark hair and a well-trimmed beard and mustache. He did not have any astounding features, but his clothes seemed to make up for that. He wore rich, fur-lined velvet with gold clasps and a crown upon his head that was heavily embellished with jewels.

"Shh," he said and gripped my chin, two ring-encrusted fingers covering my mouth so I could not speak. "You will listen. Your coven will follow my commands, and you will be the one to change their minds, understand?"

I did not know what he was talking about—my coven? Even so, I could feel myself glaring at him.

"And if you do not, I will kill every last one of you. Do you understand? Not just your coven but every witch in this land."

There was silence as the man studied me, and after a moment, he leaned closer, his lips hovering near mine.

"But for you, it will be a different end." His fingers moved from my mouth, and then his lips closed over mine. His kiss was bitter and rough, and as he pushed into my body and his tongue attempted to pry my mouth open with his, I fought him, lashing out with my blade. He staggered back. Pressing a palm to his chest, it came away bloody.

"You little bitch!"

He reached for me and yanked my hair.

"I will kill you," he threatened.

"Kill me then," I said. I spoke the words and felt the relief of them—if he killed me, I would not have to betray myself or my coven, but even he saw the truth of that within my eyes, and his hold relaxed on my hair.

"No," he said. "I think life is a greater punishment for you."

He released me with a jerk, and I fell against the shelf, still clutching my bloodied blade. He glanced at it and laughed.

"Remember what I said."

In the next second, he vanished. I blinked and realized I was alone, standing with the book and knife in my hand, unbloodied. I turned in a circle, my heart still racing from the encounter with the man, but saw no one.

I was truly alone.

I curled my fingers around the knife, wondering if it possessed some kind of enchantment, but if so, what was its purpose? I could not be certain whose mind I'd inhabited, but something inside me knew it was Yesenia. It was the same knowing I'd felt when I'd looked upon Adrian—a strange connection that I could not deny. And I'd just witnessed Dragos, the deceased king of Revekka, threaten her life.

I would have thought I was imagining things if my heart wasn't still racing from the encounter and my hand still shaking.

Suddenly, I questioned just how much knowledge I wanted about the past, because it was turning out that I knew nothing about the world I lived in, and I was angry. Angry because I had not known and angry because the one person who was telling me the truth happened to be my greatest enemy.

# SIXTEEN

**The next day, I was surprised to receive a letter from Nadia.**

"When did this arrive?" I asked Vesna, who was alone while Violeta worked in the kitchens to help with preparations for the Burning Rites feast.

Vesna had come to help me prepare for tonight's hunt, an event Adrian did not yet know I would be attending. My outfit was far more comfortable than anything I'd worn since my arrival in Revekka—a black tunic and leggings which I tucked into knee-high boots of the same color. Over the outfit, I wore a snug jacket that was cut short in the front and longer in the back.

"Just this morning, my queen," she said. "Sorin brought it."

Sorin? Was he traveling to and from Lara while searching for Ravena? I had no idea.

"Would you like some privacy? While you read?"

I smiled at her. "Please, Vesna. Thank you."

I was not sure how I'd respond as I began the letter.

I feared my own emotions at this point. My heart and chest already felt as though they were being crushed by the absence of my father and of Nadia. I wasn't sure what would happen once I saw her handwriting or read her words. There was also a part of me that felt dread— would she blame me for the coup? Would she continue to inquire as to why Adrian was not yet dead?

When Vesna left, I tore open the envelope and unfolded the heavy parchment to find Nadia's familiar handwriting.

*Issi*, she'd written, and I pressed my hand to my mouth to keep from sobbing. No one had called me Issi since I'd left Lara.

*I must admit my surprise when one of the Blood King's soldiers agreed to carry my letter to you. I suppose I should wait until I receive confirmation you have received it to be impressed. Nevertheless, I miss you. Your father misses you. I have never seen him so forlorn. It makes me ever eager for your return. Commander Killian told us of your attack, and I would not have believed it had we not had our own uprising, but, Issi, my dear, it is not as if the whole of Lara feels betrayed. There are many of us who trust your plan and know you have not forgotten your cause. Think often of us, especially your father. He is lost without you.*

*I know you are curious, so I will add only that I have read four books since your departure, and while every page was a delight, they are nothing compared to having you home.*

*I miss you.*

*Nadia*

I read through the letter twice more as a torrent of emotion tore through me. I was caught between a deep sense of guilt and a strange pain borne of my father's sadness. I had not completely abandoned my mission. I was still trying to discover Adrian's past, hoping it would lead to some great revelation, but this was the first time I let myself acknowledge it wasn't with the intention of defeat. I wanted to know him, which seemed even more ridiculous given what Gesalac had suggested last night. What if Adrian really was only trying to win my loyalty by manipulating the crimson mist? Hadn't he told me more than once that he was a monster?

The worst part about it all was that it had almost worked. I had begun to let his kindness and the things I'd learned about High Coven and Dragos overshadow the reality at hand—Adrian was still the conqueror of my people.

I stowed the letter, hiding it beneath the book I'd taken from the library last night. Then I shrugged on my cloak and pulled on my riding gloves.

Tonight, I would hunt.

I left my room and found Adrian and his council of noblesse assembled in the courtyard, scattered around the blazing pyre. I kept my distance, halting at the end of the steps, though I could still feel the heat of the fire on my face. It wasn't until the noblesse began to bow that Adrian turned, eyes sparking at the sight of me.

"My queen," he said. "What are you doing?"

"Joining the hunt," I said.

Behind them, a few of the noblesse laughed.

"Is something funny?" I asked.

Their humor abruptly ended.

"It will be a long night," Adrian said.

"I've had many of those."

His lips twitched, and he handed me Shadow's reins. "Mount up, my queen."

Once I was seated, Adrian followed, and his body pressed heavily into mine. I wasn't sure if it was intentional or if it was because his presence had more force since I'd been distant from him for the last three days. I let out a slow breath to release the tightness in my stomach.

It didn't work.

"Comfortable?" he asked, mouth near my ear.

I turned toward him, a heady flush rushing from my head and into my throat.

"Not a word I would choose," I said.

"Hmm." I felt him hum against my back, and in the next second, he signaled Shadow forward, and we departed through the gates of the Red Palace, into the village of Cel Ceredi, followed by Daroc and the noblesse.

The night was fading, and as we descended, fires raged in the village. Some were from the pyres, but there were others, smaller ones dotting the landscape. As we drew closer, I realized they were villagers holding torches.

"Will they join the hunt?" I asked, recalling how Adrian had instructed the noblesse to light fires around their villages to keep the mist at bay.

"They will watch from the gate," he said.

As we passed them, they joined the crowd, and as we came to the edge of Cel Ceredi, the gates groaned open, parting to reveal a wall of dark woods. As we approached, Adrian drew his arm tightly around my waist, and I realized I'd unconsciously leaned into him.

"It is unlike you to be afraid," he said.

"I am not afraid," I said.

"Am I to assume, then, that you find comfort in my arms?"

There was a note of amusement in his voice. I thought about grinding my ass into his raging erection to prove a point. This wasn't about comfort; it was about the fact that we had not fucked in three days, and I was angry and needy, and I wanted to take my rage out on his body the way we had on our way to Cel Ceredi.

That was where I wanted to be, unwavering in my hatred for my enemy, not here in this space where I hoped he was...*sincere.*

"What are we hunting?" I asked, changing the subject.

"Now that you're here, the question is what will hunt us?"

Right. I was the one with blood worth draining and flesh worth eating.

Adrian guided us into the woods. There was little light, only a muted, haunting red that made the sky look like a storm. Still, Shadow and Adrian navigated well enough. Behind us, the noblesse fanned out, taking their own paths through the woods.

"Sorin says he is hunting for Ravena," I said. "Did you give those orders after Sadovea too?"

"Did you come on this trip to fight with me or to hunt?" he asked.

"Why not both?"

"One or the other, Isolde, but if you choose to fight,

I will take you back to the palace. I will not be distracted out here where you are most at risk."

"Fine," I said, feeling a little silly. "No fighting then."

There was a stretch of silence.

"Sorin has been on Ravena's trail for a while, long before the attacks in Vaida and Sadovea."

"Oh."

Once again, I felt silly, and I wanted to deflect, to find a reason to be justified in my anger despite what Adrian had said about fighting. But then his hand hooked around my head and his lips crashed down upon mine. I groaned at the hunger with which he devoured my mouth, met each thrust of his tongue just as hungrily.

*Yes*, I thought. *This. This is what I want. What I need.*

I hated needing anything, but this, I could not deny, and I wouldn't have stopped if it wasn't for a high-pitched screech that made my blood run cold.

"What was that?" I asked, pulling away from Adrian's mouth. My lips felt raw from his kiss.

Adrian chuckled. "Just an owl."

"We need to leave."

Owls were an omen of death.

It was one of few beliefs my father had carried with him from my mother's culture because he had seen it—carriages overturned or attacked, squadrons wiped out, all moments after an owl crossed their path.

The hysteria in my voice must have convinced him, because his body went rigid against mine. "Okay."

But as the word left his mouth, Shadow began to neigh and shiver. Adrian held tight on the reins just as a creature came out of the tree line. It was tall and thin with nails that were long and sharp, covered in blood.

Its hair was wet and stringy, shielding a face of overly expressive features, including a wide mouth full of sharp teeth.

It was an alp, no doubt drawn to us because of Shadow, who sensed the danger.

"Isolde," Adrian said. "Take the reins and go back to the castle."

I did as he instructed, and he slid off Shadow's back, landing soundlessly on the ground. Adrian took a few steps toward the monster, but the creature did not take its eyes off me.

"This will not end well for you," Adrian said, drawing his blade.

The alp hissed, wiggling its sharp claws, and without so much as a warning, it launched itself at me.

Shadow bucked, neighing wildly before darting into the darkness of the trees, his fear keeping him moving forward. All the while, branches whipped my face, arms, and legs. I pressed my thighs into his side and pulled the reins, but nothing seemed to slow him down, so I dropped one rein and gripped the other in my hands, pulling it toward my hip. Just as Shadow started to slow, he bucked, and as I hit the ground, he darted away. The impact of my fall stole my breath, and I lay there for a moment, fighting dizziness and a sudden pain in my ribs, until I noticed something out of the corner of my eye.

I rolled and looked up into the face of the ginger-haired woman whom I'd seen in the reflection of the window and the hall of mirrors.

"It's you," I said, choking on a painful breath as I rose to my feet. "You're Ravena, aren't you?"

I kept one hand around my waist, but I was already

thinking of how I might bring her down. I only had my knives, which meant I'd need to get close to her—too close.

"Clever little bird," she said. "Though you always were."

My brows furrowed, confused by her words.

Her eyes narrowed, and it made her look critical and cold.

"So it hasn't happened yet."

She spoke more to herself than me. Still, I could not help asking, "What are you talking about?"

"Adrian," she said. "He has yet to partake of your blood."

I did not answer her, though I wondered what that had to do with her. But it wasn't a question I was willing to ask her. She was a different kind of enemy, and I felt like any information she might glean from me would lead to devastation.

Then she laughed.

"It is good that you have not changed much," she said. "Same stubborn countenance, same obvious weaknesses."

"What do you know about my weaknesses?" I asked, and as she answered, I worked to free one of the blades at my wrist. I'd prefer to attack her from a distance, uncertain of what kind of harm she might inflict once she had her hands on me.

"I know a lot about you, Issi," she said, and I flinched at her words. "Tell me how conflicted you are between the love you have for your father and the love you have for Adrian."

Once again, I did not speak, and as the knife came free into my palm, it bit into my skin.

*Fuck.*

I flinched, and Ravena's eyes shifted to my hand. A cruel smile spread across her face.

"Oh good," she said. "You are armed. You'll need it."

I reared back and threw my blade. It cut through the air toward her, but just as it was about to hit its mark—the very center of her chest—she vanished, and in her place was a familiar face, a noblesse.

"Ciro," I breathed his name in shock as the knife lodged in his chest. Where had he come from? I thought he was still in Zenovia, but I soon noticed something was wrong. The noblesse was disheveled and dirty, and his mouth, chin, and the front of his robes were covered in thick, crimson blood. He had been feeding.

"Ciro," I said his name again as he stared, motionless, at the blade jutting from his chest.

My voice drew his gaze, and I wished I'd stayed silent.

As soon as his eyes met mine, I knew I was in trouble. He squatted on the ground and then lunged.

*Fuck, fuck, fuck.*

He had been possessed by the mist. I was certain of it.

I managed to dodge his attack, only to feel his clawed hands grip the back of my neck as he twisted to reach for me, and his touched burned. There was nothing I could do against his sheer strength. He lifted me up and tossed me. I landed on the ground, my back cracking against a tree.

I groaned, already feeling tears stain my cheeks. I'd never felt such pain, and yet I moved. I had no choice. I rolled onto my hands and knees, and as I got to my feet, Ciro gripped my throat, lifting me off the ground. Though his touch was like fire and my vision blurred, I still managed to shove my remaining blade into his neck. I tried to cut through the bone and sever his head, but he released me too soon, and I fell to the ground once more, choking and gagging.

I drew in ragged breaths and stood once more, shaking. I watched as Ciro now pulled the blade from his chest. I guess I'd taught whatever possessed him how to use a weapon, and as his dead eyes met mine, he lifted the knife, but before he could strike a fatal blow, something swooped down between us—a bird that transformed into a person.

"Sorin," I breathed as the vampire manifested, his back to me. All I saw were his powerful muscles working as he swung his blade and beheaded the noblesse who had nearly killed me. As Ciro's body fell to the ground, my legs gave out.

"No, you don't," Sorin said, catching me before I hit.

I stared up at his face, but the dizziness forced me to close my eyes.

I groaned.

"Please don't tell me you can transform into an owl," I said.

I heard him laugh, but it was a distant sound, as if he were in a cavern.

"Not an owl, my queen," he answered quietly. "A falcon."

I remembered nothing more after that.

———

I woke with my swollen face pressed into the cold, stone floor of a cell.

It took me several moments to gather the strength

to lift myself into a sitting position, and even as I did, the ache in my jaw made me light-headed. I wanted to vomit but held it in; opening my mouth would just make everything worse.

I squinted into the darkness and made out the faint, crumpled outline of Adrian.

"No," I whispered.

He lay on his stomach, hands bound behind his back. He was just out of reach within a cell beside my own. I crawled to him, body shaking, having no energy to expend for breath, much less movement. Still, I managed to reach the bars and used them to pull myself closer, slipping my hand between them. I brushed my fingers over a lock of his hair.

"Adrian." I whispered his name, broken and full of the blood pooling in my mouth.

He did not wake for a long time, but I sat there and stroked the piece of hair I could reach, and when he finally stirred, I began to cry.

I tried to say his name again, but he stopped me.

"Shh," he soothed. "I know, my sweet. You cannot help who you are, and I cannot help who I love."

I jerked awake, inhaling a sharp breath as if I'd just come up for air. My skin was covered in a thin sheen of sweat, making my shift stick to me. I threw off my blankets and then fell back into my pillow.

"I'm safe," I told myself. "It was a dream. Just a dream."

But it had felt so real—the cold, rough stone against my skin, the pain and the thick blood in my mouth, the feel of Adrian's hair against my bruised fingers.

Even now I could feel the claws of guilt twisting in

my chest, because though I did not know how, Adrian had been in that cell because of me.

Now that I was awake, I realized I was also alone.

I sat up again, placing my feet on the floor, taking inventory of my body. I thought I'd bruised my ribs when I'd fallen off Shadow, but I was certain they'd broken when Ciro had thrown me against that tree. Now I felt little pain, just an ache. I touched my neck where the noblesse had gripped me and swallowed without discomfort.

I'd been healed.

I wondered if it had been Adrian's doing, since Ana used traditional healing methods. And if so, where was he now? What about Ana? I'd at least expected to wake up and find her sitting with me, but perhaps Isla had returned. Had Shadow been found after he'd darted away into the woods?

I had so many questions.

I rose to my feet and pulled on my robe. I tried to force away the hurt I felt at waking alone, at discovering that Sorin was a shape-shifter. Did Adrian not care for me? Did Sorin not trust me? I paced my room, reasoning that it was ridiculous to feel this way. Adrian had not waited for me to wake up because I was fine, and Sorin had no reason to trust me because I did not trust him... did I?

I growled in frustration just as a knock erupted at the door, sending my heart into a frenzy.

*Adrian,* I thought and raced to the door, only to find Lothian on the other side.

"Are you well, my queen?" he asked, and I knew he'd witnessed Sorin bringing me here.

"I am…as well as can be expected," I answered. "What can I do for you?"

"I have news about your mother's homeland," he said. "May I come in?"

"Of course." I stepped aside and closed the door quietly behind him. Lothian crossed to the middle of the room, turning to look at me.

"I fear I do not have good news."

*Just tell me*, I wanted to yell as a chasm opened in my chest, far larger than the one made by Adrian's absence.

"Go on," I implored.

"I could not locate any texts on your mother's people, mostly because their history is told orally. I thought to reach out to some of the elders there, but—"

"Lothian," I said. "Get to the point."

"They're enslaved. All of them," he said. "By King Gheroghe of Vela."

# SEVENTEEN

**If Lothian said anything after that, I did not hear it.**

I felt a surge of adrenaline, and at the same time, I felt sick.

And to think King Gheroghe had been *here*. He'd attempted to barter with Adrian for immortality—with the promise of my people. I could have killed him then. I could have liberated my people.

My body shook with rage.

Had Adrian known? Had he said nothing?

I turned from Lothian, tore open the door, and ran for Adrian's quarters.

"Out of my way!" I commanded as I raced down the halls, packed with servants, vampires, and their vassals.

I could not imagine how I looked, but I felt wild and angry, and when I arrived at Adrian's door, I threw them open, only to find Safira in his bed—one I had yet to occupy.

She was sitting up, naked and bent so that her breasts

were peaked. With most of her weight on one arm, she trailed the other along her raised leg. Her golden hair, unbound, teased her arm in gentle waves.

Obviously, she expected another visitor.

"Where is my husband?" I demanded, my fury rocketing.

She flinched but swallowed her fear. "Shouldn't you know? You are his wife," Safira retorted.

My hands clenched at my sides, and I wished I'd brought my knife. Still, even as I took a step toward her, she shrank back against the headboard, and I felt a small bit of satisfaction knowing she was afraid of me.

"I am his wife, which begs the question—why are you in his bed?"

It was another slap in the face—waking alone after being nearly killed, and now this? If he truly knew about my mother's people, I would never forgive him.

She laughed, a haughty sound that made me want to shatter her teeth.

"I have warmed it for three nights," she replied smugly, as if it were gossip to spread.

There was a part of me that did not believe her because I wanted to believe Adrian. I wanted to trust him. Then again, I was no fool. There were few men who would decline what Safira offered, but all I cared about was that my husband had.

"Don't take it personally, my queen. It would be impossible for one woman to fulfill every one of Adrian's desires. Luckily, many of us are up for the challenge."

"You grossly underestimate me, Safira. Worse, though, is that you have made Adrian into something he isn't."

"And what is that?"

"A god," I replied and left.

I had one guess as to where Adrian might be, and that was with his advisors, likely discussing Ravena's successful corruption of Ciro. I was sure to be an unwelcome presence among the noblesse. Only, I did not care. I flew down the corridors, my feet carrying me as if they were not my own, and burst through the doors of Adrian's council chamber.

He stood at the head of his round table with Daroc on his right, surrounded by what remained of his noblesse. My gaze caught and held Adrian's, and I took two more steps into the room.

"Leave. I wish to speak to my husband."

There was a beat of silence. No one moved, and I thought for a second I would have to repeat myself, or worse, Adrian would not support me in my interruption of whatever this was and force me to leave—a decision that would not bode well for him. But then the room cleared. I held Adrian's gaze as each noblesse passed. Even Daroc's—which was pointed and heavy—did not faze me.

Finally, the door closed behind me.

"To what do I owe the pleasure of your visit?"

I did not even know where to begin.

"Did you know my mother's people were enslaved by King Gheroghe?" I could barely finish the sentence; I was in so much distress. "Those are my aunts and uncles...maybe even my grandparents."

All this time, I'd been left to wonder if they cared about my mother, if they cared that I even existed, but it was possible they did not even know I lived or that my mother had died.

"Isolde—"

"Did you know?" My scream was so loud, my voice went hoarse.

His silence spoke volumes.

"You bastard!" I said, clenching my jaw so hard, my teeth hurt. Tears blurred my vision.

"What would you have me do?" he countered.

"Free them!" I yelled. "Kill King Gheroghe. Do you not plan to conquer Vela anyway?"

"It is on the list, Isolde, but it is not the priority."

I flinched. "Are you saying I am not your priority?"

"I never said that." He spoke with such reverence, my blood ran cold. "I care about you, far more than you will ever understand, but I can only do so much. I only have so many men. Not to mention I'm concerned about the crimson mist attacking our people."

His words took most of the fight out of me. Still, I rallied.

"Recruit more men," I said.

He tilted his head and his lips twitched. "Are you telling me to turn more people?"

I swallowed hard. I was forgoing all my values. Tonight, I'd asked Adrian to attack a kingdom of the Nine Houses, and I'd asked him to turn mortals into vampires. I'd fallen so low, and I didn't care.

"I understand your anger," he said. "I am not happy with King Gheroghe either. Even if he had something I valued, I would not offer him immortality for his crimes. His end will come, and it will be by your hand...if you are willing to act as a queen."

"And how does a queen act?" I asked, fury still coursing through me.

"Everything must be strategic, and nothing can be personal until victory is near. Do you understand?"

He was telling me we had to plan. He was telling me I had to wait to free my mother's people—*my* people. Could I handle the guilt of my own freedom? Of my own privilege?

"Everyone will want your sacrifice, Isolde. Be mindful who gets it."

"Who gets yours?"

"Do you really need to ask?" he said, his voice quiet.

I did need to ask, because he'd left me to wake up alone, because when I'd gone in search of him, I'd found Safira instead.

"I just came from your room," I said, and Adrian's brows rose, more curious than alarmed.

"And what were you doing there?"

"Looking for you," I answered. "But do you know what I found instead?" I could not even wait for him to answer, I was so angry all over again. "Safira. Naked. In your bed. She claims to have been there the last three nights."

Adrian stiffened. "And you believe this?"

"You do not get to ask me what I believe or do not believe at this point, Your Majesty. You get to explain. Now."

Asking for an explanation did not mean I did not trust him, but I deserved one all the same. Especially considering all he'd kept from me. He stared at me for a long moment, and I wondered if he was reading my mind. Were my emotions strong enough? Were they too chaotic for him to decide what to focus on? After a moment, he moved from behind the table, and on his way past me, he said, "I will do more than explain."

He strolled out of the council room, shoving the doors open with a loud bang. I followed, unflinching, noting his stiff shoulders and clenched hands.

"Daroc, I require your assistance," he said without halting his stride. His second-in-command had waited outside the room, and I wondered if he'd been eavesdropping. He scrambled after us, glancing at me.

Adrian moved so quick, I could barely keep up. His people—those I'd had to command to get out of my way earlier—moved to the side for him, and I did not know if it was out of fear or respect. Either way, it stung in a way that made me want to incinerate this whole castle.

As we approached his chambers, Adrian ordered Daroc to remain stationed outside while he flung open the doors.

"Get up!" he snapped as he entered. I followed behind him and watched as Safira scrambled to her feet, dragging Adrian's sheet with her as she held it to her chest.

"My lord—I only thought—"

"Silence," he commanded, and her mouth shut, her face paled.

Adrian turned to me then and held out his hand. It took me only a second to accept.

"I've been informed that you are suggesting I've been disloyal to my wife," Adrian said.

Safira gave a nervous laugh. "Her Majesty misunderstood. I was only speaking of our past—"

I stiffened, angered by her suggestion that this was just a misunderstanding. But Adrian squeezed my hand, and the movement was strangely reassuring. It told me he believed me. A little of my anger receded.

"Are you saying my wife is a liar?" Adrian asked. Even I was unsettled by the tone of his voice.

Safira's eyes widened.

"Of course not, Your Majesty. I am saying this has all really been greatly exaggerated."

"I see. If that is the case, you will think my punishment is most severe. Daroc," Adrian called, and the commander entered. "Escort Safira to the dungeons."

Safira backed away, bumping into the wall as Daroc approached.

"Adrian, please!" she begged.

"It's only a short while. Why not one day for every night you claimed to sleep with me?"

Daroc yanked the sheet from her hands and grasped her upper arm, dragging her from the room, naked.

"I did not mean any harm," she said, struggling against Daroc's hold. "I beg you." Neither one of us spoke as she was taken, the doors closing on her final, desperate cry. "You can't do this!"

Adrian turned toward me. "Are you reassured by my fidelity?" he asked.

A blush warmed my cheeks. I felt silly for needing this comfort and yet more confident than I'd ever been in his loyalty to me.

"I am sorry that I needed it," I said. "I suppose that's another way I am not acting as a queen, but it seems that everyone in this castle wishes to remind me I was not your first and not sufficient enough to be your last."

"I will be the judge of that," Adrian said, and he tucked a stray piece of hair behind my ear. "I did not intend for you to wake alone."

I felt a sudden rush of embarrassment. "It was selfish," I said. "Of course, you have more important—"

"Nothing is more important than you," he said and brushed his thumb along my lips, sending a shiver of arousal through me. We had been distant for four days, and the whole time, I'd been desperate for him. I only let myself fully acknowledge it now—the way I had wanted him, his body, his reassurance, his mind.

He stared at me with a soft admiration in his eyes. "Need something, Sparrow?" he asked, raising a brow.

"Can you not read minds?" I asked quietly.

"That's not how this works," he said and backed away, sitting in the chair near his desk.

I wanted to chase his warmth, but I stayed where I was, demanding, "What are you doing?"

He shrugged. "Take what you want."

My body literally quaked. I clenched and unclenched my fists.

"I can't fuck you fully clothed."

"Debatable," he said, and a cool smile spread across his lips.

"Sometimes I really do hate you," I said.

"Only sometimes?" he asked, voice quiet, and then he tilted his head to the side. "And right now? Do you hate me?"

I slipped out of my robe and pulled my shift over my head, standing naked before him. His eyes gleamed, but he did not move to touch me.

"No," I answered.

My hands came down upon his shoulders, and I straddled him, taking his mouth against mine. My body was suddenly flooded with feeling. It was a rush that filled every vein and every nerve. My hands wound into his hair, and I ground against his length, buried beneath layers of clothing.

"A truth from me," he said against my lips. "I missed you."

His fingers pressed into my hips. He sat forward, one hand moving between us to capture my breast while his lips left mine to trail my jaw, my throat, and then closed over my nipple. I inhaled between my teeth and grasped his face, holding him there as he lavished my skin. It felt good to be touched—better by him.

I pushed his vest from his shoulders and yanked on his overcoat.

"Take this off!" I demanded, and he chuckled.

"A moment, Sparrow," he said, and I shifted off him. He stood, and I helped him undress, unlacing his pants as he shed his overcoat and tunic. Once his cock sprang free, I grasped it, uncaring that he had yet to completely shed his leggings. He groaned and yanked me forward, tongue devouring as I coaxed beads of come from the tip of his cock with my fist until I pulled away and knelt on the ground.

I held his gaze as I tasted him, his flesh soft and salty beneath my tongue. Before my mouth could close over him, he sat, his hands braced on the arms of his chair.

"I think about your mouth a lot," he said. "The things you say and what you do with it."

"Very few praise me for what I say," I said.

"Perhaps they do not value the truth." He leaned forward just a little, his hand tangling in my hair. "So tell me a truth now—you fear what you feel when you are with me."

I stared at him.

"You first," I whispered.

He smiled. "I have never been afraid of what I feel for you."

I took him into my mouth. It was the only kind of answer I was willing to give at the moment, and Adrian let me. I touched every part of him, tongue sliding beneath the crown of his cock and the veins running down the shaft. My fingers teased his balls, heavy with need. I kept my pace, a slow and steady build, even as he groaned and growled over me. When he came, I kept him there a moment longer, letting the pressure of my lips glide against him until he slipped from my mouth.

He stared at me as I sat between his parted knees, my lips wet from his release.

"Can you handle me?" I asked.

He smiled. "Sparrow, I will take whatever you give."

I rose to my feet and turned, giving Adrian my back, and bent across his desk. He seemed to understand my wordless invitation as his hand parted my flesh, his fingers diving into the silken skin that had grown warm and wet while I'd feasted upon him. The feel of him there was a kind of release all on its own, and I gave a guttural cry. My hands sought his flesh and landed on one of his thighs. Adrian did not seem to mind, spending a few more moments inside me before he pulled his fingers out and sat, guiding me down upon his cock. He was engorged, and as he slid inside, I felt every rise and dip of his shaft.

"Yes," he hissed, shifting me closer to him, sealing my back to his chest as I began to move. His hands gave attention to my breasts, squeezing and kneading. It wasn't until he shifted to tease my clit that I needed to anchor myself again, moving my legs on either side of his. It gave me greater purchase, and I rocked harder and faster, turning my head toward his. Our mouths collided in a messy, hard kiss. Our bodies were slick, and there was a heat between us that warmed my cheeks and exploded in the pit of my stomach. When I could no longer move, Adrian gathered me into his arms and deposited me on the bed. He hovered over me, breathing hard, pieces of his long, blond hair sticking together in sweaty clumps.

"Are you all right?" he asked.

"More than," I replied, quiet and sated.

He stared down at me, smoothing my hair from my face.

"Just when I think you could not get any more beautiful."

It seemed that he had more to say, but he remained quiet, only tracing my face lightly with his fingertip.

He had positioned us in the same manner the night I'd asked him to leave—when I'd felt too close to him and had wanted distance. My legs were bent, his length pressed into my bottom. I might have let him have this position, but tonight, I felt like being in control.

I placed my hands upon his forearms and guided him to his back, pinning him beneath me. I was tired, but I liked the feel of him under me, liked the way my hands splayed across his chest.

"What do you want, wife?" Adrian asked, staring up at me with heat in his eyes.

"The women of your court took pleasure in telling me how you fuck," I said, and I reached between us for his cock, guiding it to my heat. "As if I did not know."

I impaled myself upon him, tilting my head back until I was completely filled. Only then did I meet his gaze, and as I spoke, I bent to press a kiss to his chest. "The next time they look at you, I want them to see your lust for me in your eyes."

We moved together until I could not move at all, until all I could do was cling to Adrian as he moved for both of us. We stared at each other, our breaths mingling until he closed the space between us and kissed me—deep and bruising and languid. When he pulled away, he whispered, breathless, "Come for me."

His thrusts grew harder, rougher, and they took me over the edge. Not long after, he followed.

We lay together in silence for a long while before Adrian spoke. "I feared I had truly hurt you," he said.

He did not need to give any more details. I already knew what he meant—the night I'd asked him to leave my room without explanation.

"No," I said, and nothing more. I trailed my fingers along his chest, over raised scars that nipped at his sides.

"Lothian tells me you have enjoyed the library," he said.

"Yes."

"What have you learned?"

"Things that scare me," I said.

"Do you mean that you have learned the truth?" he asked.

I spent a few moments tracing his skin and then looked at him, my chin resting on my hands. "Lothian and Zann introduced me to letters and journals from people who had lived during Dragos's reign. I did not know."

There was something hopeful in Adrian's eyes as he stared at me, and he lifted his hand to brush his thumb against my cheek.

"You know now," he said.

"Ravena does not make it easy to trust magic," I said and paused. "I saw her in the woods."

Beneath me, Adrian stiffened. "What did she say?"

"Nonsense." Even now, I tried to recall her words, but they escaped me. I'd been too focused on planning how I was going to kill her for any of them to stick. "What did you do to her?"

"I only took what she stole from me," he said.

"And what was that?"

"A future."

I had more questions and more things to tell Adrian, like how I'd also seen Ravena in the window at Sadovea and in the hall of mirrors, but a knock at the door interrupted us.

"Not now," Adrian called.

"Your Majesty, it's urgent," Daroc said from the other side of the door.

We exchanged a look, and I pushed off him, dragging the blanket up to my chest.

"Enter."

There was a click as the door opened, and Daroc walked into view. His face remained perfectly stoic as he spoke. "We've had another attack," he said. "At Cel Cera."

# EIGHTEEN

**Dread tore my chest in two—I had heard of Cel Cera** before. It was the home of Ana's vassal.

"Adrian," I said. "Isla was coming back from there."

Adrian looked to Daroc. "Were there any survivors?"

"Not everyone is accounted for," he answered, but that was not a promising sign. It might mean they lived but that they were possessed and were now wandering the woods in search of prey. "Sorin is still searching."

I swallowed hard.

"Send more soldiers," Adrian said. "But only those who fly. They have a better chance of escaping the mist."

I looked at him, surprised. "How many can fly?"

He shrugged. "About thirty or so."

"Are they all falcons?"

"No," he said.

I now wondered just how many times I'd seen a hawk or bat circling in the sky only for it to be a vampire.

"And if we locate anyone infected?" Daroc asked.

"They must be killed," Adrian said.

I felt sick, but I knew Adrian was right. Daroc bowed and left.

"Someone must tell Ana," I said once we were alone.

"I will," Adrian volunteered.

"Let me go with you."

Adrian did not protest, and we rose and dressed quickly. I had never been to Ana's quarters before, but she resided in the upper level of the west tower, and when we knocked on her door, she answered with a smile that dropped instantly.

"No," she said, shaking her head, already guessing why we'd come.

It was Adrian who caught her as she collapsed.

"Ana," he said, explaining the attack and smoothing her hair. Finally, he added, "She may yet live."

And as she sobbed in his arms, she begged. "Do not kill her, Adrian, please."

———

"You look stunning," Vesna said, drawing my attention from the mirror as Violeta finished lacing my gown for tonight's feast, the final night of the Burning Rites. It reminded me of water, twining waves of white and silver that trailed down my body and dragged the floor. The sleeves were long, but the neckline fell off the shoulder, adorned with icy, lace flowers that matched the floral crown atop my head. My hair was pulled to one side, trailing over my shoulder in thick waves. A pair of silvery earrings dangled from my ears, and I stared at them now, thinking of Ana.

We had spent the remainder of the night with her.

She had never stopped crying, never stopped asking Adrian not to kill Isla.

*If she is possessed, let me keep her. I will find a cure.*

And he would answer, *She may yet live, Ana.*

We had left her to sleep and with no news about her lover.

Even now, my eyes burned with her hurt.

As I had watched her, I realized she was living my fear—losing the ones I loved most. Now, I considered how safe my father would be on his journey from Lara here to the Red Palace for my coronation. Adrian had dispatched more guards—but that meant the possibility of more infected vampires.

"Isolde?" Violeta called my name, and I looked at her.

"Hmm?"

"I asked if you were all right," she said. "You look a little...sad."

I cleared my throat and swallowed the tears that had built there. "I am well, thank you."

She did not believe me, but it did not matter. There was nothing to be done about my fear.

"We should go," she said. "We will be late."

But as she rose to her feet, there was a knock at the door.

"Are you expecting a visitor?" Vesna asked.

I shook my head, but then the door opened, and Adrian filled the doorway, a dark shadow that cut through the firelight. Our contrasts were not lost on me. He embodied everything I'd imagined the Blood King to be—a looming darkness, both beautiful and dreadful. I stared at him, and my chest expanded, full of a type of anxiety I did not want to admit. It was the anticipation of his touch, of the words he would whisper in my ear later when we were alone.

"My king," Violeta and Vesna said in unison.

"I wanted a moment with my queen," he said.

"Of course," Violeta said. "We were just leaving."

She reached for Vesna's arm, looping it through her own as they left, and I couldn't help smiling at how comfortable the woman had grown in her time as my lady-in-waiting.

Adrian's eyes darkened as the door closed.

"Sparrow," he said, his voice warming the very bottom of my stomach. He took my hand in his and brushed his lips along my fingers. "You look beautiful."

"You outdid yourself on the gowns," I said. "I have never had such beautiful pieces."

"I only wish to spoil you," he said. "Though you look beautiful in any form—covered in blood or writhing beneath me."

I hated blushing, and here, once again, I was. I swallowed thickly. "How is Ana?"

Adrian's expression changed, growing serious. "Unwell," he said. "But she will be in attendance tonight. She needs the distraction."

My chest tightened.

"Violeta said we were running late. If we linger here too long, we will be very late."

Adrian raised a brow. "Are you eager to be rid of me, my queen?"

"N-no. I mean..." I stumbled across my words, irritated by how flustered I felt. It was made worse by how Adrian smiled at me—kind and gentle. It made his

317

eyes crinkle at the sides, and I felt like I'd been knocked in the chest. I cleared my throat. "You wanted a moment with me?"

"I want you for lifetimes," he said, brushing his knuckles along my cheek. "But I shall be content with now."

I held my breath until he dropped his hand and stepped away. "I want to show you something. Will you come?"

"Of course," I said and followed him out of my room, into the corridor. He took my hand, lacing our fingers. It was different from how we usually walked, and part of me worried that if anyone from home saw this—if my father witnessed us—he would be so disappointed.

Adrian took me into the east wing. It was the tallest part of the castle and happened to also be where the library was located, but we passed those doors, heading down darkened hallways with gilded accents, up flights of stairs until we came to the roof.

Atop the castle, the wind gusted around me. We were up so high, I felt as though I could reach out and touch the clouds, which were rimmed in a red light, casting the whole of Revekka in a strange, crimson-tinged darkness that was both beautiful and haunting. From here, the horizon seemed to stretch for miles in all directions—beyond Cel Ceredi and the Starless Forest to the Golden Sea.

"To the edge," he said, and I hesitated. I wasn't completely sure why, perhaps because there was no rail to hold on to against the wind. Adrian looked down at me and frowned. "I won't let you fall."

I wondered if he took my wavering as a sign that I did not trust him.

But that brought up another thought that was far more disconcerting to me. When had I grown to trust Adrian Aleksandr Vasiliev?

I gripped his arm as we neared the edge, and I looked down over our kingdom, where hundreds of fires burned across the land. I had no idea there were so many. It looked so ominous, as if we were on the cusp of battle and the fires were a mark of how outnumbered we truly were.

"The night High Coven was murdered, the world looked just like this," Adrian said.

I looked at him as he watched the flames consume the night. His eyes looked black, his face harsh. He seemed so cold, the complete opposite of how he had appeared in my room earlier. Whatever he was thinking about had changed him.

"Why do you do this?" I whispered.

"What?"

"Torture yourself with whatever you are reliving while watching this. Adrian..."

"You asked before what motivates me to conquer the world," he said and looked at me. "It's this. Two hundred years ago on this night, I lost everything."

He gave me nothing else, but I understood it all the same. Whatever had happened the night of the Burning had led to his conquest of my home. Normally, I would ask for more, but even I did not wish for him to continue to experience this—whatever this was. I only knew it was horrifying based on what Lothian and Zann had shared.

"Adrian," I said and tugged on his hand, guiding him away from the ledge. Inside, the stairwell was just as dark, and before we could descend, he stopped me and pinned me against the wall. For a moment, I wasn't sure what he intended to do, but then he rested his forehead against mine.

"I miss you," he whispered.

At least that was what I thought I heard, but those words did not make any sense. I was right here. I did not ask him to repeat himself, and we did not speak as we descended stair after stair.

As we entered the great hall, it was to a round of applause, and despite the sound of approval, I could not help feeling that it was not for my benefit. The crowd stared back, full of noblesse and their vassals, guards and palace staff. They were dressed in far finer attire than I'd ever seen them. The women were in satin, silk, and velvet, trimmed in lace and pearls, ribbons and rosettes. The men wore high collars and ruffles, gloves and gold, and they all looked back at me with a mix of approval, longing, and pure, unveiled hatred. I let all of them see me—met each one of their gazes: from Sorin, Lothian, and Zann, to Gesalac, Julian, and Lady Bella.

"Preening, my queen?" Adrian asked, and he looked down at me, a smile touching his lips.

"Are you chiding me?" I asked.

"No, by all means, continue."

He pressed his lips to my temple and then led me to the high table and where Ana and Daroc stood, waiting for us to join before they were seated.

When I saw Ana, I took her hand. "How are you?" I asked, knowing it was a horrible question, knowing there was only one answer.

"Afraid," she said and gave a shuddering breath. Her eyes flicked to Adrian and then back to me. I knew what she wanted—to beg for Isla's life again in hopes that she could find a cure, and I knew what Adrian would say: *She may yet live.*

I hoped, for Ana's sake, she did.

As we sat, I took in the amount of food on the table—dried meats and bread, fruit and cheese. I looked at Adrian questioningly, wondering why there was so much.

"It is for you and the vassals," he said and reached for a carafe. "Wine?"

He poured some into my goblet, and I took it, enjoying the taste on my tongue—a little sweet, mostly bitter. I sipped again and set the cup aside, watching the crowd descend into the heady madness of music and dance and feeding. The doors to the great hall and the front of the castle were open, and I could see into the courtyard where a fire blazed and more people danced. This was a merry contrast to how I'd felt high upon the castle with Adrian, and I thought it strange that this could be both a day of mourning for so many and a day of celebration for the same.

The music reached a crescendo suddenly and dove into a haunting melody. A line of women dressed in black and veiled cut through the crowd. I sat up straighter, a little alarmed.

"What is happening?"

"It is a mourning dance," Ana said. "There are thirteen women, one for each member of High Coven."

The crowd parted, and the women branched off in a circle. Hand in hand, they pushed and pulled upon one another, bodies undulating. One of the women spun into the center of the circle. She danced wildly, beautifully, and when she spun out of the middle, another woman took her place.

I watched, transfixed.

They moved like long shadows, like smoke into the sky, twisting, twining, twirling, their movements attuned to the violence of the music. I had never seen anything like it. I loved it and I also hated it—the way it reached into my chest with claws and pulled all my emotions to the surface. I felt so many things all at once: confusion and shame and sadness. When it was over, the sudden cheers startled me, and I was slow to rise to my feet with the others.

Adrian looked down at me, and he reached out a hand, trailing his fingers over the high part of my cheek.

"Would you dance with me?" he asked.

"Yes," I whispered.

He took my hand, holding it aloft as we made our way to the floor, drawing me against him and guiding us in smooth circles. I held his gaze, my body and brain focused on the feel of him moving with me.

"You enjoyed the performance?" he asked.

"Yes."

I maintained his gaze as he guided me into a spin, and when I came back to him, he held me tighter than before. I'd never imagined dancing with him like this or feeling the way I did now—comforted and safe. And as I looked into his eyes, I recalled a few of the words Ravena had spoken.

*Tell me how conflicted you are between the love you have for your father and the love you have for Adrian.*

I would not call this love, but it was true my feelings had grown far more complicated. And in six days' time, my father would bear witness to it.

Suddenly, I felt sick.

We finished the dance in silence and to great applause, and as we returned to our seats, I took a long drink from my goblet. As the liquid hit my tongue, I knew the bitterness was wrong. I spit the contents out, but it was already too late—whatever was in my cup had taken effect. My head spun, my throat felt tight, and my stomach knotted.

"Isolde?"

I heard Adrian say my name, but I could not focus, and then I was falling.

"Isolde!"

He gripped my arm and jerked me to him. My head fell into the crook of his arm. I could not hold it up, and as his face came into view, the only thing I could focus on was the fierceness of his eyes as he spoke my name.

"Poison," I managed to gasp as his face began to mutate. The whole world was melting. I was too.

"No, no, no," I heard him say, and I thought that he had lowered me to the ground, but I could not be certain because I could not see. "Isolde? Isolde!"

Then Adrian's voice echoed suddenly—a firm, frantic sound. "Daroc! Lock the doors! No one leaves until we discover who poisoned the queen."

I was awake long enough to feel the air swirl around me. It seemed to thicken and darken, like tendrils of smoke, and out of the darkness, once again came Adrian's voice. "Don't leave me."

———

It was so hot.

Scorching.

Sweat pooled on every dip of my skin, in every crease. I thrashed, suffocated by it, by the air, heavy with heat.

*Hush, my sweet.*

A cold hand touched my forehead.

Adrian.

*Hold on to me. I will carry you through.*

I woke, drenched, my vision blurry. I turned my head and found Adrian watching me.

For a moment, I thought he was angry with me. I'd never seen his face carved quite so severely. My brows lowered over my eyes, and I tried to speak his name, but my tongue felt swollen and sour in my mouth.

"Shh," he said, leaning forward, and some of that harshness drained from his face. He placed a cool hand upon my forehead. "Drink this."

He tilted my head, and I drank deeply.

"Not too much," he said. "You will make yourself sick."

I sank into the pillows again, my body weak. My eyes felt like lead and closed of their own accord.

"Sleep," he whispered. "I will be here when you wake."

He pressed a kiss to my forehead.

The next time I opened my eyes, I stared back at Ana.

"You are awake," she said, relief softening her features.

"About time," I heard Sorin say.

"Careful, she might stab you," said Isac.

"We are glad to have you back, my queen," Miha said.

I blinked, attempting to clear my vision and get my bearings. I realized I'd been brought to Adrian's room. Ana sat nearby while Sorin, Isac, and Miha stood apart near the doors as if guarding the entrance.

"Where is Adrian?" I asked.

"He will return shortly," Ana interjected quickly. "Let me help you sit up."

I rose as she stuffed pillows behind my back. I felt dizzy and nauseous, and I recalled how I'd gotten here—someone had poisoned my wine.

"Here, drink this," Ana said, and I was shocked by my own hesitation. "It's all right. Look."

Ana sipped from the container, and when nothing happened, I nodded, and she placed the cup to my lips. It was only water, but as it hit my tongue, I found myself more aware of the metallic taste in my mouth and cringed.

"Was anyone else poisoned?"

"Only your glass," said Sorin.

So I was the target. I was not surprised.

"We will know more soon, now that you are awake," said Ana.

"How long have I been…"

"Three days," Ana said and then she added, hesitantly, "No one's left the banquet hall since Adrian brought you here. Everyone from guards to the noblesse have been locked inside."

Three days?

"What?"

Just then, the door opened, and Adrian appeared, his eyes immediately finding mine. I could not place the expression on his face. It was a harrowing mix of anger and worry and relief, and as he strode toward me, I found myself sitting up higher, wishing to reach for him. Only he bent to me and pressed his lips to my forehead.

"My queen," he said. "How do you feel?"

"Like death," I said.

Adrian frowned but said nothing, and I wondered what words he would say if he chose to speak at this very moment, because the pain and fear written upon his face shocked me.

"Adrian?" I whispered.

"Do you think you are well enough to stand?" he asked.

I frowned. "I...think so."

"We must return to the banquet hall," he said.

My eyes widened. "Now? Why?"

"Because our people must know you are well," he said.

"How do you know they want me alive?"

"Because I want you alive, and my people want what I want," he said. "And those who do not will be eliminated."

I did not doubt his words, but I worried Adrian would make more enemies by defending me. Ana drew the blankets away, and I pushed off the bed, rising to my shaky feet. I was dressed only in a shift, but Ana helped me into a patterned robe that belonged to Adrian. He held me tightly, an arm around my waist.

"Lean on me until we are in the great hall. Once we are inside, I need you to hold your head high for as long as possible. Can you do that?"

I nodded. I knew what he was doing—showing these people I could not be defeated, that I was stronger than the poison in my veins.

We returned to the great hall. Ana walked beside me while Daroc and Sorin led, and Isac and Miha were at our back. When the doors were opened, I pulled away from Adrian and instead held his hand, my grasp tight. My legs still trembled, and the stench of urine and feces was so strong, I almost vomited, but I managed to walk the path with him, passing the gaunt faces of the men and women who had been so jovial three nights prior. They were almost phantoms of themselves. Some had shed their luxurious petticoats and jackets, now wearing the bare minimum in the hot room. Others were covered in blood, a mark that vampires at least had fed while trapped.

Adrian took me to his throne, and I sat without his help, trying not to sag, though I desperately wanted to lie down once more. Despite this, I stayed upright and watched the crowd, wondering who among these people had seen fit to murder me.

Adrian turned and drew his sword.

I realized I had only seen him fight a handful of times—once against my own people and once when he beheaded Zakharov. I wasn't sure why this felt different. Perhaps it was the way he moved—with a predatory purpose that communicated just how angry and betrayed he felt.

"One of you attempted to kill my queen—your queen," he said as he traversed the crowd. "You have committed treason against your king and country, and until I have the name of the one responsible, no one will leave this room."

A grave silence followed, and then someone spoke. "You are mad, Adrian." It was Noblesse Anatoly. "At least let your council go. We would not dare harm our queen."

I did not believe him. I knew the hatred they possessed for Adrian, and I believed that I had somehow made that worse.

"You are not my council because I trust you," Adrian

327

said. "You are my council because you are useful. But you are not irreplaceable."

Anatoly scowled. "Is this woman not irreplaceable? Is she worth losing alliances? She is only a woman, after all. There are hundreds at your beck and call—"

*Like his daughter, Lady Bella*, I thought, my fingers gripping the arms of Adrian's throne.

I expected Adrian to speak, to give some verbal indication that this noblesse had offended him, but instead, Adrian's blade cut through the air, and Anatoly's head slipped from his neck and landed at his feet as the screams of his daughter echoed in the hall.

"What have you done?" Lady Bella shrieked. Her arms were stretched toward her father, fingers splayed, but she did not touch him. She did not seem to know what to do. Over her anguished screams, another man drew his blade and charged Adrian. It was a vampire I did not know or recognize, but I assumed he had some association with Lady Bella.

His strikes were hard but no match for Adrian's strength and speed. Their blades clashed only a few times before the vampire joined Anatoly on the floor.

Lady Bella continued to scream.

"Clean this up," Adrian snapped and then glanced around the room. "A warning for you all before these doors open—you are here by my grace, by my mercy. I can unmake you all."

As his final words fell from his lips, he met my gaze, and I saw the promise in his eyes.

It was then I realized how wrong I'd been about Adrian.

He *was* a god.

# NINETEEN

***Three days later, I felt mostly recovered. Adrian assigned*** a food taster, a man who was brought into the kitchens in chains and made to sample my food and drink my wine under Daroc's supervision. It all felt very surreal, but so had my marriage and the subsequent attack by my people.

This was my life now, I realized.

This was my life forever.

I did not hate it, however. But as the day of my father's arrival and my subsequent coronation drew near, I became more and more anxious. I could honestly say, for once in my life, I did not know how to act. I'd grown so comfortable with Adrian. I liked him despite what he was. I'd grown to appreciate his past, even understand High Coven and despise King Dragos.

I had changed.

But I wasn't sure how to be this person around my father or even if I could. I faced the possibility of distancing myself from Adrian or my father, and that thought made me sick. This wasn't a world where I could have both, even though my father had surrendered to the Blood King, even though I was married to him.

I stood at the entrance of the castle upon the steps, waiting for a glimpse of my father's blue cape and his spotted horse, Elli. I could climb to the top of the castle walls and see farther—at least to the boundaries of the Starless Forest—but I did not want to fight the stairs as I raced to his side. I shifted from foot to foot, restless, worried, unsure of what my father might face on his journey to the Red Palace.

"What troubles you?"

I looked up at Adrian, who stood beside me, dressed in his regal, black robes. He'd pulled some of his hair back, and it exposed the high parts of his face to the light. He was breathtaking—a darkness in this bright courtyard.

"I am just worried for my father," I said.

"Gavriel will take good care of him," Adrian said.

"I know, but I will worry until I see his face."

I looked up as Sorin flew overhead, shifting as he landed in the courtyard below. I took a step down, anxious for information.

"Your father is well," Sorin said. "He is almost within sight."

I stepped beyond him then, to the edge of the courtyard where the trail snaked down the side of the hill into Cel Ceredi. A few seconds passed when my heart thrummed through my whole body, and then I saw my father and I broke wide open. I did not think it was possible to feel such happiness or such relief.

I took off at a run, my legs barely carrying me. I knew when he saw me too, because he set off at a gallop. He dismounted before he got to me and ran the rest of the way, and as we embraced, I sobbed.

I had missed him so much. I hadn't even realized it until this moment.

"My sweet Isolde," he said.

He pushed me away and held my cheeks, his eyes roving over my face. I felt as though he was looking for something, perhaps scars, both physical and mental. Here was the beginning of my guilt, but I quashed that thought by pulling him in for another hug.

"I missed you so much," I said.

"Oh, my gem, you do not know the depth of my sorrow."

Each word chipped away at my heart, and by the time we pulled apart, it sat in the bottom of my stomach in pieces.

It was then I noticed Commander Killian, who stood apart, waiting patiently with the delegation.

"Commander," I said.

"My queen," he said back, bowing his head. I expected his gaze to be a little severe, but instead, he looked genial, and I wondered what he had come to think of the vampires since they'd so often come to Lara's aid as Adrian had promised.

I glanced behind me, up at the Red Palace. "Come. I will show you to the palace."

My father did not remount. Instead, we walked together back to the castle, the delegation following a few paces behind us.

"How was your trip?" I asked, hoping to keep the

conversation light but also curious to know if he had encountered anything unusual.

"Thankfully uneventful," he said.

"How are things in Lara?"

Asking after my home brought more anxiety. I was not certain I wanted to know the truth. Between the uprising and Nadia's letter, I did not know what to expect, and right now, all I could think of were my father's words: *You are the hope of our kingdom.*

But so many things had changed since then. He'd said that before my own people had attacked me, before I'd learned the truth about Dragos and High Coven, before I'd learned that my mother's people were enslaved.

And suddenly I wondered if my father had known about King Gheroghe and Nalani.

*Surely not*, I thought. I hoped.

I would have to ask him later.

"Uneasy," he said. "I am not so surprised. I knew my surrender to the..." He trailed off and then cleared his throat, correcting himself. "I knew my surrender to King Adrian would cause unrest."

My father did not look at me as he spoke, and I found his understanding of the revolt a little unsettling. Still, I did not prod, continuing to keep our conversation companionable until we reached the courtyard, and my father grew silent. I looked in his direction, his eyes settling upon Adrian.

He descended the steps and approached us, placid and composed. "King Henri," he said. "Welcome to the Red Palace."

My father tipped his head back, observing the monstrous structure. "I appreciate the offer to see my daughter and the escort to Revekka, King Adrian," he said. "It is good to see you are well."

I was not certain my father meant the last part, but he was a master at hiding what he truly felt. I had once believed that made him a better king. Now I wasn't so sure.

"Of course," Adrian said and stepped aside, gesturing for us to move into the castle ahead of him.

I requested refreshments be brought up and then escorted my father to his room as Adrian saw to his men.

I had spent so long imagining what it would be like to reunite with my father, I never anticipated that we would have nothing to talk about. But as I sat opposite him in his suite, at a table laden with fresh fruit, bread, and tea, I found I had nothing to say.

"Is Nadia well?" I finally asked.

"Yes, yes," my father replied. "She misses you."

"I miss her," I said, and our conversation trailed off again.

To fill the silence, my father slurped his tea. As he set his cup and saucer down noisily, he asked, "Does he treat you well? The Blood King?"

"Yes," I said without pause. "Yes, of course."

He stared at me for a long moment, and I did not know if it was because he thought I was lying or he did not like my answer. Finally, he dropped his gaze.

"Well," he said, taking a breath. "I think I would like to rest."

"Did you know about Nalani?" I asked. The words had been building in the back of my throat, and I couldn't stop them from spilling out.

He blinked, then looked down.

"Issi—"

"Don't." I stopped him. "How could you look at me every day and not think of the fate of my people? Did you not think I would want to do something?"

"Isolde, those are not your people. You were raised in Lara."

I flinched. "But you married my mother. Did you not promise to protect her people too?"

"I promised to protect her, and I did."

"Did she know what King Gheroghe had done?"

He did not answer.

"You didn't protect her then. You lied to her."

I stared at him and realized what had weighed on me since his arrival—I no longer knew him. And he no longer knew me.

*You will come to find that blood has no bearing on who you become,* Adrian had said before, and he had been right.

I left my father's room in a daze, feeling a keen sense of disappointment and sadness. I could not quite decide how to feel about my father's decision. I tried to rationalize that perhaps he felt as Adrian had. Perhaps the threat of vampires and monsters and protecting his people far outweighed attempting to free my mother's people.

Still, why was I raised knowing nothing of their enslavement? That felt like a betrayal on its own.

I considered returning to my room to rest but decided instead to head into the garden. It had become my place of solace, just as the one in Lara had been, and right now I needed its comfort. As I wandered the worn paths of the garden, I found Adrian lingering near a pool of water. I had not been sure where he would retire while my father was here, and it was the first time I'd encountered him in the garden, though I usually came early in the morning.

He stood, framed by trees and a vine-covered wall looking brilliant beneath the red sky.

"What are you doing?" I asked, coming to stand beside him.

"Watching my fish."

He did not look at me, just stared into the pool.

"Your...fish?"

He said nothing, and I supposed he did not need to repeat himself, because as I came to stand beside him, I saw the fish too. There were larger ones and small ones; some were orange and white, and others were silver and black. They mingled and parted, a mesmerizing dance.

"Are they...your pets?"

Adrian's lips quirked. "I suppose you can call them that. They make me feel calm."

I wondered what spurred his discontent. Was it that my father had arrived from Lara? Or that Isla was still missing and Ravena was on the run?

"And you?" he asked. "Why do you come to the garden?"

My thoughts were far more personal than my answer. I came to the gardens because while I did not know my mother, the flowers felt like her embrace. And that was what I craved right now.

"The same as you."

We were both quiet for a moment, and then Adrian said my name, and it wasn't until I looked at him that I broke.

I cried. He pulled me into his arms and kissed me, and I met his mouth with mine, and soon my back was against the vine-covered wall, my legs wrapped around Adrian's waist. We were almost frantic with how quickly we came together. His fingers bit into my thighs, while mine twined into his hair. My breaths were cries, keening and desperate as Adrian moved inside me at this odd angle.

"Sparrow," he breathed and buried his head in the crook of my neck. As he did, I saw that we were not alone in the garden, and I choked on a moan as Killian's name spilled from my mouth.

I felt Adrian stiffen against me, and he slowly lowered me to the ground.

I couldn't even look at Killian, my face felt so hot. All I had worried about was how to interact with Adrian when my father and Killian were near, and here I'd been caught having sex with him. Knowing the commander, he would tell my father too. Then what? My relationship with my father already felt strained.

"Commander Killian," Adrian said, a pitch of frustration in his voice. "Can we do something for you?"

"You dishonor her," he said.

Adrian offered a shrewd smile.

"In what way? By fucking her against a wall? It feels like worship to me."

Killian gritted his teeth, and I looked between them, embarrassed both by Adrian's words and that we had been caught, by Killian no less. I hurried from the garden, heading for the secret corridors that would allow me to pass, unnoticed, to my own room, but just inside the door, Adrian caught up to me.

"Isolde!" He reached for my arm, and I twisted toward him.

"Did you do that on purpose?" I demanded.

Adrian flinched, almost like I had slapped him, and then he narrowed his eyes. "Why do you care that he saw us?"

I glared and he waited. Finally, I relented, admitting, "I don't know how to do *this*. Be with you and love them."

"No one says you cannot do both," Adrian said.

"That is not the world we live in, Adrian."

"You are queen of Revekka, soon to be queen of Cordova. You get to decide what world you live in."

I returned his gaze, my chest tightening. If that was the case, why did I feel so powerless? I watched him take a breath and then step away.

"I am here when you are ready."

Adrian left me in the corridor, alone.

———

As evening approached, I asked Violeta and Vesna to help me get dressed early in a gown that Violeta had made from fabrics gathered at the market in Cel Ceredi. It was sleeveless, the bodice a black appliqué that cupped my breasts and trailed down my stomach into a full skirt made of light pink silk overlaid with black tulle.

*Adrian would like it*, I thought, and this time as the familiar claws of guilt attempted to grip my chest, I shoved them away.

Today, I would stop feeling guilty about my feelings for Adrian.

They were complicated to be sure, but no more complicated than how I felt about the people of Lara who had tried to kill me or my father, who had kept the enslavement of my mother's people from me.

"I saw you with your father today," Violeta said. "You looked so happy."

I had been happy; now I was confused and a little angry. I wondered how she felt, having my father in her country, an enemy who agreed with Dragos's agenda, the king who had killed her family.

"I was happy to see him. He was all I had for so long, since my mother died when I was born."

He had been my world, and there had been nothing beyond that.

Now, that was not so. Now, I had Adrian, and soon I'd have a whole nation.

"Then I am glad he is here to watch you become queen of Revekka," she said, and despite my conflicted feelings around my home and my father, I was thankful for Violeta's words.

The last piece of my outfit was a black circlet. It was heavier than I expected and had black obsidian gems twisted around it. As I placed it upon my head, I wondered just how happy my father would be seeing me as queen.

"If there is nothing else, my queen?"

"No, nothing else," I said. "Thank you, Violeta, Vesna."

The women left, and I turned from the mirror and crossed the room to store my blades inside the drawer, since they could not be hidden on my person in this dress. But as I went to put them away, my eyes fell to the book I'd taken from the library—the one in which the strange blade was hidden. I had yet to open it again, to pick up the knife, for fear of reliving the encounter with Dragos once more, but something drew me to the book, and as I opened it, I realized it wasn't a book at all but a journal. The words were so precise, it looked like print.

*I would be content, if I were free to conjure spells and teach, but Vada says my gift is too powerful to waste. She puts too much faith in these would-be kings, men who say they should rule a kingdom because their blood is different, though they bleed red like the rest of us. She thinks they will use our magic to predict drought and famine, but my king—he has the heart of a conqueror.*

Another entry read:

*Today the king asked if the High Coven would support an invasion of Zenovia. I asked him how that would help his people, and when I did, he said I was here for my prophecy, not my opinion.*

*He does not understand that they are one and the same.*

*The High Coven did not agree to support the king in his wish to invade, and though I believe the right decision was made, I am filled with such dread for my present and future. King Dragos will murder me. I have foreseen it.*

I shared this woman's dread, and it kept me turning pages.

*My days in this life are waning. I do not have the heart to tell Adrian.*

*Our love will damn this world.*

I felt numb with shock. Suddenly, I could connect every instance when Adrian had spoken about the witches, defended their magic, talked of their wish for peace. He had done so with such reverence, and I had never considered that it had been because he loved one of them.

He had loved Yesenia.

It was not that I didn't believe what Adrian said about High Coven. This did not change what I had learned—what Violeta had said or the accounts I'd read in the library from Dragos's reign—but it hurt to know that I held the journal of Adrian's lover. That she had written in these pages, that she had professed her love for him here, and that everything he was doing now—conquering my world—was still for her.

She was his world.

And if she was his world, what was I?

Once again, I found myself asking a question I hadn't in a long time—why me?

I let the book fall from my hands, my shock leeching the color from my face as I struggled to reconcile this new information with how Adrian looked at me, with the words he had spoken to me. I had to reason that he could also care for me and love her, but why did that suddenly not feel like enough?

I thought I knew myself, but I didn't. I'd once been Isolde, princess of Lara, a woman who could not be swayed by pretty words or a pretty face. A woman who would not marry and would rule just as well. Then I'd been betrayed by my people, and I'd come to rule a land of monsters—a sparrow among wolves indeed.

This Isolde, the queen of Revekka, had been blinded.

A knock at the door grounded me, and I bent to pick up the book.

"Are you ready, Isolde?" Ana asked as she opened the door, and then she paused. "What's wrong?"

I could not recover enough to lie.

"I know about Yesenia," I said, because I was certain she knew too. She was Adrian's cousin, and she had existed just as long as he had.

"Isolde—"

"Why didn't you tell me?"

She just stared, and I shoved the book back into the drawer, along with my knives, shutting it so violently, it shook on its legs.

"It's not what you think, Isolde."

"Then what is it?" I snapped, looking at her. She was pale, and there was a moment when I felt terrible for bringing this upon her when Isla was at the forefront of her mind.

"Adrian cares for you."

It was my turn to flinch. "I think he loves Yesenia."

"You cannot be angry with him for avenging her death," Ana said. "He watched her burn at the stake, and when he tried to fight, they whipped him. He almost died."

A thickness gathered in my throat. I'd touched those scars, traced them with my own calloused fingers. They were raised and jagged, and they covered every inch of his skin.

"That night, he not only lost the love of his life, but he also lost his king. Adrian had been loyal to Dragos, a member of his Elite Guard."

"He should have been more discerning then," I said.

Ana looked devastated by my comment, and her distress hit me in the heart.

"You don't know what it was like," she said, her voice quivering. "We were all... None of us saw it coming."

Yesenia had, which meant she had kept the knowledge from everyone, including Adrian.

I swallowed the pain and the anger that had gathered in my throat. "Ana—"

She shook her head, silencing me. "We will be late."

She did not wait for me, and I did not blame her. I had been insensitive. She was right. I did not know what it was like to live during the Burning or the Dark Era, and I was not personally connected to anyone who had lost their lives. It was not for me to judge how someone should behave or what secrets they shared around something so traumatic.

Still, I was hurt. I could admit that to myself. And when I was hurt, I wanted to fight.

The great hall was once again packed, wall to wall. Mortals and vampires alike crowded around tables or huddled close together, making room for those who wished to dance. When I entered, someone began a chant.

"Long live the queen!"

It continued, and people bowed, though I could not help feeling like I was surrounded by enemies: people who felt Adrian was distracted by me, people who had expectations of me that I could not meet. I was a threat to everyone's agenda.

I supposed that was my power now, and I just had to stay alive long enough to use it.

It was already hot in the room. Perspiration was

gathered between my thighs and breasts. It would be an uncomfortable evening in more than one way, I realized as I crested the dais where Adrian waited. His presence was a physical blow. He was dressed in a black tunic over which he wore a fine, black velvet surcoat. He was like the night, and his face was lit like a star, framed in a halo of blond hair.

I held his gaze, and he seemed both sincere and tender. I was torn between letting go of my rage and stabbing him as he greeted me.

"My queen," he said and held out his hand. I took it, not wishing for him to know that I'd discovered his secret. Not yet. I only thought with relief that I had avoided making a fool of myself. Moments before I'd found Yesenia's journal, I would have gone to him. I would have told him I was ready to make the world I wanted.

*I could still have it*, I reminded myself. Adrian was only a vessel through which to achieve my goal.

I shoved my hurt down and lifted my head. I would enjoy this night, and I would be crowned queen tomorrow, and I would seek a way to have my own form of vengeance. And perhaps, in the end, I would rule as I was meant to—alone.

"My king," I acknowledged curtly.

Adrian raised a brow. "Are you feeling well this evening?"

"Extremely," I replied, trying to calm myself enough so that he couldn't read my mind. It was hard to imbue my voice with anything but disdain. I moved past him, headed for the high table where my father stood. Normally, I would have embraced him, kissed his cheek, but tonight, I only greeted him.

"Father," I said.

"Isolde." His voice was much softer, as if he wished to say something, but I did not look at him, and I did not even greet Killian, who stood opposite him.

Adrian came to stand beside me, Daroc and Ana on his right. As he sat, the rest of us followed. I reached for my wine, and though I knew it had been tested in the kitchens before it had arrived here at my table, I still hesitated.

"Would you like me to try it?" Adrian asked.

I swallowed, and without me even answering, he sipped.

I could not help watching how the wine stained his lips until he licked it away, and as he set the goblet down before my hand, he said, "Fine."

"Thank you," I said lightly and swallowed a mouthful.

It was not long after that I began to fan myself. The heat burned my skin.

"Warm, my sweet?" Adrian asked beside me.

Even as I turned toward him, I felt the sweat gathering upon my brow. He appeared unbothered.

"Boiling," I said.

"Perhaps movement would help," Adrian suggested. "We could dance."

"No," I breathed. "I'd rather not."

It wasn't until the words were out of my mouth that I realized how he would take my refusal. He would think I'd declined because my father and Killian were present, when the reality was that I could not face him right now. I could not be that close to him at this very moment. I wanted distance, but I had to remain at the banquet.

We drank and ate and watched the boisterous crowd,

who did not change their behavior even in the presence of my father. Vampires fed from their vassals and performed various sexual acts, small fights broke out, and when blood was drawn—by vampire or mortal—there was an even greater struggle to taste it.

"Despicable," my father muttered under his breath.

"Perhaps you should retire, King Henri, if this is too much for you," Adrian said.

I did not like sitting between them.

"Is this how you claim to take care of my daughter?" he asked. "Exposing her to this...*filth*?"

I worried over what Adrian would say. *Your daughter is no saint*.

"She has a choice, just as you."

"You make a mockery of the legacy of this castle."

"And what is that legacy, King Henri? One of mass murder and the persecution of innocents?"

I pushed my chair away from the table and rose, unable to handle being at the center of their conversation and unwilling to mediate.

"Excuse me," I said and left the great hall.

It was cooler in the corridor, and I stood near the open doors, staring at the fire that roared at the center of the courtyard. It was one that had not been extinguished since the Burning Rites. Women danced around it, flower crowns upon their head. I watched them for a moment, mesmerized by their movements and the shadows they cast. I wondered if they feared the flames like I did.

"Isolde."

I had not heard anyone approach, and I whirled, my heart in my throat, only to face Killian.

"Apologies, *Queen* Isolde," he corrected himself, though it sounded a little sarcastic. "Are you all right?" he asked.

I was suspicious of his question but answered anyway. "I'm fine," I said. "Did you need something?"

He hesitated, eyes darting to the left before he spoke. "I would like to first apologize for how we parted."

"But not for what you said?" I asked.

He looked at me, and I felt as though he was asking: *Will nothing ever be good enough?*

"What are you doing, Isolde?"

My brows lowered, confused by his question. "I don't know what you mean."

"That monster is in love with you."

"What?" My breath rushed out of me at his observation. The notion of love between Adrian and me was ridiculous, especially given what I had just learned about Yesenia. I was surprised by how his suggestion hurt.

"Isolde…"

"Commander—"

"Have you even tried to kill him since leaving Lara?"

"What exactly do you want from me?" I asked him. "I married him to protect our people—people who later tried to kill me. I stabbed him *twice*. I—"

I'd slept with him. I'd found comfort in him. I'd hurt for him.

"You love him," Killian said, and he stared at me the way he stared at Adrian.

I shook my head. "You wouldn't know love if it looked you in the face, Killian."

"I thought I did," he said.

"And you were wrong."

346

I moved passed him and entered the great hall again. My gaze shifted over the crowd and landed once again on Adrian, who sat reclined, one hand lifted to his mouth as he watched me. I stared at him, at the man who had loved Yesenia, the man who had killed a king for her, conquered a kingdom for her.

She had never really died, and I had never really been his queen, his match, or his equal.

Suddenly, the sound of drums pulsed, nearly vibrating the ground. I turned, looking around me, only to find a procession of women dressed in shimmery, beaded scarves that were so translucent, I could see their breasts and the curls at the apexes of their thighs, their hair threaded through with flowers. They spun and twirled at first through the whole crowd, but then they circled me, and the woman at the start of the line placed a floral crown upon my head while another took my hands, sweeping me into their parade. At first, I resisted as I was pushed and touched, but soon I gave in to the movements, following the beat of the drums and the thud of the dancers' feet. I let them spin me and twirl me. It was not violent or angry; it was gentle and jovial.

Before I knew it, we were outside, dancing before the large fire at the center of the courtyard, and the heat from it made me sweat. I let my hands rise into the air, and I spun beneath the starry sky while people around me laughed and danced and kissed and fucked. And I reveled in the frenzy, desperate to forget everything about Adrian and my father and my future, until the first scream broke out.

I halted in my rhythm. My euphoria was suddenly drowned in fear as the courtyard filled with a line of knights from another time. Between each pair was a woman. The first had dark hair, and somehow, I knew that her cheeks were usually rosy and that her eyes were bright blue, but right now she was pale, and there was no light in her eyes.

Her hands were tied behind her back, and the soldiers gripped her upper arms, the indentations of their fingers making her skin turn white. They only released her when they pushed her into the fire.

"Evanora!" I screamed, and I struggled but found I too was bound.

She hit the wooden pyre, and her horrifying screams filled the air. She thrashed and the wood collapsed, sparks exploding as she rolled, a ball of flame that parted the crowd until she came to a stop, dead.

The display did not stop the sequence.

The next woman was Odessa. She tried to fight, but she was subdued with a crack to the skull and tossed into the flame. She did not move but wilted there on the pyre.

I did not stop screaming, even as my voice broke and my throat bled. I screamed as my coven, my sisters, these women whose souls spoke to mine, died before my eyes. I did not know how long it lasted, but the fire began to lose its potency, and over the dying flames, I saw a set of dark eyes—King Dragos. Beside him was the woman whose magic had haunted me since Lara, Ravena, her unmistakable ginger hair even more radiant in the firelight.

When the king met my gaze, he smiled.

"Bring him," the king ordered, and my eyes shifted to a familiar face framed with white-gold hair.

"Adrian." His name rasped from my mouth, and my heart beat harder in my chest. "Adrian!"

He was brought to his knees before me, and I saw that his head was bleeding, his lips were cracked, and bruises bloomed across his cheek.

"Yesenia!" He looked up from the ground, desperate.

"Adrian," I repeated his name, and for the first time tonight, I felt a sense of calm wash over me that came from a simple piece of knowledge—he would live.

He would live, and he would damn the world.

Dragos's voice echoed in the courtyard.

"To think my greatest knight would choose a witch over his kingdom. Well, tonight, you will watch her burn. Tomorrow, you will collect her ashes. Light it."

"Yesenia!" Adrian struggled against the guards, but they beat him until he could barely rise to his knees.

As the soldiers moved forward to place torches at my feet and the smoke rose to fill my vision and my throat, I spoke. "Do not fight, my love," I said. "You are destined for this world."

"Yesenia," Adrian whispered, then begged. "Please. Please. Please."

I shook my head and spoke words that ripped my heart in two. "All the stars in the sky are not as bright as my love for you."

And as the flames lapped at my skin, I squeezed my eyes shut and clenched my jaw tight. I would not give Dragos the satisfaction of my screams.

At the end, I felt no pain.

# TWENTY

*I woke up with a start to find that I was in Adrian's* room. I was dressed only in my shift, the smell of smoke clung to my hair, and my throat was sore. I touched my neck, wincing as I swallowed. As I rose into a sitting position, I found Adrian standing a few feet away, staring out his dark windows.

He did not seem to know that I had awakened, and I was too caught up in my emotions to attempt to bury them now. I'd been inside Yesenia's head. I'd watched the people she loved die. I'd watched Adrian beg for her life at my feet. I'd heard him scream for her. I'd seen his horror and his pain.

"I know about Yesenia," I said.

Adrian turned toward me. He was still dressed as if he had come from the celebration in the great hall, but he had discarded his overcoat.

"Everything you do, you do for her."

He said nothing.

"What I don't understand is, why me? Why make me your queen?"

"Isolde—" Adrian said my name like he was desperate for me to understand, but there was no explaining this.

I pushed the blankets off and stood from his bed. "You took me from my home to fill a place beside you that I could never fill in your heart."

"Isolde—"

Again he said my name but firmer.

I pushed on. "I did not want to love, because it has only ever meant loss, but I let myself do it anyway!" I screamed, and it hurt so bad, I flinched. Everything *hurt*.

"Are you finished?" Adrian asked, a tinge of annoyance in his tone.

"I hate you," I said through my teeth. It didn't matter that I had just admitted to loving him.

He took a step toward me and then another. "You hate me because you love me," he said, and it felt like a taunt as the corners of his lips lifted.

The only thing I knew to do was fight. So I launched myself at him, but his legs tangled with mine, and I ended up on the floor with Adrian on top of me.

"Don't you dare laugh!" I struggled against him.

"I would never laugh at you," he said.

"You are! You did!" This time, I could not keep the hurt from my voice. Everything just kept getting worse. "I wish I had never met you."

"Isolde," Adrian said, and there was something in his voice that made me go completely still. He called my name, and it called to my soul. His eyes held mine as he brushed stray pieces of my hair from my face. "You have a place beside me because you fill my heart. I love you.

I have loved you since the beginning," he said, and his voice almost broke. "I have loved you forever."

His words hurt in a way I'd never imagined. This was a good kind of pain, an agony I'd die for. "If you have loved me for so long, why didn't you to tell me?"

"You would have laughed at me," he said. "But it is also the nature of my curse."

"I thought you weren't cursed."

"I am not cursed to be a vampire," Adrian said. "But I am cursed in other ways, and you are one."

I shook my head. "And Yesenia?"

"Isolde, it isn't what you think. I don't know how to tell you—"

I pressed my fingers to his lips and stared at him. I wanted to know, but not right now. Not after what he'd said, what I'd said. I needed more than words.

"Make love to me first."

Adrian captured my face between his hands, eyes searching mine before our mouths sealed together. As he did, his fingers threaded into my hair. His body moved against mine. Our hands searched for ties and clasps, eager to feel skin against skin, and when we were bare, Adrian knelt between my thighs. One hand dipped behind my knee, guiding it over his shoulder, and he parted my flesh with his fingers while his mouth closed over my clit. I let out a breath that sounded more like a sigh and twisted my fingers into his long, silken hair.

As he thrust and teased, a harder sound escaped my mouth, my fingers digging into his scalp. He looked up at me from his place between my legs, his eyes glinting, full of a furious desire to pleasure and please. And he did, sending coils of electricity throughout my body until my stomach was wound so tight, I began chanting his name and moving with him.

"Please," I breathed. "Adrian."

He rose up my body and kissed me, slow and languid.

"Hold on," he said, and I wrapped my arms and legs tight around his body as he carried me to the bed. The blankets cradled me, and Adrian covered me. His body felt so warm and solid and right. His lips left mine to trail along my jaw and collarbone before he lifted himself to meet my gaze.

"I do not pray," he said. "But I begged for you."

Then he bent and kissed the place between my breasts before rising fully and pressing inside until he had filled me, whole and deep, and paused. We took a breath and stared at each other, and after a moment, Adrian began to move—slow, lush thrusts that ensured I felt every part of him.

Perspiration built on our skin, and I held his forearms, nails digging into his hard muscle as sounds and words escaped my mouth—an erotic song he encouraged me to sing. It was in this moment that I understood I truly loved him. He had made me come alive in a way no one else had from the moment I laid eyes on him in Lara, and I'd spent every day since fighting it—but no more. Suddenly, I wondered what it would be like to surrender to him, to offer my whole being.

Would he offer the same to me?

"Adrian, wait," I said, and he froze above me, concern etched across his glistening face.

"Are you all right?" he asked, breathless.

I smiled and trailed my fingers along his cheekbone. "Take from me."

I did not think it was possible for him to become any more still.

"Are you certain, Isolde?"

I nodded, and my eyes blurred with tears. "I am certain," I said, feeling the truth of it in my chest. "I want every part of you. I want to invade your body. I want to be so heavy in your blood, you taste me when you bleed."

Adrian shook his head a little, and then he slid from my body and sat up.

"Where are you going?" I demanded, rising with him.

"There is something you must understand about your bloodletting," he said. "Before you agree."

I waited, staring up at him.

"I told you that I begged for you?" he said.

I nodded.

"And you are here now because of those pleas."

My brows furrowed, but I nodded anyway. He was acting as if I was a gift from the goddesses.

"Partaking of your blood means I...become vulnerable. Worse, it will make you a target."

"I am already a target," I said. I had been since I'd agreed to marry him. "But what do you mean... vulnerable?"

"By doing this, you become my one true weakness. If you die, I die."

"No," I said immediately. I needed him to be invincible. I needed him to be immortal. I swore I would never love if I had to lose. "Then we can't. I won't."

"Isolde," he said, and that gentleness returned to his expression. "I would *never* let anything happen to you, but I will also not exist without you again. More than that, though, I am willing to risk my life to be bonded to you the way I have always desired. I have waited centuries for this. For you."

My heart felt like it would explode.

"Does anyone know? About the curse?"

"Only those who were there when it was made," he said. "Ana, Daroc, Sorin, and Tanaka."

They were closest to him, more trusted than anyone else in Adrian's circle. I felt safe in the knowledge that no one knew beyond those four, and in the end, no one had to know of our bloodletting. There would be no evidence, no wound and no scarring, because Adrian could heal it.

I rose to my knees and twined my arms around his neck.

"Well then, you'll just have to do a very good job of protecting me."

I kissed him, and Adrian gathered me into his arms, guiding my legs on either side of his as he sat on the edge of the bed. He held my waist and slid into me, his mouth leaving mine to graze along my neck and shoulder. I clung to him and shuddered, letting him lead, and when his fangs elongated and pierced my skin, I gave a guttural cry. There was a second of pain before the pleasure of his mouth and his cock won over. They seemed to work in tandem, filling me with an ecstasy that took me under.

And then my mind was flooded with memories of Adrian.

Memories that had felt like dreams.

I met him beneath jasmine and kissed him under stars, and we made love in the dark, and that love ended in fire and damned the world.

I knew then who I truly was.

Who I had always been.

Yesenia of Aroth.

I was Yesenia of Aroth—not now, not in this body, but I had been her in another life, in Adrian's life.

The tears came when Adrian released me.

"Isolde." He cupped my face and kissed my mouth and my cheeks. "Tell me."

"I know," I whispered, and my body shook with sobs.

I couldn't explain it completely. I did not have all the memories or moments, but the knowledge of who I had been and who I was now existed simultaneously in my mind. And Adrian—*he* had brought me back. When my mind had not remembered him, my body had.

"I know you," I said and collapsed against him.

———

I lay draped over Adrian's body, his fingers moving lightly over my skin as I wrestled with my strange thoughts, dividing them into past and present.

"But how did you get here? How did you become a…"

"Monster?"

I smiled a little. "A vampire."

"I made a trade," he said. "I begged the goddess Dis to let me live and seek revenge against everyone responsible for your death, and she granted my wish."

I had a few memories of High Coven worshipping Dis as their creator.

"At the expense of desiring blood?"

"It is what I asked for—*let me taste the blood of my*

*enemies."* I heard him chuckle quietly. "Be careful of your words in deals with the divine."

"You never speak of the goddesses," I observed.

"Just because I was created by one does not mean I serve them. Gods become more human the closer you are to them," Adrian said.

I sensed there was more he could say, but he didn't, so I asked, "Do you hate her? For what she made you?"

"No. I quite like what I am," he said.

We were quiet for a few moments, and then he spoke. "I spent a long time searching for you. When I saw you in the woods, it took everything in my power not to bite you then."

"Why didn't you?"

It seemed like the easiest thing. He would have avoided all my hate, all my anger and resentment.

"I would have, but Dis is a cruel goddess to bargain with. You had to choose me, love me." He paused. "I do not think she believed you ever would."

There was something ominous about how he spoke. I halted my exploration of his skin and met his gaze.

"Is she why you began your conquest of the Nine Houses?" I asked. "Do you conquer for Dis?"

"I conquer for myself," he said. "And Dis can do nothing without me, because I am her weapon."

"But you do not wish to be her weapon," I said.

Adrian did not speak.

I rose, straddling him, his hands grasping my thighs. "If these divine beings are so powerful, why do they not come to earth and vanquish their enemies? Why do they play with mortals and monsters?"

"They have no power on earth, save what they can

do through us," Adrian said, his hands drifting to my waist.

"Can a goddess be killed?" I whispered.

"That is blasphemy," he said, though his eyes flashed at the prospect.

"Are you pretending to be pious?" I teased, just as he once had.

I bent and kissed him, then took him inside me again.

———

It was late in the morning when I returned to my chamber to wait for Violeta and Vesna's arrival. I needed to bathe and dress, and I would like to spend some time with my father before the coronation began. I was still not pleased with him, but he would only be here for a short while before returning to Lara, and I did not want to regret this time.

I came around a bend in the hallway and halted, finding Killian outside my door.

"Killian, what are you doing?"

"I came to see if you were all right after last night," he said. "But it seems you are just fine. Did you seek comfort in your husband's arms?"

I stiffened at his comment. "*That* is none of your business."

"Of course not, Your Majesty." His tone was biting, and I flexed my fingers into a fist. One day, he would feel the sting of my blade, I was certain of it.

"You should leave," I said, moving past him, but as my hand touched the handle, he spoke.

"You once hated them as much as I did. What changed?"

"I learned the truth," I said.

"You have been brainwashed."

His words made me pause, and I turned to him fully, taking one step closer.

"That has always been your issue, Killian. You think I do not know my own mind. Mark my words, it will cost you dearly one day."

I took a step back, and then I entered my room, locking the door behind me.

Violeta and Vesna arrived only a short time later, and we began preparations for the coronation. I started with a bath, and as the jasmine dropped into my water, memories of the nights I'd spent with Adrian in the pool rose to the surface of my mind. I thought of Ana then. Of my first day in the castle when Violeta had dropped the oil into my water.

*Lady Ana Maria said it would relax you.*

But it had not been for relaxing at all. She had used it to trigger my memories.

*Ana, my best friend*, I thought. There were no memories yet, just the knowledge of how close we had been.

An hour later, I was ready. Vesna had pinned half my hair up and let the rest fall in shining waves over my shoulders. After, Violeta helped me into my dress, which was designed by Adrian. It was black, fitted from the bodice to my hips, where it flared into a full skirt. Appliqués in a darker shade of black curled like shadow in strategic places, around my breasts, my hips, and the hem. The neckline was cut low and a collar necklace only drew more attention. A simple pair of earrings glittered in the darkness of my hair like stars in the inky sky, and as I stared at myself in the mirror, I felt awake for the first time.

I was ready to be queen.

I was ready to conquer.

Just then, the door opened, and I turned to find that Ana had arrived. While I knew I had seen her most days since I'd arrived in Revekka, there was another part of me that felt as though it had been forever, and for the part of my soul that knew her, it really had been.

"Are you all right?" she asked.

I opened my mouth to try and speak, but no words came out. I cleared my throat and tried again, only managing to say, "I know."

Ana's face melted into a sob, and she covered her mouth. "We waited so long."

I hugged her to me tight and only let her go because it was time to see my father.

He was in his room and sat at his small, round table eating breakfast. It was odd to see that his usual routine was not interrupted despite a change of scenery.

"Father," I greeted.

"Isolde," he said. "My gem. You look beautiful."

"Thank you."

I stood awkwardly in the middle of his room until he stood and faced me.

"Isolde, is this truly what you want?" he asked.

I drew my brows together, confused by his question. He had not asked me when I'd agreed to marry Adrian if this was truly what I had wanted, because he knew it hadn't been. But that was then, and this was now.

"Yes," I said. Perhaps it was the fact that my memories

had awoken, but it was somehow easier to admit to my desires.

"If it is a queendom you want," he said, "then I will abdicate. I will give you my throne."

"Father—"

He was talking nonsense.

"You can end this, Isolde," he cut me off, speaking firmly, and I blinked.

"What?"

"You can kill Adrian."

"No, Father," I said, shaking my head.

"End him, and whatever spell he has cast over you will end too. You will know when it is done. Please, Isolde."

"I cannot kill him!" I snapped.

"Then I will help. Killian and I. We will—"

"You would have to kill me!" I yelled, and my father blanched. We stared at each other in silence for a moment.

"What did you say?"

"I said there is only one way to kill him, and it would mean you'd have to kill me." I swallowed hard. I was not willing to tell him that Adrian had fed from me, but I could confirm other things. "You were right about a curse, but it wasn't what we thought. Our fates are tied, Father. If I die, he dies."

I stared at my father as he realized fully the impact of what I had told him. Of everyone, I could trust my father to keep the secret. He would never wish harm upon me—he had almost gone to war just so he would not have to give me up to the Blood King.

"So you see," I whispered, "there is no way."

My father shook his head. "Isolde."

"I'll be all right, Father. Adrian will protect me."

There was a knock at the door. "Your Majesties," Ana called. "It is time."

I took a few steps, closing the distance between us, pressing a kiss to his cheek.

"I love you," I said, and as I drew away, he held my face between his hands.

"You are the hope of our kingdom, Isolde."

Ana collected us, and together we made our way to the great hall. It had been decorated with flags in Adrian's colors—red and black with gold accents—but there was an addition to his crest. Among the roses and the wolf was a sparrow.

The room was packed with many of the same people as last night and some additions. Once again, there was a tension here that ate away at my skin, a tension that I was even more aware of now that Adrian and I had bonded. And though I saw a few friends—Daroc, Sorin, Isac, and Miha—we were among far more enemies.

Ana walked ahead of us, bowing to Adrian before taking her place beside Daroc on the dais. My father strode beside me, offering his arm as I made my way down the aisle toward Adrian, who stood tall and proud, dressed all in black and crowned in iron. I held his gaze, full of things he had said and wanted to say. I wondered about my father, at the desperation with which he had begged me to end Adrian's life. Had my admission been enough? Would he give up on the task and encourage others to do the same?

We came to the bottom of the steps, and my father bowed before ascending the steps to stand beside Killian as the coronation began.

"My king," I said to Adrian and dipped into a deep curtsy, the folds of my dress fanning out around me.

Adrian's lips curled. "Is Your Majesty willing to take the oath?" he asked.

"I am."

"Do you swear by your king to honor and protect the people of Revekka?"

It was strange, the notion that I was agreeing to protect vampires, to protect the kingdom I had once despised, and yet I found myself agreeing with my whole heart, because I knew the truth of this world. I had seen the murder of High Coven by a power-hungry king. Adrian was not the monster—evil could live within any creature. Adrian was the vengeance.

"And will you use your power justly and mercifully as it applies within the bounds of our rule?"

"I will."

"And will you serve beside me and upon my council to execute our law?"

"Yes," I breathed.

Adrian's eyes never left mine as he spoke, and I felt like he was seeing me throughout all my lifetimes. I wondered if he had ever guessed this future for himself like Yesenia had—like *I* had.

Ana approached holding a velvet pillow, and Adrian gathered the crown that sat atop between his hands. It was black and iron, and though it sat heavily upon my head, I knew it belonged there.

"Rise, Isolde, queen of Revekka, *future* queen of the Nine Houses."

I took his hand, and as I did, he kissed my knuckles.

"You are my light," he said.

"And you are my darkness," I replied.

They were old words, a memory from my past, and they felt just as natural as Adrian's touch.

He pulled me up the remaining steps and into a kiss that I felt deep in my belly. My hands went to his face as I devoured him just as hungrily, and when he released me, the crowd began to clap and chant.

"All hail the king! Long live the queen!"

I scanned the faces gathered, noting those who joined the hymn and those who remained silent—one of them being my father. I felt a horrible pang in my chest as I connected with his hard stare.

"All hail the king! Long live the queen!"

Adrian started to guide me down the steps when the doors to the great hall were thrown open and in ran a guard who stumbled and fell to his knees.

"Cel Ceredi is under attack!"

Dread tightened my throat as Adrian and I exchanged a look.

We both knew who it was.

*Ravena.*

The crimson mist.

"Stay," Adrian said. "Get to higher ground, and I will return." He kissed my forehead and as he left, calling for Daroc to join him, Ana hurried to my side.

"Sorin," Adrian called. "Stay with the queen!"

Several guards fell into ranks behind them, and as I watched him go, a greater sense of unease washed over me.

"You heard the king," Sorin said. "Higher ground."

But as he spoke, Gesalac stepped into the center of the room, and I knew whatever his intentions, they were not good.

I lifted my chin.

"So it appears you have made it to coronation day," he said.

"Do you have something to say, Noblesse?"

"My queen," Sorin said, coming to stand beside me. He placed a hand upon my arm. "Perhaps it would be best to retire to your room where it is safe."

He attempted to urge me toward the adjoining room where Adrian and I had waited for court, but as he did, a group of vampires—some noblesse, including the one-eyed Julian and their vassals surrounded us. When they drew nearer, I felt Sorin's body tense, his grasp on me tightening. Ana, too, turned in an attempt to block me from their onslaught.

I glared at Gesalac.

"So this is how it will be," I said.

"This is treason, Noblesse Gesalac," Sorin said.

"It is not treason," he said. "It is revenge. King Adrian *knows* a thing or two about revenge, does he not?"

"I am warning you not to touch me," I said.

The group who surrounded me laughed.

"What is a warning from a mortal? Besides, you would not want anything to happen to your father, would you?"

Gesalac nodded, and I turned to find that my father and Killian were restrained. I spun to face my captor. "You want me to pay for killing your son, is that it?"

"I want you to pay for coming here at all, for turning the king's eye away from his prize."

If he knew Adrian at all, he would know he had already claimed it.

I clicked my tongue. "Oh, that rings of jealousy, Noblesse."

"Adrian may like your mouth, but I, for one, cannot wait to cut out your tongue."

"Did he not warn you," I said through my teeth, "that I am a warrior first and a queen second?"

Just then, the doors to the great hall groaned open and a woman staggered inside. I did not recognize her, and despite her muddy clothing, I could see that she had long, dark hair and delicate features—round eyes, a small nose, and soft lips.

I heard Ana gasped beside me.

"Isla!" Ana called and attempted to sprint down the steps, but she was instantly restrained by one of the vampires.

"No!" I reached for her, but Sorin held me in place as Ana screamed again for Isla.

The vassal stumbled and fell to her knees just as Gesalac broke the circle around me and Sorin and approached her.

"Don't you dare! Don't touch her!" Ana shrieked.

He bent and picked the woman up by her hair, dragging her to her feet. He tipped her head back so that her neck was taut.

"Your vassal's looking a little wan, Ana Maria," Gesalac said. "Perhaps we should end her suffering."

As he spoke, however, Isla began to convulse.

"Isla!" Ana screamed. "Isla, no!"

What was happening?

Ana broke from of her captor and raced for Isla.

"Sorin!" I commanded, and the vampire caught Ana about the waist as a terrifying sound came from Isla's mouth. It was something akin to a scream, and Gesalac released her. Only Isla didn't fall to the ground. She stood with her arms spread wide and her head thrown back. Her long hair began to rise and float around her, and as her mouth gaped, a red mist came from her throat, curling into the air.

"It's here!" one of the noblesse yelled. "The crimson mist is here!"

A rush of bodies charged the exit, and most of the circle surrounding me broke away.

"Don't let the queen escape!" Gesalac yelled, and though he tried to hurry back to me, he could not fight the rush of the crowd as they attempted to escape the mist that had begun to consume one person after another. Horrifying screams filled the room as bodies fell, skinned, to the ground.

Sorin dragged Ana backward, away from the reaching mist.

"Let me go to her! I can help!" I heard her yell.

I was so caught up in Ana's anguish, I did not notice anyone approaching. Someone grabbed my shoulders and jerked me. As they did, I reached for my crown and shoved it into my attacker's face. He cried out and released me, and I turned to find a mortal had attempted to take me hostage. He held his hands to his bloodied face but recovered enough to growl at me, so I rammed the crown into his face once more. He stumbled back and fell, motionless.

"Isolde!" Sorin called, holding open the door to the room adjacent to the great hall. Ana was nowhere in sight, and I guessed she'd already gone inside.

I turned, searching for my father, finding him just as he bent to retrieve a blade from a downed mortal.

"I've got him!" Killian called to me.

We fled inside the small room, shutting the door behind us.

"What the hell is that?" Killian asked.

"It's called a crimson mist," I said. "It's what killed the villagers of Vaida."

Killian paled, and more screams came from the other side of the door. We did not have much time. The mist would seep beneath the crack in the door and kill us all.

"I need you to get my father out of here," I said to Sorin.

"And you, Your Majesty."

"No. Ravena is here somewhere, and I think I know what she's after."

"I cannot let you go alone," Sorin said.

"I'll go with you," Ana said.

"And so will I," Killian said. I looked at him, shocked, but he shrugged. "You are my princess."

I looked at Sorin. "Get my father out of here, then come find me."

He nodded. We split up—Sorin and my father to the west tower, Ana, Killian, and I to the library. We ran, dodging staff and servants and members of the court. I did not know how fast the mist could move or how visible it would be against all the red. Still, I looked for it and for any sign of Ravena in reflections. Now, with access to Yesenia's memories—my memories—I recalled that Ravena's magic was portal magic, though she was rarely powerful enough to create one without some kind of reflective surface, so she often walked through mirrors or windows.

"You think she's going after *The Book of Dis*," said Ana.

"I know she's going after *The Book of Dis.*"

Lothian thought it was blank, but it was only blank because it was spelled.

And I'd been the one to spell it.

We continued down hall after hall, and just as we reached the familiar ebony doors of the library, Gesalac burst from behind them.

I skidded to a halt, flanked by Killian and Ana.

"Now is not the time for your petty revenge," I seethed.

"If not now, when? I can skin all three of you alive and claim it was the mist," Gesalac said.

"You would let your people suffer in favor of my death?"

"Some revenge is just too sweet," Gesalac said, and as he lifted his blade, I noticed Ana's mouth moving, whispering hushed words. She was reciting a spell, but Ana had no magic. I could not hear the words she spoke, so I did not know what she summoned until blue lightning sparked at her fingertips, but it was nowhere near the shock she would need to attack Gesalac.

"Speak it again," I ordered.

She glanced at me and did as I instructed. The more she did, the greater the sparks grew. Each incantation made them stronger and stronger; my only hope was that she would be able to control it. Otherwise, it might hurt her.

"Killian, give me your sword," I said.

"Isolde—"

"Please, Killian," I said. He relented, and as he handed me his sword, I whispered, "Protect Ana at all costs."

Gesalac chuckled as I lifted my blade.

"Are you going to fight me, warrior queen?"

"If you insist," I said.

Gesalac's blade came down first. It was a hard move, straight down and directed at my head. I imagine he wanted to split me in two, but I moved quickly. His sword caught the hem of my dress while mine caught his arm, drawing dark blood.

He growled, and I suspected he thought that would be his killing blow.

I had to admit, I was unnerved that he'd cut my dress. It meant I had barely moved fast enough, and if he kept striking like that, I wouldn't make it.

Gesalac picked up his sword again and swung. This time, I attempted to deflect, but the impact rattled my bones, and I almost lost my grip on my blade. It was a mistake, and Gesalac used the opportunity to swing once more, knocking it from my grip. Just as he moved for what I was certain would be a killing blow, a knife whirled through the air and lodged square in his chest.

*Killian*, I thought as the noblesse roared, and I bent to scoop up my blade.

"Ana!" I called and flung out my hand. Just as I did, she reached for me, and I felt the surge of the magic she'd summoned work its way through my body into the hilt of the sword. I sunk it into Gesalac's heart, and he convulsed around the blade. I did not let go of Ana until he no longer moved.

"Is he...?" Ana asked.

"Not dead," I said. He had no beating heart to stop; the only thing it would do was paralyze him for a few hours. I stared at her. "You never said you were learning spells," I said, and Ana shrugged.

"You pick up a few things along the way."

The sound of shattered glass drew my attention.

"No!"

I ran into the library, to the glass cases that contained the High Coven's relics, and I found each case intact. *The Book of Dis* was still there, but as I stared, a face looked back at me.

"Ravena."

She smiled.

"Yesenia," she said. "Or should I call you Isolde?"

I narrowed my eyes. Did her use of my old name mean she knew my memories had been awakened? Did she know about the bloodletting and the subsequent bond between Adrian and me?

"What are you doing?" I asked.

"Taking what was stolen from me," she said.

"*The Book of Dis* was never yours," I said. It was mine—Yesenia's.

"It's not about the book. It's about what it can give me," she said.

I shook my head. "That book will take as much from you as you ask of it," I said. "Is that what you want?"

"I want power," she said, and her voice shook.

Suddenly, the case exploded, and I covered my head as I was showered in glass. Pieces of it bit into my skin, but I did not have time to react, because as I rose from the shelter of my arm, I saw that the book was gone, and in its place was a bubbling, red mist.

"Fuck!" I yelled and turned to run just as Killian and Ana caught up with me. "To the west tower! Now!"

We raced through hallway after hallway until I rounded the corner and came face-to-face with the mist.

Killian reached for me and jerked me back. It had filled most of the hallway in front of us, completely barring us from the other side of the castle.

"Fuck!" I said again.

"Isolde!" Ana called, turning to run down the opposite hallway. I knew where she was going, and I caught up with her as she was pulling open a near-invisible door—the secret corridors.

It was quieter in the passageway. Our breaths were ragged, our hearts pounding. I kept my hands pressed against either side of the wall as I followed Ana in the darkness. When we emerged on the other side, the mist was behind us, but it roiled and built, gathering like a wall of cloud and following.

"We have to get to Sorin," I said.

I wasn't even sure he would still be atop the tower. It was possible he had gotten my father to safety and left to find us. What if we did not cross paths? What if he got caught in the mist? I pushed my worry away. Sorin could fly; if anything, he had the best chance of escape of any of us.

I was in the lead, my legs burning as I tried to carry myself faster and faster to my father. As I crested the top of the stairs and ran down the center of the hall of mirrors, the mist roiled behind me, cutting off Killian and Ana's pursuit.

"No!" I screamed and turned back for them, but the mist was already up to Killian's waist. I stared at both of them, wide-eyed and fearful.

"Don't let it consume you," I said. "Get to safety."

"We can't leave you!" he said.

"You can. Get to safety!"

I watched him hesitate, and I knew he was assessing whether he could make it if he ran toward me.

"By the fucking goddess, leave, Killian! Get Ana out of here! That is an order!"

His jaw ticked, but he relented, and a wave of relief washed over me as I saw them retreat before the mist filled the end of the hall.

I turned and sprinted to the stairwell which was plunged into darkness, only to be hit hard in the chest as I reached the top. I tried to grip something—anything—but there was nothing. I tumbled backward, falling and rolling until I came to a stop at the bottom of the stairs.

I couldn't breathe, my ribs hurt so badly. I groaned, rolling onto my back as I attempted to catch my breath, confused, when the blurry image of my father walked into view.

"Father?" I asked.

"I'm sorry, Isolde," he said, and he lifted his blade. "But this is the sacrifice of a queen."

"Father!"

I rolled as his sword came down, grazing my side, and hit the stone floor beneath me. He continued toward me and tried once more to bring the blade down upon my bruised body. I tried to scramble to my feet, but a harsh push sent me to the ground again, and as I began to crawl away from my father, I sobbed.

"What are you doing?"

I was so weak and so tired. My chest burned, my ribs sent an echoing pain through my whole body, and I was more dizzy than I'd ever been.

"What you should have done the moment you discovered you were his weakness!" my father yelled and placed his booted foot against my side, sending me to my back.

"You wanted me to kill myself?" I asked, disgusted. "For whom? For a kingdom of people who turned their backs on me for my sacrifice?"

"It is for the greater good!" he said. "Not just your people but the whole of Cordova."

"Even my mother's people?" I asked, my voice quiet, calm. "Because you left them enslaved, and that does not sound like the greater good."

The mist was gaining on us. I had never been this close to it, but now I could feel its magic. It tingled with an electric pulse that raised the hair on my arms, and it reminded me of who I was and where I had come from.

I was Yesenia of Aroth.

As my father thrust the end of his blade toward my chest, I caught it between my hands. It cut into my palms, and blood dripped onto my skin.

"Father," I said, tears spilling down my face. "Please don't."

"Were you not prepared before to do whatever it took to save your people? What has changed? *Love*?"

Everything had changed.

It wasn't just Adrian. It was my whole world. The people I had once trusted were now my enemies. The people who had been my enemies—whom I had detested for so long—were the only ones I dared believe. And at the root of all of it was him—my father. The foundation from which my life of lies had begun.

I ground my teeth, jerking suddenly, knocking the blade away and shoving my feet into my father's knees. He grunted and went down. Then I kicked him in the chest, and he fell onto his back, losing his sword in the process. I scrambled for it and took it into my slick palm. As I rose to my feet, he came to his knees. I pointed the blade at him, and he lifted his hands in surrender. The mist behind him was a bloody curtain.

I shook my head, sniffing. I wanted to break completely, to fall to the floor and sob endlessly. My father had tried to kill me.

"You would be renowned," he tried to reason. "Not just in Lara but all of Cordova. Is that not what you want?"

I did not want to die a hero.

I wanted to live as a conqueror.

"I wanted to be a queen, Father, and now I am," I said. I let his blade fall to my side. "Go home." I started down the hall toward the stairwell. I wanted fresh air, and I wanted to sleep forever.

I made it two steps before he launched himself at me, and as I turned, I slid my blade through his stomach. His eyes widened in shock, blood spilling from his mouth, and as he fell to his knees, I went with him.

"I'm so sorry," I said.

The only thing my father could offer was a choked sound when he landed on his side, and as I watched him die, I cried.

"What a horrible thing to have lost a parent, and by your own hand."

Ravena's voice echoed all around, and my spine stiffened at the sound of it. I looked up and around but did not see her.

"It is horrible," I said. "The burden of a kin slayer is great, but you would know something about that, wouldn't you?"

"Oh," she breathed, and then she appeared in every mirror along the hall. She was untouched by battle—perfect hair braided to rest over her shoulder, her white robes far too pristine. It was how she always fought—through others or from afar—but one day, she would know the bite of a blade, and I wanted it to be from me.

She held *The Book of Dis* cradled in her arm, and it ignited something inside me, a deep and growing anger I did not completely understand. I was two people now, and I only knew as much as the other would give.

"The witches of High Coven were never my sisters," she said.

"They *loved* you—"

"Do not!" she shouted, and in that moment, her face changed. She looked older and hate filled. Her eyes seemed to sink into her head and darken, taking on what I could only describe as an evil expression. *This is who she truly is*, I thought. *This is what her path to power has cost her.*

"Do not say they loved me! Do not say *you* loved me!"

I stared at her, breathing hard. I recalled caring for Ravena, but she sought power beyond the rules of High Coven, and it wasn't until she'd tried to use it that she was exiled and a curse put upon her own magic.

It was why her spells did not work as they were supposed to—because she was forbidden from practicing magic.

"Do you know he never wanted me?" Ravena said.

"Ravena—"

"I was Dragos's last resort," she said.

The mist crept closer as she spoke, and I reached for my father's blade, pulling it free from his body. I had no choice but to leave him and retreat. As I did, I passed mirror after mirror, full of Ravena's reflection.

"At least you ended up by his side," I said. "The rest of us turned to ash."

I had no sympathy for her plight.

She was the reason my sisters were dead.

"Tell me," I said, continuing my slow walk down the hall. One of these was not an illusion—one of these was a portal. One of them would bring me face-to-face with the real Ravena. "Did you kill us all because you knew you'd never be his choice unless the rest of us were dead?"

Ravena's anger surged, and there was an old part of me that felt it like a tangible thing. I was getting closer.

"Your power could have been great. It was your mind that was weak."

"*My mind?*" she snapped. "Says the witch who fell in love with a mortal. Even in this life, you haven't changed. Tell me, did you enjoy the bloodletting?"

A cold sense of dread washed over me.

So she did know.

"You let him compromise the one thing you should have coveted—your life. Now who is weak?"

I took slower steps, her anger was a wall as red as the mist advancing upon me.

"Adrian's love has always given me power," I said. "It is what brought me back to life."

That wasn't a lie or an exaggeration.

*I begged for you*, he'd said.

"You are a fool," Ravena spat.

"I am queen," I said. "And despite all you have done, you are a powerless witch who hides in mirrors."

Her anger flashed bright. It took everything in me

not to react to it, not to turn then and let her know I'd found her.

"Not for long. I have the book."

I smiled. "And I wrote it."

She did not need to know that I had not recalled a single spell, that I had yet to remember why I'd even begun writing it in the first place.

"Pity you were not born with magic in this life," she now mocked. "How will you *ever* defeat me?"

"I do not need magic to defeat you, Ravena."

"Oh?" she asked, amused. "Tell me then, if not magic, what do you need?"

"Patience," I said.

Then I shifted and flung my blade. It pierced one of the mirrors and lodged in Ravena's chest. Blood spattered from her mouth onto the glass. I reached for a nearby candlestick and swung, shattering it, but I knew Ravena was gone when the mist vanished.

I stood for a moment, breathing hard, and the weight of what I had just done—of this whole day—crashed down upon me.

I screamed.

I raged.

I broke every mirror left in the hallway, and when I was finished, I made my way upstairs, to the top of the tower. There, I sank to the ground to rest beneath the red sky of Revekka, and I knew this was the pain that would make me into a monster.

———

When I opened my eyes again, Adrian hovered over me, expression grim. Anger was etched into his brows and the hollows of his cheeks. I broke when I saw him. My anguish was a physical thing that had invaded and warped my body. I would never be the same. My father was dead. The man who had raised me, whom I had looked to for guidance, whom I had idealized as a great king, had tried to end my life for the greater good.

For the greater good.

I kept repeating his attack in my head and hearing his words, but I was no closer to understanding.

Adrian knelt and gathered me into his arms, and I sobbed into the hollow of his neck. The next thing I remembered was waking up beside him. I lay on my stomach, my hand curled beneath my head, and when I met his gaze, more tears sprang to my eyes. I was exhausted, I was tired of crying, but I could not hold on to anything but my pain.

He reached out and brushed them away.

"Do you know why I call you Sparrow?" he asked, his voice a quiet whisper.

I shook my head. I had assumed it had something to do with my vulnerability here among so many vampires, and right now, I felt every bit the mortal I was.

"The sparrow is sought after by many monsters, but she is cunning and resourceful, and she always wins."

As he spoke, my throat tightened, and the tears burning my eyes were renewed once more.

"You have the heart of a sparrow, even among wolves," he said, and his lips pressed hard against my forehead. When he pulled away, he added, "It should have been me. My blade that cut him down, not yours."

"No," I said.

It was right that it had been me. If he had died by

any other hand, I could not have forgiven them, just as I would never forgive myself.

"I failed you. I promised to protect you."

"How could you have known?"

"It is not about knowing. I swore an oath."

"To my father, who could not even keep it."

As I spoke, my lips quivered, and I could see he struggled just as much, his eyes reflecting the torment of my heart. The pain and anger and sadness—even the shock. Who would have suspected I would not be safe with my own father?

"Then let me swear a new one to you," he said. "I will never let anything hurt you like this again."

Nothing could hurt like this, unless I lost him. I would have made the same oath to him, but his was already fulfilled. He would never live without me.

"Adrian," I whispered his name and touched his face, my fingers twisting into his hair. "Ravena knew."

His expression hardened.

"Ravena knew about the bloodletting, which means one of your four is a traitor."

It was a greater blow. It was not as if we had many people to trust. The noblesse were not to be trusted. The four were trusted...until now. Who between Daroc, Sorin, Ana, and Tanaka would have told? Had it been a mistake? A moment of weakness?

I also told him of the noblesse who had betrayed him—of Gesalac and Julian—but he was not surprised and admitted that they had fled.

"Sorin is hunting, but I do not think he will find them."

"What will you do?" I whispered.

380

He studied me for a moment and then answered, "We will wait. Sometimes a traitor is the leverage we need."

Strangely, I wondered if this was what it meant to be queen—never fully trusting anyone but my king.

---

We would burn my father, forgoing the traditional burial of my people. It was an insult, because no king of Lara had even been consumed by fire, and yet as I watched the final beam fall into place atop the pyre, I did not regret my decision.

I stood in the courtyard of the Red Palace, wearing blue and silver, the colors of my house. It was not for my father but for myself. I saw this as my funeral too—the death of the woman I used to be.

Few joined us for the burning. Ana and Killian stood on my left and Adrian on my right. Beside him were Daroc and Sorin and behind them, Isac and Miha. Tanaka and the remainder of the noblesse were scattered about. I tried not to look at them with mistrust, tried not to think that one among four of Adrian's closest friends was a traitor, and yet I could not let the knowledge fall to the back of my mind.

We had a traitor.

With that thought, I moved closer to Adrian, and he welcomed me, his fingers sliding between mine as my father was carried from the castle. He was wrapped in white, and what was left of his blood soaked through the fabric, his skin having been eaten away from his body by the mist.

My misery was acute, both because my father was

dead and because he had tried to kill me. I was still not over the shock of it, and I had barely slept, because each time I closed my eyes, I no longer saw burning pyres at my feet—I saw my father standing over me with a sword.

How had we gone from only having each other to this? How had I gone from being his gem—the savior of our people—to the enemy?

Was that the duty of a king?

To ensure the greater good?

I did not care for the greater good.

I wanted what was good for me, what would ensure I lived long enough to save my mother's people, protect those I called my own, defeat Ravena, and become queen of all who would harm me.

That was my greater good.

Beside me, Adrian looked solemn, and I knew it was both because he knew my hurt and because he had not been here to help me. My chest tightened at how he'd looked at me, how he'd sworn a second oath, an oath he had said he would never offer, and yet that was how I knew he loved me.

"What happens now?" I asked.

We watched as a guard moved forward to light the pyre. The fire caught quickly. It reminded me of how fast it had consumed the wood at my feet two hundred years ago.

The flames burned hot, and normally, I would try to keep my distance, the fear of flames and smoke a trigger, but this time, I did not move, and I watched my father's body burn through blurry eyes.

"We must find and kill Ravena," he said. "I imagine she will continue attempting to perfect her mist."

The attack on Cel Ceredi had taken many lives. Those funerals would be held in the coming days. Among those we would bury was Isla, Ana's lover.

I glanced at Ana, pale and quiet, and reached for her hand.

She did not look at me—she hadn't looked at anyone since Isla's death, but she squeezed my hand, and at least that was a comfort. I could not imagine what she was going through. In truth, I did not want to know, but I felt for her in a way that made my chest ache and guilt settle heavily upon my heart. I had not been able to even broach the subject with her, too consumed in my own strange grief.

"And King Gheroghe?" I asked. "When will he pay for what he did to my people?"

"Soon, Sparrow," Adrian said.

The pyre collapsed, and Father's body crashed to the stone ground, sending sparks and ash flying. I watched, unblinking as every bit of him was reduced to ash. Until there were only scorched bones left, and it was as I saw the eyes of his skull—vacant and full of smoke and fire— that I remembered why I'd written *The Book of Dis*.

It was a book of spells. It was a book of dark magic.

The kind High Coven had outlawed.

The kind that could raise the dead.

*Make someone fall in love with you.*

The words were a cruel taunt that echoed in Hades's mind as he prowled the darkness of his club to clear his head.

Perhaps he had gone too far in criticizing Aphrodite's choice to ask Zeus for a divorce, but Hades knew the goddess loved Hephaestus, and rather than admit it, she thought to force the God of Fire into expressing his feelings by goading him. What Aphrodite failed to understand was that not everyone worked like she did, least of all Hephaestus. If she won his love, it would be through patience, kindness, and attention.

It would mean she would have to be vulnerable, something Aphrodite, goddess and warrior, despised.

And if he understood anything, it was that. Aphrodite's challenge forced him to acknowledge his own vulnerabilities, his *weaknesses*. He frowned at the notion of finding someone who wanted to carry his shame, his sins, his malice, but if he failed, the Fates would get involved, and he knew what they would require if he returned Basil to the land of the living.

*A soul for a soul.*

Someone would have to die, and he would not have a say in the Fates' victim.

The thought made his body tighten, another thread added to the others marring his skin. He hated it, but it was the price of maintaining balance in the world.

A smell brought him out of his thoughts and gave him pause. It was familiar—wildflowers, both bitter and sweet.

*Demeter*, he thought.

The Goddess of Harvest's name was sour on his tongue. Demeter had few passions in life, but one of them was her hatred for the God of the Dead.

He inhaled again, taking the scent deeper. Something about it was off. Mingled with the familiar aroma was the sweetness of vanilla and a mild, herbal note of lavender. A mortal, perhaps? Someone with the goddess's favor?

The scent drew him out of the darkness in which he had lingered to the edge of the balcony, where he scanned the crowd and found her immediately.

The woman who smelled like vanilla, lavender, and his enemy sat poised on the edge of one of his sofas in a pink dress that left little to the imagination. He liked the way her hair curled, falling in luminous waves down her back. His fingers itched to touch it, to pull it until her head tipped back and she looked him in the eyes.

*Look at me*, he commanded, desperate to see her face.

She seemed to look everywhere before her gaze halted on him. His hand tightened around his glass, the other gripped the balcony rail.

She was beautiful—lush lips, high cheekbones, and eyes as green as new spring. Her expression was startled at first, eyes widening slightly, transforming into something fierce and passionate as her gaze swept his face and form.

*She is yours*, a voice echoed in his head, and something inside him snapped. *Claim her.*

The command was feral. He had to grind his teeth to keep from obeying, and he thought he might shatter the glass in his hand from clutching it too tight. The impulse to whisk her away to the Underworld was strong, like a spell. He had never thought himself so weak, but his restraint was a thin, frayed thread.

How could he want this woman so badly? What was this unnatural pull? He stared at her harder, searching for a reason, and became aware that he was not the only one feeling the effects of their connection. She fidgeted beneath his gaze, her chest rising and falling as her breath hitched, her skin turning a pretty pink, and he had the thought that he would like to follow that flush with his lips.

He would give anything to know what she was thinking.

He was so preoccupied by his own salacious thoughts, he had not felt anyone approach until arms snaked around his waist. He reacted quickly, latching onto the hands that held him, and twisted to face Minthe.

"Distracted, my lord?" she purred, amused.

"Minthe," he snapped, releasing her arms. "Can I help you?"

He was frustrated by the interruption, but also grateful. If he stared at the woman any longer, he might have left his position on the balcony and gone to her.

"Already zeroing in on your prey?" she asked.

For a moment, Hades did not understand her comment, and then he made the connection. Minthe assumed he was searching for a potential love interest, someone who could help him fulfill Aphrodite's bargain.

"Listening in the shadows again, Minthe?"

The nymph shrugged. "It is what I do."

"You gather information *for* me," he said. "Not *on* me."

"How else am I supposed to keep you out of trouble?"

He snorted. "I'm millions of years old. I can take care of myself."

"Is that how you ended up in a bargain with Aphrodite?"

He narrowed his gaze, then lifted his glass. "Did I not tell you I am not to have an empty glass tonight?"

She gave her best *fuck you* smile and bowed. "Right away, my lord."

He made sure Minthe was no longer within sight before returning his gaze to the floor. The woman had turned back to her friends.

Hades studied them in an attempt to discern the kind of company she kept, when he noticed someone he was not particularly fond of—a man named Adonis. He was one of Aphrodite's favored mortals. Why, he had no idea. The mortal was a liar and had a heart as dark as the Styx, but he supposed the Goddess of Love had a hard time looking past his pretty face.

He hoped the woman did not share that quality. He frowned, wondering if she would leave the club with him tonight, and then scolded himself for having these thoughts. His concern should go as far as fearing for her well-being for the mere fact that Aphrodite was fond of punishing anyone who gave her lovers too much attention.

"Your drink, my lord," Ilias said.

Hades glanced at the satyr, relieved that he had sensed his approach.

Ilias could be best described as another assistant. He had worked for Hades almost as long as Minthe, filling roles wherever Hades needed: bartending at Nevernight, managing his restaurants, and enforcing Hades's rule in the Upperworld. He was best at the latter. With an unassuming, pleasant appearance, Hades's enemies were often surprised by Ilias's ruthlessness.

Hades did not often employ satyrs. They were wild, prone to drunkenness and seduction, but Ilias was different and not by choice. He had severed ties with his tribe after they betrayed him, raping a woman he loved. She had killed herself and Ilias had killed them.

Hades took the glass, and before he thought too long on the subject, said, "I have a job for you."

"Yes, my lord?"

Hades nodded to the woman who had triggered him with her golden hair and green eyes.

"That woman, I want to know if she leaves with anyone."

Silence followed Hades's order, and when the god looked at Ilias, he was staring back, brow raised. "Is she in danger, my lord?"

*Yes*, he thought, she was in danger of never leaving this place. Something inside him wanted to disregard every civility and *possess* her. Something about her called to him—a thread that pulled at his heart.

He froze as those words surfaced in his mind, eyes narrowing, and thought, *It cannot be.*

Hades peeled back layer after layer of glamour that kept his vision shielded from the ethereal Threads of Fate. They were like shimmering spiderwebs connecting people and things—some were wisps, others were solid. Their strength waxed and waned throughout life. The whole floor was like a net, but Hades was only focused on one, fragile cord that ran from his chest to the woman in shimmering pink.

*Fucking Fates.*

# AUTHOR'S NOTE

I think my favorite thing about writing fantasy romance is that I can have these fantastical settings and still write characters who handle our everyday emotions and challenges. This book began with two characters fighting over a sort of arranged/sort of forced marriage and evolved into a story about identity and choosing what is best for you no matter the opinion of others.

I am only going to go into a few details about the vampire mythology and monsters in this book because I did use a particular guide as a reference for every creature you encounter in these pages. I learned from reading Theresa Bane's *Encyclopedia of Vampire Mythology* that there are actually hundreds of iterations of vampires across the world and across cultures and they are all based upon what people fear most. So as I wrote this book, I first considered what this world would fear most.

Turns out, they feared something stronger than themselves. You can see this in the history of the kings, who murdered witches for fear of being overtaken, and so Dis, the goddess of spirit, decided to create a creature that really could do that—and Adrian, well, he took it to an extreme.

Other abilities I adapted from the mythology of various vampires but also, in particular, the famous

*Dracula* are: the ability to shapeshift into an animal or a mist. You see these parallels in a few ways throughout the book. First, Dracula was said to be able to turn into a wolf (among other creatures). I did not feel like Adrian could shapeshift, so I used the wolf as a symbol for his crest. You also see shapeshifting with Sorin, who could turn into a falcon. (Other vampires were noted as being able to turn into vultures or bats). The mist reference comes in the form of the crimson mist which, at one point, Isolde thought a vampire was responsible for.

I also decided to maintain that the sun was deadly to vampires, but I had always seen Revekka with a red sky. Adrian, of course, was the first vampire and much stronger, so he, like Dracula, was still able to move in fading sunlight, and it was not fatal to him.

Outside of vampires, every monster in this book is also some kind of vampire. You will recognize many of them because you've heard them across various stories, including Lamia, who fed on children (if you have read *A Touch of Malice*, I referenced this myth).

I also must make a note that while I know many make connections between *Vlad the Impaler* and *Dracula* by Bram Stoker, I highly encourage you to read about the real Vlad III. There are many atrocities attributed to him, though I feel like it's always taken out of the context of the time and his motivations for conquering are never mentioned.

Thank you so much to my readers. I appreciate you all—without you, my dreams would not have come true. I hope you loved the story of Adrian and Isolde. I hope you loved their friends and their world. I cannot wait to share the next book with you!

—Scarlett

# ABOUT THE AUTHOR

Scarlett St. Clair lives in Oklahoma with her excellent dog. She has a master's degree in library science and information studies. She is obsessed with Greek mythology, murder mysteries, love, and the afterlife. For information on books, tour dates, and content, please visit scarlettstclair.com.